I0618937

Carbon Black

Declan Milling

London | New York

Published by Clink Street Publishing 2014

First edition.

ISBN: 978-1-909477-36-0
Ebook: 978-1-909477-37-7

Prologue

Rain in the rainforest.

Appropriate.

Big, fat droplets tumbling down from high in the canopy.

Intensity building to a rapid crescendo, then easing back to just another life-sustaining downpour.

An involuntary shiver stiffened him at the suddenness of the wet cold. Head down, looking at his feet, he knew they were wet but he couldn't really feel them, like they were somehow disconnected from his body.

Sheets of rain washing over him, soaking his head and running down his face. He couldn't get his hands up to wipe the rain off his face. But it wasn't rain. It was muddy water thrown from a bucket. Slowly he was coming back to consciousness. Back to reality. Still tied to a tree.

The guy with the thick accent was speaking again.

"So tell me, what're you ant you' friend doin' snoopin' 'round here?" He pointed the thick stump of his index finger at Glenn. "Ant don't give me that research bullshit again, ok, or I give you another fuckin' slap."

Glenn looked up at the man – thick neck and thick gnarled face to go with the accent. South African, maybe. Or Dutch. Or German. Couldn't tell; didn't care. He'd been slapped in the head so many times since they'd been held by the group of bush-knife-wielding natives purporting to be project security, led by this thick-faced thug, that he'd lost count. The thick face made the rest of his features too small, Glenn thought. Then he lost concentration and his head dropped forward again. It felt like there was a Harley-Davidson idling inside. Each throb in his temples so hard it hurt. Really hurt. The twine tying his hands cutting into his wrists, restricting circulation. Hands all pins and needles.

Contemptuously, the man scowled back. Then his thick hand shot out and his knuckles caught Glenn across the side of the head.

"Too slow again."

Glenn's head roared like the Harley taking off at full throttle. Star bursts of white light filled his vision. Blood gushed from his nose into his mouth.

"You know, this is a very primitive place. There still are head-hunters ant cannibals here."

The man looked over to where his troop of nationals – the security detail – were grouped, over past the tree where Tom Percival had been tied.

"You know 'bout antropologie?"

Glenn tried to look up at him again, but it felt like a balloon had been filled with water inside his skull, sitting above his forehead weighing down on his eyes.

"Well, no matter, let me tell you some. You see these boys of mine, they have some very funny ideas," he went on conversationally, almost friendly. "Clever uni pricks like you would call it their koltcha. OK, so they have this funny koltcha – y'know what it is? They think that if they eat the part of their enemy that makes their enemy strong, it will make them strong. Weird, eh? Personally, I'd just leave it at fuckin' killin' enemies."

He kicked at Glenn's and Tom's rucksacks on the ground in front of him, the hard edge returning to his voice.

"Now, you want to tell me what all these photos are for? You going to put them on the net, try to make trouble for our project? Make trouble for the government, the locals who are getting money from this great project? Make trouble for me ant my boys?"

It had seemed like a good idea at the time. The NGO Tom joined after uni was sending him to do what he called, euphemistically, an 'unofficial audit' of some project in Papua New Guinea; he'd suggested Glenn tag along. Reaching Port Moresby, they'd travelled to Daru, built on a malaria-mosquito infested island not far from the mouth of the Fly River. From there they headed up to Kiunga and then east, along the Elevata River. This was their jumping off point into the bush, making their way to where the forest conservation project was meant to be located, in rugged terrain between the East Awin logging concession and the town of Nomad. It was the end of the wet season, although in this part of the world it was pretty much always wet, so their two day trek to reach the project site had been a constant battle to keep leeches and other blood-suckers out of their boots and off their person generally.

Their route was simple. There was meant to be a road they could join that would take them to the location. It wasn't difficult to find: the 'road' was in fact a gouge several hundred metres wide, cut through the forest. According to their map, it was well outside any logging concession, but it had clearly been logged before becoming a thoroughfare, the detritus of tree stumps and other uncommercial bits of vegetation having been bulldozed to the sides, forming flanking ramparts against the forest. Initially they kept to this fringe, to avoid being too obvious to the occasional passing trucks. But in the wet, the uncompacted red clay stuck to their boots, sucking at them, making their progress increasingly difficult. In the end they walked in the bush itself.

On the first day, they sporadically encountered locals and, that night, stayed in one of their villages. The villagers had been curious as to what these 'tupela liklik masta' were doing traipsing around in the bush. But when Tom managed to communicate, in his bastardised pidgin English, where they were going, the headman of the village had became quite agitated, shouting at them:

"Bisnis bilong Gavman samting nogut! Masta i brukim graun, katim bus, katim diwai. Dispela ples nogut tru!!"

He knew why, now.

On the second day, when according to their GPS they were well inside the project area coordinates, whatever huts they passed were empty and derelict, some having been burnt. In spots, vegetation had been cleared and there were excavations, other cleared areas having been pegged out, as if in preparation.

They photographed everything as they went, but met no-one. No-one, that is, until late-afternoon in a torrential downpour they'd literally stumbled out of the bush into a cleared area where there were prefabricated cabins, like on a construction site. Then the security detail had bailed them up and the guy with the thick face and the accent had appeared out of one of the huts. They had been "arrested for trespassing", taken to the far end of the clearing away from the cabins and tied to trees on the edge of the bush. Then the interrogation had begun.

The man paused for him to respond, but the throbbing in Glenn's head was intense, stars were exploding in front of his eyes and, even if he had wanted to speak, the mixing of dried blood and fresh gummed his mouth.

"That makes you ant you' mate over there enemies, as far as I'm concerned. Same goes for my boys. I've told these boys of mine that you' mate who was giving all the lip is the smart one of you two. The talker. Very clever." He smirked. "Very brainy."

Glenn managed a sideways glance in the direction of the cluster of nationals. They'd moved away from the tree. He couldn't see Tom – wasn't tied to the tree any more. Then another backhander caught Glenn across the jaw, making his head snap back and forth like a speed-punching bag, stars exploding everywhere and he couldn't see anything.

Suddenly he was conscious again. More muddy water thrown in his face. Some went into his open mouth and he gagged it up. Hot, stinging, bile vomit welled up the back of his throat.

"You gonna answer me, you little shite?"

Glenn choked a painful cough, head throbbing even harder, blood ran out of his nose down his chin.

"We … research … animals … specie … "

"In that case, you shouldn't have spent so much time taking pictures of our project area. We're not animals." The man sighed. "You must think we're idiots. Our people in Moresby spotted you two the second you arrived. We've been watching you the whole time – not the other way 'round."

The man's tone indicated finality. "You know what I told these boys of mine? I told them you got ten wives back down south in Aussie ant fifty chil'ren."

Glenn stared down, uncomprehending.

"You know I can let you go. Just tell me who all the photos

ant other stuff is for back in Moresby. Is it for that German girl at the information centre?" He paused. "Don't worry we won't do anything to her, we just want to know."

Glenn tried to work his aching jaw. Searing pains stabbed up each side of his head. Water, he needed some water. The stinging in his throat, he could hardly breathe. It was so intense. But he had to respond or he'd be hit again. A barely audible "no" came out.

The man picked up a rucksack and fished a mobile phone from it. He started thumbing the keypad.

"There's a message here 'bout meeting when you get back to Moresby. Is it this guy?"

Tom said some guy had agreed to meet them when they got back to Port Moresby. Must have been him. Glenn inclined his head in affirmation.

Abruptly, the man was finished. He dropped the mobile back into the rucksack and slung both of them over his shoulder. Then he turned and walked away, leaving Glenn where he was, still tied to the tree.

As he left, the man stopped briefly and spoke to the cluster of squatting nationals who had finished whatever they'd been doing in the bush beyond the end of the clearing. After the man had been gone a while, one by one they stood, then started back across the clearing, towards Glenn.

Eyes glazed, mind dulled by the 'slaps' meted out to him, slipping in and out of consciousness, Glenn could just barely focus on their outlines. Arms hanging by their sides. Bushknives dangling from their hands.

It was getting dark and rain had started falling again.

Then his eyes closed.

1

Just before eight and already it was sticky. At this time of the morning the S-Bahn was usually congested and he was regretting not having skipped the second coffee at breakfast. Should have gone just that little bit earlier. The hotel coffee was pretty disgusting, anyway. He noticed how much he was sweating as he squeezed his way past the crowd standing near the doors, into the inside of the carriage. Maybe there might be a little more air movement through the middle. It was going to be another warm one and the humidity was as unwelcome as it was surprising, given it was only just April.

Now if he'd been on the platform trying to get on, he was sure the doors would have shut promptly. But as he was inside, they stayed open inordinately long, more and more commuters pushing and shoving their way in. Forget any idea of personal space. The carriage was tightly packed by the time they closed: he caught a whiff of the fellow squashing up against him. This guy was far too close for Emil's liking. My God, had this bloke taken a bath in the last month? He doubted it. Oh, and the bastard was letting off stinkers. 'SBDs' they were when we were kids, Emil thought. Silent But Deadly. In this sardine tin he had no escape. Holding his breath, turning his head away, he tried to inhale from the opposite direction. The conference, his presentation, work back at the office, upcoming deadlines, when he would leave for Frankfurt, his next holiday: he forced himself to think of anything other than the olfactory.

The train rolled agonisingly slowly out of the main station and onto the Hohenzollernbrücke, where it stopped. Below, the Rhine was enticing and a light breath of cooler air wafted through the windows. Emil could feel beads of perspiration beginning to make their runs down the middle to the small of his back, dampening his waistband. Tugging the back of his shirt collar up to give more latitude under his Adam's apple, he ran his index finger around the wet inside collar. A couple of torturous, perspiring minutes later, the train jolted into motion and edged slowly forward, the piercing screech of steel wheels on steel track like fingernails down a blackboard as it rolled on into Kölnmesse/Deutz station, where Emil joined the throng shuffling their way towards the convention centre. God how he hated being trussed up in a suit on days like this.

It was the second day of the *'C-world International Match-making for the New Global Carbon Trade'* Conference and Trade Fair, billed as the biggest global carbon market event of the year. Breathlessly proclaimed, by the organizer's promotional material, as more than just a trade fair and conference, but a celebration of the *paradigm shift* in the carbon market. Resorting to such an overworked phrase said it all.

A more impartial observer might have concluded that the real shift in paradigm was taking place on the streets outside the convention centre. Even at this time of the morning, arriving delegates were chided by a copse of placards exclaiming messages like 'Carbon market is problem NOT solution!' and demanding that they 'Make polluters PAY, NOT TRADE'. On the previous day, there had been protests out on Deutz-Müllheimer-Strasse and, a couple of times, protesters had managed to avoid the security cordon and make their presence felt amongst the delegates inside. The ubiquitous and increasingly militant anti-market protests railed against letting polluters simply buy the right to emit, instead of being obliged to reduce their emissions – blamed for the more erratic and extreme weather that had now become the norm. Ever since Copenhagen in 2009, conference disruptions had become commonplace, not just at intergovernmental meetings, but any climate change industry events. And with *C-world* billing itself as the main event for the year, well, that was just asking for trouble.

Entering past the security, Emil made his way up to the Congress Room on the fourth floor. Nodding to familiar faces, some friendly, nodded back to him. Others scowled or just blanked him altogether. He chatted briefly with a couple of former acquaintances as he worked his way towards the front. It might have been his imagination, but he could swear he heard one of them say "Arsehole" behind his back as he moved on. He didn't turn around, would only give them the satisfaction of knowing he'd heard it. Niggles like that just reinforced his determination to succeed.

A scrum of people had formed in front of the dais and he could see the session moderator, Christopher Manning, partner in an international law firm, in earnest discussion with a number of them all at once. Manning was English and a one-time colleague, so at least Emil had one ally, no, make that a neutral party, in the room, whom he might expect to be more balanced. Other than that, he was not expecting an especially friendly reception. While his ten minute speaking slot would be pretty much standard *policyspeak*, he expected the Q&A session that followed to be more lively.

Manning extracted himself from the cluster when he saw Emil and came over.

"Ready for it, Emil?"

"Chris, good morning. Ready for what?"

"Both barrels, my Aussie mate, both barrels," Manning replied, grinning broadly and mimicking the firing of a shotgun at Emil. "There was some pretty agro stuff being spouted here yesterday, directed at your lot. Didn't you cop any of it?"

"I sat in on the session on emerging domestic exchanges. Some guy from Sino Carbon was just warming to the theme of 'death to the regulators' when the protesters got in and brought it to a premature end."

Manning shook his head.

"Those shits! They've got to do something about those bloody protesters. It's out of hand."

"Don't you think they've got a right to be heard?"

"Those unwashed louts might have some point they want to make, but they should stick to harassing governments. They're the ones who need to get their message, whatever it is, not the business people actually trying to progress things."

"Maybe it's exactly the people here they're aiming at: the greedy, evil partakers of the rapacious, self-serving markets!" Emil grinned.

"Well, that's guilt by association for your lot, then. Besides, coming in here being pains in the arse isn't exactly going to encourage private sector investors to put their hands in their pockets." His face reddened even more. "If any of them get in here today," he said, nodding around the Congress Room, "they'll be the ones getting the pain in the arse – courtesy of my boot."

With that rant off his chest, Manning moved off to greet other panellists who were stepping on to the podium.

Unwashed louts. Emil stood there reflecting on Manning's neatly stereotypical view of the world. He himself had just had a close encounter with an unwashed lout on the S-Bahn, not much more than half an hour earlier. Only that unwashed lout was in a crumpled suit and clearly coming straight from the notorious Traders and Brokers Party that always took place on the first night of *C-world*.

The Congress Room had seating for about five hundred, Emil guessed, and the numbers of people entering looked like they might fill it. The podium was set up with armchairs arranged in an arc on the side opposite to the lectern, the current fashion being for the informal 'fireside chat'. The audience was already settling into their seats and shortly Manning was at the lectern, calling them to order and getting proceedings underway.

"Good morning, ladies and gentlemen," Emil began. "Contrary to what our two previous speakers might suggest to you, the United Nations' Global Carbon Markets Organisation is neither a toothless tiger, nor is it a restriction on the proper operation of the carbon markets. To the contrary, its principal objective is to ensure the efficient and effective operation of those markets. In this sense, the interests of the organisation are totally aligned with your own."

At Christopher Manning's prompting, it had been agreed that Emil would be the third of the four panellists to give his spiel. The session was meant to be a panel discussion format, less monologue and more questions, on the topic of governance. Since joining the GCMO, it seemed he'd been on a constant speaking circuit, trying to get a positive message out. So he was well practiced. He knew how to deal with any of the bullshit this bunch of suits might throw at him.

Quickly into his stride, he ran through the historical sequence that preceded the decision to set up the GCMO:

"Firstly, there were the inconclusive negotiations on a global treaty – whether to continue the emission limits on rich countries; whether to extend them to the more rapidly developing countries such as China, India and Brazil. There was US intransigence.

"Then there were the scams that beset projects in developing countries: the industrial polluters that increased production to inflate emissions, just so that they could reduce them again and receive more credits; the plantation developers that clear-felled virgin rainforest to plant faster growing species to increase their returns; the straight out financial frauds on investors.

"There was the global financial crisis and its aftermath. As we all know, this reduced economic output, causing an over-supply of emission allowances in the market – a problem that took far too long to sort out.

"There was growth in bilateral deals between countries, outside the international negotiations. And, of course, the promotion of carbon trading in lesser developing countries.

"These are all reasons why the organisation was established and why it is 'an important market adjunct'."

Emil had been particularly pleased when he'd come up with this description – a good grab line for any media and just the right level at which to pitch the GCMO's existence to an audience of brokers, traders, bankers and other market makers who, let's face it, really only cared about their profit margins.

"And what does the GCMO do, you ask? Well, if you look in the conference materials you've received, you'll find an outline of our mission, role and functions [Author's note: see Appendix]. I won't go into them now. They're self-explanatory, but I'm happy to take questions on them.

"The GCMO is here," Emil wrapped up his allotted ten minutes, "to ensure a smooth running, fair, transparent and efficient carbon market for all."

The fourth panellist was from an NGO and focused on attacking the first two speakers, one of whom was from a bank, the other from a brokerage firm, for their hypocrisy over governance issues. It was all a bit over the top, but Emil was quite pleased that it took the attention away from him and the GCMO. However, his respite was short-lived. The questions and challenges soon came thick and fast.

"Isn't the GCMO just another hopeless compromise to try to give the UN continued relevance?"

"Why do we need yet another market regulator feeding off the public purse – with so many financial regulatory bodies now, why is there a need for the GCMO?"

And from the head of trading at a UK bank:

"The European financial supervisory system was just a power grab to weaken London's pre-eminence as a financial centre. Isn't setting up the GCMO in Frankfurt just the same sort of lame attempt at undermining London's carbon market leadership?"

On it went, Emil fielding most of the questions, with the NGO person doing her best to get in the firing line as well, the other two content to nod their support for the questioners. He'd been careful to steer around the actual role that his unit played, but the next question from the audience brought him back to it.

The questioner was towards the back of the room and didn't identify himself or his organisation, so that, although Emil felt the nondescript North American accent sounded vaguely familiar, he couldn't quite place it.

"Mr Pfeffer, you head up the Market Integrity Unit of the GCMO. Perhaps you could elaborate for us what role that unit plays as part of the "important adjunct" to the market?"

The delivery dripped with sarcasm. An almost perceptible ripple of smirking ran across the faces of the audience. But he had expected his unit's role to crop up.

"Thank you, I'm glad you asked that question."

Beginning with that line, he meant the opposite. Who is that guy? flashed across the back of his mind.

"As the name suggests, the unit I head is concerned with the integrity of the carbon market. What do we mean by integrity? Well, we mean that there is limited scope for gaming the market, for example, by parties manipulating events to artificially inflate the price just before they sell, or deflate it just before they buy. We mean that information asymmetries are as limited as possible, so that one party doesn't have critical, price-sensitive information that allows it unfairly to get the better of the other party. We mean that the design and operators of the market limit the opportunities for crimes like those we've seen all too often to date, such as the thefts of certificates from electronic registries, which are then on-sold to unsuspecting buyers."

He let them take it in.

"The GCMO is principally a supervisory body. It oversees the operation of the carbon market; conducts research and analysis; and makes information available to governments, so as to help the market work better.

"The Market Integrity Unit, conversely, has a more hands-on, policing type role. It works closely with the national regulators themselves, to fix the problems identified. They look at how things work locally and we check and approve that they work in the global context."

The questioner was on his feet again, microphone in hand.

"So you regulate the regulators? Who watches the watchers? The Market Integrity Unit!"

The theatrical delivery brought a more perceptible ripple, some sniggers. Emil felt a slight tingling in his stomach. A sudden thought arrived: the bastard didn't introduce himself because they all know who he is. No longer relaxed and in control, Emil sat up on the front edge of his armchair, leaning slightly forward, arms folded. A defensive position. Trying to better see his questioner. But he still couldn't place him. And the questioner wasn't finished yet.

"Mr Pfeffer, why, if the Global Carbon Market Organisation is so hell-bent on integrity in the carbon market that it would have a unit with the word 'integrity' in its name," he paused for effect, "the unit that you head up," he paused again, making sure full audience attention was focused on him, "why then, Mr Pfeffer, is one of your colleagues, in fact one of your very own *integrity* staff, a Mr Gordon Davies, the senior manager responsible for *integrity* in the Asia-Pacific Region markets, currently under arrest in Papua New Guinea, and can you explain to this audience here what the charges are?"

There was a collective drawing in of breath around the room, like everyone soup-sipping in unison. Then silence. Heads that had been turned to the questioner, turned back. All the faces in the room were looking up, looking up at Emil. Slowly he stood, but later didn't remember doing so. Mouth agape, eyes wide, his face said complete and utter bafflement.

"What are you talking about?" the words sticking to the sudden tacky dryness in his mouth, making it hard for them to get out.

"Ha! I'm asking about the integrity of a member of your team, Mr Pfeffer."

At that point Emil recognized the skew-whiff grin of self-satisfied success that he'd seen on television, recognized the narky, arrogant conceit in the tone. Bradlee Nelson, the Lynx cable channel's self-appointed media spokesperson for climate sceptics everywhere had shot down another climate phoney. And he was still firing.

"I mean, exactly *what* do your *integrity* staff get up to when they're meant to be regulating the regulators?"

The noise level in the room rising, Nelson virtually shouting into the microphone.

"Can you answer my questions, Mr Pfeffer?"

"I, I really don't know what you're talking about … but if you'd like to…"

Nelson cut him off, shouting into the microphone:

"I'd really like you to answer me, Mr Pfeffer".

People were on their feet now, noise in the room escalating more, becoming chaotic.

"Hey, are you gonna answer him?" someone called out.

"Yeah, what about some answers, Mr Integrity!" shouted another.

Someone further back shouted: "Shut up so he *can* answer!"

Raised voices, shouted questions, demands – suddenly they were coming from everywhere. Christopher Manning was at the lectern banging his gavel and calling for quiet but it was too late for that. Emil looked at Manning then waded into the crowd, pushing past people and trying to get to Nelson. People seemed to be moving in all directions and Nelson had become besieged by a cluster five or six deep. Quite a number of the people around Nelson looked like journalists: there were note pads out, dicta-phones held forward under his nose, cameras flashing, and a TV camera crew had appeared from God knows where. Nelson was holding court. The penny dropped – it was completely staged. Emil's self-preservation instinct kicked in: he wasn't going to give Nelson another go, waiting to be caught and crucified by that lot. Backing out through the crowd, he turned and headed for the door, beating a hasty retreat from the Congress Room, not even stopping to collect the papers he'd left on the podium.

He darted downstairs and out of Köln Conference Centre like a handbag snatcher, expecting at any second Nelson or another journo would call out 'Stop thief' or 'Hold him', enough for the surfeit of security men to pounce and block his retreat. Grabbing a taxi to his hotel, he rang through to his office, but no one there knew what he was talking about. Davies was a British national, so he asked his assistant to call the British Embassy in Port Moresby, to see if they could shed light on the situation. He called Gordon Davies' mobile phone, but it didn't answer. That in itself told him nothing, as Davies could easily have been out of mobile range or, at that time, possibly asleep. Within an hour he was on an inter-city express to Frankfurt.

The conference went until the following evening, so he reck-oned there would be time enough for him to find out what was going on and respond appropriately to anything that appeared in the press. But he didn't reckon on the rabidity with which Nel-son's stunt infected the media.

The GCMO offices were located in Bad Eschbach, one of the satellite business hubs around Frankfurt. The intention was that eventually the organisation would take space in the recently com-pleted building that would house the European Central Bank, on the site of the old Großmarkthalle in Frankfurt's Ostend. But even though the ECB was moving soon, the space earmarked for the GCMO wouldn't be ready for another year. So for the first couple of years of its existence it would be a further, thirty-minute S-Bahn journey out of Frankfurt. By the time he reached his office, the story was already appearing on news websites.

His assistant, a young German, greeted him.

"Herr Davies' mobile phone still does not answer and the British Embassy does not answer. I think they have all gone home for the day."

"Keep trying please, Sabrina, and also try to get through to the main police station in Port Moresby, probably the one at a place called 'Boroko'. If you get anyone there, can you let me know and I'll speak to them."

As Sabrina left his office, his phone rang. It was the Director-General, Betty Greenhaugh.

"Ya wanna let me know what's goin' on?"

She was from the mid-west United States, a five-foot tall thermo-nuclear dynamo. While the overall breakdown of GCMO management broadly reflected the relative significance of the national trading regimes in place, Emil reasoned that picking the director-general must have been a demand made by the US for coming on board as part of the deal. The US would have wanted someone in place who would keep the GCMO tightly within the bounds of its mandate and Betty G was just the person to do that.

"I will when I find out myself."

"Make it fast, Emil – I've just had a third journalist call me and it doesn't look good when I have to tell them I don't know what they're talking about."

"Tell them we're looking into it and we'll get back to them."

"Don't you now start telling me how to do my job. Just find out what Davies is doin' out there in Pa-poo-a Noo Ginnee and get it under *control* – no more bad press, OK!"

"OK, OK, I'm working on it. You'll know as soon as I do," said Emil, thinking: there's her favourite word again.

She hung up. Emil had what he thought was quite a good working relationship with Greenhaugh. At least, it was better than what he had with his other colleagues on the management team. But she was not to be trifled with when the situation was not entirely and completely under control: *her control.*

He rang the hotel in Port Moresby where Davies was booked

in. The concierge was very understanding, but could not help. Yes, he knew Mr Davies, but no, he hadn't seen him since the day he checked in. However, he had heard from other staff, that the police had been at the hotel asking about Mr Davies and had visited Mr Davies' room. Emil rang the PNG Office of Climate and Carbon but got no answer. He was just starting to foment evil thoughts about lazy public servants, when he remembered it was the middle of the night in PNG.

He logged on and checked the briefing Davies had provided for his trip. Davies' purpose was to establish links on the proposed trading scheme with the government's new Office of Climate and Carbon. This had succeeded the Office of Climate Change and Environmental Sustainability, after its head had been sacked for orchestrating a scheme to sell fake US$1 million carbon credit certificates. Davies' briefing set out a history of conmen with promises of *moni bilong skai* bamboozling guileless landowners, whose predilection for cargo cult left them easy prey. Not encouraging reading, juxtaposed as it was with the following sections on the government's impressive plans for domestic carbon trading. These were to be leveraged off the successful forest conservation projects it had established under the internationally recognized 'REDD' program.

Development projects in PNG had a notorious history of conflict with traditional landowners. The giant Panguna copper mine had brought on the Bougainville civil war. At the opposite end of the country, the massive Ok Tedi gold mine, in the Star Mountains, had resulted in equally massive river pollution, causing extensive conflict. Entire mountains – places where traditional owners had their spiritual roots – would disappear when mined. Other projects had pipelines, or electricity cable pylons, dynamited because of insufficient compensation for crossing traditional lands. But with these forest conservation projects, all would be different. It would be, the government boasted, a Melanesian win-win on carbon trading. Davies' briefing concluded with the observation that success of the PNG arrangements would be critical to give impetus to carbon trading, which now was the only global response to climate change.

Sabrina brought him back to the present. Boroko police station, Port Moresby was on the line, she announced. He picked up the phone and having explained who he was, and established that he was speaking to Sergeant Wari, and that, yes, Sergeant, he realized it was the middle of the night in Port Moresby, Emil explained that he needed to find out whether they were holding a Mr Gordon Davies, who worked for him, in the police station or if not, did the Sergeant know if Mr Davies was being held in another police station. The Sergeant went away to check.

"Hello, hello, sir, are you there?" Sergeant Wari returned several minutes later.

"Yes, hello Sergeant, this is Emil Pfeffer, I'm still here. Did you find out anything about Mr Davies, Mr Gordon Davies?"

"Yes, hello, Mr Davies is currently being held here in Boroko cells."

"Can you tell me why he is being held?"

"Yes, sir, I can tell you that the entry in the register says Mr Davies is being held on suspicion for murder."

He didn't let his voice betray his shock. "Sergeant, is it possible for me to speak to Mr Davies?"

"No sir, no phone calling to the prisoners is allowed."

This wasn't going much further.

"Thank you, Sergeant. Is there anyone else in the station who might be able to tell me more?"

"Ah, it's night-time here, sir. I am the only police officer on the desk, so if you want to talk to the Commander, you will have to ring back after seven o'clock in the morning."

Emil's deputy, Dominik Baumann, had been checking through Davies' desk and the papers in his office for anything to indicate what Davies might be involved with in PNG, apart from his work. He came in just after Emil finished the call.

"There's nothing in his office to indicate what's going on."

He looked at Emil, whose motionless state and unfocused stare into the middle distance suggested he might have died, sitting upright at his desk.

"Are you alright?"

"Oh, ah Dom, yes. Yes, I'm fine, but I don't know about Gordon. I just spoke to the police in Port Moresby – at the main lock-up. They said they're holding him on suspicion of murder."

"What? That can't be possible."

"That's what Sergeant Wari of the Royal PNG Constabulary said."

Then after a moment's further thought, he picked up the telephone and dialled Betty G.

"I just got through to the police in Port Moresby. They said they're holding him on suspicion of murder."

Emil jerked the handset away from his ear. Across the room, it sounded to Baumann like there was a needle being violently scratched back and forth across an old vinyl phonograph record at the other end of the line.

"Yes, that's all they would say," said Emil, when there was a pause in the electronic screeching, still holding the handset slightly away from his ear as a precaution. "I'm going to try to get onto someone more senior when he arrives in a couple of hours' time."

Emil listened for a minute, then said: "I'll get something to you before I go tonight."

He cobbled together what information he could about the situation for a briefing to Betty G. He recounted the episode at the conference centre, without going into much detail, the shock of the moment having temporarily wiped most of it from his memory. He thought about trying to ring people whom he recalled had been there, such as Christopher Manning, but he doubted they would be able to shed any more light on the matter. He shrank from the thought of calling anyone at Lynx Cable, or Nelson himself. No, that was utterly out of the question. That arsehole. He'd probably illegally record the call. Emil was reluctant to provide details that might show how inept he'd been in front of so many people, how flummoxed he'd been by Nelson. That arsehole.

Dominik Baumann came back into his office about half past ten. He'd just got through to the British Embassy.

"They said they understood a Mr Gordon Davies, a British citizen, has been arrested, but the police have not allowed any consular access and have provided no other details, except what we already know – that he's being held on suspicion of murder."

At eleven he rang and was amazed to get straight on to the Commander of Boroko Police Station, whose name was Kehara.

Emil asked what details he could give surrounding Mr Davies' situation.

"We were in the course of carrying out a police investigation, when we intercepted Mr Davies," said Kehara. "When we made a search of the surrounding area, we found two bodies, bodies of two boys. So now Mr Davies is helping us with our inquiries into what happened to these boys."

Just before midnight he provided his briefing to Greenhaugh.

"Chessus! I thought Davies was happily married?" she said when she read the information from Kehara. "You'd better get out there and sort this out A-S-A-P. I don't want to start jumping to conclusions, but didn't any of the background checks on Davies show up anything like this before he came on board?"

"He came to us with excellent credentials and references. He's been around the Asia-Pacific region for the best part of his career."

"Maybe *that* should have given us the hint," Greenhaugh replied, with just a whiff of sarcasm.

"I don't like what you're implying, Betty. You might remember that I come from that part of the world and worked there for a few years too! There's absolutely nothing to suggest he's been anything more than in the wrong place at the wrong time." Then he added: "Apart from a spot of supposition and innuendo, that is."

"Alright, don't get on your high horse. I'm not serious. I don't think this is in character for the Gordon Davies I know, either. But you'd better get this sorted out quick! Some of your fellow directors are less than happy to share this organization with your unit as it is, not to mention the people who want to close us down altogether. When word gets around about this tomorrow," she looked at her watch, "today, as it inevitably will, there'll be more than supposition and innuendo to deal with. And since I'll be the one dealing with it here, you'd better not leave me in it too long."

Emil was back in his office by seven the next morning. Greenhaugh came in while he was hanging up his jacket.

"I thought I heard you," she said. Her office and those of some of Emil's fellow directors occupied the second level of the building. Sabrina's desk was directly outside his office but the rest of his staff were scattered all over the place, a sore point that hadn't really helped his team building efforts.

"Did you go home at all last night?" he said, looking at her.

Greenhaugh had plonked herself in Emil's visitors' chair. The skin under her eyes was dark and had taken on prune-like qualities.

"I managed to find out some more details through my connections back home. You wanna hear the bad bits, or the worse bits, first?"

"What about you give me both over a coffee?"

In the office kitchen, she set out what she'd gleaned overnight from her various US State Department contacts, the US Embassy in Port Moresby and her 'other sources', whom she said would have to remain nameless.

"Davies was picked up in a police stakeout. The police got a tip-off that a crime was being committed at a particular place at the back of Port Moresby harbour. It's a remote spot on the road heading around towards the oil refinery and new LNG plant – just bush and mangroves, apparently – and it was at night. The police were waiting in the bush, but then they realized someone was walking around at the spot, so on went the lights and they moved in. It was Davies, caught like a rabbit in car headlights."

"What the hell would he be doing in a place like that?"

"When the police questioned him, he was apparently very evasive – wouldn't give a clear answer about why he was there. Then they found the bodies in the mangroves."

"Jesus."

"Turns out they were a couple of foreign boys – not locals, early twenties. They'd entered PNG on tourist visas a week or two earlier. Their passports indicated one was British and the other was Australian."

Emil felt like his jaw was dropping lower the more Greenhaugh went on.

"The bodies had ... Things had been ... cut off ..."

"God almighty! It's unbelievable. Davies couldn't have anything to do with something like that!"

"There's so much riding on this PNG application, Emil. Not just for this organisation. This is really the last throw of the dice. Globally. I know it. You know it. Davies should know it. Whether he's responsible or not, how could he let himself get into a situation like this?"

"I just don't know. I can't explain it. Gordon knows just as well as we do how important this is."

"He's one of your team. So get out there and find out what's going on. Sort it out. Quick!"

Betty G rinsed her empty coffee cup and, with a final direct look at Emil over the top of her half-moon glasses, was gone.

2

A key in the lock woke him. Gordon Davies struggled to sit up on the concrete slab that had been his bed for the past three nights. The sergeant motioned for him to stand, which he did, straightening his burly, hulking, once-upon-a-time rugby forward's frame only with difficulty. The cold slab had been murderous for his lower back.

"You are being bailed, Mr Davies," the sergeant said over his shoulder as Davies followed him through the reeky breezeblock corridors to the front desk.

With laborious precision, in the sergeant's neat but slow hand, the necessary forms were filled out, then signed. All in Melanesian time, Davies murmured to himself, with a little nod of self-acknowledgement. His watch, wallet (miraculously still with contents, he noted) and the other possessions he had on him three nights earlier returned and signed for, he made his way out to the compound where his hire car had been left, being careful to shade his eyes from the intense mid-morning sunlight. Slightly disoriented by the brightness, with sunglasses and air-conditioning on, he sat behind the wheel of his car, doors locked and eyes closed, collecting himself. In his mind's eye, he could still see the vision of the bodies in the mud beneath the mangroves. Every time he'd closed his eyes since that moment, it had been there, as if the image had been tattooed indelibly on his retina.

Davies opened his eyes. On his lap was a letter the desk sergeant had given him. It was from the Minister with whose office

Davies was meant to be dealing, the Minister for Climate Change, Sir Gideon Kukuraimi. The desk sergeant had told him it was Sir Gideon who had posted his bail. He ripped open the envelope and read the handwritten note. It confirmed that Sir Gideon had put up the bail. The note requested Davies meet the Minister that afternoon at Sogeri, in the foothills of the Owen Stanley Ranges behind Port Moresby, at the Owen Stanley Motor Lodge. Davies was not to mention the meeting to anyone.

It would take over an hour's drive to get there, so Davies headed back to his hotel in 'town', as the port area of Port Moresby, around the eastern side of the mouth of Fairfax harbour, was still known. Boroko, where he'd been held at the main police lock-up, was half-way between town and the airport and was the main shopping precinct. North of Boroko was Waigani, where the parliament and most of the government offices were located. But Davies always stayed in town, at the hotel at the top of Hunter Street, above Ela Beach, with views to both the harbour and Coral Sea. Over the years it had become like a second home to him.

The clothes he was wearing were imbued with three days' sweat and a rankness only Boroko police cells could impart – reminiscent of the pooey, stale sewage smell that emanates from drains in old cities during prolonged dry spells. Luckily, no other hotel guest or employee needed to share the lift with him. He showered, and although they probably should have been thrown away, put them in for laundering. Once on the road again, he retraced his route back out to Boroko, through the early afternoon shopping traffic, past the roadside shanties to Six Mile, past the airport turn off and out of the city.

A few kilometres further on, where the highway headed to Brown River, he turned into the Sogeri Road, passing the crocodile farm and Bomana gaol, shuddering at the thought he might end up inside the latter – or either – for that matter. The road began to climb, running parallel to the Laloki River. It was lush and green along the river, but away from it the landscape quickly gave way to a burnt brown. Past the Bluff Inn, the road ascended steeply into a series of long switch backs, punctuated by hairpin bends, some of these bends so improbable, Davies wondered whether his hire car would actually negotiate them. Apart from a smattering of rusted panels of Marsden steel matting – a World War Two relic – it was devoid of any attempt at a safety rail, one side simply giving way to a precipitous drop, the other a wall topped by the switchback above. It was the tail end of the wet and the Laloki was thundering over Rouna Falls, throwing up a fine mist that nurtured verdant overhanging shrubbery, but beyond that burnt patches of yellowy-brown grass, or simply bare rock, covered the erect cliff faces and surrounding hills.

Shortly before reaching Sogeri, he turned off the road through what passed as a gateway: two sawn logs about four metres tall, with another across the top, giving access to an oval of flat, beaten dust perhaps twenty metres in diameter. It was rimmed by a number of fibro cabins with corrugated iron roofs, a larger structure standing at the far end. To describe the Motor Lodge as unpretentious wouldn't be unfair. Nature had come to its aid, though, and a profusion of red and yellow hibiscus blooms on a sea of green foliage hid much of the constructed ugliness. A single vehicle stood outside one of the guest cabins – not the Minister's, but another hire car, identical to Davies' own. The only sign of life a cassowary, carefully picking its way through a rubbish bin.

Giving the cassowary a wide berth, Davies entered the larger building through the bar area and made a quick scout around, confirming the Minister wasn't in the dining area, the bar or the seating area off the bar that constituted the lounge. He went back to the bar and ordered a beer. Apart from Davies, Herbie, the owner, who was sitting at the end of the bar, and the national serving behind the bar, the place was empty. In Davies' experience of previous visits, Herbie's current position was more or less semi-permanent, as was the polystyrene bottle holder clamped in his hand like an extension of his arm and the regular turnover of cold beer bottles that passed through it.

Davies moved into the lounge area to wait for the Minister. A short while later, a couple entered and sat in the dining area. The lunch menu consisted of steaks – beef or crocodile – which came with a salad. Onto his second beer, and still with no sign of the Minister, Davies had started giving the menu more serious consideration when there were raised voices from the dining area.

The diners, apparently the only guests at the Lodge, were complaining loudly to the barman-cum-waiter:

"We ordered tossed salads, fella, but all you've brought us here is," as the husband demonstrated by holding up between his thumb and index finger with mock delicacy, "just some very sad li'l ol' lettuce leaves."

They were from the Decatur, Illinois, USA and had stayed in good and bad places all over the world, the man was explaining, but in most, when they'd asked for a tossed salad, it hadn't been *too difficult* for the management to provide one.

Herbie stood just a shade under two metres tall, the wobbling rolls of belly overhanging his belt not even sumo-like, just looking excessively corpulent, in spite of his height. It took a lot of both physical effort and provocation to get him to haul himself off his bar stool. But he didn't broach no shit, not from Americans or anyone else, either, and now he was on the move, heading for the dining area.

"Don't youse fuckin' yanks do anything but complain?" announced his arrival. "Yesterday it was the fuckin' towels not bein' replaced offen unuf, today it's the fuckin' food."

He reached the table and picked up their plates, then heaved the contents skywards, up into the vaulted roof of the dining area, into the overhead fan, spraying the meat and salad, such as it was, all over the room.

Herbie leant forward as far as he safely could without toppling over, sticking his face close to the stunned couple.

"Is that fuckin' tossed unuf feryer now?"

Then he straightened and waddled back to his stool.

Watching this sideshow in the next room, Davies didn't notice Sir Gideon had slipped in and was now sitting opposite. Turning back, he started.

"Good to see I can still surprise you fellows," said Sir Gideon, giving a weak smile.

Davies smiled back. "I'm sure you have plenty of surprises for us up your sleeve, Minister," he said.

"Well, order me one of those," Sir Gideon gestured at Davies' half empty beer bottle, "and I'll share a few more with you."

The Minister sounded business-like. So it would seem this was not meant to be a social meeting. The fracas in the dining room had settled down, the couple having left in disgust and not a little intimidated, Davies got the barman's attention and another beer was promptly delivered. They clinked their bottles and each took a swig.

"Do you have your car here, Minister?"

"No, I just had my driver drop me and go back down. I didn't want to broadcast my whereabouts or who I was meeting."

"Thank you for posting the bail," Davies began, "but for the life of me, I have no idea what this business is all about. It's true what the police have been saying: I was there to meet those boys. But they were the ones who wanted the meeting – I didn't even know what they looked like."

Sir Gideon listened sitting forward in his chair, elbows resting on knees and fingertips pressed together, head tilted slightly down. As Davies finished speaking, he lifted his head and their eyes met. They stared at each other for a moment, before Sir Gideon wiped the dampness from his eyes with a thumb. Looking at Davies very directly, he spoke slowly and so softly that Davies could barely hear him, even though he was less than a metre away.

"This is entirely my fault. I accept full responsibility."

"Why? How, Minister?"

Sir Gideon shook his head slowly. "I have been a fool. A real fool … the deaths of these boys … I can't begin to tell you how upsetting this is. On my watch, my ministry. It's entirely my fault."

He took another swig from his bottle. "I have been an absolute fool," he repeated, with a slow, regretful shake of the head.

"Minister, how?"

Sir Gideon Kukuraimi: tribal big man; chief of his Highlands village; long-term, well-respected public figure. A former ambassador to the United Nations, as well as one of the longer serving politicians in his country's short political history. Now, just a glassy-eyed, sad, old man sat in front of Davies.

"I must come clean. It's too late for those boys, but at least I can still do it for myself."

Sir Gideon's eyes made a quick sweep of the bar and what he could see of the dining area over Davies' shoulder. There was no-one except the barman to be seen, even Herbie was temporarily away from his stool.

Sir Gideon leant forward, even closer to Davies' face:

"I have taken money from people that I shouldn't have. My trading company, back up home, was in trouble. I don't know how they found out, but they said they would pay some consulting fees to get the banks off my back. They said they just wanted to help me through with some extra cash. I was stupid, I didn't think. But I've stopped it now and made some inquiries. The company that was paying me exists only on paper. Now these two boys are dead and I know the same people that were behind it are responsible." Sir Gideon's eyes widened. "I know they killed these boys and now I know why!"

Outside in the white light of mid-afternoon there was barely a movement. Even the cassowary had stalked off, with slow, deliberate steps, somewhere else into the shade. Inside, Sir Gideon had Davies' full and undivided attention. He began his story.

3

The pilot's voice came over the intercom, announcing that they'd soon be crossing the coastline. Emil struggled to open his eyes, to straighten up from the position into which he'd slumped, forehead against the window. He'd dribbled in his sleep. He got the back of his hand across his chin just before a member of the cabin crew leant over and asked him to put his tray table up. The papers he'd been reading were on the floor around his feet. They'd have to stay there until they landed.

It had been a long journey. He'd been on the flight out of Frankfurt the same evening as his early morning exchange with Betty G. Booked at such short notice, he was routed via Singapore to Sydney, then back up to Port Moresby. He was tired and stiff and, even though he'd managed to grab a quick shower in the lounge at Singapore, he needed to get to his hotel and change. He felt like shit, probably smelt like it, and expected he looked like it, too.

Crossing the outer reef, in the distance to the west lay Port Moresby, shrouded in the ever-present smoke haze from fires the locals lit everywhere at this time of year. Ignoring the greasy mark his forehead had left on the window, he stared out into the shimmering blue of the Coral Sea and back twenty years to when he'd been on a similar flight, looking out on the same view. He'd been a newly qualified lawyer, heading to a new job, in a new country. It had been a big adventure. Even sat in a similar window seat. He remembered the passenger next to him introducing himself as George Smiley, as the man gulped into his fourth G&T. He'd wondered if the guy was a Le Carre fan, or just a fantasist. Port Moresby, he'd come to learn in his three years there, had more than its fair share of such characters.

"The only people who go to PNG," someone in Sydney said to him before he'd left, "are missionaries, mercenaries or misfits."

He wondered which description fitted him.

The aircraft rolled around to make its landing approach into the afternoon onshore breeze – a permanent feature other than in the wet season. Tipping down, beneath him the red earth and sparse tree cover around the shacks dotted about the airport perimeter fence, he recalled his arrival that first time. Stepping out of the plane, the heat had pressed in on him like it was trying to force him to the ground. There, in the scorching sun, behind the cyclone wire fence, sweating like the crowd of sweating nationals around him, had been the piggy face of Piers Birch, with its veinous snout and beady brown eyes. Piers was gone now, not *gone pinis*, like ex-pats usually did, but *dai pinis*. The fags and the grog. Another feature of ex-pat life back then, Emil recalled, as the aircraft wheels touched the tarmac at Jacksons International Airport.

He noticed the tightness across his shoulders. Taking a couple of deep breaths, rolling his shoulders like he was belatedly putting into effect exercises recommended on the in-flight video, he tried to expunge the unwelcome visitors that were crowding their way into his memory. He'd arrived that first time a blank canvas, without pre-conceptions, or even views on many things; just brimming with the sense of the different, the unknown, the adventure, and the competitive, unquestioning faith in one's ability to deal with anything that blesses youth, before it countenances the disappointments that life can throw-up over you. He'd found his peer group – the ex-pat lawyers – to be less than engaging, to the point of rejection, establishing few connections with them and maintaining none. His social contacts had come mostly from the local community. He wondered whether he'd been drawn to them or driven to them, his choice or his fallback; had his natural inclination been to friendship with the locals, or had they just been his safety net? When he'd left PNG, he'd closed it off from his mind, like an unfinished book he'd lost interest in reading. Now it was down from the shelf, open in front of him again.

The baking hot, tin shed he'd entered the country through on that first occasion had gone, too, replaced by a new terminal and an arrivals hall that had working overhead fans. This time, too, instead of queuing for hours to have his bags searched, his diplomatic passport smoothed his entry passage. Exiting the arrivals area, Emil was greeted by a national carrying a large, white card on which his name was neatly printed. He introduced himself as Hoko. He would be Mr Pfeffer's driver. Hoko said his director, the head of the Office of Climate and Carbon, had asked if Mr Pfeffer would mind coming to the offices before checking into the hotel, as there had been some developments. From Sydney, Emil had spoken to Dominik, who had informed him of news from the British Embassy that Davies had been bailed the previous day. So perhaps Davies would be at the OCC to greet him.

In his weary state, it didn't occur to him that if Davies knew he was coming, Davies would have been the one collecting him from the airport.

4

Waigani. The building that housed the OCC. So much was different, yet so much the same. Oil and gas finds in the previous decade had ensured there were plenty of new buildings, advertising hoardings, shops and roadside stalls, but there was no boom town feel to the place. If ever there had been, it was gone now. Even here in the government sector, new buildings had sprung up, but their appearance belied their age. Already there were signs of a lack of maintenance, or even simple up-keep. The roads leading to them were just as potholed as ever. The omni-present betel nut sellers still sat around them under the rain trees, plying their trade to red-mouthed customers who loitered in the shade, periodically breaking the rhythm of their mastication to hoick out dollops of red spit. That hadn't changed.

Hoko led Emil over the red-splodged, concrete footpath up to the building. A battered lift took them to the seventh floor. Emil noted, from the yellowing directory, that the Department of Justice Executive was located in the building. He made a mental note to seek out his old friend and former legal sparring partner, Gerry Johnstone, who now headed it. Leaving the lift lobby, they crossed an open plan area scattered with desks devoid of occupants. On the far side, a large office housed a single desk. The incumbent looked up as they approached, then came out to greet them.

"Hello, I'm Tomas Siroi," he announced. "Please come into my office, have a seat."

A loaded ashtray crowned the desk, the air thick from the most recent addition to it. Siroi signalled for Hoko to wait outside. Emil noticed the bright red of Siroi's mouth.

"I'm very pleased you could come here straight away," he said. "There have been some developments."

Emil was a little perplexed as to Davies' whereabouts. He'd been expecting him to be there to greet him.

"Yes, I understand Mr Davies has been bailed. Is he joining us?"

Siroi was focused on the cigarette lighter he was turning over and over in his hands. Emil wondered how long this was going to take. He really needed to have a shower and change his clothes. And talk to Davies; find out what was going on. He wished Siroi would get on with whatever he'd dragged him here for.

"Ah, I'm afraid I have some bad news, Mr Pfeffer," Siroi began, his gaze still focused on the lighter.

Emil sat up straighter in his chair. Where was this going?

"Don't tell me Mr Davies has been re-arrested, or something."

Siroi's hands stopped turning the lighter over. He looked up at Emil and as their eyes met, Emil immediately had the sense that he knew what Siroi was about to say.

"Ah, I'm sorry to have to tell you this, … Mr Pfeffer…but, Mr Davies is, ah, Mr Davies is … deceased."

Emil stared at Siroi.

"Dead?"

Siroi went on quickly.

"There was a motor vehicle accident. He was with my Minister, Sir Gideon Kukuraimi. They were both killed. The car was found this morning, it's only just been recovered from the Laloki River."

Emil couldn't think of what to say. It might have been the shock. It might just have been tiredness from the long journey. He sat speechless for a minute, dissonant thoughts competing in his head, like someone had just thrown a deck of cards into the air, and he was waiting for them to float down again, to see how they fell. Laloki River? What on earth were they doing there? Why would Davies be there with the Minister? What the hell was Betty G going to say?

"Do you know what happened?" he asked eventually.

"I'm sorry, Mr Pfeffer. I don't know anything more at this moment."

"Where is Mr Davies now?"

"Probably, the bodies will be at the morgue by now. Do you want to see Mr Davies? I think the police will ask you to identify him officially."

There were voices in the open office area outside. Emil, recognizing Gerry Johnstone's Kiwi tones, turned in his chair as Johnstone came in through the door. It was the same tanned, smiling face, the same dangerously disarming charm, that Emil remembered. The full head of wavy locks greying now, but in a distinguished sort of way that probably enhanced, rather than detracting from, his weathered good looks.

"I heard you were here. It's been a long time, mate – good to see you," said Johnstone, holding out his hand to Emil and at the same time nodding to Siroi.

"Thanks, Gerry. Yes, it's been quite a while. Good to see you, too. I was going to call by later to see if you were around. I'm a little bit stunned by the news Tomas has just given me."

"Yes, it's a bit of a shock for everyone. I'm sorry about Davies."

Johnstone's and Davies' paths had crossed occasionally over the years.

"Listen, mate, I'm going to be up at the Parliament for the rest of the afternoon, but I'll call by your hotel this evening. If you don't already have arrangements, maybe we can go up to the club for a drink."

"Thanks Gerry. Well, I was thinking that I'd be seeing Gordon, so no, I don't have any plans. I'm at the old Travelodge. I'll see you later then."

As Gerry left, Emil suddenly wondered about the wisdom of the arrangement he'd just made. Apart from being a notorious Lothario, whose own marriage was long over and who had tested the resilience of many other Port Moresby ex-pat marriages over the years, Gerry was, at least back then when Emil had been there, a renowned party animal, who never let his age or his professional seniority get in the way of some serious drinking. A drink at the club with Gerry could easily transmogrify into an all night wake for Gordon, Emil thought, if he wasn't careful. Not really what he needed just at the moment.

After some brief discussions with Tomas Siroi about Davies'

work and meetings, before the business with the police, it was agreed that Hoko should take Emil to his hotel, then to the morgue. Having checked in, he called Betty G. It was early morning in Frankfurt but, predictably, she was in her office.

"Hallo Emil. To what do I owe the honour of this early morning call?"

"Bad news, I'm afraid, Betty. Actually, terrible news. Gordon Davies is dead. He's been killed in a car accident."

Whatever shock she experienced was immediately subordinated to thoughts of damage control. Maybe that was just her way of dealing with it, Emil thought. Or maybe she'd already been notified, by her 'unnamed' sources. He said he'd call her again as soon as he had more information.

The afternoon heat was ebbing by the time they were heading out to Port Moresby General Hospital, to the morgue. Tomas Siroi had notified the police inspector in charge of the investigation – in fact both investigations, the murder of the boys and the fatal road accident – since they were linked by Davies. The inspector would meet them there.

As they approached, a large crowd of nationals, congregated outside the hospital gates, started spilling out over the roadway so that Hoko was forced to slow, then stop altogether, as the vehicles ahead of them had their passage blocked. The ochre mud-caked highlanders began working their way down the line of traffic. Emil had a sense of déjà vu.

"They're highlanders, *wantoks* of Sir Gideon. They're here to pay their respects," explained Hoko. "Don't look at them, it's best just to just look straight ahead."

"Yes, I know. I've made that mistake before."

As a younger man, he'd returned the stares. Normally, the highlanders would destroy just their own property as a mark of respect for a deceased big man. His cultural naivety, on that earlier occasion, had resulted in his vehicle receiving special 'respect' attention from the mourners. Windows had been broken, windscreen wipers and wing mirrors ripped off.

The mourners were all around the vehicle now. Orange smeared faces staring in at Emil, slapping the bonnet and roof with the ochre mud, or just their open palms. A face pushed up against the windscreen in front of Emil, staring eyes challenging, an open palm hit hard and flat onto the window next to his head, startling him. Surrounded by them, trapped in the car, puzzlingly, the image conjured by Emil's mind's eye was of the black hooded, anti-market troublemakers at the Köln conference, and other climate protests. They couldn't be more different, he mused. Then another flat-handed blow landed on the roof above his head and, instinctively, he flinched.

"It's OK," reassured Hoko.

The crowd moved on and they were able to turn into the hospital grounds and park. Getting out of the car, Emil's legs felt like he'd just cycled very hard up a steep hill. He lent on the vehicle and flexed them, trying to release the tension from his thighs. A policeman came forward to greet them.

"Mr Pfeffer, I am Inspector Dawani," he said, extending his hand.

"Pleased to meet you, Inspector. I understand from Tomas Siroi, at the OCC, that you might want me to identify Mr Davies."

"Yes, that would be very helpful, sir."

As they moved through the hospital grounds around the side of the building to the rear, where the morgue was located, the air seemed to become fouler with every step. The stench was soon over-powering, the air so offensive, that Emil had to put his arm up around his face, his nose and mouth covered in the crook of his elbow. The source of the offence was two shipping containers located outside the back of the hospital, besieged by clouds of flying insects.

"These are where the unclaimed bodies are stored, until mass burials are organized," said Dawani on seeing Emil's reaction. "They are mostly victims of AIDS."

The doctor in charge, Steve Grahame, hearing them from inside the wire screen door of the morgue, came out and introduced himself.

"Rape and promiscuity are pretty common in Moresby, in both cases almost always unprotected," he went on. "The stigma of being HIV positive or having AIDS means that most never admit it until they can't hide it, by which time they've probably infected a number of others. It also means, unfortunately for the hospital, that the bodies of AIDS victims are rarely collected – so that's where we store the overflow," said Grahame, nodding at the shipping containers.

"Even more unfortunately," he continued in his laid-back drawl, "the refrigeration units in both containers failed last week. Haven't been able to get an engineer in to fix 'em yet."

The formality of identifying Davies was over quickly. Emil's final memory of the rambunctious, rugby-loving Welshman would be of that bruised, greying corpse laid out on a mortuary slab, overwhelmed by the smell of decay emanating from other, unwanted, fellow corpses.

Grahame indicated that both Davies and the Minister, who was laid out on a table adjacent, had multiple fractures.

"There's signs from the bruising that both of them were wearing a seat-belt, but I doubt it would have saved them anyway. They both drowned, so they would have been alive when the car went into the river, but my guess is from the degree of head and other trauma they were both unconscious."

As they were leaving the hospital, Inspector Dawani came up beside Emil and enquired how long he would be in Port Moresby.

"I'm not sure, Inspector, it depends to some degree on when you release the body of Mr Davies. I will need to make arrangements for it to be repatriated to the United Kingdom."

"Well, sir, the deaths have been reported to the coroner, so the bodies are now under his control – he needs to issue a warrant for a body to be released," said Dawani. "He's already indicated that he will be holding an inquest, since it appears Sir Gideon and Mr Davies drowned – this is required under the Act. I expect that will be within the next week. When Mr Davies' body is released will depend on his findings."

The Inspector thought for a moment.

"If the finding is just that it was an unfortunate accident, then I think you will be free to take Mr Davies' body immediately."

"And is that likely to be the finding, Inspector?" Emil asked.

"I don't want to pre-empt the outcome, sir, but it looks that way."

5

Back at the hotel, Emil rang Betty G.

"I'll arrange to contact Mrs Davies. I haven't had to do something like this before, but I'll sort something out," she said, to Emil's relief. "And I'll contact New York about getting the wheels in motion for the repatriation and other arrangements. But you, Emil, can have the pleasure of following up on the voluminous amounts of paperwork this will generate."

He'd booked into the same hotel as Davies for convenience. Instead now, the limited floor space of his room was occupied by Davies' suitcase and personal effects. The duty manager had them dropped in, apologetically explaining that the hotel would either need to continue charging for Mr Davies' room, or make it available to other guests. While he waited for Johnstone, he went through the papers in Davies' briefcase. The laptop was password locked, that would have to wait until he returned to Frankfurt. At the hospital, Inspector Dawani had given him Davies' mobile phone, wallet, passport and the other personal effects the police had recovered. The vehicle had been hired by Davies, so Emil added a visit to the car hire company to his growing list of unhappy tasks.

He was in danger of falling asleep by the time Johnstone arrived. Even though they were only going to the Paga Hill end of Douglas Street, a distance of about five hundred metres, they took Johnstone's car. As Gerry reminded him, there was no point in Emil getting rolled by a gang of *raskols* on his first night back in Moresby.

The club was just the same as he remembered it. In fact, to his amusement, he found that he was still listed as an out-of-town member, in spite of the fact that he hadn't paid any fees since he'd left. The barmen still wore royal blue lap-laps and starched white shirts. The interior decorations were the same, just more faded. The same old, worn, leather armchairs were in more or less the same positions as when he had last been there, about twenty years earlier.

"Yeah, nothing has changed," said Johnstone as the waiter delivered their drinks. "Women still only allowed in on the same three occasions a year; no money, just got to keep your bar tab in credit; and if you're caught talking business you have to ring the bell."

Ringing the bell meant you had to buy a drink for anyone who came into the club for the rest of the day. Members also had to ring the bell on the day they joined and on their birthday. On top of the subscription, Emil had found his membership to be an expensive luxury. There were other clubs and places to socialize, but the Niugini Club, located in a big old house on Paga Hill with expansive views over Fairfax harbour from its wide verandah, shuttered doors and slowly turning overhead fans, had all the allure of being a true relic of the colonial days. When he'd first stepped through the door as a young man, he'd felt as if he'd been transported into the pages of Somerset Maugham. Now, he noticed, the shutters were supplemented by security grills, armed guards roaming amongst the bougainvillea and hibiscus below the verandahs and the interior was just shabby.

Despite the length of time since they'd last seen each other, inevitably, they talked about Davies. Emil was sure Johnstone would be able to fill in some of the gaps.

"Well, so far as I can tell from the police, they don't seem really to have anything linking him to the two bodies other than the fact that he was at the scene. Mind you, that in itself raises some questions. He claimed to the police that he'd been asked to meet someone at the place, but he couldn't say who or why. He said he didn't know the people who he'd arranged to meet or what the meeting was about. It all sounds a bit odd to me," said Johnstone.

Emil agreed.

"Do you know what he was doing with the Minister?" he asked.

"It seems he and the Minister had been up at the Owen Stanley Lodge. Herbie has given a statement to police that they'd been there all afternoon."

"What, so he's saying that Davies was pissed?" Emil didn't like the sound of this.

"I don't know. All I heard is that they'd been there for a quite a few hours."

"Great! This is getting better and better all the time."

Johnstone changed the subject.

"So how did you come to be involved in carbon trading?"

"Before I joined the GCMO, I'd been in-house counsel at a couple of corporates, financial sector related. Then I ended up working in the nascent carbon market, you know, project finance, buying and selling carbon credits. We started getting into trading in a big way, so I was putting my experience to work."

"If it was such a good wicket, how'd you end up as a regulator then?"

"Well, with the impasse over Kyoto, the talk shifted – in the international negotiations, that is – to how a compromise could be reached. Part of the compromise involved setting up the GCMO and I found out that there was going to be this unit for market integrity. They were looking for a lawyer with market experience to head it up. I was looking for a change of scene anyway…I needed to get out of London."

"Sounds like trouble with a woman, mate," said Johnstone, subconsciously defaulting to his own particular area of expertise.

"Actually, you're sort of right, Gerry. I had a partner, we'd been together quite a few years. Just over ten. In fact, it was just after we celebrated our tenth anniversary – she found out she had breast cancer. Then they found secondaries."

"Shit, the native dancer. I'm sorry, mate."

"Don't worry, Gerry. It was a fair while ago now."

Johnstone moved back to more comfortable ground.

"Have you run across the PM's Special Advisor on Climate and Carbon yet? We call him the Special Advisor for Everything."

"I haven't, but I'll have to at some stage, I guess. I'm glad to see you still have a healthy bureaucratic disrespect for your political masters and their appointees. So then, Gerry, tell me what's happening here about climate change?"

Johnstone cocked his head slightly:

"You know this place as well as I do, Emil. The crooks and conmen are woven into the fabric. As soon as that REDD idea, you know the forest conservation stuff, started to get traction, every Aussie conman who wasn't already here, suddenly appeared out of the woodwork, trying to buy up the rights to any credits that might become available for traditional landowners. Only problem was, the Chinese were in ahead of them. And the Chinese had a shitload more money to throw about."

"Yeah, my people have been keeping an eye on what's been happening here," said Emil, feeling a pang of melancholy as he thought of Davies' briefing he'd been reading a day or two earlier.

"Of course, the joke is on both the Chinese and Aussie spivs. The landowners up in the bush just keep on accepting money from whoever gives it to them – don't know any better. As far as they're concerned, these people are giving them money for something they couldn't see and didn't know they owned – the air, in effect, money for nothing! There'll be a problem, of course, when these spivs try to claim the credits from any conservation projects, but we'll deal with that when it crops up."

Funny, Emil thought, that's a totally different perspective from Davies' take on things.

"So what'll happen? You sound like you don't hold out too many hopes for this trading exchange the government's pushing?"

"Emil, mate, don't get me wrong, I'm a humble servant of the government!" Johnstone exclaimed with his hand on his heart. "My department's finished the legislation to set up the exchange. The government will initially own any credits generated, which it will then sell on the exchange. So no problem there. All we need now are genuine investors to bank roll things and there'll be *moni bilong skai* for everyone."

Then, as an after-thought:

"But don't let my jaundiced views colour your appraisal!"

"Don't worry – I'll keep an open mind, Gerry. Speaking of things that drop out of the sky, did you ever find out what happened to that guy Shaun what's-his-name who used to play indoor cricket with us?"

"Shaun … ?"

"Mmm. Maybe it was Shane. You know, he was a researcher out at the uni. Used to drop out of a helicopter onto lily pads to count the eggs in croc nests. Good cricketer, but then he suddenly stopped coming. No-one heard from him again."

"Oh God yeah, him. Sometime, maybe a year, I guess, after you'd left, we heard that there'd been trouble with one of his female student assistants. The male students took exception to it, so apparently he went *pinis,* rather abruptly."

Then he added: "Back to Adelaide or wherever he came from, I think, as opposed to down a croc's throat, that is."

"Well, I guess he was a risk taker," observed Emil. "What about the others that used to show up for the cricket, do you ever hear from them? Whatever happened to old Charlie Broadbent?"

"Oh, they all go *pinis* eventually. Charlie's bank sent him to some godforsaken place in South America, I think. Asuncion, or Quito. Somewhere like that."

"You remember the day he forgot to put the bungs in and sank the bank boat right outside the yacht club?"

"Yeah, with the bank logo on the bow the only part visible, right next to the launching ramp! Everyone in Moresby knew what the silly bugger had done. Mind you, he still managed to put on a pretty good piss up that night back at his place, if I remember correctly …"

"So what about these two tourists that Gordon was supposedly meeting. What do you think the story is with them?"

Johnstone was thoughtful for a moment or two, then asked:

"Do you remember me telling you about the first case I had when I came up here as a junior prosecutor?"

"You mean the cannibalism trial with all the chattering in the public gallery?" said Emil laughing. "That story got better each time you told it!"

"Yeah, and it was true, by the way. They all had lockjaw from eating human flesh. Anyway, I saw the autopsy photos of those two boys. They had body parts missing. Really reminded me of the victim in that trial, although mind you, in that case he'd been dead a day or two before he ended up on the menu. But it was just the same sort of way pieces had been removed, almost selectively...."

"So what are you saying – Davies had picked up some unusual dietary tastes?"

"No, no, not at all, mate. Look, since the last lot of oil and gas finds, it's really changed. We get so many people coming through Moresby ... I wouldn't be surprised what sort of things are going on in the squatter settlements that've sprung up all 'round the place in the last few years. That's all I'm saying. You know, traditional beliefs, a bit of sorcery and witchcraft, compounded by settlement criminality. These boys probably just fell in with the wrong crowd – especially at that spot where we found them, it's a bit notorious around there now."

Emil wasn't sure whether Johnstone meant it was a place to buy illicit drugs, a gay pick-up spot, a spot to get robbed and murdered, or what. But he didn't want to broadcast his ignorance, so stayed silent. Not long after that they decided to call it a night, agreeing to catch up for dinner before Emil left. Johnstone also offered to provide one of his bright young legal officers to tag along with Emil and make sure he didn't have any problems, an offer Emil readily accepted – anything to smooth the way was welcome. Then Johnstone dropped him back at the hotel.

They'd only had a couple of beers and it wasn't late at all, so it seemed his earlier misgivings had been misplaced. Since he left Port Moresby, Emil hadn't kept in contact with anyone directly, only hearing of developments there second-hand through third parties. But he managed to extract from Johnstone during the course of the evening the fact that he was now in a stable relationship, which was having a calming influence on his lifestyle. He said he'd 'settled down'. Their friendship, the only one amongst Emil's former ex-pat legal peers, had developed out of one of the more extreme moments of Gerry's earlier self-destructive behaviour, when he was very much 'unsettled down'. At the Law Society dinner in the year Emil arrived in Port Moresby, Emil had retrieved Johnstone from some bushes where he had passed out, dead drunk, while trying to urinate. He was a mess, and Emil had extricated him just before the Chief Justice and Attorney-General, together with visiting legal dignitaries, would have found him as they were leaving. Emil had got him home safely. When Gerry heard about it from third parties, not actually able to remember any of the evening himself, he'd done his best to make sure that Emil was accepted by a professional fraternity unwelcoming of unconnected newcomers.

Those days were now long gone for both of them, Emil reflected. But Gerry certainly hadn't lost any of his talent for spinning the bullshit, like his old chestnut, the cannibalism trial story.

6

Emil spent the next few days shuttling between various locations, wrapping up Gordon Davies' last visit to Papua New Guinea, thinking of himself as some sort of executor's assistant.

He sorted out the situation with the hire car – luckily Davies' had taken out full replacement insurance. Just a sheaf of forms needing to be filled out. Then, having made several visits to the police to discuss the complications of Davies' status as both a bailed person and a motor vehicle accident victim, and to the British Embassy concerning his rights as a British citizen, Emil turned his attention to picking up the threads of Davies' official purpose in being there: the PNG request for recognition for international carbon trading.

In spite of these tasks filling his days, and the tropical heat and jetlag disrupting his sleep and wearing on him physically, he couldn't get out of his head the nagging questions why Davies would want to meet these tourists in the first place, why Sir Gideon would put up the bail money for him and what they had been doing together up at Sogeri. He started conjuring up all manner of fanciful explanations. Maybe the pair of them were part of some sort of cannibalism cabal – perhaps they'd been doing it for years! Maybe Betty G's off-the-cuff assessment had been accurate after all. Or, maybe, the boys were rough trade that Davies and the Minister picked up, but things had got out of hand. Maybe Gerry was right about the boys. Or, maybe, all of them had just been in the wrong place at the wrong time.

He had to end this baseless speculation going on in his head. He needed some answers.

A couple of days before the inquest he had Hoko drive him – and Robert, the young legal officer Gerry had sent – to view the spot where Davies' vehicle had been retrieved from the river. When they got there, the only sign of the location was a remnant of police accident tape. Ahead and behind them, the steep, narrow bitumen strip was more or less straight. To their left was the precipitous, rocky drop down to the river, still raging with the last of the wet season rains running off the Sogeri plateau. Above them, the near vertical rock face reaching up to the next switchback section of road. But apart from the tape, there was no sign of an accident.

"Well, it doesn't look like they tried to brake," Emil observed, scrutinizing the road surface.

Robert was a Papuan, with the finely chiselled features, the slim, sinewy frame of the coastal people and big, afro-style hair, which made him look like he'd time travelled from a 1970s rock band. He came from a village just down the coast from Port Moresby and reminded Emil of some of the local friends he'd made years earlier, but with whom he hadn't kept in touch.

Robert had been standing for a couple of minutes looking up the rock face.

"Up there, see," he said, pointing. "It looks like glass."

They headed up to the section of road above, from where they could clearly see broken glass and what looked like scrapings of paint on some of the more protruding rocks below. But there was nothing to indicate the vehicle had run off the road there either. So they headed up to the next switchback. At the top, the road continued past the stopping point for the Rouna Falls lookout – this sat on a huge exposed mound of rock topped by an electricity cable pylon – before running on to Sogeri. Up here, two switchbacks above where the police had determined Davies' car left the roadway, it was clear from the scrapings through the dirt and grass fringing the road that this had been the vehicle's actual point of departure. It was a long way down. The rock face irregular, nearly vertical. Little wonder the vehicle had been so battered and their bodies so broken.

When Emil had seen enough, Hoko used the lookout parking area to turn around and Emil commented that the Huli wigman was in his familiar position, standing in traditional dress waiting for tourists to stop and take his photo, for a fee.

"That can't be the same guy who was standing there for the tourists twenty years ago, when I was here, surely?"

"No, it'll be the son or cousin or a wantok of the guy who was there then," said Robert. "The guy who was there, when you were here, is probably enjoying his retirement down in Cairns now, he had so many photos taken over the years."

They continued back down to the next switchback, when Emil suddenly exclaimed:

"Stop! We need to go back. The wigman might have been there that afternoon. He might have seen the accident."

With exaggerated caution, Hoko reversed back into the hairpin bend and did what was more like a ten point turn, before heading back up to the Rouna Falls lookout. The wigman was still squatting there and when they pulled up, stood ready to be photographed.

"Ask him how much for a photo."

Robert and the wigman had a brief conversation. "Twenty-five kina, but I told him that's too much."

"Sounds like his price is indexed for inflation. Used to be about two kina when I lived here. Ask him if he's the same wigman who used to be here twenty years ago."

Robert had another rapid exchange with the wigman. "He says that would have been his uncle."

"OK, tell him I have a photo of his uncle and I'll buy one of him, but first I want to know if he saw the motor car accident that happened here a couple of weeks ago with Sir Gideon."

Robert translated, and the wigman gave forth a torrent in Huli. Robert stopped him and he started again in Motu, the local language, but just as quickly.

"He said he saw the accident. He remembers because he was just about to head home that evening – the day had been very quiet with hardly any cars at all – just the white car that had the accident heading up in the early afternoon, and one or two others."

"Did he tell the police?"

Robert translated but there was no response. The wigman

had turned and was running down the track towards the viewing platform for the Falls, away from them and away from the road. Behind them, a vehicle could be heard approaching from below. Soon a long wheel-base Landcruiser pulled over the rise and stopped adjacent to where their vehicle was parked, the occupants hidden behind tinted windows. They stood there looking at it, then it slowly continued on up the hill, towards Sogeri.

"They must have thought we were raskols," joked Robert.

"Well *they* scared off our wigman, he didn't even wait for the photo. I guess we'll have to wait for the inquest to hear what he's got to say."

The following day, when he was at the OCC, Emil decided, on the spur of the moment, to call into Sir Gideon's Ministerial office, to see if he could glean any more information. Inquiring whether Sir Gideon's Chief of Staff might be available for a quick chat, he was asked to wait. Half an hour later he was just about to give up and leave when a stocky, balding, bearded highlander appeared out of the offices. He introduced himself as Sam Kaumi, Sir Gideon's Chief of Staff, and invited Emil to join him in his office. The cut of Kaumi's pressed white shirt and grey pinstripe trousers, his club tie and patent leather shoes, gave Emil that uncomfortable underdressed feeling, like arriving at a formal function in an open neck shirt. He felt more like a tourist, than someone conducting official business. Perhaps he should have made an appointment, he thought, but oh well, it was too late now. He'd just press on.

When they'd finished exchanging condolences over the deaths of Sir Gideon and Davies, Emil explained how there were aspects of Davies' situation that he was at a loss to understand. Sam might be able to help.

"For example, do you have any idea why the Minister would post bail for Mr Davies, or why, on Mr Davies' release, they would meet at Sogeri?"

"Don't you think you should leave those questions for the police and the coroner, Mr Pfeffer?"

The voice was distinctly North American and it came not from Sam Kaumi, whose mouth hadn't moved, but from behind Emil's back. He's a ventriloquist, was Emil's first crazy thought, but then turning around his gaze met that of the tall, slim figure standing in the doorway, perfectly groomed, staring at him intently, obsidian eyes boring in like a sintered diamond drill, the hair straight and black, swept back and across his head, gelled in place.

He moved into the room and held out a hand.

"Gregory Hudson. Special Advisor on Climate and Carbon to the Prime Minister's Office," he said, mouth crookedly half-cocked in what Emil took for an attempt at a smile, but closer to a grimace.

"Pleased to meet you. Emil Pfeffer," he responded, shaking his hand, "but you obviously already know who I am."

Emil observed Hudson as he sat down in the other chair in front of Kaumi's desk, crossed his legs then resumed his black stare. So this is the Special Advisor for Everything, Emil thought, as he watched him, how long has he been there listening to me? Everything about him is smooth: his skin, his features, the hand he'd just shaken, his attire, his manner. He seems to ooze smoothness. Elegant, is the image being cultivated here, Emil thought. He would look out of place in Moresby. But instead Emil was the one feeling distinctly out of place, even more underdressed. It was easy to see where the influence on Kaumi's dress sense came from.

Hudson was continuing: "As I was saying, I'm sure your questions will be answered by the police and coroner. I think it would be counterproductive for you to be second-guessing them when you've only been here in Port Moresby five minutes, don't you?"

The line was delivered lightly, but there was no mistaking the sting in the tail. Emil decided he could come back to that later.

"I hope you're right, Greg, as from my…"

"It's Gregory." Hudson interjected quickly, smoothly, firmly, like he'd been waiting for it.

"Well, Gregory," said Emil, his voice betraying slight annoyance, "I lived in Papua New Guinea myself, a number of years ago … from that experience I have reservations that the police or coroner will be able to answer all my questions about what happened here."

"As you say, Mr Pfeffer, it was a number of years ago – twenty, wasn't it? Papua New Guinea has changed since the old days when you were here."

So he's done his homework. *I wonder what else from my background he's picked up.* Emil decided on another tack.

"I understand that PNG will be lodging its formal application for recognition of its trading arrangements soon."

"Yes, there's been a lot of hard work put in over the last twelve to eighteen months to bring that to fruition. You might also be aware of the government's flagship Debepare forest conservation projects: credits from these will be amongst the first listed and traded on the market, when it opens. The Department of Justice has prepared the necessary legislation to implement it. Technical work on setting up the exchange is progressing well. Of course, we aren't there yet, but we hope to be soon."

Hudson's voice took on a softer, sincere tone.

"Your organisation's recognition is very important for giving investors confidence, as I'm sure you know. We'll be taking a marketing roadshow to a couple of selected locations in Europe, later in the year, to encourage some first world governments and companies to invest in the future, rather than just talk about it. Perhaps you'll have time to come along to one of our events and be impressed."

Like most of his type, Emil thought, *this guy likes the sound of his own voice. It only takes a small prompt to get them going.*

"I might just do that, Gregory," he responded. "But like your advice concerning the police and coroner, I'll wait and see, before I decide whether I'm impressed. More to the point, the GCMO itself will need to be impressed before you get to use its endorsement as a marketing tool."

Hudson gave his half-cocked smile again, then stood, Emil thought, to leave.

"You'll be sure to work through the appropriate liaison channels for any future enquiries, won't you, Mr Pfeffer? Tomas Siroi and his team at OCC are doing an excellent job, and if they can't help you, they can refer matters through to the right part of the government for response. We need to make sure we do things properly," he finished, holding out his hand again.

But this time it was not to shake, it was gesturing towards the door. Emil was being dismissed! He felt his hackles rise. He let them settle, before slowly easing himself out of his chair. He wasn't going to give Hudson the satisfaction of ushering him out quite so quickly. With a show of great warmth, he reached over the desk and, picking up Sam Kaumi's inert hand from the desk, pumped it vigorously.

"Sam, thank you so very much. It's been a great pleasure meeting you. We must catch up again sometime when work matters aren't so pressing. Perhaps we can have a drink or something," Emil beamed at the daydreaming Kaumi who, until that point, had sat sphinx-like behind his desk, a non-participant.

Releasing Kaumi's hand, Emil momentarily held Hudson's sloe-eyed stare, then turned and walked out.

7

Hoko collected him early on the morning of the inquest. Robert met them at the court with the news that the inquest into the deaths of the two tourists would immediately follow on from this inquest. Two days had been scheduled in the court lists for each.

Due to the amount of interest concerning Sir Gideon, the proceedings had been removed from the small, low ceiling, stiflingly hot, plasterboard rooms that were Boroko District Court to the comparatively salubrious precincts of the National Court at Waigani. The allocated court room was large, with high, thick, preformed concrete walls. But it was a hot Moresby day, the heat and humidity magnified in the court room by the number of wantoks and onlookers. It was airless. Emil sat there, fanning himself with a Manila folder, waiting for the appearance of the coroner. His shirt was already wet and sticking to his back. Pulling it out, flapping it up and down, he tried in vain to cool himself. As more and more people tried to get in, the court room was becoming increasingly claustrophobic. Eventually the coroner entered, but then ensued another delay as he ordered the overflow out of the court, so that the doors could be closed, to give the feeble air-conditioning a chance to work.

Opening formalities over, the coroner's assistant, a government lawyer, called the first witness, Inspector Dawani. He provided the background – the initial accident report, recovery of the vehicle from the river and the victims from inside, and the police investigation into how the accident may have happened – which was scant on detail – really drawing no conclusion other than that the vehicle drove off the road, and rolled down the embankment into the river.

"The vehicle was upside down in the river when found, causing the victim's heads to be under the water. It appeared from the position of the victims' bodies," Dawani concluded, "that Mr Davies was the driver of the vehicle and Sir Gideon was the passenger."

After discussions with Davies' widow, Betty G. had agreed that Emil should hire a lawyer from a private firm to represent Davies' family (and, as far as Emil was concerned, the GCMO) in the proceedings. The lawyer now tried to extract more information from Dawani.

"Inspector, were there any witnesses to the accident?"

"Ah, no sir."

The lawyer looked at Emil, then back to Dawani. "None at all, you're absolutely sure?"

Dawani hesitated.

"Yes, sir."

He wasn't. The lawyer looked at Emil again, then continued.

"Inspector, it is possible that Mr Davies' vehicle left the road just after the Rouna Falls lookout. Does that tally with the police accident investigation assessment?"

Dawani referred uncertainly to his notebook. He flipped a couple of pages, then peered into it for what seemed like minutes. Finally he looked up.

"Ah, sir, we don't have any information along those lines."

"Objection."

The coroner's assistant had let Dawani suffer enough.

"Yes, upheld," the coroner intervened. "Counsel, unless you propose to introduce specific evidence along the lines you are alluding," he said to Emil's lawyer, "of which you have given no indication before these proceedings commenced, I don't see the point of your line of questioning. Do you have any specific evidence?"

Emil's lawyer looked at him again then back to the coroner.

"No, sir, not at this time."

A deposition given by Herbie was admitted into evidence and Dawani called upon to read it into the transcript of proceedings.

According to Herbie, Davies and the Minister had been the only customers in the bar at the Owen Stanley Motor Lodge and they had been there for about four hours, drinking consistently.

Emil lent forward and hissed in his lawyer's ear:

"This is highly unusual procedure, is this normal here now? Where's Herbie – he should be here to be cross-examined on this."

The lawyer could only shrug. "The coroner has pretty wide powers under section ten of the Act."

Emil tried again: "Interject and ask if Herbie is being called to give evidence and be questioned by the represented parties."

The coroner's answer was no. Herbie, it seemed, had unexpectedly needed to travel back to Queensland and was not available, so no Summons had been issued for him to appear.

The autopsy report was next, but there was no sign that Steve Grahame was going to be called either. Instead, Inspector Dawani again was called upon to read out the medical examiner's findings as to cause of death, but that was all. Emil was perplexed. He lent forward again and whispered in his lawyer's ear:

"Ask what were the autopsy findings as to their blood alcohol levels."

Again the answer was unhelpful. It appeared the samples from the two deceased had been mixed up in the lab, one was tolerably low at 0.05 milligrams per litre, but the other was much more. Emil's lawyer asked whether there was a plan to take further samples, to help resolve the issue, to which the coroner's assistant answered that there didn't seem to be any reason. After thirty minutes of to-ing and fro-ing on this point, the coroner had had enough and adjourned for lunch.

A frustrating morning was compounded by the non-reappearance of the coroner, extending the luncheon break. Emil found he had to keep reminding himself he was back in PNG, to stay relaxed. When the afternoon session did commence, Emil was surprised to see Sam Kaumi called to give evidence and even more surprised by the direction in which that evidence went.

"Sir Gideon had been depressed for some time," said Kaumi, with more than a little prompting from the coroner's assistant. "He'd been having financial problems with his businesses in the highlands, but then things started to improve."

Emil really couldn't see what the point was of this evidence. He was just leaning forward to issue more directions to his lawyer when the coroner's assistant produced documents to the coroner, which he wished to tend as evidence: bank statements from the holding company for Sir Gideon's trading businesses.

"It appears," the assistant advised the coroner, "that this company, Yumbitchi Holdings, had been receiving regular payments from a Hong Kong company."

The assistant asked Sam Kaumi to speculate on why Sir Gideon would have been accepting such payments.

"The only possible reason I can think of," Kaumi responded, "is that this Hong Kong company was hoping Sir Gideon would use his influence with the government in some way."

Sir Gideon's family wasn't represented. Emil thought about getting his lawyer to interject, but on what grounds? He was appearing for Gordon Davies' family, not Sir Gideon's. And while the evidence was remote and Kaumi's opinions irrelevant, as Emil's lawyer had told him, it was open to the coroner to explore all avenues, and ultimately up to him to determine what was relevant in reaching his findings of fact.

Sam Kaumi stepped down and the coroner's assistant announced that there were no further witnesses. Even though they'd barely been going an hour since lunch, the coroner adjourned proceedings for the day.

"This is ridiculous! None of the evidence is being properly tested," Emil fumed as they left the court. "The coroner might have a broad discretion, but we should at least be able to test this evidence under cross-examination."

"It's difficult to do more than we are," the lawyer responded defensively.

"Yes, I know. I'm not blaming you. Everything about this inquiry is botched. The police didn't even wait for the medical examiner before removing the bodies from the vehicle. They just hauled them out and bagged them off to the morgue. It's a joke. No wonder they didn't want Dr Grahame here giving evidence!"

Robert and Hoko were waiting for him on the steps leading to the car parking area. He concluded his discussion with the lawyer, then started in their direction, too late his peripheral vision catching the group standing just around the corner, outside the judge's entrance to the court. He could sense Gregory Hudson's black stare on him. Hudson and Kaumi were in discussion with the coroner's assistant. Emil looked back at Hoko and Robert and, with the slightest nod of his head, indicated that they should clear out. By the time he looked back, Hudson was on his way over.

"I see you're making full use of the resources of the government of the Papua New Guinea, Mr Pfeffer," he stated matter-of-factly.

"The use of a vehicle is a courtesy that your colleague, Tomas Siroi, has extended to me, in the circumstances."

"And the Department of Justice lawyer another courtesy?"

"Well, since the Davies incident, perhaps the Department of Justice has decided that GCMO visitors to PNG need a chaperone."

"I'm glad you mentioned the Davies matter. I was going to raise it with you anyway," Hudson responded quickly. "There seems to be an unresolved issue concerning the bail money."

"Really? What's the problem?"

"Well, it seems the police are treating the bail money as theirs, since Davies did not comply with the terms of his release."

"Oh, for God's sake," said Emil. "The man was dead within hours of his release."

"Nevertheless," Hudson went on, "we also have a problem. It seems the money put up for Davies' bail was not Sir Gideon's, but, in fact, was a cheque written on the office of the Minister for Climate Change. So, in fact, it was the government's money and the government now wants it back."

"This is absurd. The government has it – the police have it and the police are part of the government. In fact."

"That's not the way it works, Mr Pfeffer, as you should know. Is that what you would say back in your rich country – in Australia, in Europe? No. I don't think so."

Emil was about to ask whether that was the way it worked in Hudson's country, which he presumed was the US, but thought better of it.

"I'll look into it," he said turning on his heel and heading towards the car park.

"That would be much appreciated by the citizens of this poor third world country, Mr Pfeffer." Hudson called after him.

Betty G was furious when he reported the day's proceedings to her, that evening.

"Shoot. It's a hatchet job. They're stitching up Sir Gideon, and by implication, Davies and therefore us. I can't begin to imagine what the fallout's gonna be for the GCMO. The Governing Council'll be jumping around like they've all stepped on a bull ant nest."

"The proceeding is unusual, to say the least, but we've made some inroads with our questions. There may even have been a witness to the actual accident they haven't bothered to call. If the coroner makes a finding of fact that Davies caused the accident, we're keeping to door open for a judicial review."

"OK Emil, just don't go making too many waves with this hotshot lawyer you've got. We need to limit the press coverage of this business, not increase it!"

No witnesses were called on the second day of the inquest. If there'd been any point to it, Emil would have tried to call Herbie and Steve Grahame to test the evidence, in spite of Betty G's warning ringing in his ears. The day devolved into the coroner retracing his steps through the evidence and then delivering his findings, which Emil duly reported to Betty G.

"He found they died of drowning as a result of 'an unfortunate motor vehicle accident'," Emil read from the notes he'd quickly jotted down in court. "He didn't actually make any finding as to how it happened. But you're not going to like the next bit."

"I don't care, Emil, just give it to me. Just give me the facts."

"He observed that the two deceased had been in the bar at the Owen Stanley Motor Lodge at Sogeri for some hours before the accident. And made some not-so-subtle references to what he described as a 'drinking binge', that preceded the accident. Of course, in the absence of the correctly identified blood samples – remember we had an argument over these yesterday – his observations in this respect don't have any real weight, but they will cause some bad press, I'm afraid, Betty."

"So we can expect reports saying that Davies was drunk and simply drove off the road?"

"That's about the long and the short of it."

Emil skipped down through the rest of his scribbled notes.

"OK, Emil, there wasn't any mention of the GCMO, which I have to say is my primary concern at this point. That's a good result. The best thing we can do now is give it time to fizzle out of the media. Let sleeping dogs lie."

He thought about ignoring her and doing a bit of legal stirring, but ultimately he didn't really have enough evidence to make it worth his while. He'd have to go along with her and let the dogs lie – for the moment.

8

Boroko District Court hadn't changed. No mining boom money had trickled this far down the government budget. It reminded him of the classrooms he'd spent years in as a schoolboy, growing up on the outskirts of Sydney. The permanent temporary type.

It was another hot one and, even with all overhead fans turning, the atmosphere was close. All they were doing, Emil thought as he sat there sweating, was moving the heat radiated off the expanse of bitumen car park outside, in through the open windows, around the bodies inside, like a big, slow convection oven.

The crowd of interested observers had dwindled to almost no-one, those milling around outside the windows mostly just not having anything better to do. Unlike the preceding days, they got underway promptly, the same coroner presiding but this time with no lawyer assisting, just a police sergeant.

Again, it was Inspector Dawani, sitting in a chair next to the coroner's table, who provided the police evidence concerning the stake out, the apprehension of Davies, the discovery of the bodies and Davies' arrest.

The autopsy findings were read into evidence by Dawani. At least it's time efficient, Emil thought, even if there isn't a proper examination of the evidence. The boys had suffered appalling injuries related to the excision of various organs. The report surmised that if the other injuries hadn't killed them first, then loss of blood from the wounds related to the excisions would have done so.

"The first deceased's body is missing the front half of its tongue and part of its head – the scalp has been removed, the skull has been fractured and a section removed and the parts of the brain adjacent to that opening in the skull have been removed. The second deceased's jaw had been completely dislocated. The face and head of this deceased has suffered extensive and severe haematomata."

Dawani read on, even more awkwardly:

"There is evidence of violent head trauma causing intracerebral haemorrhage, that led to cerebral oedema. This would have caused increased, possibly severe intracranial pressure. The most probable cause of death is traumatic brain injury."

Both bodies were missing their genitals. These, the report concluded, had been removed post mortem.

When Dawani had finished, the coroner offered the parties the opportunity to put questions. Emil's lawyer jumped to his feet, holding a list of points Emil had been scribbling down while Dawani had been giving his evidence.

"Inspector, you said that in mounting the stake-out on the Napa Napa Road, the police were acting on information they had received. From whom was this information received?"

Dawani hesitated, then answered:

"It was an anonymous call."

"So the police received this information by telephone?"

"Yes, sir."

"And at what time was this call received?"

Dawani took his notebook out of his pocket and flipped through a few pages.

"Ah, the call was taken at 3:30pm at the front desk."

"And what steps did you take to verify the information or determine the source?"

"Ah, we mounted the stake out, which verified the information," Dawani responded confidently.

"So the information you received was that Mr Davies would be on the Napa Napa Road, and that you'd find two bodies there as well?"

"Ah, no, ah, the information, ah, the information was that there was a crime going to be committed at that location," Dawani responded, now less confidently.

"So you received this information and acted on it without a thought as to whether it might be a hoax?"

Dawani didn't respond.

"Inspector, do you know who provided the information?"

"No."

"Have you made any attempt to find out who it was that provided this information?"

A pause.

"No."

"Did you ever think that whoever provided the information, might be the same person who killed those boys and put them in the mangroves?"

Again Dawani hesitated, then answered:

"We have, er, had, a suspect, who we caught at the scene."

"Yes, Inspector, and that suspect, Mr Davies, gave a statement to you that he had been asked to meet someone at that location."

The lawyer then produced Davies' mobile telephone, which Emil had given to him that morning.

"Inspector, do you recognize this mobile telephone?"

The lawyer showed the mobile to the police sergeant, then passed it across to the coroner who looked at it, before giving it to Dawani.

"It's the one you gave to Mr Pfeffer here," he said, indicating Emil, "as having been recovered from the vehicle in which Mr Davies and Sir Gideon Kukuraimi were killed."

Dawani looked at it, turning it over in his hand.

"Yes, I remember. This was part of the personal effects we recovered from Mr Davies."

"Inspector can you go to the Inbox for messages on the telephone please."

They waited while Dawani thumbed the necessary buttons, then looked up.

"Got it?"

Dawani nodded.

"Good, then can you scroll down to the third last message and open it." Dawani did so. "Now, Inspector can you please read the message to this court."

Haltingly, Dawani read:

"Plan changed. Meet 7:00pm Napa Napa Rd. 1km past Tatana causeway. Park where mangroves start."

"Thank you, Inspector," the lawyer continued, "can you tell the court please the time when that message was received on that telephone?"

Dawani scrutinized the phone display carefully for a few moments, then read out:

"15:24"

"And that was on the same day that you went to the Napa Napa Road and apprehended Mr Davies?"

Dawani scrutinized the display again then checked his notebook.

"Yes, sir, that was the same day."

"Thank you, Inspector. No further questions."

9

After Dawani stepped down, the coroner adjourned proceedings for lunch. But as they were leaving the room and stepping out into the bright midday sun, the police sergeant approached them and the other parties' representatives with the news that proceedings were adjourned for the day: the coroner would only be reconvening the following morning.

Emil had Hoko take him back to the hotel. He was sick at the thought of the injuries suffered by the two boys, and he was feeling the heat which, combined with residual jet-lag, was making him unsteady on his feet and slightly nauseous. He spent the next couple of hours lying on his bed, slept and woke feeling better, but with something nagging at the back of his mind. He had the feeling he'd missed or forgotten something and couldn't quite put his finger on what it was. After again going through Davies' things, which still littered the floor of his room, in the hope of jogging his memory, he decided to walk down to Konedobu. There was an EU-funded Environmental Library and Information Centre located there in the old buildings that once housed the pre-independence Australian administration. When going through Davies' papers he'd noted from his diary that Davies had visited there just after he arrived in Port Moresby, so perhaps they could shed some light on Davies' activities.

It was approaching late afternoon, but Emil wasn't concerned about the threat of *raskols*, in spite of what Gerry Johnstone would have advised. The sun was nowhere near setting and in the late afternoon harbour swell, whipped up by the onshore breeze, the light winked at him off the water. He headed down Hunter Street, then right into Champion Parade. Maybe the walk would help him remember. But he was quickly lost in much earlier memories.

The container terminal had expanded from what it had been when he lived on the hill above it. As he got further around he noticed that Champion Parade now went behind the Yacht Club, rather than in front of it, allowing for a substantial expansion of the club along the foreshore, and of the marina into the harbour. He used to go jogging along this stretch of road but he hardly recognised it now. After the Hubert Murray Stadium, he crossed Spring Garden Road into Government House Road. The colonial style fibro huts were surrounded by wide verandas with corrugated iron roofs. At least these were as he remembered them, standing under an umbrella of large mango trees, fringed by neatly-cropped buffalo grass and clean-swept paths. Like the Niugini Club, this place belonged to another era. A large sign, showing a circle of stars on a blue background, guided him to the hut housing the Environmental Library and Information Centre. The office consisted of a front counter on which various information materials were stacked in neat piles, encircled by full bookshelves lining all the available wall space. Half a dozen desks were arranged around the office behind the counter, the occupants working quietly at their desktop computers. A European women got up from her desk and came over to the counter.

"Can I help you?"

"Hello, my name is Emil Pfeffer. I'm with the Global Carbon Markets Organisation. I understand a colleague of mine, Gordon Davies, visited you here about two weeks ago. Unfortunately, Mr Davies has been killed in a car accident. I'm just following up on his visit."

"Yes, we know about poor Gordon. I'm Johanna Dorn," she said, with the German pronunciation of the 'J', so it became Yo-hanna. "I'm the director of the centre."

"Pleased to meet you, Johanna," said Emil, briefly taking the proffered hand. She smiled and returned the gentle pressure on his hand.

"Please, come in and have a seat, Mr Pfeffer. Would you like a cool drink?"

Emil went around the counter and sat in the chair in front of her desk.

"Thank you, I walked here from town, so that would be nice. And please, it's Emil."

His eyes followed her figure as it retreated to the small refrigerator at the back of the office. It was like a magnet had been turned on. There was something about her that he found instantly attractive – he found himself noting the line of her legs, the curve of her buttocks and that her singlet top made no attempt to hide her midriff. He caught himself just in time, as she returned with a glass of chilled water. She had clear, even features and intense blue eyes but what caught his attention most of all was her skin, which was fair to the point of being translucent, like very fine porcelain. He wondered how she survived in the tropics with such a complexion.

"We were greatly saddened by poor Gordon's death," she said, as he took a sip from the glass. "He was a nice man. He always called in to see us, when he was in Port Moresby. He was interested in our work."

"How did he seem when he called in this time?" Emil probed tentatively.

"Same as normal. It was before this matter with the boys in the harbour, of course."

"Yes, I realize that. Did he say anything about meeting with these boys?"

"No. Why would he say anything to us about his arrangements?" she responded, the bright intense eyes looking directly into Emil's.

"I was just wondering," he retreated. "I'm trying to piece together what I can to clear his name from anything to do with their deaths. Had you met these boys?"

"The expatriate community isn't so small that you meet every tourist that comes to town," she said, smiling at him, "even for single girls like us," she finished, acknowledging one of the other workers, like Johanna, a blond European who was watching them and smiled at Emil. "But it was horrible what happened to them.

I think your lawyer made some good points this morning, asking about the timing of those phone calls."

"Oh, you were there? I didn't see you," said Emil, surprised. "We hope the coroner will…" his voice trailed off mid-sentence: suddenly it came to him, the thing that had been nagging at the back of his mind all afternoon. "Yes! That's it!" he muttered to himself, loud enough for Johanna to hear.

"I'm sorry?" She gave him a puzzled look.

"Excuse me. You just reminded me of something that I've been trying to remember," he explained. "Where was I? Oh yes, we hope the coroner will make a finding that clears Gordon's name."

"Yes, poor Gordon. He was such a nice man. He was always joking and happy."

"You said he was interested in your work – what exactly is it you do here?"

"Essentially we gather and publish information on the PNG environment. It's available to students, researchers, the government, basically anyone who wants it. This is an extraordinary country – environmentally, geologically, anthropologically. It's so diverse – you can go from coral reefs and mangroves, through rainforests, to glaciers and snow-covered peaks – all only a few degrees south of the equator."

"Mmm. Fascinating…" He hadn't expected such an enthusiastic response. It made him wonder whether they had many visitors call in.

"But it's under a lot of pressure, too. Of course, I expect you would be aware of the impacts here from climate change?"

"You mean coral bleaching?"

"And the increasingly irregular monsoon rains. And the more frequent storms coming off the Pacific. Do you know about PNG's climate refugees?"

"I know there's a problem with some of the more remote islands out in the Pacific, but I wasn't aware PNG had a problem," said Emil.

"Some of the first instances of climate refugees were here. Probably ten years ago, now. In the Bismarck Sea, near the Duke of York and Credner islands. It's been getting worse, every year, since then."

"I didn't realise."

"Yes, the more severe the storms become, the more coastal communities have to be permanently relocated. It's putting pressure on communities in other parts of the country."

She was bursting with information that she was going to share with him, since he'd asked. If he hadn't been so instantly attracted to her, he might have been inclined to take her less seriously. He even resisted his natural inclination to make a smart remark when she insisted on providing him with a sample bag of the resource materials they'd developed.

"Well, I think I've disturbed your afternoon enough now, I'd better be going," said Emil as they moved back around the counter towards the door.

"Not at all. It was very nice to meet you. We don't get a lot of visitors, so we're always pleased when we do."

"I've enjoyed very much chatting with you." Then, on the spur of the moment, Emil stuck his neck out. "Look, um, if you're not busy, perhaps we could continue chatting over a drink, maybe later?"

"Oh, ah....I...," she hesitated, caught off-guard, then making up her mind. "Alright, that would be nice," she smiled, with a little tilt of her head to one side.

She checked her watch, then looked over to her blonde colleague:

"It's almost finishing time now Luisa, can you lock up? I'll walk over to the Yacht Club, with Herr, er..., Emil, you can join us there with the car, when you're ready."

On the way to the Yacht Club, Emil learned that Johanna had been in Port Moresby almost two years running the information centre. She was from Berlin, but had been working for the EU, mostly in Brussels, since completing her doctorate in biology five years earlier.

"How did you come to have such an old traditional German name," she asked, after Emil explained he was Australian.

"My great grandparents were from Baden. They came to German New Guinea, as it was, in the early 1900s, as missionaries – ended up running a coffee plantation, near Namatanai, on New Ireland. With the outbreak of the First World War, they were interned. Afterwards, they settled in northern Queensland, where my grandfather was born, but then they died from some sort of tropical disease, maybe malaria, while he was very young. He was brought up in an orphanage in Brisbane. Emil was my great grandfather's name."

"You have quite an exotic family history. My family are all scientists. Very boring. They mostly work in academic institutes, or for the German government. I'm the only one who has travelled to this part of the world."

"So what inspired you to leave Germany and come to PNG, of all places?"

"My doctorate was on the mating rituals of tropical birds, especially birds of paradise. I travelled here, and also to some Indonesian islands, as part of my research."

They were in the bar of the Yacht Club, sitting looking out over the marina.

"This club has really changed," he said looking around. "Lots of things have. I came up here from Sydney to work years ago – looking for my family roots in a way, I suppose. I was working in Port Moresby and this place was much more basic then. Do they still have the Thursday night disco?"

"Disco?!" Johanna almost choked. "You're giving your age away a bit there!" she said laughing. He laughed too – with embarrassment.

"So what was it you remembered when we were talking in the office?" she asked.

"Oh, oh that. It was just something that came up in the evidence today that I need to check."

"Is it important?"

"It might be, I don't know yet."

He explained it related to the timing of the calls.

"It's just one of those things. You know how something will niggle in the back of your mind, on the tip of your tongue, but you can't quite get what it is. You triggered my recollection, so thanks."

She smiled, engaging him with her eyes. "How much longer will you be here?"

"Well, once the inquest is over, I need to finalise the arrangements for repatriating Gordon's body to his home in Wales. And I need to conclude the work that he was here to do. Maybe another week, or so, at most."

Luisa joined them and they ordered food. Luisa was a European Commission trainee who had joined Johanna in the last six months. She was from Copenhagen, in her early twenties and liked going out, but had to take 'mum' everywhere.

"All the ex-pat boys think we're a couple of lesbians, I'm sure," she complained.

"Aren't you concerned about your safety in a place like Port Moresby?"

"We have twenty-four hour security. It's discreet, you may not have noticed it at the centre," said Johanna. "However, it's also quite expensive, so we're being replaced at the end of the year: by a couple of males. I suppose the Commission thinks that their security requirements will be less costly."

"Back to Brussels?"

"Luisa will be. I'm taking some time off before I go back there. I might spend time in Berlin, or travelling."

Emil was becoming more interested in Dr Johanna Dorn, as the evening progressed, and it was progressing very pleasantly. Until, that is, he thought they might be interested in his work, since it was environmentally related, and started describing what his job involved.

"I don't agree with all this carbon 'market' business," Luisa interrupted him. "It's letting the polluters off the hook. Look at the free allocations of emissions rights they get. Why should multi-billion euro energy companies get free allocations? Then they charge their customers for the same thing? It's giving them windfall profits, at our expense!"

"It's not letting them off the hook, they still need to change their behaviour, to emit less. The market approach just gives them time to do it, time to adjust."

"Oh, you mean like the time to adjust they give us, when they increase their prices?"

"We *all* need to change our approach to using energy – not just the companies."

"I'm on Luisa's side," said Johanna.

She had been quietly observing the increasingly animated exchange. He was pleased she intervened, to let Luisa cool off a bit. Besides, he was more interested in what *she* thought.

"Even where these polluting companies buy credits from countries like PNG, that just lets them keep doing what they're doing."

"But the screws get tightened and eventually they will need to change."

"I don't see why we need to tread so softly when we want to change their behaviour."

"Why not?"

"Because the concentration of gases in the atmosphere is at what scientists say is the tipping point, the point beyond which change is irreversible. Why don't we care more about the victims, the climate refugees – the environment? Fragile ecosystems like you find here in PNG are being devastated."

"What would you do?"

"Act firmly! Impose limits on companies – if they don't reduce their emissions, we penalise them, or stop them operating altogether."

"Hmm. Sounds to me you like a bit of discipline!" said Emil, raising an eyebrow.

Johanna shot a glance at him then looked away, checking with Luisa if she'd locked the office properly. He'd irritated her. Should've taken her more seriously. But then he noticed the corner of her mouth curl upwards into the briefest flicker of a private grin.

Better not to push his luck.

"But look, let's talk about something much more interesting – tell me more about how you came to be here. I'm intrigued as to why the EU would be funding an environmental library in Port Moresby."

"Well, PNG is one of the most biodiverse places on earth, but it's still largely an unknown quantity. For example, just over twenty-six thousand species of plants and animals have been recorded, but estimates are that there could be well over two-hundred thousand."

"But you're not out searching for new species, are you?"

"No, no. We make sure that resources on what is known are

available to people who are interested. The more that is known about the biodiversity here, the more people who are aware of it, the better the chances are to protect and conserve it ..."

Once he'd started them, their philosophical objections to his work were forgotten. He was happy to listen to them enthuse about their work instead. And they did, showing off an encyclopaedic knowledge of the local fauna and flora.

"... and it's not just the mega-biodiversity," Johanna was continuing, "size *does* matter."

Emil had been studying her face, not really listening to what she was saying. He was caught unawares.

"I'm sorry, did you say *size* matters?"

"Yes, it does! They specialize in 'big' here. The world's largest egg-laying mammal, largest butterfly, largest bat, largest pigeon, largest lizard – the crocodile monitor – they can get up to almost four metres!"

"Largest orchid," chipped in Luisa, whose specialisation was tropical trees and plants. "We like them big," she said, smiling suggestively at him.

"Oh, I see," said Emil, colouring a little and avoiding eye contact with Luisa, trying to give the impression it was Johanna's words that had his full attention.

"And in some cases, it's not just the biggest, but the only," Johanna continued. "You might think that you have to be careful of the deadly spiders and snakes, but you also have to be careful of the birds."

She's winding me up, he thought.

"Oh, you must be referring to the giant man-eating sparrows?"

"No," she frowned at him, "I mean the only species of poisonous birds ever discovered are found here."

"Poisonous birds?" said Emil, raising his eyebrows in disbelief. "You're kidding me."

"No. Certainly not. There are two identified, so far. Who knows, there may be more. It's fascinating."

It was Johanna's turn to smile suggestively at him.

"If you call into the centre again, I'll show you."

That was an opportunity too good to miss. Emil promised to call in to the Information Centre again to see what these dangerous birds looked like. And, of course, to spend time chatting up Dr Johanna Dorn a bit more, he thought to himself.

The security detail that had escorted Luisa over was waiting outside the club with the car, when they left. Emil could see why this sort of arrangement was due for the cut, in times of the financial strictures affecting the EU. It must have cost a lot, even in PNG terms. They dropped him back at his hotel and he was pleased Johanna reminded him to call in again, before he left Port Moresby. He assured her he most certainly would.

10

Someone else Emil hadn't noticed, at the back of the coroner's court, was the journo from the local daily paper. Splashed across the front page, next morning, were all the graphic details of the victims' injuries. Just what you need with breakfast, he thought, sitting in the hotel coffee shop finishing his own. The story was supplemented by interviews with various self-appointed experts, politicians, commentators and police, the overriding theme being the need to clean up the squatter settlements that had mushroomed around the city. These were the incubators of crime and more recently, the consensus seemed to be, a breeding ground for transposing village superstitions into the city. Maybe Gerry was right on that score.

To everyone's surprise, when proceedings got underway the coroner brought the inquest to a prompt conclusion. Apart from establishing the identities of the victims, and how they died, the coroner's findings were light on specifics. But, at least he found the boys had been killed by a person or persons unknown, rather than Davies, thereby exonerating him.

"Thank the Lord!" intoned Betty G, when he rang with the news. She almost sounded relaxed, for a change.

"I expect I'll be back in Frankfurt within the week. I just need to finalise the arrangements for the release of Davies' body, then sort out the last details for its repatriation. I'll feel much better when Gordon's mortal remains have been extricated from that malodorous morgue."

He called Dominik Baumann, to check on the operations of the Unit.

"No, everything is fine here, Emil. You're not being missed here, at all," advised Baumann with his wonderful, Germanic directness.

With both inquests finished, as he had expected, Emil's questions remained mostly unanswered. Betty G might not want to rattle cages, but Emil wouldn't be happy until he had more answers. Having completed his calls, he decided to put the rest of the day to good use by doing a little unofficial investigating of his own, suggesting to Hoko and Robert that they drive up to Sogeri for lunch. As they passed the Rouna Falls lookout they slowed, but there was no sign of the Huli wigman. Sogeri was cloaked in low cloud and chilly, compared to the stifling dust bowl they'd left below. Maybe it was too cold for the wigman, Hoko suggested, only to be scoffed at by Robert: Huli got much colder than this.

The Motor Lodge parking area was almost full when they arrived, as they found the dining area on entering. They settled at a table in the area off the bar and waited for the barman to take their order. When he returned with their drinks, Emil asked if he had been working the day the Minister, Sir Gideon, had been there. The man finished putting the drinks down then just stared at Emil, uncertain, so Robert spoke quickly to him in Motu. The barman looked around furtively, then leaned forward and made out he was wiping the table.

"Yes, I was here when Sir Gideon was here with that other man," he said quietly.

"Did you serve them a lot of drinks?" asked Emil, as the man continued to wipe the table where he had already wiped.

"Not really a lot. Sir Gideon had five or six SPs. The other man only had ..."

"Hoi, get a move on, ya' lazy coot…there are other customers here too…."

It was Herbie. He was easing himself onto his stool at the end of the bar, waving his polystyrene beer holder around furiously, to demonstrate its emptiness. The barman hurried away to satisfy the demands of his employer. Eventually their meals arrived, crocodile steaks with a poor excuse for salad. When they'd finished, Emil went to the bar to pay.

"Hello Herbie, I thought you were down in Queensland."

"Who the fuck are you? Whatsit the fuck to you where I am?"

"I was at the inquest into Sir Gideon's death. They said you couldn't attend because you were in Queensland, that's all," said Emil, trying to make the exchange less confrontational, although Herbie being Herbie, it was moot whether there was any point.

"Yeah, well I'm back. So youse ken pay, then fuck orf and mind yer own business. Who the fuck d'yer think y'are anyway, a fuckin' copper or sumthin'?" Herbie glowered at Emil.

Discretion was the better part of valour, in a situation like this, he decided. The barman returned behind the bar from delivering orders and Emil paid him, then headed out with Hoko and Robert in tow.

"That was a success!" he remarked as they left.

But it wasn't entirely a waste of time. Robert had managed a few quick further words with the barman while Emil had been at the bar, and he'd finished saying what he'd been trying to say, that the man with Sir Gideon only had two beers then switched to mineral water.

The cloud over Sogeri had lifted when they left, so they took their time, visiting the Surinumu Dam and Variarata National Park before heading back towards town. Emil had Hoko pull in at Rouna Falls lookout, but there was still no sign of the wigman. He decided to wait there a while to see if the wigman would show up.

An hour later there was still no sign of him and the huge orange ball of a sun was dipping towards the horizon. Vehicles, carrying now well-lubricated Motor Lodge lunch patrons, were passing regularly in the direction of town.

"The wigman's missing a lot of potential customers," observed Emil. "Where do you think he is?"

"Back at the squatter settlement. He probably looked at the weather this morning and decided there wouldn't be any tourists," said Robert.

Emil thought for a moment.

"Is it far from here?"

"Maybe ten minutes through the bush. Much longer if we drive around."

"OK, let's see if we can find him. Hoko, you stay here with the car. If you're worried about raskols showing up, just go back up to Sogeri and call us on the mobile."

They set out in the direction the wigman had disappeared on their previous visit, half trotting in the rapidly fading light, Robert leading and Emil doing his best to keep up.

"Watch you don't step on any snakes," Robert called over his shoulder as the track began diverging into longer and longer grass. "Papuan taipans are most active about this time of day."

"Thanks for telling me now!" said Emil, high-stepping like he was doing sprint training and straining to see where each of his footsteps would land.

After what seemed, to Emil, more like thirty minutes of the track running in and out of long yellowy grass, up and down hillsides, they approached a clearing cluttered with corrugated iron lean-tos and rough shanties made of refuse wood, hessian sacks and what looked like had once been fruit packing cases. There were cooking fires in the centre but the smokey smell couldn't disguise a stale putrefying waste odour that gave the place the air of a landfill, suggesting the source of the building materials.

Robert called out as they walked up through the structures into the clearing, but the first woman to see them coming out of the bush through the blue-grey smoke just started screaming and pointing at them as if they were a pair of ghosts. Other women, around the cooking fires, on seeing them began screaming as well, the men jumping up around the two of them, brandishing bush-knives and sticks and shouting as if they were going to kill them.

"Hey! HEY!! Calm down! HEY! BACK OFF!!" Emil shouted back at them, hands in the air. Robert shouted at them in pidgin to more effect, eventually managing to quell the angst their arrival was causing. After a lengthy discourse with the men in pidgin, he explained to Emil.

"They thought we were *kumo* people, come to kill them."

"And exactly who or what are *kumo* people?"

"The kumo are the bad spirit people. They come in the night

and cause harm. Similar superstition to the *sangguma* you get up in the Sepik, just the highlands version. They said that they could hear the kumo hovering around the settlement last night – there were spirit noises in the bush. That's what's spooked the wigman – he's been too afraid today to leave – he thinks the kumo will kill him when he's on his own over at the lookout."

They found the wigman sitting cross-legged in his shack, rocking backwards and forwards, smoking tobacco rolled in newspaper. Having a source of income, his shack was marginally better constructed, being built up off the ground and having four walls, unlike some of the others. He looked up apprehensively when they stuck their heads inside, eyes wide with fear at the sight of Emil, but when he recognized him from their earlier meeting at the lookout, he relaxed a little.

"Ask him why he didn't wait for the photo the other day."

Robert translated. "He says the kumo was coming to kill him, he had to get back here to his wantoks."

"Hmm. Ask him again about the white car running off the road."

Robert translated, and the wigman gave forth a torrent in Huli. Robert stopped him and he started again in Motu, but just as quickly.

"He said he was just about to head home that evening, just as he told us before – the day had been very quiet with hardly any cars at all – just the white car heading up in the early afternoon, and one or two others. But when it came back past him, it was trying to escape from the kumo, they were fighting. Then as they passed him, he saw the kumo win and push the white car so it rolled over the edge."

"Kumo? What the hell is he talking about? What's he mean 'they were fighting' – what did it look like?"

"He says it's like a big car, but controlled by the kumo – there is no driver or passengers."

"Very helpful. So did he tell that to the police?"

There was another machine gun fire response.

"He says he reported the accident and when they came, he told the police. Then, later, one of his wantoks, who is a policeman, came and warned him that the kumo was sending people to kill him, too. He told him not to say anything and to go away for a while, so he went back up to the highlands. He's only just got back. He said while he was away some *masta* came here looking for him, but went away when they were told he'd gone back to the highlands."

As Robert finished, they could hear another commotion starting outside. Robert asked the wigman what was happening.

"He says they can hear kumo coming again."

Emil got up out of the wigman's hut. The men and women were running around the clearing in a panic, shouting as they had earlier when Emil and Robert appeared. The sun had set and the intermittent light from the cooking fires left the area surrounding the camp as dark as pitch. There was a sound alright, it sounded like vehicles approaching. Being unfamiliar with the place, Emil couldn't work out from which direction they were coming. Then blue flashes started on the black trees and hills: it was clear who they were. It was clear, too, that they were pretty much all around the settlement. Robert and the wigman were outside now.

"Shit, it's a police raid. We'd better not be found here," said Robert looking around. But as he spoke the headlights of the vehicles lit up the clearing, the white light dispersed through the cooking smoke giving an eerie, nether world appearance to the silhouetted, shouting figures dashing back and forth. It was too late to get back to where they had entered the clearing from the track.

"Quick, get behind here," said Emil.

They jumped behind the wigman's hut, squatting down out of the bright white light now bathing the clearing. Emil looked around for the wigman, but he'd disappeared into the darkness. All the other squatters seemed to have disappeared into the surrounding bush as well – it was as if he and Robert were the only ones left in the place now. Police were fanning out around the shanties and lean-tos.

"Fuck, we're stuck, this is going to look good," whispered Emil peeking around the corner of the hut.

Robert tapped him on the arm and pointed beneath the hut. Emil mouthed the word 'Snakes', but Robert was already down on his belly and sliding in under the hut. Emil didn't have much choice: he followed him. There was just enough height for them to fit lying face down and with their heads turned on their side. The only sounds audible over the vehicle engines now being the police calling to each other as they confirmed that the settlement was clear.

Boots crunched over the gravelly soil up to the front of the wigman's hut. Above him, there was a voice. It spoke in English, the accent was difficult to pick, but there was clearly one there. Some sort of European maybe, Emil thought.

"Is this where he lives?"

Someone stepped inside then out again. Emil could feel the structure above him lurch under the weight, as if it would collapse and bring the policeman down on top of them. Then there was a sudden vibrating sensation in his trousers. His phone! Hoko, oh fuck! In a second the vibration would become a ring. He transferred his weight to his opposite side and shovelled his hand quickly down into the pocket. His fingers scrabbled for the answer button and just as quickly the power off button on top, holding it down long enough to be sure it was off. He froze rigid.

"Burn it. Burn it all."

Orders were called out in Motu. There were more boots, running, then splashing sounds. The sound of jerrycans having their contents sprayed over the huts and lean-tos. Robert looked urgently at Emil, their faces only inches apart. He mouthed the word 'Out', but he needn't have bothered, Emil was already looking for a way out, but the boots were still there, in front of the hut. If they moved now, they'd be caught for sure. A jerrycan arrived and the contents splashed out over the structure above them. Emil could smell the petrol, feel it dripping down through the saturated packing case floor of the wigman's hut onto his back, his head, droplets running down across his face. Burning sticks and logs were being hauled out of the cooking fires and hurled into the petrol soaked shanties. Brief conflagrations were exploding all over the settlement as the pathetic structures immolated then died out just as quickly. The boots in front of the hut moved away to meet an approaching torch-bearing policeman.

"Here, give it to me," said the European accent.

"Now," Emil mouthed at Robert, wriggling as fast as he could out from under the back of the hut and scuttling into the bush behind it, Robert hot on his heels. They flung themselves into the grass as the wigman's hut exploded in flames and was consumed in a matter of seconds.

The policemen began moving back to their vehicles, not even bothering to search for the former inhabitants, now that the settlement had been reduced to burning embers. Crouching there, Emil thought he felt the grass move under his leg. He looked around and in the dying light from the pyre that had been the wigman's hut, saw the sleek, glistening black line with an orangey-red stripe down it, standing vertically erect. His first thought was how beautiful it seemed in the light, then in the next split second as his brain registered the danger, it was already lunging forward, fangs just reaching the arm of his jacket, venom wetting through the fabric.

"Snake!" he yelped, belatedly reacting and pulling his arm back.

"Taipan!" Robert yelled jerking Emil's arm further away, just in time to avoid a second more aggressive lunge that would have reached the flesh under the jacket sleeve. They both jumped up, back out of its immediate range.

"Hey! Who's there?" The shout came from across the clearing. The bright, white beam of a torch shot out in their direction.

"Run!"

Robert disappeared deeper into the bush, Emil, not bothering about the high-stepping and careful foot placement, right behind him. They ran hard and fast, in the dark lucky to stumble onto the track. They covered the distance back to the lookout parking area in a fraction of the time they had taken to reach the settlement. It was empty, Hoko and the car were nowhere to be seen. Robert stood bent over next the power pylon, one hand on a stanchion, the other on his knee, sucking in breath. Emil called Hoko to collect them.

"Since when have the police been clearing squatter settlements, like that, at night?" he asked when he finished the call.

"Beats me," said Robert between asthmatic gasps. "There's been plenty of talk ... in the press ... about it. But that's all. Nothing has come through our department. That's for sure."

Ten minutes later they were beginning a slow and cautious descent in the dark, down the switchbacks. Hoko had taken refuge up in the Owen Stanley Motor Lodge car park, after the convoy of police vehicles passed the lookout. All the windows were down and Emil had barred Hoko from lighting a cigarette – with all the petrol fumes reeking out of their clothes, he didn't want to spontaneously combust.

"So what's your take on the wigman's story – was there a second car involved in the accident?" Emil called from the back seat to Robert who was in the front directing Hoko away from the edge if he showed signs of getting too close.

"It's possible. I think it's likely. What I mean is, I don't think the kumo is completely a figment of his imagination."

Hoko flashed a nervous look around at the mention of the kumo.

"Yes, I think I agree with you. They all thought the police were kumo. At least they were right that the cops were there to do some harm. Maybe it was a police vehicle."

As he finished speaking, there was a flash of light across Hoko's face. Emil sat up and looked around from the back seat. Two intense white lights were racing up immediately behind them, forcing him to shield his eyes with his hand.

"That idiot better slow down and get his high beam down," he said.

Down the straight run, the vehicle had come up very close behind their car. It was some sort of high wheel base vehicle, its lights now shining directly in on Emil's head. He sat forward to get out of the line of light, better to block the light in Hoko's face from the rear-view mirror.

"Back off, you moron," he called out, waving his hand behind him to give the driver the message. He'd barely got the words out before the vehicle shunted into the rear of their car, shoving it forward.

"Shit! You bastard!" he shouted, waving his hand more frantically but the vehicle just shunted their car again, and then again.

Hoko was going as fast as he dared down the precipitous, uneven surface in the dark, but the vehicle was on top of them, nudging the back of theirs like a predator toying with a cornered quarry, before executing the coup de grâce.

"Slow down, keep your foot hard on the brake," Emil shouted in Hoko's ear, as the pursuer shoved into the back of them again.

With Hoko's foot hard down on the brake, instead of bumping their car forward, the two vehicles locked together, moving forward as one for a stretch, the pursuing vehicle pushing, forcing their car forward. They reached the bottom of the last switchback and, as they rounded the corner, the road began widening out. Hoko accelerated to put some distance between them and the maniac behind, wind and dust rushing through the open windows. But the pursuing vehicle was far more powerful and roared up alongside them. It was a Landcruiser, tinted windows hiding the occupants. It drew level, suddenly veering towards them.

"Brake! BRAKE!!!" Emil screamed in Hoko's ear, almost ending up in the front seat as Hoko responded.

The Landcruiser flew off across in front of them, illumination from its powerful spot lights through the cloud of dust it threw up creating crazy dancing figures out of the trees along either side of the road as it disappeared into the distance. Then, suddenly, the light was gone. Their vehicle had gone into a four wheel slide in the dirt. Hoko controlled it and brought them to a complete halt. The trailing dust cloud caught up with them and wafted past, filling the cabin.

"Let's go. Before we all die. From dust consumption," said Robert, a pursy wheeze punctuating each of the phrases.

"Did either of you get that bastard's number?" asked Emil.

"No ... Those big Landcruisers ... are everywhere."

They started on their way again slowly, pulses still racing. Suddenly two bright spot lights exploded into their eyes, rapidly bearing down on them, barely a couple of hundred metres away. Directly in front. Fuck, this maniac's really out to kill us, Emil thought, detachedly, as if he was having a bad dream, staring at the lights, until urgency snapped him out of it. He looked at Hoko. He seemed to be in a trance, mesmerized, staring into the lights.

"HOKO!!!"

Hoko swerved to the left. The huge steel bull-bar shot past the open windows on their right: the vehicle so close, the air pressure wave it created buffeting them. They weren't going very fast, but still careered along for a hundred metres on the wide dirt verge before stopping. Emil jumped out and looked back through their dust after the assailant's lights, this time receding far into the distance back up towards the switchbacks. He slumped back onto the seat. A millisecond slower and they'd have been completely annihilated by it.

"Well, guys, I think we just survived an encounter with the kumo."

As they headed into town Emil rang Gerry Johnstone, who was not impressed when Emil finished narrating their exploits to him.

"Listen, mate, you really shouldn't be nosing around, 'specially now that the coroner's made his findings. As for the Landcruiser, if you didn't get the rego, there's not a lot I can do. There must be a thousand of 'em in Moresby now."

"So, Gerry, are you telling me that there isn't a cover up? The barman could've even given evidence as to what they drank. The bloody wigman says he saw the accident, for God's sake. What the hell was Dawani doing? What was the coroner doing? Come to think of it, you're the head of the Department of Justice, who was in charge of the inquiry in your department?"

"It wasn't Dawani's fault. He was just following the instructions of the coroner's assistant, who was being instructed, as was the coroner, by the PM's office. It was taken out of the hands of Justice. I didn't have any say in it."

"Well when did it become police policy to clear out squatters and burn their settlements?"

"Don't know about that either. You'll have to ask the PM's office about that, too."

Emil held his tongue. Any more he could say would only criticize Gerry in front of Hoko and Robert, making him look as impotent as he now seemed to be, with the PM's office controlling everything.

"OK, Gerry, you're right. But I must at least report it to Dawani and get him to follow up on it. I owe that much to Gordon."

They rang off, neither very happy with the other. But it was too bad if Gerry was pissed off with him for making his own inquisitorial trip to Sogeri. As he had said, it was the least he could do, he owed it to Gordon.

11

It was two days after the Sogeri trip and Emil was still angry.

He was angry with Inspector Dawani, to whom he'd reported what the barman had said, the fact that Herbie was sitting up in Sogeri and could have been made to appear at the inquest, and the eye witness account of the Huli wigman, which had been actively discouraged by the police themselves. Dawani had dutifully written everything down in his notebook, assuring Emil it would be taken up with his superiors. Fat lot of good that will do, Emil thought, they're the ones who are trying to bury this all quietly in the first place. He was angry with Gerry Johnstone, for the way he'd discouraged him from taking the information any further. He was angry with him for kowtowing to Gregory Hudson and whoever else was orchestrating matters out of the PM's office.

But, mostly, he was angry with himself. He'd let Gerry persuade him to back off. What was more, he didn't really have any evidence, just the brief conversations with the barman and the wigman, neither of which were recorded in any way. Gerry had hinted, without saying as much, that government policy was to clear out some of the squatter settlements. If that was the case, it was going to be difficult to find the wigman again if he didn't go back to plying his trade at the lookout, which was unlikely now. So even the statement to Dawani seemed lame in retrospect, as he stewed it over in his mind. And as for the Landcruiser maniac, he'd asked Hoko and Robert to keep an eye out, to see if it appeared around town, but without the wigman, turning that into evidence was a remote prospect, as well.

He'd finalized the arrangements for the repatriation of Davies' body that morning and all that remained for him to do was to lock in his own travel arrangements, which he'd now done. He would be leaving the following day. He'd wrapped up things out at the OCC offices, discharged Robert back to his work as a government lawyer, and was sitting in the hotel lobby drinking coffee. He'd done everything he had to do in Port Moresby and, with time on his hands, was left with the feeling of frustration that he was failing Davies. His reflections were giving him the shits. The only redeeming feature was meeting Johanna. At any rate, he wasn't going to let these thoughts spoil this evening – his last here. He would be having dinner with her. And, unfortunately, her shadow.

When he'd revisited the information centre to find out about the poisonous birds, he'd tried to entice Johanna out on her own, but she'd been unwilling to leave Luisa by herself, even with the security guards (or, maybe, because of them). He'd relented graciously, hoping, at the same time, that he'd put up enough of a protest for her to get the message that he was interested. Then again, maybe he'd been too subtle. He sat there stewing over his coffee, lost in his thoughts a while longer, then headed up to his room for a shower.

The sun was setting below a thickly banded, peach-coloured cloud, striated mauve and red, below it, an intensely golden horizon, mirrored in the millpond-still harbour. Emil sat on the balcony of his room and watched it to its conclusion. It was like a ritual clearing of his mind, before he headed down to meet his guests. He'd invited them for dinner in the hotel's dining room – it still seemed to be the best place in town to eat. The evening flew past, so engrossed were they in their conversation, that they didn't notice they were the last patrons left in the dining room, until the maitre d' arrived to present the account to Emil. As he was paying, it crossed his mind to invite them back to his room for a nightcap, but he dismissed the thought just as quickly as it arrived. That might be pushing things a bit too far. He escorted them down to their waiting car and security detail, received a peck on each cheek and a promise from Johanna that she would be in touch. Then they were gone.

Next morning, Emil was on the ten o'clock flight to Singapore, where he would pick up a flight directly to Frankfurt. With his diplomatic passport he didn't need to rush, so he spent time checking his email before leaving the hotel. There were update reports on assessments his team was carrying out, but he knew Dominik was following up on these. There was the usual array of administrative notes and the endless updates from the news lists and information services to which he subscribed. Emil noted that in spite of higher level security introduced after the last attack, there had been another episode of security breaches in national registries. These had been happening on and off for years, and although each time measures were taken to improve security and catch the perpetrators, after a while it all faded into the background, until the next incident occurred. It was always a case of too little, too late. The thefts had little effect on market trading activity, they were more a police matter. Nevertheless, this would arrive on Emil's desk too, eventually, for follow up by his Unit. Part of his Unit's role was to devise a long-term strategy to deal with this problem; clearly that would now need to be elevated in the priority list. The last item was a confidential report of an attack on a trading platform operating in Poland. This could affect trading, he thought, and sounded much more serious. He made a diary note to follow up.

The trip to the airport was uneventful and having checked in and passed security, he wasn't in the lounge more than a few minutes before the boarding call. If only it could be this easy every time, he thought. Once in his seat, waiting for the other passengers to board, Emil texted Johanna on the pretext of checking that they had made it home safely the previous evening. He hoped there would be an immediate response, but there wasn't. He left his mobile turned on anyway – just in case – and, as had become his habit whenever he boarded an aircraft these days, dozed off.

The stragglers were still boarding, as a member of the cabin crew came through offering reading material. Emil took a copy of the morning's newspaper, folded it on his lap and went back to dozing. Shortly afterwards, they were taxiing and he was roused by the crew going through the safety procedures. He opened up the newspaper on his lap and was assailed immediately by a dominant bold headline 'SO THIS IS WHERE THE MONEY GOES' over a large grainy picture that covered much of the rest of the front page. Still drowsy, he puzzled at it for a moment, then suddenly flushed with the horror of recognition. It was a photo of him sitting at the table with Johanna and Luisa in the hotel restaurant the previous evening. The caption below read:

'GCMO boss finds money to treat EU library staff, but can't find funds to reimburse Davies' bail money. Story page 2.'

He ripped the page open, tearing it in the process. The story inside told of how the GCMO boss, Emil Pfeffer, in Port Moresby to sort out the mess left by the death of his staff member, Gordon Davies, shouted the ex-pat staff of the EU Environment Library in Konedobu to a 'slap up dinner' at the Crowne Plaza hotel, in spite of the fact that government money posted for Davies' release on bail had not been repaid. The story then went into detail of what they had ordered, how many drinks they had, what the bill came to and the fact that Emil had paid for all three. It then rehashed details from stories it had printed earlier about Davies' arrest, the car accident, the inquest findings and coroner's remarks about the drinking session and musings on the purpose of the meeting at Sogeri, coloured, of course, by the information concerning Sir Gideon's finances. It finished with a diatribe on how the behaviour of these international bureaucrats was affecting PNG's progress into the carbon trading market, referring readers to the editorial page.

Emil knew what it would say. Masochistically, he turned to it and read the four paragraphs of sanctimonious harping on how rich countries are happy to tell poor countries how to manage their finances and cut costs, especially through inter-governmental organizations like the IMF. But these IGOs should take their own advice, until they can manage their own staff, and pay their own way, instead of relying on the good graces of poor countries like PNG. It couldn't have been worded better if Gregory Hudson himself had written it, Emil thought. He probably did.

He finished reading it, slumped back in his seat and closed his eyes.

"Oh fuck. Oh fuck," he uttered, audibly enough for the passenger next to him to turn and frown.

At Singapore, Emil raced off the aircraft and up into the lounge. He was in the process of getting online when his mobile phone rang. He fumbled to answer it and was disappointed when it turned out only to be Dominik, not Johanna.

"I thought you might be there by now, so I would try to ring," Dominik explained. "I have to tell you that all hell has broken loose here. Betty is *very* angry."

"You mean the bloody newspaper story? I didn't know anything about that until I was on the plane. They must have taken the photo with a mobile phone and no flash – I never saw this happen. All we were doing was having a meal, anyway. This is an outrageous invasion of my privacy. It's a complete beat up."

"You haven't heard then?"

"Heard what?"

"About the EU library, where the friends you had dinner with work."

"What? What? Tell me!"

"It seems the newspaper story stirred up some hotheads. They were protesting outside library. It must have been while you were on the flight to Singapore. The situation got out of control. They broke into the library, smashing it up … pretty badly, from the reports we're getting … really trashed it …"

12

Emil stood leaning against the bench-top in the kitchen of his shoe-box apartment in Bad Eschbach. The kitchen was so small, he could reach every part of it, into every cupboard, without moving from where he stood. It wasn't yet six in the morning and the sun had just risen, already fashioning the day to be another unusually hot one. Not that the days here compared to his recent experiences in Port Moresby. But at least in Port Moresby there were more air-conditioned places into which one could retreat.

Breakfast consisted of two pieces of fruit, consumed standing where he was standing, looking out the window. He would have coffee when he got to the office. Immediately outside was a path around the building, along which Frau Hoerler, his landlady, would pass, not at this time of the morning, of course, but often in the evenings, only the profile of her head visible, bobbing up and down, back and forth, directly outside the window, like a hand puppet in a children's show. Ostensibly, her activity would be tending the vegetable patch that covered the rest of the yard, but he suspected that an important supplemental, perhaps secretly, the primary purpose, was to peek through the windows to check on the apartment. He'd caught her doing it, being inside when she'd been peering in. It seemed that the garden activity had really only begun in earnest after he'd confronted her about making unauthorized visits to his apartment while he wasn't there. Her claim was that she was just tidying up. But he'd return to find that her 'tidying' visits had included turning off all electric power points and turning the level of the refrigerator down, since electricity usage was included in his rent, so she would be paying for any wastage. It was irritating enough to continually need to reset the electric clock and the DVD timer, but when food in the refrigerator started going off, he'd been forced, in as friendly a way as possible, to ban Frau Hoerler from entering his apartment when he wasn't there, unless she asked first.

He thought about Johanna, as he had done, standing in that spot, every morning since his return from PNG. There was still no word from her. He'd tried to contact her, without success, every day. The Environmental Library and Information Centre had been closed, temporarily, he was assured by someone in Brussels. The EU staff had been repatriated and, despite his most persuasive importuning, nobody in Brussels was going to breach EU privacy regulations to provide contact details for Dr Dorn, even if they had known where she was to be found. The best they could offer, was that if she were to get in touch, they would pass on that he had been trying to contact her. He looked up Dorn in the Berlin telephone directory, but there were too many for this to be realistically pursued. He googled her, but that only provided background on her academic publications. Sabrina had even come to his assistance and found out that, amazingly, like him, Johanna wasn't on any social networking sites.

Emil finished his breakfast, wiped the bench and rinsed the knife and plate he'd used. It was the same plate he'd used last time and the same one he'd use next time – the only one he owned. He rationalized he didn't need more than one, since he only needed to cater for himself. Most of the other paraphernalia of his previous existence he'd either sold, or given away, when he left London. He didn't want to be burdened by too many superfluous possessions, things to evoke memories or bring on self-pity. No, that would be an indulgence he would do without. He cherished his memories of Catherine, but there was a time and place for everything, he told himself. But thinking of her as, inevitably, he did now whenever he thought of Johanna, left him slightly maudlin.

Enough! he thought, rousing himself to action. Before leaving for the office he went through his usual routine of locking the windows open enough to get some air flow and closing the shutters enough to keep the sun out. His morning routine had been the same since the day he moved into Frau Hoerler's ground floor apartment. He was a creature of habit. It helped.

At this time of the day, the low-angled sun shone directly along east-facing Heinrich-Heine-Weg, making it prematurely warm. He walked in what shade there was, then crossed Eschbacherstrasse and waited at the bus stop outside the railway station for the bus that would take him a couple of kilometres up the road to his office. His eye ran back over the grimy front of *Zum Löwen*, the local pub, to *Autoecke* next door, across the road to Mr Pizza Thai takeaway on the opposite corner and down the line of drab, grey stuccoed, satellite dish festooned buildings fronting each other across the bitumen of Heinrich-Heine-Weg. What would Heine have found to write about this sad little street named in his memory? Someone must love it, he thought, just not me. When the office relocated to central Frankfurt he'd promised to find himself a nice older apartment with high ceilings, in Nordend, or Westend, somewhere close to good bars and restaurants. Then he'd never come back to Bad Eschbach. Well, no, that wasn't quite true. He would come back to the local bakery whose *Dinkelvollkornbrot* was the best bread he'd ever tasted. Yes, he'd definitely make the trip back for that. The bus pulled up in front of him, snapping his gaze back into focus, dragging his thoughts back to the present.

In the two weeks since Emil's return to Frankfurt, the pressure on him had been increasing like a rash crawling up his body from his feet. Dominik provided great support and Emil couldn't wish for a better deputy, but he'd greatly understated the situation when he had called in Singapore. Betty G wasn't just angry, she was absolutely, furiously ropeable.

"How could you let things get so badly out of hand? How could you do it, when you'd just assured me down the telephone line that everything was hunky dory?" She mimicked Emil calling: "Yes, Betty, everything out here in Pa-poo-a Noo-Ginnee is just peachy!"

"Betty, it was a set up!"

"I don't care whether it's a set up, beat up or any other kind of up – or down – for that matter. I've had people from UN headquarters in New York on the phone constantly wanting updates on what's been happening. I've had functionaries from Washington, London, Berlin and lord knows which other national governments calling. Brussels has gone berserk that its library's been trashed. It's now in a diplomatic spat with Pa-poo-a Noo Ginnee. And of course, there is still the little matter of the dispute over the bail money, for me yet to resolve."

She stopped for breath.

"That's all YOUR handiwork, Emil!"

Media interest, and especially that of Lynx cable channel's Bradlee Nelson on his now top-rating show, *Citizens' Truth*, didn't help matters. *Citizens' Truth* was like a video blog from every lunatic conspiracy theorist, right-wing ratbag, racist, protectionist, climate change denier imaginable on prime time US television, syndicated into Europe. Emil's director colleagues expressed sympathy over Davies' death, but Emil was sure they were secretly pleased about his own personal travails. They'd made no secret of the fact that they thought the MIU was an unnecessary part of the organisation and that it only created an atmosphere of mistrust in the market, whereas they sought to nurture a more collegial relationship with market participants, leaving the regulatory side to the national authorities. But they were all still giving him a wide berth, conscious of not becoming collateral damage from any of Betty G's frequent broadsides. At least that meant he wasn't being bothered by them for the moment.

To make matters worse, however, there had been an upswing in both the number and severity of criminal cyber attacks on registries and market participants, resulting in thefts that were showing initial signs of affecting market confidence. Emil and his team were working overtime, with the various national regulatory bodies, to devise appropriate responses to the situations. He had little time to do anything other than fight fires. And the picket of anti-market protesters, which had now set up a permanent tent encampment on the nature strip across the road from the entrance to the GCMO building, was making everybody irritable.

But today was shaping up particularly badly. This morning, there would be an Executive Board meeting: the only substantive item on the agenda, being the MIU's recent activities in PNG and the fallout from those activities. The only paper for the meeting was his report, covering everything from the beginning of Davies' trip, until Emil stepped off the aircraft back in Frankfurt. It had taken him most of his first week back to compile it. After the Executive Board meeting, there was to be a short memorial service for Davies, at which he would speak, followed by a wake for Davies, organized by some of the other anglos in the organisation. First, however, there was the Executive Board to deal with.

13

An inconclusive debate had rolled on for a number of years, on the fringes of climate change politics, over the need for a better institutional framework for the burgeoning international carbon market.

While the Kyoto Protocol continued to apply, there had been a failure of agreement in the broader negotiations on emission limits and other issues, resulting in no agreement to extend or replace it. Individually, however, the BRICs, the US and other countries had committed to the carbon market in their own ways and so, by default, it had become even more the focus for a global response to climate change. There was no escaping the conclusion, though, that the GCMO was a consequence of the failure of agreement on the global level. It was unfortunately, "the outcome the world got on the rebound", the "bastard offspring" of the total collapse of negotiations on global climate relations.

However, in the on-going wake of the global financial crisis, the GCMO had been seen as a good policy option by governments. As a result of the horse-trading to get a deal to follow Kyoto, parties involved in carbon trading had perversely agreed to set up and fund it to monitor and, in conjunction with national agencies, to police market activities. The funding commitments were put in place and the initial pilot period before its operations were to be reviewed was set at seven years.

But there was an array of groups with vested interests whose intentions with respect to the organisation did not necessarily coincide. To some of them, the GCMO was just a pawn in a much bigger game. There were many parties interested in controlling or influencing the GCMO, as well as many whose interest was to see it fail. And if it didn't fail by itself, to destroy it.

14

The Executive Board assembled in the meeting room by nine. Betty G made Emil wait, spending an hour running through administrative matters before handing over to him.

"You all should have read the paper circulated for this meeting, so I won't repeat the basic facts," he began. "Some of the events that have taken place recently, in PNG, are terribly unfortunate for personnel of this organization, but also for the organization itself. However, we need to keep these events in perspective. And that perspective is clearly PNG's proposals for a domestic trading regime and bilateral trading arrangements. This is to be based, initially, on credits generated from avoided deforestation projects. To some extent – in my personal view, to a significant extent – the way events have unfolded in PNG is due to positioning by the government, to put pressure on this organization, while we are assessing the proposals."

"Do you seriously expect us to believe that a sovereign government would behave in such an inappropriate manner?" interjected Havinda Singh, deputy director of the Economic Analysis Unit.

"Exactly what assessment is that going to be? Positive or negative?" added Jonathon Playfair, the deputy director in the Market Policy Unit.

"Alright, alright," Betty G cut them off. "Let him finish, before we start the discussion." 'Discussion?' Emil thought, you mean summary trial, conviction and execution, don't you?

"Gordon Davies was in the wrong place, at the wrong time,

which resulted in his arrest. He had been asked to meet some people who, in fact, turned out to be dead, even before he received the last message which purported to be from them. We still have virtually no information as to who these people were, or why they wanted to meet him. We have no information on who sent that last message, apparently from them."

This tidbit of information Emil hadn't included in his written briefing, although he had told Betty G. One or two of his colleagues looked up more attentively when he mentioned it, but most showed no recognition of its significance.

"Davies and the government minister he was dealing with in his work for this organization were subsequently killed, in a motor vehicle accident. The accident was not fully investigated and, from my own limited inquiries, it would seem that there may have been another vehicle involved."

Susanna Tüchner – Dr Tüchner, as she wouldn't hesitate to advise, in no uncertain terms, any unfortunate who addressed her otherwise – the Swiss director of the Economic Analysis Unit, uttered a loud, disapproving tut-tut sound. Emil returned fire, shooting an equally disapproving glare at her.

"The PNG police have made no attempt, so far, to follow up this information, which they have had from the beginning of the investigation. Both the inquest into their deaths, and the inquest into the deaths of the two tourists, seem to me to have been brought to a premature conclusion. The investigation into the facts by the coroner, in both cases, seemed very cursory, to put it politely."

He looked at the faces around the table, before continuing. Some were attentive, others non-committal. In Tüchner's case, openly confrontational.

"Whatever the reason for the murder of those two tourists, which doubtless had nothing to do with Gordon Davies, the government has sought to shift attention away from its law and order issues and on to the GCMO. As for the proposals themselves, there are some issues that we will need to take up with the government and its advisers. Provided they can assure us that these issues are being addressed adequately, from a market integrity perspective, they should be able to receive GCMO endorsement."

As soon as he uttered those last words, there was a commu- nal release of held breath around the table. Emil knew that this would be an important milestone for the organisation. PNG was the first of the lesser developed countries to bring forward trading proposals – and for his colleagues sitting at the table, it was criti- cal to the GCMO's future.

Betty G looked at Emil: "OK, well, if that's all from you Emil, I'll open the meeting up to discussion. I'll make the first point, which concerns publicity and the impact these events have been having on our public image. Disastrous, in a word. Whatever the truth in all these events, there's no doubt the PNG govern- ment has exploited the media in relation to this business about the bail money. We left ourselves completely open to this," she was looking at Emil, "something which, with our profile, we simply cannot afford to allow. The press – especially the likes of *Citizens' Truth* – have been loving it. It's like manna from heaven for them. We simply cannot give them that sort of opportunity. It will kill off our organization in the minds of the public, and with our supporters, in no time at all. We need to be on the front foot, getting positive news out – like how efficiently and well the market is operating, thanks to this organisation's diligence. Not this other bullcrap!"

"Yeah, and by the way Emil, the Liaison Unit actually had a report arrive from the PNG government this week. They were very unflattering about your visit," said Otis McDowell, director of the Liaison Unit and the other American on the Executive. "This sort of feedback is really unhelpful, it makes our job very difficult."

This was news to Emil. McDowell must have decided to save it up, Emil thought, just so he could spring an ambush in front of the others at this meeting.

"Don't tell me, but would that have been written by one of your countrymen, Gregory Hudson?" Emil asked sarcastically.

"It doesn't say who wrote the report, but it was signed by Sam Kaumi, Chief of Staff to the Minister for Climate. The report sets out a number of instances where he says you were making inquiries outside your authority. Acting like some sort of private detective, second-guessing the police inquiry and the coroner's findings. They're pretty serious allegations, if you ask me. The sort of thing that could well be fodder for the next round of media bashing that Betty's talking about. And Gregory Hudson happens to be Canadian, by the way."

"OK, so it was ghost written by a Canadian."

"What about the substance of these allegations?" McDowell pressed. Others around the boardroom table murmured their support for McDowell.

"What about them? One of my staff had been first arrested, then killed. I was sent there – by Betty – to find out what was going on."

"You were there to get the situation under control."

It was Orlando Suarez, Betty G's Brazilian deputy.

"That's right, Orlando, yes, I was there to get the situation under control. On arrival the first thing that greeted me was the news that the situation had deteriorated well beyond what I was supposed to be there to deal with. And as things progressed, it became clear that neither the police, the government generally, nor the coroner were really going to get to the bottom of what had happened to those four people. They were not even attempting to do so."

"But that's not your job, nor the job of any of the members of this organization," blurted Susanna Tüchner angrily. "That's properly for the police and juridical agencies. They should be left to do their job, and we do ours! Your actions have been seriously prejudicial for this organization, for all of us!"

"So you still haven't provided a useful response on how we can deal with the allegations in the report sent to Liaison, Emil," McDowell persisted.

"And I won't be able to, Otis," Emil retorted, "until I've seen the report and had a chance to consider what it actually says."

"Otis, you should have tabled that report beforehand if you wanted it considered by the meeting. We have procedures and they should be followed." Betty G intervened. Thank you, Betty, thought Emil, looking skyward.

Wang-jin Li, director of Market Policy entered the fray:

"I have two questions for Emil. Firstly, how do you know that Gordon Davies did not know these tourists from somewhere else?"

"Dominik and our IT people have been through all the electronic records of Gordon Davies' work here with GCMO. They've made a forensic examination of his laptop and mobile phone. The only interaction with these tourists was an exchange of text messages, when he was in Port Moresby, on this most recent visit. The fact that, in the first text he received from them, the writer even needs to introduce himself, suggests pretty strongly that Gordon didn't know them. The text messages are basically aimed at setting up a meeting, but we don't have any information on what was the purpose of that meeting. Telephone records show that there was a call between them, so I assume they must have discussed this during the call. I've also been in touch with Davies' widow, in the UK: she had no recognition whatsoever of the names. Never heard of them."

"Thank you Emil," said the ever polite Li. "My second question relates to what you said earlier – that the last message Davies received would have been after these tourists were dead. Can you explain?"

"Thanks, Wang-jin," said Emil, using his Chinese name, although Li preferred his colleagues to call him Walter. Some of Emil's MIU staff had, in fact, coined a new adverb in his honour, being to do something '*walter-li*' or '*walterly*', defined to mean 'creating the impression of making a difference, but in actuality being completely ineffectual'. Emil thought it a bit unfair on poor old Li, who in his view did a reasonable job for an economist (it was just that to Emil, all economists, especially the likes of Tüchner, were meretricious). But all the same, he liked Li and always steered well away from the risk of any *faux pas*, by using Li's Chinese name.

"I think this is an important point. It illustrates the lack of investigation actually carried out by the PNG authorities. Davies received a text message re-scheduling the time and place of the meeting with the tourists exactly to the place where their bodies were found. He was arrested there because, at the same time, the police had been tipped off anonymously – probably by the same person who sent the message to Davies. At the time the message went to Davies – and this has been verified with the telephone service provider, so there is no question of the message having been sent earlier and been delayed – those tourists were already dead, perhaps for days, according to the autopsies presented at the inquest into their deaths."

A number of the others realizing, at last, the significance of this information, further questions ensued. The discussion became less recriminatory and more sympathetic towards Davies and, by association, Emil. What could they do to find out more about who had sent the text? Should they be involving Interpol, or Europol? What about involving Scotland Yard?

The discussion was directionless and Betty G only let it run for a few minutes before she cut it off. The meeting ended without a resolution concerning the PNG episode, other than the need for Emil to propose an appropriate response to the report sent by Sam Kaumi. Susanna Tüchner and Otis McDowell were clearly displeased by this outcome and said as much. Playfair and Singh also looked less than happy with the lack of any formal outcome but, as deputies, were not really in a position to voice their thoughts more forcefully. From their scowls as they left the meeting room, Emil knew this wouldn't be the end of the matter, as far as they were concerned.

After the others had departed, Betty G asked Emil to join her in her office to discuss the way forward. She sat behind her desk, Emil opposite.

"You know we can't leave this as it stands," she said.

"Yes, I agree, Betty. We've got to find out what happened to Davies and the Minister, and who sent that text luring Davies into a trap."

Betty G shook her head in frustration.

"That's not what I meant, Emil. There are a number of Governing Council members who want you disciplined, or even sacked over this matter. They appear to have been fully briefed already by the PNG government on your visit to Port Moresby."

The skin on Emil's face tightened. "Sounds like the kangaroo court has already sat."

"If I could finish," she shot back. He had to remember who was the boss.

"We need to take steps to manage the immediate situation and get the GC members back on our side. I'd like to find out what happened to Davies, just as much as you and your team do. But we simply cannot afford – you can't afford – any more public relations disasters."

"I certainly understand that."

"The first thing we need to do is assess the PNG proposals. If you and MIU can do that, without stirring up another controversy, it would be a start. I'm meeting later in the week with the GC members who are making the most noise about you. You should probably attend, to put your side of the story to them. I'll get Orlando to organize that and let you know."

She looked around her cluttered desk, briefly eyeing her desk diary, then her watch.

"Now I think we're both overdue down in the lobby to say some nice words about Gordon, so we'd better not keep the troops waiting any longer."

"Before we do, Betty, there's a further aspect to this matter that I didn't include in my report. Remember it was that jerk, Bradlee Nelson, who kicked off all this business at the *C-world* conference?"

She looked at him sharply.

"Well, as I reported, in the second inquest there was evidence as to when the police received the anonymous call that led to the stake-out, and we know that Gordon received the text about the same time. Working back from those times, the only conclusion that can be drawn, is that Nelson knew in advance – that's how he was able to perform his little stunt at the conference!"

Betty G fidgeted with the pens on her desk for a few moments, then looked back up at Emil.

"If that's the case, then Nelson must have some link with the person who made the call to the Port Moresby police," she said. "And as you've said, that's probably the same person who called Davies to set him up."

"Who probably also has something to do with the deaths of those boys."

"OK, you're right. This can't be allowed to rest where it is. Can you email me the time sequence with the supporting evidence. We can't let Nelson or anyone else get away with this."

Then she added: "But don't think this gives you any sort of license, Emil. We keep this confidential, until an appropriate course of action is sanctioned, OK? You're still within a hair's breadth of having your contract terminated by the UN employment office. That's warning enough, isn't it?"

They headed downstairs to the entrance lobby of the building, where there was sufficient space to assemble the sixty or so staff that constituted the GCMO. Chairs had been arranged in rows, a lectern at the front creating a makeshift auditorium. It was a brilliantly sunny day outside and sunlight was pouring in through the glass front of the building. Emil couldn't help noticing how nice it looked, in spite of his aversion to the heat and humidity. The foliage on the trees seemed especially green in the bright light and some of the picketers, on the opposite side of the road, were lying on the grass soaking up the sun.

Dominik met them as they reached the bottom of the stairs. He had things ready to go. People stopped moving about and sat down as Betty G took to the lectern, where she gave a précis of Gordon Davies' career and family background, sensitively and sincerely, but, Emil thought, with not a lot of depth. After she'd been going about fifteen minutes she surprised everyone by asking them all to stand while she recited the Lord's Prayer, since Davies had been a Christian, then observe a minute's silence in memory of him, their colleague, who had died while on assignment.

When everyone was re-seated, Emil replaced Betty G at the lectern and tried, as far as possible, not to repeat Davies' career details. Instead, he confined himself to a couple of funny anecdotes he'd heard, either from Davies himself or other former colleagues, about Davies' adventures over the many years he'd worked for international agencies around the Asia-Pacific.

"Then there was the time Gordon was part of the observer group making a visit to the civil war torn island of Bougainville. For some reason best known to Gordon, he managed to get separated from the rest of the observer group and was accidentally left behind, when the group's boat departed. Now these blokes on Bougainville didn't muck around and as soon as the boat left, the ceasefire was considered over and they were at each other again with machineguns, going hell for leather! When it was discovered they were one short on the observer side of things, the captain was unwilling to go back in because the fighting had resumed. Can you blame him? With all that heavy machinegun fire that Gordon used to tell us about! Seemed like there were more machineguns every time he retold it … but anyway … the upshot was that he had to spend a couple days sheltering under a hut, until another ceasefire could be organized so the boat could return. And, as I'm sure those of you who heard this story from Gordon himself will recall, when he got back to head office, his boss at the time wouldn't believe his story – made him book the extra days as annual leave!"

Emil managed to raise a few laughs with his stories, and even drew a moist eye here and there.

"So, devastating and untimely though Gordon's death is, I think he would at least be pleased that he was doing the type of public service work he loved, in the part of the world he loved. I just hope that…"

He stopped, mouth open, mid-sentence. He couldn't believe his eyes. Over the heads of his colleagues, outside the glass front, he could see Bradlee Nelson, in the bright sunshine, setting up to do a 'face to camera', right in front of the building. That arsehole! It was a flagrant provocation! And he wasn't going to let the scumbag get away with it.

Emil started walking down the aisle through the middle of his seated colleagues.

"I don't believe this, I don't fucking believe it," he was muttering to himself, almost audibly, striding towards the glass front doors.

Dominik, Betty G and some of the others at the front had stood and turned, when he had stopped speaking. Now they were moving too, after Emil. Betty G turned to Dominik:

"Stop him! Now!"

Dominik covered the distance to Emil quickly and grabbed his arm, just as he reached the doors. Emil turned and looked at him momentarily, then shook his grip off and pushed through the doors.

"You've got a gall coming here today Nelson," he shouted.

Nelson and the camera turned towards Emil in unison.

"And you have some questions to answer, Mr Pfeffer, so let's start getting answers before you disappear again," Nelson called back, smiling.

He began advancing towards Emil with the cameraman in tow.

"Not as many questions as you have to answer, Nelson. Like how you knew Gordon Davies was going to be arrested before he was arrested. And what your links are to the people who murdered those boys in Papua New Guinea."

"I'll ask the questions, Pfeffer, you give the answers."

But Nelson wasn't smiling now and he waved his hand for the cameraman to cut filming.

"What's wrong Nelson," Emil shouted, louder, even though Nelson was only a couple of steps away. "Lost your nerve all of a sudden?"

Nelson had turned and was walking away, together with the cameraman. Emil started after them, but Dominik's grip on his arm – this time much firmer – restrained him.

"Come on, leave it. Building security is coming: they are not allowed to film here. They're going anyway."

Across the road, the lounging picketers had stood up, watching the pantomime being played out in front of them, with interest, amused.

Emil turned and walked back inside. As he entered, spontaneous clapping from the MIU staff started and some others joined in. But it died away quickly. Betty G stood glaring at him from the bottom of the stairs.

"There's proof enough of his complicity, if you needed it!" Emil called to her.

She said nothing, then turned and left, followed by Suarez, Tüchner, McDowell and the other acolytes.

15

The *Frankfurtburghof* was in a not very attractive part of town. Just a block or two from the main station, which made it convenient to reach from the office by train, but that was about all. Emil had heard some of the anglos in the office referring to it as the '*Fornicatorhof*', the Forni for short, almost as a term of endearment, perhaps reflecting the strength of their connection with the place. He wasn't sure whether the nickname derived from their own personal experiences there, or merely from the fact of its location adjacent to the red light district, just over the other side of Baselerstrasse. Anyway, Emil thought the place was a dump and they would have been no worse off at *Zum Löwen*. At least, if they'd gone there, he wouldn't have had far to get home if he drank too much, which, after the morning's events, was a distinct possibility.

Quite a number of the staff had shown up and were lunching, intending to take the afternoon off work. Betty G, Orlando, Walter Li and his deputy Jon Playfair made appearances, although apart from Playfair they were pretty brief. Other members of the Executive Board were conspicuous by their absence, Emil noted. Betty G did the rounds speaking to people, but slipped past Emil without acknowledgement. It was better if she had some time to cool off.

Eventually the numbers began to thin out and Emil found himself sitting at the bar surveying those of his MIU staff still there. They were mostly professionals from financial or regulatory backgrounds, not economists but scientists, lawyers or accountants, with a broad range of experience. Europeans, with a couple of other nationalities thrown in for good measure. They even had a 'star' environmental regulator in Dominik, who had transferred from the BMU, the German Federal Ministry for the Environment, Nature Conservation and Nuclear Safety. In spite of his young age, he had already made a name for himself there for hunting down illegal traffickers in hazardous and toxic wastes. His other claim to fame was having exposed and prosecuted companies importing timber products, from illegally cleared tropical forests, into Germany in breach of EU law. As a consequence, a number of Indonesian and Malaysian conglomerates had found themselves blacklisted by European investors and retail chains.

By late afternoon it was just Emil and Dominik. Earlier, they'd relocated from the Forni to a marginally more acceptable wine bar, further up towards the main business district. Emil kept leading the topic of their conversation back on to women. He was keen to talk about meeting Johanna Dorn, to get Dominik's thoughts on how he could find her. It amused Dominik to have his boss using him as a sounding board on 'matters of the heart', as he put it.

Dominik ordered another bottle of cabernet and, turning back to Emil, said:

"If you don't mind me saying, you really shouldn't let that Nelson character get under your skin. He's not a nice person, we all know that. But what he was doing today was clearly aimed to provoke a reaction – that's his modus operandi – and you gave him what he wanted."

"I know, I know, it was stupid, but I couldn't let him get away with it."

Emil thought for a moment.

"That bastard is up to his neck in this business with Gordon. I'm going to find out exactly what his involvement is and expose him."

"What do you mean? The tip-off he got that Gordon had been arrested?"

"Tip-off? My arse!"

Drinkers at a table across the room looked up from their conversation. The wine had made Emil bellicose. Lowering his voice, he went on:

"Nelson knew Gordon was going to be arrested before he was arrested – I'm sure of it."

"That's not possible. How can you be sure of it?"

"What time was Gordon's meeting rescheduled for?" Emil asked rhetorically. "Seven o'clock in the evening – PNG time. What time did the session at the conference begin – the one where Nelson ambushed me? Nine-thirty on the dot – Central European Summer Time – I remember Chris Manning was very punctual getting started. Time difference between PNG and CEST? Eight hours."

Emil was leaning further and further forward, as he spoke. Just in time, Dominik moved his wine glass out of the sweep of an extravagantly gesticulating hand.

"Thanks," he said, taking the glass back from Dominik and sipping from it.

"Even if Nelson had come in to the session just before he started asking questions, which I don't think was the case – I think he was there the whole time – but even if he had, at best it would have been contemporaneous with the actual arrest taking place in the backblocks of Port Moresby. Now if that's the case, firstly, how did he find out instantaneously, and secondly, how did he line up his little media stunt? Answer: he knew in advance that the arrest was going to take place."

He sat back with a satisfied look and exhaled. Dominik sat looking at him, taking it in. Emil leaned forward again and spoke softly:

"And if Nelson did know about it in advance, that means he knows who called the police and who texted Davies. And that person, or those people, are probably responsible for the boys' deaths."

"Does Betty know this?"

"Yes."

"What does she propose to do?"

"For the moment, nothing. Her words were to the effect that we should keep it confidential until an appropriate course of action is sanctioned – presumably this means taking it to the Governing Council, but God knows how long that would take, or how appropriately they react. She also warned me that if anything else goes wrong, they'll probably withdraw my contract. So, Dom, after today's events you might already be sitting in my seat!"

"Emil, don't suggest such a thing! Besides, it would be publicly advertised, so I wouldn't be guaranteed to get it."

"Always looking at the practical side of things, eh Dominik?" he said, sitting back again, with just a faint smile.

They talked work a while longer, Emil speculating that the increasing cyber attacks were being coordinated by criminal gangs in Russia, or the Caucuses. He was convinced they weren't random individual attacks, but were quite organized. Dominik still had his doubts, but agreed that it was a possibility.

With the second bottle empty, they decided it was time to head home. As they stood to leave, the news came on the television at the end of the bar. It was the Lynx cable channel news. The lead story was the harassment to which Lynx current affairs anchorman, Bradlee Nelson, had been subjected, while trying to film outside the GCMO headquarters in Bad Eschbach, Germany, earlier in the day. Footage came up on the screen, without any sound, of an angry, gesticulating Emil approaching the camera, then cut to footage of the building security guards moving in to request they leave. Taken on its own, the footage was pretty innocuous. But together with the near hysterical voice-over, the impression was that a great injustice had been done to the visiting American.

"They must be getting desperate if they need to use their news bulletin to promote their other programmes," Dominik observed.

"That fuckwit!" growled Emil. "But you're right, I shouldn't let them wind me up, it only plays into their hands. That little cameo could just about cost me my job."

They walked out into Niddastrasse.

"You could do something about it."

"Like what?"

"Fight back, give Nelson some of his own medicine – leak the story to another journalist. I'm sure there are plenty who would just love to take Nelson and Lynx cable down a peg or two."

Emil said he'd sleep on it and they went their separate ways.

But a seed had definitely been planted in his mind and, in fact, he didn't stop thinking about the possibilities all the way back to Heinrich-Heine-Weg. That night, he went to sleep basking in thoughts of Bradlee Nelson being skewered by a relentless, competitive colleague, no not just one, by dozens of them hounding him until he coughed. Then it would be time for Nelson to taste the same public humiliation as Emil.

16

He slept heavily and woke early, but feeling dull-headed. They shouldn't have had that second bottle. Oh well, he hoped Gordon would have approved of him having a hangover in his honour. As he was going through his morning ritual of breakfast standing at the kitchen bench, looking out the window, Dominik's parting words came back to him. Yes, maybe it was time Nelson was given some of his own medicine. But he would wait to see what Betty G came up with first. In the meantime, he would chase up Dawani to see what had come of his assurance that Emil's report would be 'taken up with his superiors'. He'd already tried emailing him, without response, so now he'd try to pin him down by telephone.

The MIU workload was continuing to increase. Over the coming weeks, he would be short a couple of staff in Bad Eschbach as his Latin American team were visiting countries. In Europe, fund managers had started issuing forest carbon asset backed bonds, packaged in a way that was reminiscent of the collateralized debt obligations that had featured prominently in the global financial crisis, a decade earlier. For the moment, this was a concern of Wang-jin Li's Market Policy Unit, but Emil had asked Dominik to liaise with Li and keep an eye things, in case the use of these structures began distorting the market. There were reports of hacking attacks on market participants to be followed up with the relevant national authorities, not to mention the business with the trading platform in Poland and then, last but certainly not least, Emil had to finalise and sign off the MIU's report on the PNG domestic trading arrangements. The GCMO, as Emil's executive colleagues reminded him frequently, was on a critical time path to conclude its assessment of the PNG proposal – and approve it.

"A lot of people have invested a lot of political capital in this decision," Susanna Tüchner harped at him. She and Havinda Singh had bailed him up in the corridor, outside his office.

"Yes, and not only in PNG itself," said Singh. "But in the countries promoting global trade, promoting this organization, such as my own."

"And especially the United States!" clarioned Tüchner, although why the US was so important to her he didn't understand. Still, it was easier to humour them.

"Yes, yes, I realise all of that. I will be working over the week-end to get the PNG report finalised."

"Well make sure your finalised report is positive. Otherwise we can all be looking for a new job!"

Tüchner was almost threatening him. 'Oh, you mean as opposed to just me looking for a new job?', he thought to say, then stopped himself. That would be giving away too much.

"As I indicated at the executive meeting, it will be!"

Towards the end of the week, Emil sought out Orlando to ask about the proposed meeting with the Governing Council members, only to be advised that Betty G had already met with them. He finally caught up with her later that day.

"The entire matter's been referred to the UN Office for Internal Oversight Services," she advised. "It's out of my hands, Emil. It was the best result I could get out of the GC members who want your head. All we can do is get on with our work and wait for feedback from the IOS."

This was not good news. Not only did it mean that the IOS would be looking at the fallout from his trip to PNG, but it also meant that the whole issue of what happened to Gordon Davies and how Bradlee Nelson may be implicated in the matter would be lost on some UN bureaucrat's desk, in the New York head-quarters, indefinitely. Late in the week, he also finally got through on the phone to Inspector Dawani, who provided assurances that everything he'd reported was being followed up. But what that actually meant was anyone's guess!

He was chewing over these developments on the Friday morning of what had been, all in all, a pretty unsatisfying week, and the fact that work would consume his weekend as well, when his mobile phone buzzed with a text message. Going into a meeting, he forgot about it until later, when he was just about to join some colleagues for lunch, but suddenly remembered to check:

I heard you have been trying to contact me. You can call me on this number. Johanna.

He felt elation. And a sense of trepidation. The message seemed a bit cool, but he had to call her straight away. He told his colleagues to go ahead and he'd catch up later.

Back in his office, he shut the door and pressed the dial back button. The phone answered immediately.

"Hallo Emil."

"Were you waiting for me to call?"

He felt stupid for saying it the second the words were out of his mouth.

"No, I was just about to dial another number and I recognized your number when it rang."

"I was only joking," he lied, unconvincingly. "I was very concerned when I heard about what happened at the library. I was worried about you and Luisa, so I've been trying to get in touch to make sure you were OK."

"Oh, that's nice of you. Yes, we're OK, but they made a bit of a mess of the library. It wasn't really as bad as the media may have made out. I think the entire episode was quite stage managed by someone – maybe the government, I don't know. Anyway, we tidied up the resources they threw around as best we could, but there were broken windows and broken furniture."

"What about your expensive security detail? Where were they?"

"The security guards were useless, they just stood back and let it happen. After that, the Commission decided to repatriate us immediately and re-think the set-up, before they get the library going again."

"Have you been back long?"

"No, I've been travelling, as I planned to do when I left PNG anyway. I got back to Brussels this week and heard that you had been ringing. Many times! They said you had been very persistent!"

"Well, I was worried about you ... and I'd like to see you again."

There was a pause at the other end of the line.

"And I'd like to see you again, too, Emil."

"When can we meet? Are you in Brussels?"

"No, I'm in Berlin now, but I'll be in Stuttgart from later next week, for two weeks. I'm looking after a friend's apartment and her dog, while she's away. Perhaps you could call down and visit while I'm there?"

So it was arranged. Johanna would arrive the following week and Emil would take the train down on the Saturday. It was only about an hour by train from Frankfurt, but Emil hadn't been there before. He went off to join his lunch colleagues feeling like the weight of the weeks since his return had lifted. His elation persisted through the afternoon, he worked late that evening and called into the local pool on the way back to his apartment. By habit, he would swim in the evenings as a way of purging the day's troubles from his mind. This evening he felt invigorated, it being more a case of burning excess energy. He swam much more than usual and, as a result, his legs were cramping by the time he finished.

Zum Löwen was full of its usual Friday night contingent and Mr Pizza Thai takeaway had a queue at the counter. He even thought he recognised a couple of the picketers from outside the office, standing there, waiting to be served. But Heinrich-Heine-Weg itself was quiet in the summer evening twilight. Entering through the main door of the house, he didn't bother with the hall light but just went straight into his apartment, closing the door behind himself. Frau Hoerler was on her summer holiday for the next month, and the tenant in the basement apartment (whom he heard, but rarely saw, anyway) was away as well, so he would have the place to himself for the next few weeks. Just the way he liked it. He reached for the switch on a standard lamp and clicked it on. Nothing happened. Frau Hoerler must be operating telepathically now, he thought. He checked the plug, but it was still in the socket. He put his bag of swimming gear and laptop bag down and went into the kitchen. No light there, either. The refrigerator wasn't working and it smelt like the milk had gone off. Damn. He went back out into the hall, in the dark stubbing his foot on his swimming bag as he went. The fuse box was to the right, above the front door. He reached up and opened it, felt his way across the panel and flicked the safety switch up. The lamp came on and he heard the refrigerator motor begin whirring from in his kitchen. What could have triggered the safety switch with no one in the building? Must have been a power surge, or something, during the day.

He went back into his apartment, turning on more lights as he went about settling in for the evening. Then he noticed it. He couldn't quite put his finger on what it was, or on what made him notice it, but all of a sudden he had the feeling that someone else had been in the apartment, that they could still be there. Adrenalin flushed through him. The words *kumo* and *sangguma* flashed into his mind. He told himself to stop being stupid. Slowly he pivoted on the spot where he stood, looking all around him. He felt like a child, afraid of the bogeyman. There couldn't be anyone else here, he told himself. The apartment was so small, he'd been into just about every part of it already. No, there's no one there, it was his imagination. But just to be sure, just to reassure himself, he started going back through each room, opening the built-in hall cupboards and looking behind doors. He felt silly, but he went through all of them just the same. He stood in the middle of his sitting room and looked around. There was no doubting it, they may not still be there, but somebody had definitely been in here since he had left for the office that morning. It couldn't be Frau Hoerler, unless she'd made a special trip back from her cottage on the Friesian Islands. Still, he couldn't put his finger on what it was that was giving him that feeling.

The sitting room opened onto a small, added-on, glass sun room or conservatory, through which the garden could be accessed. Frau Hoerler had described this to him as the "California room", when he first viewed the apartment, as if this might somehow add to its allure. Emil hadn't been into the California room since his return from PNG, and one of its endearing qualities was its propensity to gather dust. He stood at the doorway and looked into the California room. In the light cast from the sitting room, he saw it. There was a clear set of footprints in the dust, entering from and leaving by the door to the garden. They came into and out of the door where he now stood, the carpet concealing their path from there on.

Careful to avoid disturbing them, Emil checked the door to the garden. It was locked. Just to be safe, he took a chair and jammed it under the door handle. At least if someone tried to come in that way overnight, he would hear them. He went around and checked everything in the apartment again. So far as he could see, nothing was missing, nor even really out of place. It just seemed to him that things had been moved and put back. Or was that his imagination? He went back and carefully examined the footprints on the conservatory floor. They were definitely not Frau Hoerler's. From the size, he guessed they would have been made by a male foot. And to be certain, he checked them against his own foot: they were clearly bigger. Maybe Frau Hoerler had left a spare key with someone to check on the power, while she was away. He'd take it up with her when she returned. By the time he retired for the evening, he felt sheepish about leaving the chair under the door handle. But, better safe than sorry.

Before he left for the office the next morning, as an added precaution against another anonymous visitor, he locked the door from the sitting room to the California room and took the key with him. He went around twice, checking all the window locks. As he walked down Heinrich-Heine-Weg, he couldn't help looking back a couple of times to see if anyone was watching his departure, but then told himself to stop being paranoid. He spent the day in his office, working through the PNG report, periodically stealing glances out his window at the protester encampment. They didn't seem discouraged by the fact that it was the weekend, nor the distinct lack of activity around the building, maintaining the same placard and banner waving vigilance as they did midweek. He was probably the only person in the building. He wondered whether their vigilance was a show put on purely for his benefit. By five, he'd had enough and decided to call it a day, instead of waiting for a bus, walking back to his apartment, exchanging looks with the picketers, but no words, as he left the building.

He was alone in the office again on Sunday and, with the help of a couple of strong coffees, was soon into his stride and finished by mid-afternoon. He emailed the report to Betty G. and his Executive Board colleagues, copied to the MIU, packed up and headed for the swimming pool. After an early night, he was in the office early again on Monday morning. He hadn't been in long before Betty G. called him to get into her office, quickly.

"What the hell is this?" she said pointing at her computer screen as he came in the door.

Emil moved around behind the desk to where he could see the screen. She had his PNG report open at the first page, but the letters and characters were slowly tumbling down and off the screen and a message in bold, red, 24-font letters was flashing diagonally across it:

'DO NOT APPROVE DO NOT APPROVE'.

"What's going on?" he stammered.

"Precisely my question."

"It looks like some sort of virus, but how did they get into that document? I only finished and circulated it yesterday afternoon."

Betty scrolled down the document. Each new page started losing letters and characters as it came up on the screen, with the red letter message flashing across it.

"We cannot allow this to happen!" she stated blandly, as if by saying so would make it stop. "How did a virus get into your document?"

"I, I don't know. I can't explain it. I haven't even worked on this outside the office."

But as he said it, he remembered he had opened up the document on his laptop at home on Saturday night, before he fell asleep. No, nothing could have happened then. He didn't even go online.

"Orlando isn't in yet. Can you chase down IT and get them onto it immediately."

Fortunately, Emil had printed a hard copy of the report, which he was able to give her. He found Stefan, the head of IT, at home in bed, having worked on the servers most of the weekend until late Sunday night. Betty G. appeared in the doorway to his office.

"What's the position?"

"Stefan and his guys were working on the servers all weekend. If there had been a hack during that time, they would have detected it and stopped it. He says it's not necessarily a virus that I introduced in the document, but could have been lying dormant in the system waiting for some sort of trigger to activate it. A trigger which must somehow appear in that report."

"Well, we need to get it out of that report. I've got a GC meeting on Thursday at which the members expect to be approving our endorsement of the PNG proposals. They need that report in advance of the meeting. As it is, it should have been in the agenda papers forwarded to them last week. Emil, you know how much is hanging on this…"

"Betty, I just worked all weekend to get it finalized. You don't need to tell me. I know!"

There wasn't anything else Emil could do. IT had to assess the situation and provide a technical solution. By afternoon, Stefan had quarantined the malignant program and removed it from the system. Its source, and how it got in past all the security measures, was still a mystery that Stefan guessed would take weeks more work to resolve. At least for the moment, however, Betty G. had calmed down and felt she was in control again. But there was a lingering sense of injustice in the back of Emil's mind that she had immediately assumed he was somehow responsible for the IT security breach.

Emil didn't let on to Dominik that Johanna had contacted him. He thought it was better not to burden his deputy with too much of his private life. But he did tell him about his suspicions that his apartment had been entered.

"If nothing was missing, how can you be sure there was an intruder?"

"The footprints for one thing."

"But you can't be sure they weren't already there from some previous visitor. You said yourself that you never go into this room."

"I'm certain someone was in the apartment. It's too much of a coincidence, with my landlady and the other tenant away. And the power being off. And with me working to finish this PNG report – which then is afflicted by a virus from these people trying to stop our endorsement. And with those bloody protesters, over there, watching our every move ..."

Dominik couldn't quite see how these things all could be linked and remained unconvinced. To his mind, it seemed quite plausible that there were completely separate explanations for what could well be unrelated events. But then, he saw these things from a very different perspective to Emil. And, for now at least, he'd keep his own counsel on these matters.

17

'The best laid schemes o' mice and men.'

Emil sat at his desk, trying to remember how the rest of the sentence went. What was it? Often go awry ...? Something like that. Which was apposite here, anyway.

Dominik's liaison with the Market Policy people on the forest carbon asset backed bond issues had become a troika, with Susanna Tüchner not wanting to be left out and insisting on the addition of Havinda Singh from Economic Analysis. With others copying the initial issuer, there was potential for these bonds to start generating market developments in their own right – like out-of-control wild fires creating their own winds. Now the troika was doing exactly that: Emil intended Dominik's early involvement to curtail workload, instead the creation of the troika was starting to generate its own firestorm of additional administration, with briefings and emails and minutes of meetings being fired around left, right and centre.

Late in the week, an invitation arrived for Emil to attend a PNG government event for investors, to take place at the Zürich Neue Börse, in late August. The invitation was issued on behalf of the government by the *Bankgesellschaft Kohlenstoffermäßigungen Zürich*, the BKZ, signed by none other than Gregory Hudson.

But other than these minor distractions, work had slipped into a temporary mid-summer torpor. After the frenzied pace of the preceding weeks, this week was dragging interminably and Emil had far too much time on his hands: time spent thinking about seeing Johanna again. He found himself thinking about it all the time: what he would say, the things they would talk about and do: he found himself thinking a lot about sex. Sex with Johanna. He stopped himself. He was behaving like an adolescent. In the years since Catherine's death there hadn't been anyone else, not even a one night stand. Sex had become irrelevant and he'd begun to wonder whether he'd lost interest in it altogether. Now, at least, he knew that wasn't the case. In the end, he decided to work as much as he could, to leave as little time as possible for his mind to play these games, and to exercise a lot to burn off energy, so he would relax. He had to leave the weekend to resolve itself.

By the Saturday morning of the trip to Stuttgart, the expenditure of physical and nervous energy caught up with him. He slept through the alarm and had to race to catch his train, then fell asleep again once he was on it. He woke with it sitting at the platform in Stuttgart and got off in a hurry, feeling disoriented and a little dishevelled. Not quite the arrival he had been envisaging all week; but, at least, now he was there. He walked along the platform with the crowd of alighting passengers, stepping around clusters of Stuttgarters waiting, embracing arrivals or farewelling departing passengers. Through the crowd he saw Johanna and, weaving his way over hugged her, not noticing the Jack Russell terrier under her arm until its teeth pierced his forearm. He recoiled, pulling his arm back sharply and hitting a man passing behind him in the face with the back of his hand. All three stood there for a moment, too surprised, to react.

"Entschuldigung. Sorry! My apologies!" said Emil, recovering first.

The man rubbed his cheek, giving Emil a look that said '*Ausländer!*', then kept walking. Johanna was laughing at his behaviour, until she saw the blood smeared over his forearm. She put the dog on the floor and examined it.

"I'm beginning to think you're jinxed," she said, then looking down at the dog. "Schnupsi, that's no way to greet our visitor."

Schnupsi looked up innocently, then away at something more interesting.

"Well, if you're going to be tending to my injuries – every cloud has a silver lining, as they say."

"And what do they say about smooth talkers like you?" she said, continuing to hold and examine his forearm. "Come on, we need to get it looked at."

The arm was hurting, but he'd relaxed, the week's tension dissolved in that absurd moment. There were about half a dozen small puncture marks in the fleshy part of his forearm from Schnupsi's needle like teeth, so escaping from the bedlam of the main station, they jumped on a bus to Killesberg where there was a weekend surgery not far from the apartment Johanna was looking after. Punctures cleaned and a tetanus injection later, they left Schnupsi – who by now had befriended Emil – to amuse herself at home. Johanna thought it would good for Emil's introduction to Stuttgart to begin with a short walking tour, so they set off, Emil protesting that what he needed more was a couple of strong espressos, Johanna leading him off up a steep hill to an open area of parkland capped by a stone tower, one of Bismarck's Towers.

"I love this view of Stuttgart," she said as they reached the top, "the hills immediately around the city centre: the view over all the surrounding areas, but at the same time, there is the city centre, protected inside this ring of hills. This is an industrial city, but it's nice, don't you think?"

He surveyed the panorama laid out in front of them. The hills ringed three sides of the city centre, like a horseshoe – an appropriate analogy Johanna told him, since the symbol of Stuttgart was a horse. To the north, the view took in a coal-fired power station, industrial buildings and hillsides swathed in grapevines, stretching away into the heat haze. Behind the hills opposite to the east, however, vast stacks of dark clouds were banking up ominously, like giant piles of grey cauliflower about to tumble over the side of those hills and into the centre of the horseshoe below.

"We'd better keep moving," said Johanna, "there are storms forecast. It looks like they will be here sooner than expected."

They wound their way back down to the centre and, reaching Konigstrasse, weaved up through the throng of Saturday shoppers around the Schlossplatz.

"It's not normally this busy, so early. Konigstrasse and Schlossplatz only become crowded with shoppers in the afternoon, but there is a food and wine festival taking place this weekend."

As she finished speaking, the clouds out-ran the sun and it grew very dim. With rumbles of thunder reverberating all around, Johanna led him through an archway behind the Alte Kanzlei into Schillerpaltz, around the back of the Alte Schloss and into the Markthalle. Upstairs they were just ahead of the crowd, managing to claim a table by the window in the restaurant. People were filling the tables behind them, they sat and just looked at each other for the first time since Emil had arrived.

"That was very interesting, thank you," he said, their eyes exploring and gauging each other. She was lightly tanned, more so than he remembered her from Port Moresby, and seemed slimmer and fitter than before.

"It was my pleasure. A bit rushed, but perhaps there'll be more time later, if the weather permits." Johanna was scrutinizing him with her direct look, friendly, not confronting, but assessing him nonetheless.

The thought ran through Emil's mind whether 'later' encompassed the possibility of tomorrow. The question of whether he was visiting just for the day, or was staying for the weekend, hadn't really come up. They'd just agreed he'd come down to Stuttgart on Saturday morning, the timing of his return to Frankfurt hadn't been discussed. Looking at her, he wondered whether she was thinking the same thing as she looked at him. A waiter appeared and the moment was gone. They both ordered linguine and a glass of Riesling. Rain began to dump down outside, scattering the food festival patrons and shoppers.

"When it rained in Port Moresby, this is how it used to fall: hard and straight down," said Emil after the waiter brought their wine and some water.

"Yes, but there wasn't much during the time I was there. The climate has changed. The dry season in Port Moresby seems to encompass most of the year now. There was plenty of rain up past Brown River, and up on the Sogeri plateau, of course, but Moresby itself was mostly dry."

"When I lived there, we would have periods in the dry season when the water level in Surinumu Dam was too low to generate any power. All the businesses and apartment blocks had back-up generators. It was just bad luck for the locals if they couldn't afford one. From what I've heard these incidents are frequent all year 'round now."

"Yes, certainly that was my experience, but as you said, we had back-up power. We never really got much of an idea how it was for the average Papua New Guinean. That's typical for expatriates, don't you think?"

"So do you see me as a typical ex-pat in Germany?"

"Only to the same extent I see myself as one in Brussels," she smiled.

Another peal of thunder trembled through the building, but the worst of the storm was moving on. Emil mused at how deftly she had deflected his oblique attempt to get some idea of what she was thinking about him. Or was he reading too much into it?

"Is the PNG government still planning to purchase those heavy oil generators from China as a back-up for the grid – there was something about it in the press while I was there."

"Actually, while I was in Brussels just recently I read that the China deal has been put on hold. It's all been referred to a Parliamentary inquiry, I think."

"Hmm, sounds to me like someone won't be getting their kick-back. No doubt the inquiry panel consists of members with no financial interests in the outcome … as if!"

"Emil, you're very cynical," she chided, a more serious note in her voice.

"Your cynic, is my realist, when it comes to governance. Perhaps they are one and the same."

"Perhaps."

A waiter arrived with their food. They clinked glasses and sipped their wine, then both moved the parsley garnishing to the side of their plate.

"For Gordon," Johanna intoned softly, as she did it.

Emil looked up at her.

"What did you just say?"

" 'For Gordon'. He used to move the garnish to the side of his plate. I was just doing it in memory of him."

"That's exactly what I was thinking when I moved mine."

They shared their memories of Davies and, inevitably, this led Emil on to talk about the memorial event a couple of weeks earlier and with it, his run in with Bradlee Nelson. To put it in context, he had to explain the background, including the warning about his job that Betty G had given him just before the latest of the Nelson incidents.

He was nervous talking about these matters in such a public place, as he did, furtively looking around the restaurant. It was full now, with a queue of wet patrons standing at the entrance waiting for tables to become available. Outside, the rain had eased but continued to fall. Inside, the hubbub of conversations, of orders being taken, of meals arriving and being eaten, made for considerable background noise. Still, Emil leaned forward and lowered his voice when describing events in the Executive Board. Johanna leaned forward so their noses were almost touching.

"Are you worried about being overheard?" she said in a hoarse stage whisper.

Emil sat back smiling.

"Have you told the authorities about him – the timing must surely implicate him?"

"I have raised it with my boss: we have to leave it until 'the appropriate course of action is sanctioned', whatever that may be, and whenever it may happen," said Emil, not going into the New York referral and resisting the urge to tell her about Dominik's suggestion that he fight back, to which he'd been giving serious consideration.

She could see he was still uncomfortable talking about it where they were.

"We should get the bill and go. There are lots of people waiting – you don't want a dessert, do you? We can have a coffee at the Holanka bar around the corner and find somewhere private to talk."

"Yes, that's a good idea, let's go somewhere private …" he suggested.

She slapped his hand.

"That's not what I meant! I was thinking we could walk around the Kunsthaus."

The waiter came and they paid the bill. The queue now extended back down the steps. They huddled under Johanna's small umbrella, making their way up and around the corner to the Holanka bar, but it was full with a queue to the door and with rain continuing to fall, they decided it would probably be the same most places. Johanna suggested they return to the apartment she was minding for a coffee and check on Schnupsi – at least until the rain stopped. Emil wasn't going to argue. So they huddled off under the umbrella, Emil's arm around Johanna's shoulder, holding her more tightly to him than perhaps was absolutely necessary, but she wasn't resisting, back across the wet and empty Schillerplatz and into the U-bahn. At the main station they changed onto a bus to Killesberg, where the rain was falling more heavily, in drenching vertical lines. The apartment building was set up and back from the road, so they huddled under the umbrella again, jumping up steps and along pathways running like small streams. In the minute it took them to reach the cover of the building, they were soaked.

"At least your shoulder is dry," said Emil removing his jacket, the left sleeve of which had been around Johanna's shoulder and was now dripping wet.

Johanna disappeared to find something that he could wear while his jeans and socks were dried. She came back with a pair of shorts that belonged to her friend's boyfriend, having herself changed into a robe. Schnupsi was in her basket asleep, oblivious to their voices and movement around the apartment. It was on the ground floor, but because of the elevated position of the building still had a wonderful aspect, or, at least, would have a wonderful aspect over the city below once the cloud lifted. Johanna made coffee and they sat on the sofa where she had her laptop set up.

"I've been meaning to ask you about your time working in PNG – when you used to go to the Yacht Club 'disco'," she said, a mocking inflection on the word.

"You've got a good memory."

Emil gazed out at the rain for a few moments.

"I worked in Port Moresby for a man called Piers Birch. He was OK, we got on. Piers was a bit of an eccentric – probably been out in the tropical sun for too many years. Drank a lot. Really a lot. Red wine. Gin. Whisky. Anything, you name it. Smoked unfiltered Camel cigarettes, about sixty a day. So you can see, Piers was not a very healthy specimen. Pretty much like a lot of the older expatriates there at the time.

"A lot of the other ex-pat professionals were into property deals. Basically, they had 'get-rich-quick' agendas. Piers wasn't like them. He would have seen that as ripping the place off. He set up a sports centre for kids from the local squatter settlements, paid for it all himself. But because he was different, the others used to peddle rumours behind his back about his 'interest' in young national boys.

"When I started working there, I used to stand up for him when I heard these rumours. As a result, I became a target as well. They started calling me 'Birch's catamite', like I was some newly discovered local species. This eventually became 'BC'. They didn't have the guts to say anything to Piers directly, but because I was new and young and, I suppose, looking for acceptance, they would taunt me by calling me 'BC' to my face. My rare visits to the Yacht Club disco usually ended with confrontation."

"I would have told them all to fuck off!" said Johanna, real vehemence in her voice.

"I did, more or less. I didn't have many friends amongst them – probably only one, actually. Unfortunately, in the end it was from me that Piers found out about the rumours. Looking back, it seems silly, and unnecessary, but I guess it was different then. We argued. It was over money and conditions – I wanted more than he was willing to give. In the end, I walked out – resigned. Left Pier's firm; left the country. But, in the heat of the moment, I told him I was sick of defending his reputation to his professional colleagues. He had no idea. I didn't realize what a shock it was to him to find out what his peers said behind his back. A year later I learnt that he was dead …"

He looked out at the rain. Neither spoke. Eventually Johanna broke the silence.

"Would you like to see some of my pictures from PNG?" she asked, beginning to click through the folders on the screen.

She ran through some folders of photos, but her most recent

were still on her camera, so she held it in front of them clicking through the photos from around the time of Emil's visit, talking through each one as she went. To see the small screen, their faces were very close together, cheeks almost touching. They were so close Emil could feel the warmth of her face, her beautiful skin. He realized that she had stopped talking and was just clicking slowly through the photos. He turned a little towards her, the corner of his mouth touching the corner of hers. She turned towards him and their lips touched. Photos ceased to be relevant, the camera found its way to the floor and they were locked together, finally.

There was a rustle in the basket. Johanna broke away and standing, pulled Emil up by the hand.

"Not here. We don't want another Schnupsi incident, do we?" she said, leading him into the bedroom, Emil all too aware of the straining at the front of the borrowed shorts.

She closed the door behind her and they kissed. She wrestled him out of the shorts, then pushing him to sit on the bed, dropping the robe, she removed her underwear and straddled him, lightly tanned breasts standing out in front of his face. He pulled her to him, falling back with her on top. If he'd had time to think about it, there they were, exactly as he'd been subconsciously hoping, dreaming they would be since the moment they'd met. He rolled on top of her but then, with a sudden convulsion, it was over. He rolled off her, slumped, deflated, feeling he'd disappointed her.

"I'm sorry. It's been a long time."

She gave him a gentle smile, running her fingers up and down his body before she spoke.

"Don't worry. What is it you say in English, 'practice makes perfect'?"

18

There it was again. Emil opened his eyes. He wasn't dreaming: next to him, he could feel the warmth, smell Johanna's body, hear the evenness of her breathing. But there it was again, that was definitely a noise. He had thought for a moment that, maybe, it was just the fact of being in a place, an apartment, he'd never slept in before. But this noise didn't seem normal. He sat up, at which Johanna woke and turned to look at him. He put his finger to his lips, then to hers. There it was again.

Johanna sat up.

"It's probably Schnupsi," she whispered.

Emil took his watch from the bedside table. It was just after three in the morning.

"Does she normally wake up at this time?" he whispered, but Johanna was already getting up and putting on her robe.

Emil got up and pulled on his now dry jeans and they both went out into the living area of the apartment. Johanna switched on a lamp. Schnupsi was at the door of the apartment, moving up and down sniffing along the gap at its base, making a low, growling sound.

"See, I told you it was Schnupsi," said Johanna.

She went to the door and opened it and Schnupsi immediately darted out and down the steps into the basement.

"I'll get her," said Emil as he pulled on his t-shirt. "Where's the light switch?"

"There's a button at the top of the stairs and at the bottom. It's a timer, so just push it in again if it goes off."

Emil pushed the button at the top of the stairs and headed down after Schnupsi, who had disappeared from view. At the bottom of the steps he found himself in an open area with a concrete floor, cold on his bare feet, from which led four doorways, two on either side, each one in darkness. He went to the first on the left. In the light from the landing he could see it was the washing room and he found the light switch. The room was large but there was no sign of Schnupsi. He turned off the light and checked the other doorway back under the stairs, on the left. It led off into total darkness, but he could see the wooden slats and padlocks of cellar rooms belonging to individual flats.

"Schnupsi, come."

He listened, but there was nothing.

He couldn't find a light switch, so he edged his way down this corridor, stopped and listened again. Nothing but silence. Then blackness, total blackness. The timer button for the light on the stairs had clicked off. Emil worked his way back along the wall, around the doorway into the stairwell and along the wall until he found the button.

He went to the doorways on the right. The one opposite the laundry room was just a corridor that disappeared towards the front of the building into blackness.

"Schnupsi! Here Schnupsi, come here!"

He listened but heard nothing, so he went to the other one back under the stairs, on the right. This was directly beneath Johanna's apartment and he could hear her moving around above him. He moved down along the line of wooden slats of more cellar rooms, calling softly as he went.

"Schnupsi? C'mon Schnupsi. We want some sleep! Schnupsi, come."

Maybe she didn't understand English.

"Kommen Sie hier Schnupsi, jetzt!"

Still he couldn't find a light switch. Then the timer button went off and total blackness closed in again. He'd walked in further this time, hadn't been as careful with his steps as he had been at first on the other side, now he felt a little disoriented. He had a weird sensation that he could see things but knew he couldn't really. It was like a white-out in the snow, or green-out when scuba-diving, when tiny microbes immediately in front of one's mask could be a fish twenty metres away – you just couldn't tell. Except, the difference now was that there was no light at all, so whatever he thought he could see was in his mind's eye, not his eye itself. He reached out with his hand and felt the reassurance of the brick wall. But he had to stop and think: which way had he come in? He hadn't been paying attention when he came in and half turned, or had he fully turned, when the light went out? He listened, hoping that some movement from Johanna above might help him, but there was nothing. Well, it didn't sound like Schnupsi was in here either, so he'd just have to work his way back along the wall ... he stopped and held his breath. He had a sudden feeling that he wasn't alone in the blackness. A rush of adrenalin sent a tingle up his spine to the base of his skull. He sensed the horripilation on the back of his neck. Stop being crazy, he told himself. He waved his arm around him in the blackness without touching anything. Just go back and get the light on in the stairwell. He began edging along the wall but there was no doorway. He kept moving slowly forward, hand along the wall, until it felt wooden slats. Damn, he'd gone the wrong way. He turned and began edging his way back, still getting tingles up his spine, still with the feeling he wasn't alone in the blackness. He worked his way along the wall with his left hand now, keeping his right out in front of him as protection, just in case someone was there, trying to make as little noise as possible. His hand felt the edge of the doorway. For a second, he felt relief. Suddenly, something hit him very hard in the stomach. A boot, a knee, a fist, knocking the wind out of him. He doubled up, staggering forward. A swinging boot crunched him again, in his mid-rift. He grabbed the leg attached to it. A thumping blow hit him at the top of his back, in the shoulder blade, then another, knocking him down. His grip slipped off the leg and he hit the floor. The light came on, he heard the sound of boots running away down the darkened corridor. He heard Johanna's footsteps on the stairs. He tried to get up, but couldn't take his weight on his left arm, the side he'd been hit. He rolled onto his back, brought his legs up and sucked in air.

Johanna was kneeling over him. She helped him sit up.

"What happened? Emil, are you alright?"

"There was some one here. Where does that go?" he gasped, still sucking in air, nodding in the direction of the fourth doorway with its darkened corridor.

"The garages - under the grassed terraces at the front. Is that where they went?"

"I didn't see. It sounded like it. Didn't you see them?"

"No, I was wondering what was taking you so long, so I came to the door and it was all dark, but then I heard noises - it sounded like a scuffle or something."

Schnupsi appeared out of the door to the cellars on the other side and strutted over to them. She had something in her mouth which she dropped in front of Johanna. It was an almost dead mouse; it twitched and Johanna jumped away from it. Schnupsi squatted back on her haunches, ready to pounce on it again if it showed any sign of escaping. She looked very pleased with herself.

"I thought she must have been investigating the intruder, but it was just a bloody mouse she was after," said Emil.

"She helped flush out the intruder as well."

They returned to the apartment, Emil having disposed of the unfortunate mouse to the garden. Before returning to bed, he went around the entire apartment, checking windows and doors, even behind doors and in wardrobes. Johanna thought he was being overly cautious: it was just someone trying to steal things from the cellar. He didn't share his suspicions with her, but he wasn't so sure it was just the cellar they were interested in. He hadn't told her about the uninvited visitor to his flat in Bad Eschbach. She might think he was paranoid. But it seemed a little bit too coincidental – first there, now here. And thinking about it, the attack seemed to have a violence to it that was more than a simple intruder trying to make sure of their escape.

His back, just above the left shoulder blade, was throbbing intensely. Johanna found some liniment in the bathroom and massaged his shoulder and neck.

"Twice in one day – these clouds really do have silver linings," said Emil as she finished. They got back into bed. She fell asleep immediately, her head on his chest, his right arm holding her to him. He lay awake for a long time, his shoulder aching, listening for every sound. The rain which had stopped began to fall again lightly. Sometime later it eased and through the curtains he could see the sky had lightened imperceptibly and could hear the first bird calls of the day. He was experiencing a strange mix of intense pleasure at the warm, supple body pressed against his side, one leg entwined with his, her small pad of pubic hair pressed into his thigh, but at the same time, an uneasiness which wouldn't let him sleep.

Eventually he dozed off and when they woke they were still in the same positions. It was late morning and Schnupsi roused them. They lay together for as long as they could, before Johanna felt she needed to deal with the dog's incessant attention-seeking from the other side of the door. The clouds had cleared to a bright blue sky and the city below them looked sharp and clean washed. How could anyone not feel good on such a day?

Trains to Frankfurt were regular, so Emil didn't leave until later that evening. They returned to the apartment in the afternoon and didn't even make it to the bedroom, rolling off the sofa onto the floor, clothes half on, half off, urgently, more physical with each other than earlier, in spite of the pain in his shoulder. When they finished, they each fell back laughing.

"You are so randy! Like a bull," said Johanna, breathlessly. "Are you trying to do all the Kama Sutra positions at once?"

"We only tried the first sixty-eight," he gasped.

Before he left Stuttgart, he made Johanna promise she would talk to the other tenants about the intruder and they would decide whether to report it to the police. He was still concerned there might be more to it than just an attempted theft. There was no evidence of a break into the cellars, not that it meant much – he may have disturbed the intruder before anything could be stolen. He called her each day that week, then on the Friday evening, left the office as soon as he could and caught the train back down to Stuttgart. Johanna and Schnupsi met him again, but this time they went straight back to the apartment, not via the surgery.

Dominik noticed the change in Emil's demeanour first thing Monday morning, at the MIU weekly meeting. There was definitely a spring in his step, but Dominik thought better of making any comment. It was pretty obvious, even if Emil wasn't saying anything. But eventually Dominik had to comment on the way Emil was favouring his left arm.

"What have you done to yourself?"

"I think I've pinched a nerve in my shoulder – too much swimming, maybe. I just need to let it heal before I get back to the pool," Emil responded.

In fact, he had a large bruise on his back where a clenched fist had come down several times very hard.

Dominik was away for the fortnight following Emil's second visit to Stuttgart, which meant Emil was stuck in Bad Eschbach, tied down with work. The UN paperwork relating to Davies' death, that Betty G had threatened would be coming his way, had arrived. And with it, returned his sense of guilt over the still unanswered questions concerning Davies' death. They had been nagging away quietly at his conscience since the referral to the IOS, like a skin irritation that could be endured. But with the arrival of this task, it was as if the skin had become inflamed, more irritable and, with it, an air of inevitability that, sooner rather than later, he would need to resolve it, once and for all.

19

Rodger Beckwith was happy with his lot.

He enjoyed being a banker, at least, now that nasty Financial Conduct Authority investigation, which had dogged him in London, was a few years behind him. He enjoyed especially working as a British banker in Zürich, where the locals seemed to place great store in the fact that he was a Brit, that he had forsaken the drama and excitement of the City, to be here, amongst them, the gnomes of Zürich.

Yes, he enjoyed his lot, his nice English wife and kids over in Luzern, both near enough and far enough away to be a comfort, his nice little specialist banking operation, dealing in carbon – well, maybe not Master of the Universe just yet, but who could tell, soon perhaps there would be much more, especially the way his shareholder was bankrolling things.

And, of course, there was Gisela, his assistant, who as usual on a Wednesday evening he'd be 'working back' with. Yes, Gisela was a great comfort, especially when she was performing ... he checked himself. Better put those thoughts aside for the moment, at least until he'd done this last bit of business for the day.

Rodger was sitting at his usual spot at the bar in the Kronenhalle, waiting for the summons. This was the only part of his lot that he had some reservations about, the 'secret agent bit', he called it. His backers were very guarded when it came to their privacy and had emphasized to Rodger the need, at all times, to be discreet when it came to them, their involvement or their identity. He was excited by it, what he thought of as extreme Swiss banking secrecy and the clandestine meetings. He had to admit it even gave a special edge to the rest of his evening with Gisela – not that he needed any extra incentive with her – but after these meetings, he felt super sensitized with her, like every nerve end was jangling, in a state of hyper-excitement.

He finished his gin, poured the remainder of the bottle of tonic into the glass, swirled it around and drank it down, then fished out the sliver of lemon from the bottom of the glass and chewed it. His mobile phone, lying on the bar, vibrated. He picked it up and looked at the message:

10 minutes Giacometti.

Hmm, sculpture this time, instead of the Impressionists. He wondered whether there was any significance in the choice. He left a twenty franc note on the bar and nodded to the barman, then headed up Raemistrasse to the Kunsthaus, where he bought a general entry and went into the Giacometti gallery. There was a large tour group, Koreans or Chinese, he guessed, making its way around the gallery, so he slowly worked his way around the exhibits they'd already passed, lingering for minutes in front of *Le Chien*, a stick figure bronze from the artist's mature period, before moving on to *La Cage*, which he found altogether impenetrable.

"Complex, wouldn't you say?" the man next to him observed.

Beckwith hadn't noticed him sidle up, but he recognised Davis Crooter's voice without turning.

"Too deep for a humble banker like me."

"That's an oxymoron."

"Which bit, the humility or the 'like me'?"

"Both."

They moved onto the next exhibit.

"But I'm not here to be your analyst, there's more important things to discuss."

As the tour group moved out, they very slowly made a circuit of the room, casually moving from exhibit to exhibit like any other two visitors to the gallery, coming together for a minute or so in front of each, before Crooter would move on, eventually arriving back at La Cage.

"So you say that Pfeffer has been in touch with you?"

"Yes, Hudson invited him to the roadshow event here. I didn't see who he'd added to the final list until they sent it back through from Port Moresby, by which time all the invitations had gone out. Now Pfeffer wants to meet me before the event."

"What about?"

"That's what I asked him. He said just background on our role, but he's emailed a list of points."

"OK, that's his job. Meet him. But you're just the marketing side of things, OK, so if he starts asking questions about the PNG side of things, that's not your area."

"Perfectly fine by me, I know exactly how to deal with him."

"Yes, so do we."

Beckwith stood for a few moments longer, not really looking at the work of art in front of him, thinking through the instructions he'd just received from a person he knew only as the agent of his majority shareholder, then he looked around and saw that he was alone in the gallery. He headed for the exit and the first tram across town to his apartment, which was just past the office on Ernst-Nobs-Platz, his thoughts already moving on to Gisela, his anticipatory tumescence making him ever so pleasantly self-conscious.

20

It was Emil's habit to ensure that either he or Dominik was always in the office in Bad Eschbach. It was just safer that way, both from the point of view of ensuring that there was someone in charge if an emergency cropped up, and to keep an eye on the intrigues of his director colleagues. The Zürich trip would be an exception. He and Dominik would take the train down, meet with the CEO of BKZ, attend the roadshow event and stay a couple of nights. Hopefully there would be an opportunity to catch up with Gerry Johnstone, for dinner. Maybe, Emil might even improve his rapport with Gregory Hudson. No, on second thoughts, he doubted that would happen.

Still, Emil felt he needed to be seen to be making an effort to ensure things went smoothly with the PNG delegation, in spite of, or perhaps because of, the hackers' threats that had been appearing on the GCMO computer system, warning against supporting carbon trading in PNG. In the week before the function, he'd pressed Otis to provide what background he had on Hudson, although this produced only a grudgingly shared one-page biography, that read more like a press release. The official ceremony for GCMO endorsement of the PNG arrangements was the responsibility of the Liaison Unit, but Emil wanted to build rapport ahead of it. The ceremony was scheduled to take place after the last investor event.

The other thing he needed to do was find out from Gerry Johnstone what had happened to Inspector Dawani. Emil had called a number of times to follow up on the progress of his report, but Dawani had become uncontactable. On his most recent attempt, he'd been told Dawani had been posted to Morobe Province. But when Emil rang police headquarters in Lae, they had no record of him. It was clearly time to call for Gerry's assistance to find out what was going on.

They travelled down on the day of the event and, having checked into their hotel, found their way by tram to the BKZ offices. The chief executive, Rodger Beckwith, had provided non-committal answers to Emil's emailed points. In person, he was cordial and informative on the generalities of his organization, but little more.

"Thanks again for making this time available to meet with us, Mr Beckwith. We were hoping you could give us some more details about the role of the bank for the PNG government?"

"Our function is purely marketing and brokering, as I think I've already indicated in my email. In broad terms, we source potential investors for public and private sector clients in the resources sector – which, in the instant case, includes carbon assets. We facilitate and arrange the introductions, answer questions the investors may have, pass through the information supplied to us by the client and so on."

"So the bank acts as a post-box?"

"*Au contraire*, Mr Pfeffer, we add value! Why, just the introductions themselves would justify our involvement. Arranging for the 'right' people to be here tonight, for example. But we do more, let me assure you, once that initial contact has been made. We tend and nurture the relationship, in the hope it will bear fruit. We'll elaborate on this in our presentations tonight."

Emil was already starting to dislike the dandy sitting across the desk from him, ducking and weaving evasively, like a politician, around every question.

"Well, it's very useful background for us to be here tonight, seeing who the 'right' types of investors might be, but you'll appreciate in our role we're more interested in the set up and operations in PNG itself. What's your role on that side of things?"

"Obviously, Mr Pfeffer, this bank would not be representing the government of PNG unless we had the highest regard for what we are marketing. We have our reputation, a very good one I might add, to uphold. We present only the best opportunities to our investor clients."

"So what are the particular qualities on the PNG side that you'll be holding out to investors?"

"Well, I think you'll hear it all at the event tonight. Beyond that, I'm afraid client confidentiality precludes me from saying more. I'm sure your organization has made its own investigation into the arrangements the government has in place."

"We have, but I'm just looking to see what else you can shed light on for us. We need to be thorough in these matters."

But, unfortunately, there was nothing else forthcoming. The only way they were going to get more out of Mr Beckwith would be if he was legally compelled and, so far as he understood the purpose of the meeting, that was not the case. He had his assistant usher them out, after little more than half an hour, on the pretext that there were a lot of last minute preparations to be made for the event.

"Well, that was a complete waste of time," said Emil. They were standing under the horse chestnut trees in Ernst-Nobs-Platz.

"Not completely, I think Mr Beckwith told us something without realizing it."

"Like what? That he's rich and fancies his assistant wearing a very tight-fitting blouse and skirt?"

"Well, she may not have been trying to hide much, but he definitely was – did you notice how anxious he seemed? Maybe he's trying to hide the fact that he's having an affair with her."

"I doubt he'd try to hide that, characters like him would be more likely to boast about it."

In fact, Emil hadn't noticed and Dominik's remark set him thinking. But then the button-popping curves of Beckwith's assistant's blouse kept finding their way into his mind's eye, so he decided he'd do better to move on and concentrate on how they would fill in the rest of the afternoon instead.

Immediately across the Sihl, past the stone lions guarding each corner of the Selnaubrücke, stood the Neue Börse – ironically appropriate: the New Exchange – that evening's venue, it's entrance like the open mouth of the Morlocks' cave. From a distance, Emil thought the people hanging around outside were workers having a cigarette break, and some of them were smoking, but as he and Dominik crossed the bridge it became clear that these smokers would definitely not be going back to resume seats in front of trading screens. The green brigade was here in their army disposal dungarees and dreadlocks, preparing their placards for greeting the attendees later that evening. Emil couldn't fathom how the protest groups always knew about events, even private business events that were not general public knowledge, and were well prepared for them in advance, in this case, the placards clearly identifying Papua New Guinea as a place NOT to invest.

"How could they have known an investor event for PNG would be on here tonight?" he asked rhetorically.

With the pre-emptory termination of their meeting, they had even more time to fill in before the function, so they kept going, past the Börse on the opposite side of the road, to avoid the motley crowd, continuing in the direction of the lake. At Gartenstrasse, they joined the path along the Schanzengraben, the zig-zag remnant of the fortifications that had surrounded the city. It now provided a link between the Lake and the Sihl, hosting dinghy moorings and bathing facilities, as opposed to pikes. They eventually ended up at Bellevue, looking at the granite-blue, white flecked alps, sharp and rigid, framing the end of the lake beneath an almost cloudless, blue sky. The afternoon had a soft warmth to it, leavened by the occasional cooler ripple of air off the lake, that lent itself to speculation on the sexual proclivities of their evening's host. They stopped for a drink at an outdoor café before continuing their leisurely sightseeing tour along the Limmat, walking up into the Niederdorf, the old part of the city rising on its eastern side towards the university, before eventually heading back to the Börse.

When they got there, the crowd outside the Börse was already spilling off the pavement onto Selnaustrasse, where the police were trying to keep traffic moving. A cacophony of whistles, hooters, assorted drums and a poorly played bugle was being rejoined by the tooting horns of impatient passing drivers. They edged through the crowd towards the area the police were keeping clear for arriving guests and managed to get out of the throng into the building. There was a security check with the mandatory metal detector archway and bag x-ray.

"Next it will be full body scanners at places like this, not just at airports," observed Dominik.

Exiting the lift there was more security. At the door they were greeted by representatives of the PNG delegation, including Gerry Johnstone. Emil introduced Dominik and agreed to catch up later in the evening. Inside, Gregory Hudson greeted Emil like a long lost friend and introduced the new Minister for Climate Change, a short, thick set, bearded highlander, who Emil thought could have been Sam Kaumi's twin and who, Dominik observed to Emil later, was wearing the most amazing pair of crocodile skin boots. They moved on to let others have their hands pressed by the Honourable Minister. A waiter presented a tray of drinks from which they selected champagne, another tempted them with hors d'oeuvres and they were each presented with an investor package.

"It's a production line," said Dominik.

"Yes, with Gregory Hudson's hands on the levers, I'd say. Did you see how he greeted me? I almost asked him if he'd been told to be on his best behaviour tonight, like me."

"I don't think that would have been a good idea. He's just being friendly – perhaps he felt guilty about the way he treated you in Port Moresby."

Everyone else coming in seemed to know each other already, happily going straight up and joining groups of suits. Not knowing another soul, Emil latched on to a Swiss financial regulator – an easy target really, as the man was standing by himself. They were soon joined by a couple of representatives from the Swiss development agency. What was it, Emil wondered as he exchanged small talk with these sharply dressed, affable bureaucrats, that made all the public sector people stand out like shags on a rock at an event like this? Their clothes were more or less the same as everyone else; their behaviour was indistinguishable from the bankers and private finance people; but somehow, one just knew they were public servants, not money men. They're probably thinking the same thing about me, too, he mused.

A slick video presentation on PNG began proceedings, followed by a welcoming speech from the new Minister, memorable only for its brevity and lack of coherence, both of which were made up for by Gregory Hudson. Emil grudgingly had to admit to himself, Hudson was a good speaker and very persuasive advocate of the proposals. If the roadshow failed to attract investors, it wouldn't be due to lack of effort on Hudson's part. Rodger Beckwith and some other financial spruikers followed, then more drinks and canapés appeared following the presentations.

"Did you bring your cheque book?" said Gerry joining them, grinning and raising his eyebrows, a mannerism which reminded Emil disturbingly of Piers Birch. Maybe it was something you picked up after being in the tropics too long, he thought. Emil admitted that he was impressed by Hudson's performance.

"He sounded like he really believes in it."

"Oh, don't worry, he does," responded Gerry. "Depending on the audience …"

They all concurred that the Minister's contribution needed some work.

"Thankfully that's Sam Kaumi's responsibility, not mine," said Gerry.

"Yes, I thought I saw my old friend Sam across the room earlier. I must go over and say hello."

"You probably won't get a chance. He'll be baby-sitting the Honourable. At the last one of these events in Hong Kong he, the Hon that is, was so pissed we had to put him in a broom closet until all the guests had gone. Then we forgot about him and he ended up in there all night. He was in awful state when we fished him out again next morning."

Dominik looked incredulously at Gerry, then to Emil, then back to Gerry.

"He's probably not bullshitting," said Emil, laughing. "These ministers are all the same once they get on some overseas junket. When I was there, a scandal erupted about a government Minister on a plane to Singapore, who was so drunk he worked his way down from first class and urinated over the partition separating business and economy, including passengers in the front row of economy! He tried to explain it on the basis he thought he was in the toilet. Irony is, of course, Singapore airlines economy class is actually quite good."

"Very funny," said Dominik, bemused.

Emil changed tack: "Gerry, what can you tell us about these BKZ people? We spoke to the CEO, Beckwith, today and he was singularly unhelpful."

"He's got a fantastic looking assistant."

"We've got eyes."

"What do you want to know?"

"What are they doing for you? If they're the money men, then in my experience they'll be at the heart of everything, but Beckwith made it seem like they're only on the periphery – marketing and investor relations type things, which is hard to swallow."

"That's what his assistant says too."

"Gerry!!"

"OK, sorry mate. Bit rude. Listen, here isn't the place. Let's chat about it over lunch."

Leaving it at that, they took their leave to let Gerry get on with his spruiking, having made the arrangements for the following day.

At the ground floor, the lift doors opened on a scene that could have been taken from Dante's *Inferno*. The protest was in full swing now and the police had brought in reinforcements. The din from the clashing of metal cans, chanting protesters, constant whistle-blowing, drums and police loudspeakers seemed remote in the spotlessly clean, plushly decorated foyer of the Exchange, muffled as it was by the thickness of the blast proof security glass; but there was a sense of impending threat in the chaos of constantly moving people and sporadic scuffles, compounded by the red and blue lights flashing through a fog of purple smoke from flares, that they would encounter as soon as they stepped outside.

Emil was hesitant. "Do you think we should wait inside until this lot dies down a bit?"

"We could go back up for a few more drinks ... " Dominik offered hopefully.

But before they could act on it, a security guard in the foyer gestured to them, so they followed him away from the Sihl side of the building to the Schanzengraben side, fronting the Rimini bar and baths which, in stark contrast to the other, was quiet and in total darkness. Aha, a back exit: our hosts must have been expecting trouble, Emil thought. Without a word, the guard ushered them out into the dark and they heard the door click locked behind them.

"Well, that settles that. We might be better off heading towards the lake to avoid the ..." Emil began.

But he didn't finish.

They were still a distance from the light of Selnaustrasse when there was the sound of running from close behind them. Lots of boots, heavy boots, running quickly.

Running at them.

21

The black hooded mob was on them before they could turn to run themselves. Dominik felt a whack on the back of his head – was on the ground before he knew what happened. The mob passed over him, as it did, a couple of stray boots caught him in the ribs, knocking the wind out of him. He'd stayed there for what seemed like minutes, then slowly, with difficulty, clambered to his feet.

By the time he reached the street, a posse of police was pursuing the black hoodies into the distance along Selnaustrasse, in the direction of the lake. He looked around for Emil, but couldn't see him. It was hopeless trying to make him out from the constantly shifting sea of people, police and placards. Flashing lights and flares made recognition of any but the nearest faces impossible. He tried Emil's mobile phone – just diverted to voicemail. After searching fruitlessly around the fringes of the melee for an hour, without a sign of Emil, he headed back to the hotel.

Emil hadn't been back to his room, so having arranged for the concierge to call him if Emil came back, Dominik returned to the Börse. The police there couldn't help, directing him instead to the Kantonspolice on Kasernenstrasse, to file a missing person report. At the Kantonspolice, when he finished explaining the situation, the desk officer just looked him up and down: yet another German time-waster. The night had been completely taken up by damn German troublemakers at the Börse and now here was yet another.

"How many drinks did you say you had at this function?"

Dominik was taken aback. "I didn't. But since you ask, I might have had three or four glasses of champagne, and my colleague probably had the same."

The desk officer snorted his disbelief. He was now well into a double shift because of the trouble at the Börse and he really didn't need this sort of shit.

"You're telling me that they were laying on free drinks on the top floor at the Börse and you only had three or four. You ought to see how you look. You look like you've been drinking all night."

Fortunately there were officers in the building who were able to partially corroborate Dominik's story. They'd been part of the section of police attacked by a gang of black-hooded hooligans that had emerged from Badweg at the back of the Börse, hurling rocks and other missiles, before being chased off down Selnaustrasse. The desk officer still took some persuading, but eventually he compiled a report of Emil's description and placed it in circulation.

Dominik had then sat down in the waiting room. And waited.

That was more than ten hours ago.

22

Emil opened his eyes, then quickly shut them again. He covered his face with his hands. It was so bright. He was lying on his back, facing up, facing up at a bright sky. And he was wet and cold – the cold, that's what roused him. He'd been dreaming of swimming, but he was swimming fully dressed. Then his mind had wrestled its way back to consciousness. He rolled onto his side and peered out between his fingers. He was lying in long grass. Long, wet grass in a sort of ditch. Through his fingers he could see that it was sunny, but he must be lying in shade. He was sopping wet and he was lying in the shade. And he was cold. Slowly he was piecing things together. Even that effort was making his head spin and he felt like he was going to vomit. He decided to lie there for a few minutes longer, before trying anything more strenuous.

Eventually the cold forced him to move. He rolled onto his front and pushed himself up onto hands and knees, still looking down to give his eyes time to adjust to the light. He sat back on his heels and just as he began to look up a deafening crack rang out, immediately followed by a thud above his head. Then a series of ear-piercing cracks and bangs. Thuds above. Zings from behind. He threw himself forward, flat on his face, the sudden effort making him retch. There was a brief lull, then another fusillade of cracks, this time with more zings from behind him and whizzes through the grass not far from him. He flattened himself deeper in the grass. When it stopped he looked up to his right. He could see the bare earth of the mound that formed the ditch where he lay. Mounted along it on posts, at even spacing, were large, thick rectangles. There must have been about eight of them. He looked around to the other side. The grassy ditch was about two metres wide then the earth rose up much higher and was topped by a pock-marked concrete wall. Another barrage of cracks rang out, much louder. He flattened again, hands over his head, his ears ringing. A chunk flew off the corner of one of the rectangles and bounced back off the wall into the grass. He flattened himself harder and lay there, waiting.

There was a longer lull in the firing: Emil managed to look up and down the ditch. Ten metres either side of him the mound ended, although the concrete wall behind seemed to extend further. He tried calling out for help, but his throat was reluctant to cooperate. Stinging from the dried reflux that coated it, making it hard for him to swallow. Then more volleys of shots flattened him again.

Finally, having started to find his voice, each time the firing stopped, he called.

"Hey, HEY! Don't shoot! HELP!!!"

But then it would just start up again, drowning out his feeble calls.

At the other end of the range, he realized, there was no way they would hear him anyway. He gave up and lay there, timing the gaps between the volleys to see if there was a pattern, but they seemed completely random.

But he couldn't stay there. Keeping as flat as possible, in between the volleys of shots he wriggled his way out of his wet suit jacket, then out of his soaking white shirt. Taking a firm hold of the collar, he waited until the next lull in firing then made a single quick wave of his arm, with the shirt fluttering above. After a couple of seconds silence he repeated the movement. He waited again, this time longer. He was about to swing his arm again, when a single crack rang out and the soil of the mound directly above his head instantaneously exploded all over him. Fuck, they think I'm a rabbit or a fox or something, he thought, flattening himself as deeply in the grass as he could.

Urs Hofstetter was nominally in charge of firing safety this morning at the Schuetzenhaus. It was pretty much the usual bunch of guys keeping their eye in, apart from one newcomer, who said he had just moved to Meilen and was trying out new sights for the first time. It was Urs who saw something white moving beneath the targets and called a halt to firing, which everyone observed except for the newcomer, who got in a last, poorly directed shot. I'll have a quiet word about firing range safety with that fellow later, Urs thought as he headed down the service road to the targets with a couple of the other shooters. But when they returned, having found the crazy, drunken *Ausländer* lying behind the targets and the police had come to take him away, the newcomer was nowhere to be found. None of the others had even noticed him leave.

23

"I've just had a call from my colleagues in Meilen. They are holding a drunk *Ausländer*, found lying half naked behind the targets at the Schuetzenhaus in Beulen. His identification papers show his name as that of your colleague – Pfeffer, wasn't it? And he fits the description you gave."

Dominik had nodded off to sleep, sitting in the waiting room at the Kantonspolice. The desk officer needed to shake him quite hard to rouse him, causing him to wince with the pain from his ribs at the sudden movement.

"Yes, Pfeffer. Drunk?"

"That's what I was told. He's suffering from exposure – they said he looked like he'd been swimming in the lake, fully clothed."

Dominik's eyes widened in astonishment.

"They are taking him to Männendorf hospital to be checked over – I'll arrange for you to be taken down there. We'll get some statements from you both after that."

He's changed his tune, Dominik thought, as he waited for the police car to take him to wherever this place was.

At Männendorf hospital, they took one look at Dominik's laboured movement and insisted that he be examined as well. Apart from the swelling and contusion behind his ear, x-rays revealed hairline fractures to three ribs beneath the bruising on his side. Emil was suffering from hypothermia and had a few bruises as well. They both had a full set of blood tests taken, although Dominik suspected that this was more at the insistence of the police, than for any other reason. Happily, his showed little in the way of alcohol, so the desk man back at Kasernenstrasse would have to be disappointed on that score.

Emil's was another story. The blood tests revealed an interesting melange of drugs, which probably explained why he was behaving in such an odd manner. He was having trouble maintaining concentration for very long. The police had given him a drink, which he'd vomited back up and he had dry-retched a couple of times since Dominik had been there. The doctors decided to keep him in overnight for observation. He was put in a room on a saline drip and immediately went to sleep, so Dominik went back to the hotel for the night.

Emil was almost back to normal by the following afternoon. Dominik collected him and together they went to Kasernenstrasse, to make their statements to the police. Having dictated accounts of what they could remember, a couple of officers investigating the disturbance outside the Börse interviewed them. As the session proceeded, it became evident they were only interested in Emil's account, a large portion of which, unfortunately, was missing.

"We were coming out of the Börse. We'd been shown out into the side away from the trouble – I think you said it's called Badweg, didn't you?"

He looked at the officers. One made the barest of nods in agreement.

"It was all dark, much quieter." He thought for a moment. "That's all. I don't remember anything else. As I said in my statement, next thing I knew, I was lying in the grass behind the targets."

The officers waited for him to continue, motionless, staring impassively. He gave a final offering.

"I'm not sure, but I have a vague sort of recollection of being in water at some stage during the night. But I don't know whether that's an actual recollection, or whether it's because you've said my clothes indicate I was in the lake."

After a few moments, the policemen exchanged a brief glance, then one of them spoke.

"Well, our toxicology tests on your blood samples seem to be much more informative about your activities, Herr Pfeffer."

The officer had a Manila folder on the table in front of him, which he opened and browsed through.

"It looks like you were having quite a party the night before last, after you left your colleague at the Börse. Was he too boring for you?"

"I don't follow."

"They indicate you had a lot to drink. And it would seem you were also taking barbiturates. They've identified traces of sodium thiopental, but there were other drugs in your system as well - quite a cocktail. You like cocktails, Herr Pfeffer?"

"Not particularly, why?"

"The medical examiner speculates here that, even though in the state you were in you might have drowned, your midnight swim probably saved you."

Emil and Dominik looked at each other.

"Saved me from what, exactly?"

"Death, exactly, Herr Pfeffer. At the concentrations they have extrapolated, there is a chance your body could have shut down – or more precisely, as the report says, your cardiovascular and respiratory systems may have become depressed in such a way as to be fatal."

Emil returned the officer's stare. With the fog in his mind slowly clearing, he was uneasy with the thought that whoever did this had come so close to killing him. Equally disconcerting was the fact that they probably knew exactly how far to go.

Emil needed more moral support.

"Herr Pfeffer had the same amount to drink at the function as I had, which was quite moderate," said Dominik.

"Whatever other substances the blood test shows in my system, I didn't put them there. As I have been trying to get across to you, as I tried to explain to your colleagues in Meilen yesterday, I think I must have been abducted."

"But why would someone wish to abduct you, drug you, drop you in the Zürichsee, then leave you behind the targets at a shooting range?"

"I don't know. Perhaps it was a practical joke. Completely

random. I was just the unlucky sod they picked on."

Or maybe, Emil thought, it was completely premeditated and they knew exactly who they were picking on. He almost voiced this possibility, then thought better to keep his concerns on that score to himself. These guys would probably think he was psychotic – have him psychologically profiled.

The officer wasn't the type to be interested in practical jokes.

"Based on the information in front of me, there is a good argument for charges to be laid against you for trespass, public nuisance and wasting public resources."

"What? WHAT?! What the hell are you talking about?" Emil screamed in the man's face, to Dominik's alarm. "You have information before you that we were attacked. That I was abducted. What are you going to do about that?!"

"Herr Pfeffer, calm down!" The officer's voice, raised over Emil's, was itself anything but calm. "The information I have is that you were full of drugs and alcohol, an unfortunately all too common occurrence in the people we deal with these days. Police time and resources have been spent on you. There is no evidence, other than your assertion, that you were attacked and kidnapped. Your own colleague here, with you at the time you allege it happened, saw nothing. The only people who could have done this would be environmental protesters and other troublemakers who were there outside the Börse – many of whom are from foreign countries," he looked at Dominik, "such as your own. This is the information on which we have to base our response!"

The man stared at Emil, jaw set, like he was ready for a fight. His colleague, on the other hand, was the 'good cop'. All reason and logic.

"So you see, Herr Pfeffer, the alternatives for us are that either you are telling the truth and you were abducted by these protesters and hooligans, or you are lying about being abducted and were, in fact, partying with them. We are simply trying to establish from you which it is."

"I was abducted."

It was late by the time they returned to the hotel. When Emil finally got his mobile working, there were messages from Gerry Johnstone, which became progressively more abusive as he waited for them to show for the lunch appointment the day before. Gerry would have to wait a little longer for an explanation. Emil called Betty G.

"I was wondering when I was going to hear from you two."

Emil detected something in the tone of her voice. He wasn't in the mood for this.

"Dom is here, so I'll put you on speaker and let him explain."

Dominik gave an abridged version of events since their arrival in Zürich.

"That's not how it's been reported in the press here today," was her only comment when he'd finished.

"And I suppose by 'press' you mean Citizen's Truth?"

"Don't push your luck Emil. Just forget about Nelson, OK? As a matter of fact, it's the mainstream press, although I imagine it won't take long for Lynx to pick up on it."

She said she would follow up with the Swiss authorities and make sure the police report was copied to GCMO and the UN Office of Internal Oversight Services in New York. It was agreed they should return to Frankfurt early the next morning. It would be the weekend, but she wanted to meet privately, in the office: she had an important matter to discuss with them.

24

The train eased slowly around the bottom of the Schwarzwald at the most south-westerly point of Baden-Württemberg, towards Freiburg, following the Rhine back up to Mannheim, then on to Frankfurt. To the west, the Vosges mountains were silhouetted sharply by the morning sun against a blackening sky. The predicted cold front was sweeping in and a curtain of grey hastening towards them. Soon the shroud enveloped them, lashing the carriage with rain. Emil stared out into watery impressions of scenery slipping past.

"Don't worry about the media." Dominik broke into his thoughts. "Especially don't worry about Nelson. The evidence is clear. I know what happened. You know what happened. The police report and medical evidence support what we know happened."

"Do we? Do we know what happened, really?" Emil looked at him. "I have no recollection of events between leaving the function and waking up at the shooting range."

"Yes, but the police had to admit the medical examination showed puncture marks in your shoulder. It's clear, you were drugged. And somehow given alcohol while you were unconscious. But why?"

"That's the easiest part of it. Look at how quickly it found its way into the press: obviously to discredit me. And the GCMO. Maybe they're hoping that if my reputation is destroyed, somehow this will stop, or slow down, or affect the validity of the PNG endorsement."

"Seems like a pretty ineffectual way to stop the endorsement. If you don't do it, then I will, or someone else will. They can't destroy the reputation of everyone at GCMO."

"Maybe by destroying my reputation, they think they'll critically wound the organisation – as a whole."

"It seems a bit out of character. Hacking attacks maybe, but not physical intimidation and abduction."

"Dominik, you've seen for yourself how militant these people are getting. They want to stop us. They've become more extreme. Extremists will do whatever it takes to achieve their ends."

"Still, it is a bit odd."

Dominik shifted his position on the seat, catching his breath at the sharp pain from his rib cage. He exhaled cautiously. Adjusting his position again, more tentatively this time, peering out at the dim, blurry landscape. The rain was mounting an increasingly ferocious assault, the train surging on past flat fields of partially harvested late summer crops, dissected by rivulets fast becoming teeming currents. They had the compartment to themselves and the thundering outside accentuated their silence as each toyed with his own thoughts.

Emil gazed into the middle distance, somewhere out in the sodden fields and villages they were flying past, his thoughts running back over things again. He couldn't understand Dominik's uncertainty, his reticence – he got a good kicking out of them as well – but he seemed to be making excuses for them. And why else would they be targeting me? Emil withdrew into his thoughts, their conversation over long before Mannheim. Then, with a start, he realized they were crossing the Main and rolling down into Frankfurt main station. Low cloud had settled over the city, swallowing the tops of the taller buildings. The rain would be with them for the next few days. Leaving the train they went their separate ways only to reconvene with Betty G later that afternoon.

His flat smelt musty from having been closed up, so in spite of the rain, he threw open the windows to circulate some air through it. Having done that, he suddenly wondered whether he should have first checked for signs of another uninvited visitor. Damn it, he was too dozy to make a good detective. But then he rationalised that it was unlikely, since Frau Hoerler was now back in residence on the first floor, having returned from her summer break, as had the tenant in the basement apartment – where he had spent his first weeks in Bad Eschbach, until the ground floor apartment had become vacant. He couldn't understand how the woman who was down there now could stand it – literally the converted basement, which still shared the area with the heating oil tank and a lot of Frau Hoerler's junk. It was probably completely in breach of the planning laws; the only natural light coming from a light well. And the adequacy of the ventilation was open to question. He called it the coffin flat. Even now, he was haunted by it every time the woman used the water as, after a couple of seconds' delay, the pump which cleared the wastewater would rattle itself into action. Since the pump was located outside his bedroom window, whether he wanted to be or not, he was aware of every time his neighbour used the bathroom during the night.

He did some chores, closed all the windows again and headed to the office. Perversely, he didn't mind Heinrich-Heine-Weg in these dank weather conditions. The dreariness of the place melded seamlessly with the leaden sky. Others might find it grim, but to Emil, the closed-in sky and consistent light rain gave a feeling of comfort, almost reassurance. Conditions like this always made him think of London and his time there with Catherine. Comfortable, cosy, happy times under grey skies.

He decided to take the train the one stop to the office, rather than walk, or wait for the infrequent Saturday afternoon bus. The *passage de pissoir*, as he called it, by which the platforms were reached, still reeked astringently, courtesy of the previous evening's last guests at *Zum Löwen*. The rain would eventually flush that away. Looking out from the platform, he could just make out through the gloom a person in the fields on the other side of the line walking their dog. Neither seemed to be enjoying it, heads down and steps deliberate. But Emil liked the rain.

It was still raining when he left the office. The protesters had retreated undercover, inside their makeshift tent home, although that didn't stop Emil glaring at them as he arrived and again as he left. Contrary to his expectation, the subject of the meeting was not the events in Zürich. There had been other developments, during their brief absence from Bad Eschbach.

"Just in that short time while you were gone, the cyber attacks have gone through the roof. Stefan's team can't deal with it, it's so bad. I had to bring in security consultants. These guys cost a fortune, so we need to get it fixed. Soon!" said Betty, eyeing them closely. "I wanted to see you today to bring you up to speed. What they've reported so far, causes me a lot of concern. Someone inside this organization is facilitating these hacking attacks, either unwittingly, or more likely," she scowled, "by deliberately creating access gates for viruses and malware. This treachery is completely and utterly unacceptable! It must be stopped. I want you two to find the culprit."

"What about the other directors?" asked Dominik.

"They've been told about the problem, but that's all. I'm not telling them you two are investigating, so don't you! These attacks are a direct threat to the MIU's role, just as much as they are to the organization as a whole. They are specifically directed at the Pa-poo-a Noo Ginnee trading scheme, which, I needn't remind you, principally falls within the MIU's responsibility. And, by the sounds of what you say, it might have something to do with what happened to you in Zürich."

"I don't think there's much room for doubt." said Emil, despite Dominik's non-committal shrug.

"So it seems you two are the most qualified persons for the job. And to be perfectly blunt, believe it or not, I trust you two to sort it out, more than I do the rest of them."

Emil thought about doing some laps at the pool on the way home, but the refrigerator needed restocking, so instead went to the supermarket before it closed. Nothing would be open on Sunday. Once home, he called Johanna, then ran a hot bath. He lay in it longer than he had intended, getting out with shrivelled fingers and pink skin. Pulling his towel from the rail, he sent whorls of settling steam spiralling upwards again, wrapping the towel tightly around his shoulders. Then he saw it, on the fogged mirror. Fingertip drawn crude block capitals slowly defining themselves in the steam read:

"LAST WARNING"

He stood staring, as it began to disappear again with the evaporating steam. Those bastards. Bastards! He wrapped the towel around his waist and made a circuit of the flat's doors and windows. They were all closed and locked, as he'd left them when he went to the office. He dried himself and dressed, found his mobile phone and went back to the bathroom. The message was invisible again. So he closed himself in the room and turned all the hot taps on full, until there was enough steam to bring it back. Then he took photos of it until he was satisfied he'd captured as much detail as he could. If anything would firm up his resolve in favour of the endorsement, that would.

25

Chin resting in the butt of his hand, Emil sat at his desk, deep in thought.

Following the initial misleading press reports of an officer, with an international agency, getting excessively drunk at a function and needing to be rescued from Lake Zürich, Citizen's Truth had taken up the baton. Daily reports: 'details as they come to hand' – death by a thousand cuts – with all the facts carefully twisted to put them in the worst possible light. Emil had had enough of Nelson. Earlier in the week, he'd spoken with a freelance journalist, introduced by Dominik.

They met in a Frankfurt bar one evening – a long way from the Forni and any potentially eavesdropping colleagues. Emil was surprised by how young he seemed. Dominik had assured Emil the young man was discreet, good at his business and well-connected. Once they were safely hidden from view, in a booth at the back of the bar, Emil outlined the story, giving him a copy of the time sequence details and supporting evidence he'd prepared for Betty G. The journalist took notes and proposed a drip feed of information – not full stories, but enough to stir up interest – to news syndicators, like Reuters and Associated Press, over a period of, say, a month. He assured Emil nothing would be traceable back to him. It was new ground for Emil, he couldn't feel totally relaxed about it, but he'd done it now, there was no turning back, he told himself.

The phone on his desk rang.

"The boys are back in town!" a distinctly Kiwi voice, sounding very unlike the way the song went, croaked at the other end of the line.

"Gerry, you sound as sick as a dog."

"I am, mate, I am," he croaked back. "It was the final session in London last night and we went all out to get the investors in, and then all out to drink the place dry! I almost ended up in the broom closet with the Minister this time."

"You're too old for it, Gerry. So you're in Frankfurt?"

"Yes, mate, just checked into the Westin Grand and after a bit of kip we'll be getting ready for the big session this evening. I hope you're all prepared, Uncle Gregory is looking forward to your glowing endorsement."

"He'll be sadly disappointed if he's expecting something from me. Our Director-General, Betty Greenhaugh, will be making the speech and the official announcement will be up on our website this afternoon."

Since their return from Zürich, Emil had vacillated over whether, as Dominik was advocating, to propose a postponement of the official endorsement ceremony. He expected that opposition to such a suggestion would be extreme, both from within the GCMO and externally. Equally, however, cyber attacks on the organisation's IT system were beginning to seriously impede its operations, with daily denial of service attacks on the website where, for legal reasons, the official announcement needed to be posted.

He and Dominik had tried to keep their search for an 'internal collaborator' as low key as possible, but it was like trying to orienteer at night, blindfolded, without a map or compass. The cyber attacks themselves had none of the hallmarks of prominent activist hacker groups, such as Anonymous or Lulzsec. There were no messages, other than that PNG must not be endorsed for carbon trading. No elaboration or explanation was given. Just warnings. The absence of hard evidence, but rather only supposition of internal assistance for the hacking, left them with no starting point for their inquiries nor a direction in which to move. In short, as Emil concluded to Dominik, it looked to him like they had been set up to fail.

Whatever small window of opportunity there may have been for Emil to do anything about postponing the event, if he'd been so minded, it had closed. The event planning had commenced immediately after he circulated his report in favour of endorsement. The Liaison Unit was responsible for organizing the event and Otis McDowell was focused like a laser-guided missile. For Otis, the event would re-establish the relationship between the organisation and the PNG government. Otis had developed quite a rapport with Gregory Hudson, speaking glowingly about 'Gregory' in Executive Board meetings, especially for Emil's benefit. If Emil had wanted to have the event postponed, Otis would have been the first and most difficult hurdle to overcome.

In the end, Emil's vacillations were to no avail. The day of the event had arrived and he had done nothing. Not that he hadn't considered it, it was just that, in the end, he hadn't acted. He and Dominik had talked it through on several occasions, Emil admitting he still had reservations about what was going on in PNG. But these had more to do with the death of Davies and that, for the moment, was in the hands of the IOS, in New York.

"The opposition to it proceeding is irrational: the people opposing it – the people mounting these attacks – don't give any reasons. They just keep mounting these senseless attacks. Then there are the attacks on me – personal attacks! If anything, they've galvanized my view in favour," said Emil, rationalizing and justifying his inaction to Dominik.

"What do you mean 'personal *attacks*'? You were abducted in Zürich, but that was only one occasion …"

Emil showed Dominik the photos of his bathroom mirror with the scrawled warning.

"And remember I told you about my apartment being broken into, the weekend I was working on the report."

"Yes, but even you weren't certain, you couldn't find any definitive evidence."

Well there was plenty of evidence when I was attacked in Stuttgart … "

"Stuttgart? When were you in Stuttgart?"

"When I, er, I ..."

Too late. The cat was out of the bag. Dominik dragged out of him the whole story about Johanna getting in touch, and the fact that they had been seeing each other, as regularly as they could manage, given the geographic constraints.

"You cunning fox, you kept that very quiet! I'd wondered why you'd stopped talking about her – it was because you didn't need to, you were talking to her instead! Hmm, this also explains why you've suddenly been going away for weekends, which you never used to do. It's all becoming much clearer now!" He prodded Emil in the ribs. "Yes, much clearer now."

Great care was being taken to ensure that the PNG ceremony would remain unknown to any protester groups, seeking to disrupt it. It was to be held in the reception rooms located on the forty-fourth floor of the old ECB building. Most ECB departments had relocated already to the new building in the Ostend, on the Großmarkthalle site. While this, in itself, made the function venue inconspicuous, Otis had gone to the extraordinary length of having the invitation-only guests arrive at the new ECB building, before being shuttle-bussed to the real venue. This little security twist hadn't even been disclosed to the PNG contingent, not even Otis's special new friend, Gregory.

Emil made a point of drawing to Otis's attention the fact that the ceremony was largely just that, a ceremony, since the official legal announcement had been made by publication on the GCMO website that afternoon, before it crashed under yet another denial of service attack. But Otis ignored him. Otis was in charge for the day and, unlike Emil, he was going to make sure things went right. Even if it was only ceremonial.

All the same, when he arrived at the ECB Großmarkthalle building, Emil was surprised by his sense of disappointment. He'd been bracing himself for the same sort of crew that greeted him and Dominik at the Neue Börse in Zürich. He was half hoping it might jog some recollection from his missing twelve hours there. Instead, he emerged from the U-Bahn into a crowd consisting only of workers exiting their workplaces, scuttling off into a glorious autumnal evening. The air was crisp, with a slight edge, and an unblemished blue sky was slipping effortlessly into black. Since the rain had gone, the nights had been still but much cooler, so he'd brought a coat, but it was such a pleasant evening he wondered why he'd bothered. Inside, he joined the guests being corralled by one of Otis McDowell's functionaries at one end of the lift lobby, where a lift had been commandeered to ferry them to the underground car park.

"All a bit excessively cloak and dagger, isn't it? Just to jolly along some fuzzy-wuzzies," Emil overheard a distinguished looking senior banker-type comment to his wife (later in the evening, Emil realised it was, in fact, the British Consul-General).

The venue was a great choice, he had to admit to himself. For a second, it even provoked a twinge of guilt for his earlier petty digs at Otis. But only a second. An expanse of evening lights, from Bad Homburg round to Wiesbaden, Mainz and all the way down to Darmstadt, winked up at them as the last red vestiges along the horizon disappeared. Glasses of champagne in hand, Emil and Gerry stood admiring a sunset worthy of the many they'd watched over Fairfax Harbour, then with beer glasses, from the club balcony. It was a smallish event, fifty guests all told. Gerry just wasn't up to any more schmoozing, now that the roadshow was over, and Emil wasn't interested in making small talk at these events at the best of times. They had some catching up to do.

But they both noticed Rodger Beckwith arrive, accompanied by his assistant.

"Her name's Gisela," Gerry whispered conspiratorially. "My money says Beckwith's bonking her, no doubt about it. And who wouldn't, for Pete's sake? I'd give her a good rogering, if I had half a chance."

Emil didn't respond, preferring to ignore this throw back to the Gerry he'd known twenty years earlier. He was more intent on tracking the progress of Gregory Hudson and the thermo-nuclear powerhouse that was Betty G., each diligently doing their rounds of the guests. There was no doubt, they both worked hard, albeit in very different causes.

"Did you ever get the bottom of what happened in Zürich?" asked Gerry.

"No, it's still in the hands of the Kantonspolice, although I don't expect they'll get anywhere in a hurry. I think their view is I made it all up. That I was really just bombed off my head."

"I can empathize with that. Been there, done that before!" said Gerry, again making that grinning, eyebrow-raising face that gave Emil a disconcerting sense of being in conversation with the long dead Piers Birch.

Black-clad waiters bearing trays of canapés and champagne, attempting to waft past, were bailed up and their loads lightened.

"Speaking of Zürich, we never got to have that chat about BKZ."

"I can tell you all you need to know about BKZ: she's standing just over the other side of the room and she's eminently fu …"

"Thanks Gerry, I've got the message!"

Emil noticed Dominik arrive and waved. Dominik didn't see him, instead bailing up a waiter and getting into what looked like a very involved discussion with the man. Eventually, he noticed Emil and made his way over.

"I was delayed at home and had to come here directly," he said grabbing a glass from another passing waiter. "Emil, we need …"

Before he could say any more, someone blew into a microphone. Then cleared their throat into it, which stopped every conversation dead in its tracks.

"Honourable Minister, Excellencies, distinguished guests, ladies and gentlemen," Otis began. "First, let me extend a very warm welcome to all of you here tonight for this ceremony to acknowledge the official endorsement today by the Global Carbon Markets Organisation of the framework and arrangements for carbon trading established by the Government of the Independent State of Papua New Guinea."

A round of polite clapping punctuated the monotone.

Gerry leaned over to Emil and whispered:

"Why is it that all the drink waiters always disappear at this point, just when you need them the most?"

Dominik turned to Emil:

"We need to…" he tried again.

But Otis was continuing and Emil held his index finger up and mouthed "Later", oblivious to the anxiety in Dominik's expression.

Otis launched into a long-winded outline of the background to the GCMO, the critical role his Liaison Unit played as the nexus between the international bureaucrats and the governments of carbon trading, or soon to be carbon trading, countries and the excellent working relationship and wonderful rapport that existed between the Government of Papua New Guinea and the GCMO. He then announced, mercifully Emil thought, that he would hand over to Gregory Hudson, Special Advisor on Climate and Carbon to the PNG Government, to say a few well chosen words, before Betty Greenhaugh, GCMO Director General, would propose a toast and the Honourable Minister would respond.

Emil noticed Dominik looking, searching around the room, straining to see something or someone he couldn't find. Gerry wasn't the only one after another drink, Emil thought. Hudson moved to the microphone and opened his mouth to speak, but that was all he did. Suddenly the room was plunged into darkness. There was silence, momentarily. Then the murmur of hushed conversations began to grow back to normal volume. Just as suddenly, there was light everywhere – not the lights that had been on seconds before, but bright eye-piercing spotlights, hand-held and sweeping over the crowd.

"Get on the floor! GET ON THE FUCKING FLOOR! ALL OF YOU! NOW!" a voice shouted into a megaphone. "Get on the fucking floor or we'll blow your fucking heads off!"

Cries, shocked, panicked screams. Women and men, moments before all convivial, polite attention for the speaker, cowered before a very different one. Shouting was coming from all sides. People were being shoved down onto the floor. Screaming. The smell of fear replaced perfume. Spotlight torches swinging back and forth over them. A knee jabbed viciously hard into Emil's thigh, corking it and he collapsed onto the floor. Dominik and Gerry seemed to follow quickly of their own volition, then, from where he lay, he could see Gerry's hand up to the back of his head, rich red trickles working their way out between his fingers.

"Anyone still standing in five seconds will be shot," the megaphone shouted. There were scuffing sounds and the last couple of recalcitrants complied. Emil could hear sobbing, and panicked, asthmatic, gasping breaths near him. Spotlights continued to swing over them.

"Handys. Mobile phones. Get them out. NOW! Hold them up in your hands. STAY ON THE FLOOR!"

Some sort of confrontation was happening on the other side of the room, but trying to see what was happening a boot in the middle of his back forced him flat on the floor again.

"Mobile! Give it to me!"

He got his mobile phone out, holding it up, for it to be snatched from his hand. He noticed the orders were being given in English and German. Very quickly. The voices sounded European, but he couldn't be sure they were all German. Some of the German was being spoken by non-Germans, he was sure. He tried to see where Dominik was, but outside the continuously sweeping arcs of the spotlights, he couldn't make him out.

Suddenly the lights were back on.

"Stay down. STAY DOWN!"

Mobile phones were still being snatched from hands all over the room. Somebody got half up and was knocked back onto the floor. A woman was crying uncontrollably. At least now he could see them. They were head to toe in black, wearing balaclavas, only slits for the their mouths and eyes. They had shoulder bags into which the mobile phones were going. The megaphone was on the podium from which Gregory Hudson had been about to speak, from where he had a good view over the room, calling the shots. Somewhere else in the room, a man was protesting he had no mobile phone. Emil could hear him being dragged to his feet, a quick search revealing one in the inside pocket of his suit coat before he was shoved unceremoniously back down to the floor. Gregory Hudson stood up to protest. The barrel of a gun was poked straight into his mouth and used to force him onto the floor on his back. Emil could just hear megaphone say to Hudson quietly:

"Nothing would give me more satisfaction. Don't tempt me."

Megaphone removed the gun from Hudson's face and stood up. All the phones seemed to have been collected.

"You parasites deserve to lose more than your mobile phones. Their confiscation will give you a small taste of the inconvenience most people in places like PNG live with all their lives. But we aren't thieves, like you lot are. We don't steal people's livelihoods, like you do. This entire event is about theft. It's a travesty. What an insult to the humble villagers of PNG, living in their thatched huts, eking out a subsistence living from their traditional land, until they are thrown off so their timber – their carbon rights – can be appropriated and traded to make the rich thieves in Europe or America even richer.

"The leaders of PNG are fools, in the pockets of thieves, selling out their country to you market people, aided and abetted by the Global Carbon Markets Organisation, which exists only to legitimize these thefts and help launder the proceeds."

He paused, pointing to where Rodger Beckwith lay, keeping as low a profile as possible. Two of the other black clad figures moved in.

"This is the only speech you'll get tonight. You're getting off lightly, for such parasites. But the parasite providing funding for the operation to steal from the people of PNG, he's coming with us."

Beckwith was hauled to his feet by the two standing over him, and imploring them, squealing like a stuck pig, dragged across to the door. Suddenly the lights were out and just the spot lights swept across them lying on the floor.

"The first one of you I see trying to get up gets their head blown off!" said megaphone, now from somewhere over the other side of the room, near the door.

Then, no spotlights. They were in darkness. There was silence, except for sobbing and constrained breathing. Nobody moved for minutes. His eyes adjusting to the dark, Emil looked from side to side to see who was around him. Someone near the edge of the room stood up.

"I think they've gone."

For his sake, I hope he's right, Emil thought, when the lights were turned back on by the same brave soul. Emil saw Gerry getting up off the floor, still holding the back of his head. Emil pulled his hand away and confirmed that it was just a small contusion, the blood already having congealed around the wound. With that, Gerry headed over to where the rest of his colleagues were standing, to make sure the Minister was alright.

Dominik appeared at Emil's side:

"We should go after them. God knows what they are going to do to Beckwith."

Emil nodded and they waded through the guests gradually getting to their feet, over to the door. The forty-fourth floor could only be reached by stairs from the forty-third floor which was the direction they headed. There had been security screening, both at the ground level and when they arrived at forty-three. They tumbled out of the stairwell, Dominik leading and Emil hobbling after, as fast as his corked thigh would let him. The security man was startled by their sudden appearance in the lobby on forty-three.

"Did anyone come through here?" Emil asked urgently.

"You're the first people I've seen since the last guests arrived, about two hours ago. What's the problem?"

"There's been an attack. Radio your colleagues downstairs. Call the police, immediately… And emergency services, people may need medical attention."

The man did so.

"Is there another way out of this building ?"

"Only up to the roof and jump."

Emil looked at Dominik. "They must be up there. How do we get there?"

"The only way is back up these stairs to the forty-fifth floor, which is closed off, but there's a further stair and a door onto the roof," said the guard.

"You'd better come back with us, and help the other guests," said Dominik.

"No way," said Emil pointing at the holstered gun on the man's hip. "They're armed, he's coming with us."

They made their way back up, Emil limping a distant third, looking in on the function room. People seemed to have calmed down considerably and the bar was in operation again, on a self-help basis.

Emil saw Betty G, calling to her: "The police and emergency

services are on their way. We think they've taken Beckwith up to the roof. We're going up to see."

"Don't be crazy. Wait for the police."

"We don't know how long they'll be. And we don't know what they're doing to Beckwith up there."

He pulled back out of the doorway and closed it behind him before she could respond.

They climbed up the next flight more cautiously, the security man in front, gun in hand. At the forty-fifth, they found the separate stair to the roof and, even more cautiously, began edging their way up. At the landing, the security man held his hand out behind him for them to stop. Emil could feel cool night air on his face; he couldn't see it, but the door must be open. The security man gestured for them to move forward and as he turned onto the final flight, Emil saw that the door was wedged open slightly by a thick rope jammed under it. Then he saw the note. They all did. Pinned to the rope it read:

LIFE HANGS IN THE BALANCE. OPEN THIS DOOR WITH CARE. DG.

"We have to wait for the police."

It was Dominik who spoke.

"At least hold the rope, or tie it to something, without disturbing that door," said Emil.

It was another ten minutes before the police arrived. The first police there wanted to wait for the helicopter to arrive, to check the roof. But that would be at least another ten minutes: a decision was taken to go onto the roof. Better you, than me, making that decision, Emil thought, looking at the young commander. So, rope secured inside, the door was pulled open quickly and two police lunged out and grabbed it on the outside as other heavily armed officers poured out through the doorway, spotlight torches (very similar to the ones used by the attackers, Emil thought) attached to their gun sights sweeping the roof surface. There was no sign of anyone. The roof itself had a chest high wall around it and various structures, such as the housing for the air-conditioning motors and the top of the lift well. The rope led not to the wall, but over one of these structures, on the other side of which a hessian sack was hanging, about half a metre above the roof surface. As they approached it, those closest recoiled, covering their noses. Someone shone a torch on it – the bottom of the bag was dripping. When Emil got close enough, he too recoiled at the stench, like someone had slapped his face. A pathetic voice came from inside.

"Help me, please. Somebody."

"It's Beckwith. Help me get him down."

It wouldn't be long until dawn.

They were just finishing up an ad hoc executive meeting Betty G had convened, back at Bad Eschbach. They'd only managed to leave the ECB building after the police had interviewed everyone and taken statements, which was sometime after three. Poor Beckwith was in a terrible state, when they got him out of the sack. The assailants had told him he was being left hanging over the side of the building, with the rope jammed in the door, so that as soon as someone came to find him he'd be gone. He'd pissed and shat himself, anticipating the forty-six floor drop to his death. He had to be hospitalized. Oh well, maybe Gerry would be consoling Miss what's-her-name tonight, after all. Wouldn't be surprised, Emil mused to himself.

There had been no sign of the assailants. There was nothing even to indicate where they had gone. It could only have been off the top of the building – but how? And even if the GCMO endorsement was now official, they'd succeeded in ruining the ceremony, making their statement and making good their escape. The most substantive clue, the police later found, was due to tracking devices on some of the phones. These led to a three hundred metre stretch of the Main, but few of the phones were ever recovered from it.

"Who the hell are these people?" said Betty G., looking around the room at her tired Executive.

Emil was rubbing his corked thigh, which had become quite stiff and sore.

"The police seem to think they were the waiters, since there was no sign of any waiters when the police arrived. I think that's the lead they're following up," replied Dominik. "As to how they escaped: it all seems to point to base-jumping, but who knows."

"But who the hell *are* they? Emil what did you say was on the sign on the stair?"

"It looked like it was signed 'DG'. Although that could mean just about anything – *Dei gratia* ... Dolce & Gabbana ... even Director-General," he replied looking at her, but she clearly wasn't in the mood for levity and ignored him.

He went back to rubbing his leg. None of the others had anything to offer.

"OK. I can see we're not going to get much further now. Otis, you'll need to give me a full – and I mean full – briefing on all the arrangements you had in place: security, invitations, catering, where these goddam waiters came from, who was involved in the preparations, everything. I want to know every potential source of how this information leaked out. Clearly, there is someone in this organization who is hell-bent on undermining us, trying to destroy our work, even if we haven't been able to find them to date." She looked at Emil. "But we will. Otis, I'll need the briefing, in writing, by the end of business today, at the latest. That's all, we'd all better go home and get some rest, so we're ready when the shit hits the fan in a couple of hours' time."

The meeting ended and they dispersed. Emil nodded for Dominik to follow him, as he limped back down to his office. When they got there, he went around and sat at his desk and gestured for Dominik to close the door. Dominik sat opposite.

"You know who they are, don't you?"

Dominik sat staring directly back at Emil. If he was surprised by the point-blank accusation, he didn't show it. He remained silent, returning Emil's stare.

"I saw you speaking with that waiter when you arrived, and I'm willing to bet he was the guy with the megaphone."

Dominik stayed silent, staring at Emil.

"Are you one of them? Are you the one who's been helping these people hack into our systems? That'd be ironic, if you were searching for yourself. Pity you didn't 'find yourself' – or maybe you need to take a trip to Nepal, or Bhutan, to do that."

For long seconds Dominik just continued staring back at Emil.

"Those break-ins to my apartment. The intruder in Stuttgart.

The attack in Zürich. I wondered why you were so equivocal, unconvinced, when it was clear who was behind it. Now I know why."

"That's offensive, Emil. To even think that I would be involved in any of those things, is really offensive. And for the record, no, I'm not the 'mole' or 'spy' or whatever you want to call it."

Emil said nothing, returning Dominik's stare, waiting.

"I tried to warn you. I told you we should have postponed it, given it more consideration."

"So you knew this was going to happen, but did nothing to stop it?"

"I knew *something* would happen, but I didn't know what, or when. At least, I didn't know until tonight. That's why I was late. When I found out what was happening I tried to stop them, but it was too late. I even tried to warn you when I arrived, but you told me to be quiet just as the speeches started."

"Christ, it was a bit bloody late by then, wasn't it?"

"I didn't know any earlier!"

Emil exhaled noisily, exasperated. He stood up behind his desk and looked out at the night. How did that old Crosby, Stills, Nash song go, '... the darkest hour is just before the dawn'. It was pretty black outside.

"This is a great fucking mess, isn't it. How do you know these people, anyway? Who are they? You still haven't told me yet whether you're one of them," he said, turning back to Dominik.

Dominik looked down, face contorted as if he was wrestling in his mind with some great moral conundrum.

"They aren't some sort of eco-terrorist group, as our esteemed colleagues, Tuechner and McDowell, would undoubtedly say. They're a loose grouping of people, who share common concerns and a common commitment. It's not a 'movement' and it's not connected with any of these militant anti-market groups. And it's definitely not an NGO. Just a grouping of people who know they can trust each other. That's the principal connection.

"I share their concerns and common commitment and, for what it's worth, yes, I agree with their reasons for wanting to stop the PNG endorsement: it will put money in the hands of the wrong people, it will entrench and give international recognition to a government that's probably far too closely associated with foreign business interests. But I disagree with the decision to attack the function. One of the principles of ..." he hesitated, as if he didn't want to name it, "DG ... is that to remain effective, we need to stay under the radar. Unlike some other green groups or movements – especially these radical anti-market activists, who do things to draw attention to themselves. We only measure success in change."

Emil continued staring back at him, motionless.

"This stunt tonight was completely wrong, I agree. But I guess it was borne out of frustration that some people feel about unbridled, unquestioning commitment to the market. When I learnt about it, I thought it was crazy. And dangerous. I tried to stop them but, as I said, it was too late. And as for that stupid note on the stairs – that was insanity, completely anathema to what we stand for ..."

"So who or what is the 'DG'?"

"It's not a name or anything like that. It's just an embodiment of the shared concern and commitment. It stands for Diego Garcia."

"The US Air Force base in the middle of the Indian Ocean?"

"The main island of the Chagos Islands, home of the Chagos Islanders who were expelled when it was expedient for the US and Britain to have a base there. Expelled by the Western government that purported to be their protector, which then conspired to have these people permanently prevented from returning after the air base had finished, by having the islands declared a national marine park. This was despite the fact that the air base construction had more or less rendered the area of little value for such a purpose. So much for any right of self-determination. What cynicism! But for modern governments, expedient, business as usual, I guess. We use this simply as a symbol, a rallying point, if you like, for what's wrong with the status quo, nothing more."

It all sounded a little bit too anarchic for Emil's liking. But he kept that thought to himself.

"So you are one of them?"

"I told you, I share their concerns and commitment, didn't I?"

"If you believe this, why did you choose to work here?"

"Change from within. Collaborate to compete. You can describe it in any of a number of ways. I believe, and the others I know in DG believe, that you need to be part of the system to be effective in reshaping it to a better model. I don't want to destroy it, just make it work better."

"Fuck, Dominik! That's just great. Terrific. Here I am busting a gut – or having it busted for me –and all the time my 2IC is keeping this dirty little secret to himself. But you still expect me to believe you're not facilitating these cyber attacks, or incidents like in Zürich ... that you weren't in on tonight's little exercise?"

"Look, I told you Emil, it's a loose grouping. There are common concerns and shared commitment, but everyone isn't necessarily in on everything. As for the 'mole', obviously there is someone, as tonight proves. But it's not me, and I don't know who it is, alright! They might not even be part of DG, just remotely linked. They could be affiliated with some other group that's totally opposed to what GCMO is doing. Mind you, after what you said was done to those boys and what happened to Davies, I'm beginning to think direct action like they're taking might be warranted. But nobody I know attacked you, OK?"

He stabbed a cautionary forefinger in Emil's direction.

"I'll tell you this, Emil, it's not DG you should be concerned about. You ought to be more worried about the people who fund and feed information to someone like Bradlee Nelson. These sort of people don't pull stunts, like tonight, with replica guns purchased at a *Waffenladen*. They are the sort of people who break into apartments, who abduct and even kill people who get in their way. *They're* the ones you ought to be worried about."

"What do you mean? Who are they?"

"I mean the sort of people whose financial interests are to see developing countries stay well and truly in the mining, resource-exploitation fold. They don't want them being swayed into becoming too conservation-minded – buying into the 'sustainability' model. And I'll tell you this, too, they definitely have a plant in this organization who keeps them informed. That's the 'mole' we should be trying to find!"

As Dominik finished speaking, there was a noise from the open office area outside. Emil recognized the sound that Sabrina's chair wheels made hitting the leg of her desk, something he heard, to his irritation, about fifty times every day.

"Who's there?" he called out, moving around his desk as fast as his corked thigh would let him.

Dominik was up out of his chair in a flash and whipped the door open. The outside office was in complete darkness, if someone was there, one of them would need to get to the floor light switch, at the other end of the general office area, to see who it was. Dominik took off into the darkness, down the central corridor between the desks and offices. He was just out of Emil's sight when there was a thud.

The general office was dark and suddenly silent. Momentarily, déjà vu of the basement in Stuttgart came and went.

"Dom?" No response. "Dominik!"

There were footsteps, hurried footsteps, running into the fire stair. The fire door slammed behind them and they were gone. Emil hobbled up into the darkness until he found Dominik.

"Stay there."

He continued up the rest of the way and turned on the lights. Blood was coming out of a wound in almost the exact same place as Dominik had been hit in Zürich. Emil helped him up and back to a chair in his office, retrieved the First Aid box from the kitchen and bandaged the wound.

Emil offered to see him home, but Dominik said he would be fine. He sat for minutes, head in his hands until, eventually, he felt recovered enough to get up.

"You realize that they'll be on to me now."

"What do you mean?"

"I mean that, whoever was outside the door, they would have heard everything I said. DG is exposed. I am exposed. Whoever it is, now knows that I know about them, but not who they are. They'll be reporting in to their real paymaster, probably as we speak. I expect they'll try to take some action against me," he paused. "And you too, probably. Maybe you should be considering why you chose to work here."

"What do you mean – what sort of action?"

"Your guess is as good as mine. But I'm not going to wait here, until they arrange for me to have an accident. I have a lot of accumulated leave that I carried over from the BMU. I'm entitled to take it and that's what I'm going to do – starting immediately. All I ask is that you trust me – about what I've said. Whatever you do, don't expose my links any more than they have been already – otherwise we'll never find out who was there listening."

"Trust! Hah, that's a bit rich after what you've told me! And it'll be bloody inconvenient without you here – especially after tonight."

"I'm sorry if it inconveniences you, Emil, but if I'm dead, you'll be inconvenienced just as much. And it will be a lot more inconvenient for me."

With that he left.

Emil felt an overwhelming tiredness wash over him. It was suddenly like he was in a raging river, being sucked into a vortex and all he wanted to do was relax and let go, let fate take its course. But he knew he couldn't. He couldn't afford that luxury. He knew he would have to act. The only question was, how?

He stood at his office window and watched as pale light began to infuse the eastern sky. It was going to be another beautifully serene, bright blue, autumn day in Frankfurt.

26

Six-forty two, according to the clock on the bedside table.

Emil rolled over and felt the warmth, the immediacy of Johanna's body next to him, her chest rising and falling in a slow, easy rhythm. He lay facing her for several minutes, their bodies almost covered by the duvet, enjoying the intimacy of the moment, savouring the translucency of her skin. The sensuality of her naked body so close, the softness of her to touch, stirred him. Propping himself up, he lent over her and slowly, delicately began working his lips down her chest, over each nipple then carefully around the cup of each breast. Slipping under the duvet, he ran his lips lightly over the gentle curve of her stomach, across the top of her thigh, then down her leg.

As he moved lower, her legs moved slightly. Then he felt two hands on the back of his head, the fingers of each closing tightly around a clump of his hair.

"Not so fast, mister. I think you missed a spot," she said quietly, pulling his head back up by the hair, crossing her legs over the back of his neck.

They'd met at the Sofitel Le Grand Ducal, the preceding evening. With Dominik away, any chance of Emil getting to Brussels had become remote, and with Johanna busy settling into a new job, there wasn't much chance of her getting to Frankfurt. Not that he really wanted to entertain her at Frau Hoerler's. It had been weeks since they'd been together. Before he had met her, sex, or lack of it, had not really been an issue. Now, however, he found himself thinking about her like he was a concupiscent schoolboy. The new objective, therefore, was to organize weekend trysts at midway points, that they could get to easily on a Friday night. This weekend it was Luxembourg.

In the week immediately following the PNG ceremony, an item on one of the online news services had caught Emil's eye. Headed 'Coroner returns open findings', it was a commentary on the two inquests, noting the link, through the involvement of Davies in the police inquiry concerning the two boys' deaths, but that he had been exonerated by the coroner's findings. A week later, a carbon market news service picked up on the story and tied it back to the pandemonium caused at the *C-world* event in Köln, the previous April, by Lynx cable channel's Bradlee Nelson questioning of Emil Pfeffer, Davies' boss at the GCMO. In the weeks following, blogs were posing questions about how much Nelson knew and when he knew it. It was too good to be true, Emil thought. It was just a shame Dominik wasn't around to share the pleasure with him.

Betty G, however, wasn't smiling when she strode into his office and tossed the wad of papers she'd just collected off the printer onto Emil's desk.

"What d'you know about this?" She stood glaring down at him.

Emil had been expecting a reaction from her eventually. He was prepared. Picking up the papers, he leafed through them.

"I've read some of them, I know as much as you do. You know how these things take on a life of their own, once they get started. It had to come out eventually, when people remembered what happened and began thinking about it."

"With the help of a little *aide-memoire* provided by you, no doubt!"

"I'm not one of these bloggers and I don't know any of them. It looks like it's all coming out of Port Moresby."

Later he wondered about the wisdom of making this last statement – it might look to her like he'd analysed the situation a little bit too carefully.

Betty G took the papers back from him and left. He wasn't sure whether she bought his response or not, but he didn't really care. He was enjoying his dish of revenge, served cold.

But he did care about the cyber attacks on the GCMO, which the disruption to the ceremony had done nothing to lessen. The website was still regularly targeted by distributed denial of service attacks. The fact of PNG's induction to the 'carbon trading nations' club', had been a lightning rod for the upswing. Before he left, Dominik had warned Emil that the only way to get the activists to back off was, at the very least, to announce that there would be a review of the endorsement, to delay the domestic trading arrangements from proceeding.

"But can't you speak to these people, try to convince them?" Emil had asked him.

"Even if I could find them, which is unlikely, why would they listen to me? For them, I'm just as much a part of the problem as you are, working for this organization. Besides, there's nothing I could offer them by way of compromise."

And despite Stefan's earlier confidence that the virus problem had been sorted out, it had started reappearing each time 'Papua New Guinea' or 'PNG' appeared in documents on the system, causing letters to drop off the screen when the documents were opened. To Betty G's annoyance, Emil was no closer to finding the suspected internal mole who was supposedly facilitating it.

"The malware keeps updating itself," said Stefan when Emil dropped by the server room which also served as Stefan's office.

On warm days during the summer, Emil used any excuse to call by for a chat with Stefan, as the servers were the only beneficiaries of air-conditioning in the building.

"We keep isolating it, then a little while later it appears again, it's replicating itself."

"If that's the case, then there could have been just a single security breach, any time before I finished my report."

Stefan shrugged. "Ja, it's possible."

"In which case, it's a complete waste of time trying to catch anyone now. They don't need to do anything more. It's already there on our system."

In spite of what was happening, Emil was reluctant to propose that the GCMO take the steps Dominik advocated. Emil tried to justify this to himself on the basis that he hadn't been entirely convinced by Dominik's story, wasn't sure he believed the warnings Dominik had given. Sure, people with vested interests would always try to protect the status quo – with lobbyists and media campaigns and political influence. However, Dominik was talking about something altogether different. Or was it really *that* different? But where was his evidence, anyway? Dominik had been altogether too vague about these threats, for Emil's liking.

Deep down, however, in the innermost recesses of his conscience, he wondered whether his reluctance to question or recant the PNG endorsement was, in reality, because he would be a lone voice if he did. His executive colleagues, especially Betty G, who just wanted him to track down the mole, considered the cyber attacks a serious nuisance and, like the attack on the PNG ceremony, a police matter. He was stuck between a rock and a hard place – after all, it was his MIU report which had cleared the way for the endorsement. He'd look like an idiot if he now proposed that they review their position just because of the criminal acts of people opposed to it on ideological grounds.

On the other hand, existential threats to the GCMO seemed to be multiplying. Dominik had also warned that more extreme activists were working on ways to breach the multi-layered security of exchange trading systems.

"They aren't there to steal, just to disrupt. The attack on the Polish exchange was reconnaissance. The security was so lax at the clearinghouses it was easy for them to get a Trojan in. Luckily, the exchange used its own language, so the breach was limited. But I think they would have learnt a lot."

As if to substantiate Dominik's warning, he was receiving more regular reports of cyber attacks on traders, registries, clearinghouses and trading platforms: stealing electronic certificates, blocking sites from operating, inflicting malicious damage on their systems. They were all small and isolated events, but frequent enough, over time, to become a threat to market confidence. The German federal and other national police forces, as well as Europol's eco-terrorist unit and Interpol were coordinating criminal investigations, overtaking his attempts to manage responses in conjunction with the relevant national regulatory bodies. It seemed to Emil the situation was spiralling out of his grasp, threatening his unit's relevance and, consequently, ultimately, the reasons for its very existence. But it was difficult for him to do more. He couldn't discuss Dominik's information, because Dominik's sudden departure on extended leave, coming as it did immediately in the wake of the PNG ceremony debacle, was already provoking tricky questions. How Dominik came to be so knowledgeable on the intentions of the activists, and why he hadn't revealed it sooner, was something he definitely did not want to be obliged to explain to his executive colleagues.

And anyway, he didn't know which of them he could trust. The episode in the darkened office with the eavesdropper had left him feeling guarded with all of them. He found himself on edge every time Dominik's name was mentioned. His sleep was suffering: each time the basement neighbour's wastewater pump woke him now he would lie awake for hours, working over in his mind the different courses of action of open to him and their potential consequences. Even the swimming, which normally helped clear his mind, couldn't ease his concerns that the situation was slipping irretrievably out of his control.

Then the rumour mill swung into operation, prompting another visit from Betty G.

"It can't have escaped your notice, Emil, that there's a lot of gossip flying about this organisation concerning your deputy," she said closing the door of his office behind her and standing with her back against it, as if she was trying to prevent anyone else entering or, for that matter, him leaving.

"Not that I listen to, or place any credence in gossip, but have you heard what's being said about Dominik?"

Emil felt himself tense, hoping she hadn't noticed, could feel the wetness of his palms.

"There are suggestions floating around that Dominik's sudden departure on leave is because he's the mole, that he's one of the eco-terrorists who attacked the ceremony."

"Yes, I've heard what's being said. Nobody's had the guts to say anything to me directly. It's a load of rubbish, Betty, utter rubbish. How dare they suggest that Dominik would be involved in this business, in any way, other than by trying to stop it. If I find who's spreading this crap, they're going to be sorry."

"That won't be necessary, Emil. I'll put a stop to it."

He really didn't want to mislead her, but equally he felt he couldn't 'out' Dominik, especially since having delayed so long, he would be implicated himself. What else he could do? Whatever it was, he'd have to do it soon because, as Betty G had taken to reminding him regularly, she was relying on him to sort it out.

The only respite from it all was getting away to meet Johanna, when he could, on weekends.

"Oh, I think I've had too much now," said Emil, pushing his plate away, more in order to remove the temptation to gluttony, than as an act of self-denial.

The breakfast service had almost finished by the time they made it down. It had taken longer than he planned to get there from Frankfurt, so Emil hadn't arrived until quite late. Johanna had waited for him, so both of them had missed dinner. When he did arrive, it had been straight into bed. By the time they made it down to the breakfast room, they were famished.

"You can work it off, I've planned our itinerary for today and it involves plenty of exercise."

"We've already had plenty of exercise this morning. Isn't that enough?"

Johanna's cheeks coloured, momentarily. "You've had enough of that for now! No, we're walking. And I have a surprise for you."

They left the hotel and headed over the Avenue de la Gare Viaduc into the old centre, spending time wandering around the Saturday morning market in the Place Guillaume. It was a grey, icy morning with a fog in the Vallée de la Pétrusse and a portentous white sky, but the walk and the bustle of the market warmed them. Having done the rounds of the market stalls they moved on, Johanna setting a cracking pace. Down to the Alzette, crossing and up the other side to the Kirchberg Plateau, Johanna talking all the while about her new job and the colleagues she was getting to know, the nice ones and the odd ones, the ones she'd already been warned to watch out for. She seemed so happy he was content just to let her ramble on and listen to her. Her cheeks were flushed and she was short of breath, but kept up the pace until they made it to the Museum of Modern Art. Inside, having removed their coats and scarves, they adopted more of what might be described, Emil observed, as a brisk saunter.

"Are we on schedule?"

Johanna made a show of examining her watch.

"Almost, but we can't afford to dally too long. We'll have to skip some of the galleries and come back another time."

"I was only joking. You mean we are on a schedule?"

Johanna smiled and led off to the next gallery.

They hadn't been there more than twenty minutes before Johanna announced it was time to leave. Emil looked at her.

"Now I know you're up to something," he said, wrapping his arms around her in a bear hug. "Just exactly what have you got organized?"

She wrestled herself free.

"A surprise."

Their route took them back across the Parc des Trois Glands and back down to the Alzette, but this time they followed the path along the stream. The fog had settled down here and periodically they would walk into a thicker bank where visibility was practically nil, the shroud around them seeming to swallow up any utterance immediately.

Emil stopped and held up his hand. Johanna looked at him.

"What is it?"

"Voices – I thought I heard them just behind us," he whispered.

They stood there, not moving, looking back but the only sounds they could hear were remotely from above in the old town centre, so they continued on.

"I'd be surprised in this fog – unless they were standing right next to us. I hope you're not starting to hear voices in your head," she said, frowning at him.

There were quaint old houses along the path, but no sign of anyone.

"I don't know how people could bear to live down here," he

said looking at the traditional residences. "It would be damp, all the time. It's so steep they'd get all the run-off as well."

"Yes, a few years back when there were those particularly wet summers I think a lot of these houses were inundated. They look nice, but you're right, they might not be that practical to live in."

As she finished speaking they both noticed that there were footsteps coming from behind them, not quickly, but definitely catching them up. He looked at her and she smiled back, then stopping they turned to see a figure looming up towards them out of the fog.

"Dominik!" exclaimed Emil.

"Hallo, mind if I walk for a distance in the fog with you two romantics?"

Emil turned to Johanna: "Is he the surprise?"

Momentarily, she didn't know how to respond. Realising, Emil went on "…and what a wonderful surprise it is, too!"

Dominik looked quizzically at Johanna, then at Emil.

"I hope you don't mind, Emil, but I thought the safest way to get in touch with you was to take the liberty of introducing myself to Johanna and asking her to arrange this meeting."

Emil didn't respond.

"I've had some problems – my apartment was broken into. They weren't as careful as they were at yours. They wrecked everything, tore it apart. Now people are watching it, so I'm staying with friends."

Emil was still trying to deal with the jumble of thoughts suddenly crowding into his head.

"No, it's fine, Dom. I'm sorry to hear about your apartment, but aren't you being a little melodramatic?" he said, absently. "Couldn't it have just been a robbery?"

Johanna looked ashen-faced, her eyes momentarily glistening. He put his arm around her shoulder and squeezed her to him. His underwhelmed reaction wasn't quite what she'd been expecting.

"Yes, that's fine, Dom," he repeated. "It's just that I'm a little, well … surprised."

"I'm sorry for interrupting your weekend, but it's important that we speak. I wanted to make sure that we are not being listened to, or watched. I asked Johanna to take you around town a little, so that I could see if anyone was following you."

This was becoming a little too much.

"And are we being followed? By anyone apart from you, that is."

"Well, if you are, Johanna's route has managed either to discourage them or lose them by now."

Emil looked around at the envelope of white that entombed the three of them.

"Well, we should be pretty safe here in this 'cone of silence'," he said, smiling to belie his sarcasm.

"After what happened, I don't trust the telephones at the office. And, I think, if I am being watched, you are definitely being watched, too. I don't trust your mobile either. I thought it would be better to meet instead."

"I got your text about the boys."

"I shouldn't have sent that. I should have waited until now, but it was the first useful information I had come across. My phone is blocked, but that probably wouldn't stop people with the right equipment from tracing it. Anyway, as I texted you, the boys were working for an NGO called TrueUpREDD, or at least one of them was. The other was just tagging along, to help his mate."

"Talk about drawing the short straw," muttered Emil.

"They were there to do a check on the Debepare projects, which according to TURD – that's what most people seem to call it – is where they should still have been, not in Port Moresby."

"Why is that?"

"They had some quite good gear with them. Cameras, laptops, GPS NavSat. It was to help them carry out their task, but it was also so that TURD could track them, for their own safety," Dominik paused to catch his breath. "The interesting bit is that none of this gear was recovered, or accounted for in their belongings found with the bodies, as you know from the police report."

"It was probably stolen before the bodies were found."

"But the GPS has been beaming out still – from somewhere in the project site!"

They continued walking along next to the Alzette until it met the Pétrusse where they turned right, following the narrow sliver of a water course under the Avenue de la Gare Viaduc, into the Vallée de la Pétrusse, where the fog was as thick as a cream soup.

"I wasn't happy about having my heavy overcoat when you had us racing all over the place earlier," Emil said to Johanna, "but I'm glad I've got it, now that we're hanging around down here in this fog."

"You don't think I would have let you come out here to catch your death of cold, do you?" she shot back edgily.

"No, you planned things very well."

They were almost at the end of the pathway and the occasional car could be made out through the fog, passing along the road.

"So now, Emil, what you are going to do?" said Dominik. "I think you should take leave and help me get the bottom of what happened to those two boys. This is the lead we needed to find out what Davies was doing – whether his death really was an accident. If you still want to find out what happened to Davies, that is, if his car really was run off the road?"

Emil looked from Johanna to Dominik.

"Dom, you know I'd do it if I could. Especially if it would stop these bloody cyber attacks. But with you not there, how can I? The place is in enough turmoil as it is, without me walking out. You've forgotten that the knives are out for me. There's still the threat of New York deciding to dump me altogether, and I'm not sure whether I could count on Betty G for any support."

Dominik looked resigned.

"Keep me up to speed on what you're doing."

"But the fact that the GPS is still at the site, don't you want to investigate?" persisted Dominik.

"Isn't that a job for the PNG police, as our esteemed colleague Dr Tüchner would no doubt remind us?"

"Emil, you know, as well as I do, that the signal would disappear the second we mentioned this to anyone in PNG. As for them investigating, ha, you're the one who sat through the two inquests. It's very disappointing that you don't seem as keen as you were to find out what really happened."

He knew Dominik was right.

"Let me think about it. I can't just shoot off back to PNG, but maybe in a while some sort of visit can be arranged through the office."

But Dominik wasn't paying attention. He was looking over Emil's shoulder. Johanna had noticed and was following his gaze. Emil stopped speaking and turned. A vehicle was stopped in the fog at the end of the pathway.

"They went past and came back, before stopping there," said Dominik still watching the vehicle. "I think it's time for me to head off and maybe you two had better go up these stairs, back into town. It's not healthy staying down here in this fog too long," he said, starting back in the direction they had just come.

"Keep in touch," Emil called after Dominik's receding back. Dominik gave a parting wave over his shoulder, then his figure melded into shapeless grey and he was gone.

27

"You are annoyed with me."

It was half question, half statement. They were sitting in a bar having a drink, before heading out into the cold again to find a restaurant for dinner. They had been sitting there for quite a while, without saying anything, Emil's mind somewhere else. Johanna's tone of voice brought him back.

"I have spoiled the weekend."

"No, no you haven't."

"What then? You've hardly said anything since Dominik left. You weren't pleased to see him, were you?"

"That's not right. I was pleased to see him – no, that's not right either – I was neither pleased nor displeased. It was just a surprise. Like you promised."

He tried to turn the emotional joust back on her.

"Aren't you happy that it was such a surprise for me?"

"The purpose wasn't to make me happy. I thought it would make *you* happy for Dominik to be able to contact you discreetly. Not that it seems to have worked out that way."

That car with the two goons in it, staring at them, had been unsettling. Emil sat silently looking at her.

"I'm a little unhappy that Dominik contacted you."

Johanna gave him her intent, ice-blue stare.

"He talks about these mysterious 'other people', the ones that he thinks have a 'mole' in the organisation, and who broke into his apartment. The ones that he says are dangerous and are the reason he's more or less in hiding; but then he goes ahead and uses you as his agent, without even thinking that by doing so, he might be putting you at risk – especially if these people really are as dangerous as he makes out."

"I freely agreed to do it. I don't mind, if you're at risk from them."

He reached out and took her hand in both of his.

"That's nice, something we can share – risk from persons unknown."

She smiled and leant forward, kissing him on the lips.

"And, of course," he went on, "I'm as angry as hell that Dominik contacted you without my knowledge."

"That sounds more like it," she laughed. "You're jealous."

"Madly, insanely," he hissed, grabbing her in a bear hug until she squealed and they almost fell off their seats.

He turned this conversation, and the earlier one with Dominik, over and over in his mind on the return journey to Frankfurt. And the image of the two crew-cut thugs gawping at them from the car in the fog. Immersed in these thoughts, the return journey seemed over as quickly as it had begun, although in reality, being Sunday afternoon, it was even longer than the trip there.

They made the most of the last night of their weekend together. He implored her not to agree to any more Dominik surprises on future weekends. Emil was hoping that Dominik wouldn't contact her again, but didn't want to push it too hard. He'd just need to work out another way to get in touch with Dom himself, so that there wouldn't be a need for him to involve her and expose her to any risk, whatever that might be.

Fuck it! Why did he have to react that way to Dominik's appearance? It was his behaviour, not hers, that almost ruined the entire weekend for them. He wanted to direct his anger at Dominik for presuming on his private time with Johanna, but instead all he felt was guilt. The same guilt he'd felt before he left Port Moresby. For letting Davies down. If he were honest with himself, really he was angry with Dominik for reminding him of that fact. Which also reminded him: Gerry Johnstone had promised to get back to him about Dawani's report, but that was weeks ago now. He would have to chase him up.

With the onset of the colder weather the *passage de pissoir* was meeting even greater Friday and Saturday night demands such that, even now, late on Sunday afternoon, its polecat fustiness was pungent enough to make him screw up his nose in offence. He made his way out into Heinrich-Heine-Weg quickly, trying to escape the tendrils of stench which seemed to chase him. As he approached Frau Hoerler's, he noticed a figure in the darkness at the door, but on drawing closer, he realized it was his landlady herself. The light over the door hadn't come on and she was fumbling about in her handbag for keys.

"Have you had a nice weekend?" asked Emil after they had exchanged greetings.

"Ja, I've been visiting with my brother who lives just past Aschaffenburg, in the direction of Würzburg."

Finally she located her keys and they went inside. Frau Hoerler tried the hallway light switch, but they remained in darkness. A face appeared at the outside doorway, making him start with fright. But it was just the basement flat tenant who had also been away, to Leipzig for the weekend.

"So, now we are all back here but we aren't getting very far in this darkness," announced Frau Hoerler.

"Let me see if I can find the fuse box safety switch, perhaps it has clicked off," he said, reaching up the wall and opening the small plastic door. He worked his fingertips over the recessed board of switches, found the larger safety switch and pushed it up. The outside door light and hallway light came on. Emil pushed his bag against his door with his foot.

"If this has been off all weekend, the milk in your refrigerator will be sour by now. I'll go down to the service station on the Landstrasse and get some," he volunteered, "so we can at least have a cup of tea or coffee."

"Thank you very much, Herr Pfeffer. I don't think I could stand tea without milk after a Sunday afternoon on those Deutsche Bahn trains."

As he headed out towards Heinrich-Heine-Weg again, with a flush of satisfaction he remembered the last time this had happened there had been an uninvited visitor to his apartment, through the California room. At least his detective awareness skills were improving. He quickly retraced his steps around the side of the house and confirmed the integrity of the California room door and other windows. In what light there was from the street, he examined the window sill and doorstep, but there was no indication of anyone having been there, so he turned and headed back out towards the street.

He was barely a dozen steps from the building when it hit him. The blast caught him at the top of his back, in the back of his head, throwing him metres forward, sprawling face down, showering him in a universe of tiny shards and splinters of glass. He lay there. Ears ringing. Dazed. Puzzled. For seconds that seemed drawn out into minutes, he lay where he landed, his mind trying to work out why he was where he now was: flat out on the ground.

Senses recovering, he was suddenly aware of the heat behind him, above him. He flexed his arms and legs, feeling if anything was broken. Picking himself up, he could feel the pricks of tiny glass fragments in his hair. He shook his head, sending lines of blood from the lacerations they'd left coursing around his face.

The building was awash with bluish flames, leaping out of every window of his apartment. Where the California Room had been moments before, the remains of the framework that held the glass panels were flailing about in the heat like broken tree limbs in a storm. Realising the others were inside, he took a step towards the house. The heat was so intense he could feel it singing his eyebrows and hair. He put an arm up to protect his face. It looked like a figure was at a window on the first floor. It seemed to be waving with both arms. That was the last thing he saw.

A huge, yellow fireball erupted out of the gaping ground floor, the building disintegrating, masonry flying out in all directions, the force cart-wheeling him backwards, his head catching a glancing blow on the rear panel of a parked car, before hitting hard into the tarmac of Heinrich-Heine-Weg.

28

Voices in the darkness. Hushed voices, so he couldn't make out what they were saying. Then silence again.

He opened his eyes, then blinked hard, several times. The light around him was dim but he still needed to adjust. He could make out the end of the bed and beyond that, a curtain screen.

"So you've finally come 'round," a voice said softly near his ear.

An American voice, that he hadn't heard speak so softly before. He moved his eyes to the left, and saw the beaming face of Betty G.

"How do you feel, or is that a silly question?"

"What happened?" was all he could squeeze out, before his frame was convulsed by coughing.

"Take it easy, take it easy," said Betty, positioning the plastic straw from a water bottle in the corner of his mouth. "Have some of this, but just take it slowly, or you'll have another coughing fit."

A white-coated doctor appeared through the curtain and gave him the once over, shining his pencil torch in each eye, making some notes on his patient card, then disappearing through the curtain again.

"Do you remember anything?" she asked.

Emil thought for a while but everything was a blank, everything. Then images gradually began returning to him: the train journey from the main station to Bad Eschbach, the stench of piss in the tunnel from the platform at the station, the milk, something about the milk.

"There was an explosion in the house where your apartment was," Betty began filling in. "The house and the one next to it were both destroyed. You were very lucky. Apparently you were outside when it happened. You got a bang on your head and were badly concussed. But apart from cuts from broken glass, that seems to be the only damage. The lady you rented from and the other tenant weren't so lucky."

Emil just looked at her blankly. Then his eyes closed and he lapsed back into sleep again. So she left.

The next time he woke the doctor appeared and gave him a more thorough checking over. He was being kept in for observation for another couple of days, he was informed. He ate some food, then slept again. When he woke, two green uniformed police were waiting at the end of his bed to speak to him. They asked what he could remember, but it was all so vague, he felt as if someone had pressed the delete button on his memory. Slowly, with the policeman's gentle cajoling, it started to come back to him:

"I was going to the service station, on the Landstrasse. I was going to buy milk, I think. Yes, I was going there to get milk for all three of us, because the milk would be sour."

"Why would the milk be sour, Herr Pfeffer?"

He thought for a few moments.

"Because the electricity had been off."

Little by little, he was piecing it back together.

"You see, we had all been away. We arrived back to find no power – the electrical safety switch had been triggered. So I said, as the milk would probably have gone off, I would go and get some for each of us, then we could have tea or coffee."

The police found this very interesting and made lengthy notes. At least, they were writing for what seemed to Emil a very long time. They asked a few more questions about where Emil had been, and with whom, then thanked him and left. The effort to think and recollect things for the police proved to be too much for him. He dropped off back to sleep as soon as they were gone.

When he woke, a nurse informed him that it was Thursday, and that he was going to be discharged later that day. Some colleagues would come to collect him. The nurse left and Johanna, who had been sitting quietly at the end of the bed stood, came to his side and held his hand. There were rings beneath her eyes and her usually lustrous complexion was pallid. She smiled, leant over and kissed him.

"I have been so worried about you," she whispered in his ear.

"How long have you been here?"

"Since yesterday evening. When you didn't ring, I tried your phone, but you didn't answer. Then I was called by the police. They told me what had happened, so I came immediately."

"Betty G was here before. She said there was an explosion at Frau Hoerler's – the building and the building next door destroyed. All my things were there – clothes, personal stuff, everything."

"At least you're alive, that's all that matters. Frau Hoerler and the woman in the basement were inside. They're dead. The site is a crime scene, Emil, so it's unlikely you would be able to recover anything. But I doubt any of your things would have survived, anyway."

She said she would go and buy him some clothes, so having confirmed his sizes, she left. By the time she returned, Betty G and two of Emil's staff were sitting around his bed chatting. They were waiting for her return, so he could be discharged. As he now had nowhere to live, they'd booked him into a hotel near the office. But when he swung his legs out of the bed and stood up to dress, the lingering effects of the concussion returned, and he promptly fell back onto the bed. Overcome by dizziness, all he wanted to do was throw up. Fortunately for Johanna, he didn't. When he felt balanced enough to continue, supported by her, he slowly dressed himself. Then, after brief resistance, acquiesced to being wheel-chaired out to the car.

After Betty G and the others had left them, Emil surveyed the hotel room:

"It's not much after Le Grand Ducal, but at least it's not *Zum Löwen*."

"I must get back to Brussels. I didn't give much explanation when I left. My new boss is quite understanding, but I don't want to abuse it. Anyway, I have much work to do," she paused, then said: "Why don't you come and stay with me next week? It'll be a squeeze in my tiny apartment, but it would be good for you to get away from this."

"I'd love to. It would be wonderful being in a squeeze with you. But first, let me see what it's like in the office tomorrow."

"Why do you worry so much about the damn office? What if you had been in your apartment – the office wouldn't matter then, would it? What if you had been meant to be in that apartment when it blew up?"

"What do you mean, 'meant to be in the apartment'?"

"The police are treating it as a crime scene, Emil. They must have suspicions – what if it was deliberate?"

The fact that the site was being treated as a crime scene hadn't had sufficient time to transmute into such a possibility through his dulled brain. He could see now she was worried, another thing he hadn't picked up on earlier. But she had to leave, if she was going to get back to Brussels that evening, so they didn't take it any further.

The following day he eventually made his way into the office, greeted with a hug from Sabrina, but less enthusiastically by his fellow directors.

"What are you doing here?" was all Otis McDowell could utter, looking up from the papers he was reading and seeing Emil.

"I work here, remember?" responded Emil, thinking: but if bastards like you had your way, I wouldn't.

When Betty G heard he was in, she called into his office, closing the door behind her.

"I had the policeman who is heading up the investigation here yesterday evening. You know it's a double murder inquiry, Emil? It could have been worse if the family in the next house hadn't got out before their home burnt down as well."

"Murder?"

"Yes, murder. They think you might have been the target! At least, that's one theory. They think the initial explosion was due to a gas leak in your apartment which could have been deliberate. When you turned the safety switch back on, the pilot light in the hot water system would have tried to re-ignite. It would only have been a matter of time, once it did come on, before the gas exploded. If this theory – and they're emphasising at this stage it's just a theory – is correct, then you would have literally walked straight into the explosion."

"But what if it hadn't been me who arrived home first and flicked the switch back on. In fact, now that I think about it, I wasn't first. Frau Hoerler was trying to find her keys in the dark when I arrived."

"Well, look, it's their theory. I expect they have other theories, as well. Based on this, they want even more to find these people who disrupted the PNG ceremony and are attacking our systems. It's possible this is an escalation of their tactics. And they want to talk to Dominik."

Emil began to protest but Betty G quickly cut him off:

"I know, I know. I know what you said before, but it's the police that want to talk to him about it, not me, or the GCMO. They'll have their reasons."

Emil realised he was sitting forward in his chair, tensed up. He slumped back.

"So you could help if you know where he is, or if you see him. The policeman yesterday said Dominik doesn't seem to have been back at his apartment since the day after he went on leave. His landlady said Dominik told her he would be away travelling for some weeks, but he didn't look like he was taking any clothes with him. The police were wondering whether he might be staying somewhere local."

"If he was in my apartment, he's not there now," said Emil humourlessly. "But for the record, he wasn't."

"Well, if he gets in touch, or if you see him, can you get him to contact the police. The sooner he's eliminated from their considerations, the better it will be for this organization. By the way, I forgot to ask – how are you feeling today? You're looking a lot sharper."

"Thanks Betty, I felt a lot better when I got up, not dizzy or unbalanced like I was yesterday. But I'm not sure how long it will last if I keep on getting news like that."

"That's all you'll get from me," she said getting up to leave.

Right that does it, thought Emil, Brussels here I come.

The Frankfurt Christmas market had begun.

On Saturday, Emil met Johanna off her train at the main station and they stayed in Frankfurt, wandering up and down the Zeil, sauntering between the stalls. By mid-afternoon the mulled wine was just barely compensating for the falling temperature. They were standing at one of the stalls in the square next to the Paulskirche, which was packed tightly with people, most tightly around the mulled wine stalls, of which there were many.

"It's going to snow," Johanna almost had to shout in Emil's ear over the merrymaking din of the drinkers. "Can you feel how cold it is getting?"

Emil nodded.

"That means more glühwein and wurst, then back to the hotel and into bed."

She was about to tease him for being preoccupied with sex, when she stopped herself.

"Oh, I am forgetting, I have something for you. Thank God I remembered!" she said, handing him her glass to hold and fishing about in her shoulder bag, jostling the nearest drinkers enough to make them shuffle and look around.

She produced an opened envelope, addressed to her postmarked Dubai. Inside was another sealed envelope which just had Emil's name on it. He handed her both glasses and tore it open. It contained a handwritten note from Dominik:

Emil I hope you receive this safely, it's slow but probably the safest way to contact you. As I tried to tell you in Luxembourg, there is something wrong with the PNG set up. I have located a source of information that will help prise open those arrangements. Investigators often say follow the money, and I am doing that. The source is in India, where I am travelling now. You must join me and help evaluate this information, for Davies' sake and for the sake of the GCMO's on-going credibility. Fly to Hyderabad. Book with Air India and I will know when you are coming. But do not try to contact me. I'm relying on you, Dom.

Emil finished reading and looked up at Johanna. Her expression was of concern: he wondered whether it was a mirror of his own. He passed the note to her and took the two empty glasses. She read it quickly then looked at him. They had spent most of the time since she arrived talking about what they were going to do in Brussels that week. She folded the letter and handed it back to him. Fat snowflakes had begun wafting down around them.

"Get me another glühwein please, I think I'll get drunk."

The snow fell thickly, wet and heavy for the rest of the afternoon and evening and overnight the temperature fell with it. They returned to Bad Eschbach and didn't venture out again that evening, retiring early to his room. Emil wanted to talk over everything that had happened, but Johanna quickly drifted off into a heavy, mulled wine-induced sleep. He stayed awake, dwelling on what Dominik had said when they had been overheard in his office, until he, too, fell into a fitful sleep. When they woke, they found the snow still falling and piled up everywhere, in places lying over twenty centimetres deep. Johanna just felt seedy.

"I've decided to go to India, to see what Dominik has found," Emil announced.

Johanna was lying face down on the bed, Emil sitting beside her massaging her shoulders and neck.

"Oh, that's so good. Just a little harder there, yes, right there."

Her eyes were closed and she looked as if she was dozing off again.

"I thought you would. As soon as I saw you read it, I knew."

"I'm not that transparent, am I?"

"Yes, it's what I like about you, Emil."

"Is that all?"

"That, and your massages…," she smiled. "Now, what about a little lower down my back. Yes, that's it."

He kept massaging. It partially assuaged his guilt.

That afternoon, after he'd seen Johanna off from the main

station, he went to the office and rang Betty G. She reluctantly agreed some leave was a good idea to help his recovery, but that he should keep in touch in case any matters flared up, as they were wont to do. Returning to the hotel, he went to the business centre and looked up Air India flights from Frankfurt to Hyderabad, booked on the flight leaving the next morning and paying for his ticket online, before advising the front desk that he would be checking out. Heading back to his room, he realized he didn't have anything to pack, apart from what Johanna had bought him, and he only had the plastic shopping bags it arrived in to pack anyway, so he decided to fill in what was left of the afternoon clearing what he could in his office.

It was getting dark and the snow was still falling lightly. As he passed the protester encampment, he noticed that their tent structure had been substantially consolidated to accommodate the colder weather. Clearly they intended to tough out the winter there. Hardy bunch. Walking up to the main entrance, passing the spot where he had last encountered that arsehole, Brad Nelson, he looked up at his office window: it seemed that the lights were on. His office was along towards the end of the building, so that reflections of the street lighting off the window panes made it difficult to be sure, but it certainly looked like the lights were on. On reaching the second floor, however, he found the place in darkness. Pencils of orange pointed in from the street lighting, but that was all. His office seemed to be as he had left it, not that he could really remember. He spent half an hour sifting through the paper and electronic clutter that had built up in his absence, before reaching the conclusion he could go away and leave it all and not be missed. Either it could wait, or could be handled by one of his team. He was packing up a few papers to take with him when there was the familiar, annoying sound of Sabrina's desk chair wheel hitting the leg of her desk, startling him. A face appeared at the door.

"Don't tell me you've recovered enough to be working weekends already?"

"Oh, Orlando, it's you. No, just tidying up. I'm taking some leave. What are you doing here on Sunday evening."

"The usual, preparing for the week ahead. Executive tomorrow, although you'll miss that if you're going on leave. Betty will be travelling later in the week, too, so there's a lot to organize before then."

"I just sent you a note to tell you that I'll check out of the hotel tomorrow."

"Where are you going?"

Orlando's inquisitorial tone immediately put him on his guard.

"Oh, just here and there, you know, taking it easy," he responded slowly, watching Orlando closely.

"But obviously not in Bad Eschbach?"

"Who in their right mind would take a holiday in Bad Eschbach, if they worked here?"

"Yes, you've got a point there," said Orlando, disappearing again, calling from the darkened outer office: "Enjoy your break."

Even very early on Monday morning, the check-in hall at Frankfurt airport was throbbing with people – business travellers, holidaymakers, workers – queuing, scurrying, sauntering, waiting, refreshing themselves, getting worked up. Emil regarded them all with suspicion, as he completed his check in and kept the small, newly acquired canvas backpack, containing all his worldly possessions, as hand luggage.

His suspicions were well placed, but his observations not, missing the guy further back in the same queue talking on his mobile phone, who had come scurrying into the hall, urgently searching around until he sighted Emil, who left the queue as soon as Emil had finished his check-in, and followed him, at a discreet distance, as far as the entrance to the security gates.

Once he was sure Emil had passed through and was not coming back out, he turned and quickly left the airport.

29

The security doors slid apart and the customs hall disgorged another clump of travellers. Beyond the brace of shiny black-haired, bald, sari and turban covered heads in front of him, all Emil could see was a vastly dense and varied array of faces. From deep in the thicket an arm shot into the air attracting his attention, then between the ebb and flow of the crowd he saw that the shoulder and head attached to the arm were Dominik's.

If Frankfurt had been busy when he left, Hyderabad's Rajiv Gandhi airport was positively buzzing. Emil was impressed by it – big, well maintained and fresh-looking, a symbol of the new India and the power of high tech investment. And it was exceedingly busy. Along with Bangalore, Hyderabad was continuing to grow as an IT and telecommunications sector hub, unaffected by the ructions that were still plaguing the economies of western European-based competitors. It was a major recipient of data for processing and storage, outsourced from global, mostly European and North American, businesses.

After battling his way through the mass of bodies, Dominik reached him, clapping Emil on the shoulder while vigorously pumping his hand in the most enthusiastic greeting Emil had ever known him to give, capped by an embrace around the shoulder.

"I'm delighted that you decided to come. When my friends told me that you were booked, I said I wouldn't believe it until I saw you come out of the customs hall. Now here you are!"

Emil was flattered and momentarily lost for words.

"What else could I do when I got your letter?" he asked lamely, then recovering: "Of course I had to come, I wanted to come."

Dominik had a driver waiting. When they finally edged their way through to the exit, outside it was hot and dusty and disordered, as the India of Emil's expectations should be, in stark contrast to the interior they'd just left.

"Is that all your luggage?" asked Dominik, pointing at Emil's rucksack.

"It's a long story, I'll tell you once we get inside the car and the air-conditioning is on full."

They were heading for a part of the city called Jubilee Hills, Dominik informed him when they were en route, where his friends' company compound was located. They would be staying in the guest house in the compound.

Emil told Dominik about the explosion at his apartment.

"I'm sorry, Emil. But I did warn you that you might be targeted, like me. I guess that became especially the case after we were seen together in Luxembourg. That business – the attack on the PNG ceremony – I knew it would cause trouble, but they wouldn't listen to me and call it off. All I can do is apologise."

"Dom, look, it's not your fault. This business didn't start with the disruption of the ceremony. I was thinking the other night, these things, you know, like the break-ins to my flat, they seem to have been happening for some time. I don't know who's responsible, but what's clear is that it's all related to PNG and the carbon trading arrangements they're putting in place."

"I can assure you, Emil, DG people wouldn't have had anything to do with blowing up your apartment. Do you think that Beckwith would be alive today if killing was their modus operandi? Do you think I'd have anything to do with them if it was? I can understand Betty G being fixated on DG after what happened at the ceremony, that would have been a bit of a shock for someone like her …"

"Not to mention the others that were there."

"… but she's completely wrong. She just hasn't opened her eyes to what's really going on in this space," he paused, "… unless she knows what's going on and doesn't need to open her eyes."

"If you think she's part of this other lot, I think you're wrong. Besides it wasn't her, it's the police who are following the theory that your DG friends are responsible for the explosion. I think she's pretty straight. Orlando, on the other hand, warrants closer observation. He showed particular interest in where you had gone, when you went on leave and, on Sunday – yesterday, yes that's right – I'm losing track of the days already – on Sunday, I went into the office to sort some things out and I could have sworn the light was on in my office when I arrived out the front. It wasn't on when I got up there, but a little while later, guess who appears at my door. I don't know how long he'd been there, but if I was a suspicious person – which I am – I'd say it was all just a little bit too coincidental."

"I hope you didn't tell him you were coming here – or that you were going to see me."

"Don't be crazy, Dom. What do you take me for? I hope he got the message that it was none of his business where I was going, or what I was doing."

They were scooting along a near empty flyover road from the airport, above the unfathomable congestion of cars, buses, trucks, hawker carts, pedestrians and animals all struggling for ground space below, until the flyover came to an abrupt end and they found themselves down on the ground again in the middle of it. Eventually the chaotic profusion clarified itself enough for them to wind their way, haltingly, through it and up into the marginally less congested Jubilee Hills area, off the main road, into a series of smaller back streets, the locale verdant, less dusty.

Entering through wrought-iron gates and a high fence surrounded by shrubbery, they were dropped at a small cottage, away from the other buildings in the compound.

"So who are these people whose hospitality we're receiving? Do we have a host whom I can thank?" asked Emil, once they were sitting inside. It was basic, comfortable but simple.

"We're guests of the family that owns the company, in fact group of companies, that are headquartered out of this compound. The patriarch is an old contact of mine – friend of a friend, you might say. He's normally very busy, but there should be time for us to meet him, at some stage."

"OK, so now that we're sitting in this guest house here in Hyderabad and we've each got a cold drink in our hand, you'd better tell me why I'm here, Dom."

"Yes, I suppose I had. Well, to start at the beginning, apart from making inquiries about these two boys Davies was to meet, one thing I wanted to do was to get to the bottom of what happened in Zürich. I don't like being mugged and letting the muggers get away with it."

"I can agree with that!"

"I didn't think there was much point going back to either the Kantonspolice or BKZ, especially after what happened to Beckwith in Frankfurt, which in fact turns out to be just as well, as I'll explain. So I went out to find as many people as I could who'd been protesting that night, to see what I could find out about the guys who attacked us. I eventually managed to find some activists around Frankfurt who had been there and, yes, before you ask, some of my contacts are DG related, but that's not really relevant for these purposes."

"*Bestimmt*," muttered Emil, smirking.

"This led me back down to Zürich, which at first looked like it was going to be a, what's the English expression ... a red herring?"

"That'll do."

"But then I was introduced to a couple of guys who were would-be anarchists: you know the types, the hooded losers who antagonise the police, do some criminal damage and run off. I wouldn't normally have much time for these characters, but these ones had an interesting story. They claimed they'd been in the gang that attacked the police out of Badweg that night: been recruited the day before, by some Germans."

"They didn't recognise you from Badweg?"

"Not a chance – it was so dark there that night. Anyway, these recruiters were really bad news, they said, real neo-nazis – big, vicious-looking characters from the north-east – Berlin – or thereabouts. But what was more interesting, is that the guys who were giving the orders on the night, the ones who were organizing the whole thing, were definitely not German. They spoke German very well, but when they spoke to each other, it was in English, and they had American accents.

"These two losers I spoke to were really angry with the Americans – and the Germans, for that matter. The Americans had said: when the police chase them, split up and regroup an hour or so later in the bar at the Volkshaus, on Helvetiaplatz – they would get paid when they got there. But when these two got to Helvetiaplatz, there was no sign of the Americans, just a couple of the Germans, so they went into the Volkshaus and found it was full of police! They got taken in for questioning and never saw the yanks or the Germans again."

"How does that help us?"

"Don't be so impatient! There's more to the story yet." Dominik was enjoying himself. "So I travelled up to Berlin. I didn't mind, because I thought at least it would give me a chance to catch up with some old friends, former colleagues. But it's a long train journey from Zürich, even by ICE. My arse was sore from all the sitting on Deutsche Bahn seats by the time I got there!"

Dominik took a sip from his drink, Emil a gulp from his. An image of Frau Hoerler, at the entrance to her apartment, joking about Deutsche Bahn flashed across his mind's eye.

"My purpose was, as I wrote in my note, to 'follow the money', or in this case find the money, or at least, the person who was supposed to have been providing the money, but didn't. So I spoke to a lot of contacts and someone said I would be able to find a guy called Reiner, who hung out at a particular bar; this Reiner had been one of the Germans that the Swiss had met at the Volkshaus. Only he wasn't just questioned, he'd been deported on the spot. The person who gave me his name said Reiner was still angry about it all this time later, so I shouldn't have any trouble getting him to talk.

"I wasn't crazy about the idea of going out to where they said Reiner hung out. It was a dingy little bar out in the eastern part of Berlin, although when I got there, the area wasn't as bad as I expected. It's being gentrified by yuppies. As for Reiner, I'm glad I found him in a good mood. He was huge! Balding, but not the shaven-head type: what was left of his hair was snow white. He had a really ruddy face, like he'd been out in the sun, or a strong wind, for too long, which was striking against the remnants of his hair. He looked like he could drink anyone under the table! God knows how he thought he could avoid being spotted by the police, he would have had real trouble hiding, or disguising himself!

"Fortunately I had an introduction, so Reiner was more open to talking to me than he might otherwise have been. I told him that some people in Zürich had been ripped off by these Americans and had asked me to find out what I could, and I'd heard he'd been ripped off, too. That made him laugh. He was, in fact, very happy because he'd been paid just a few days before and – get this – they'd paid him extra, to cover the delay and inconvenience. So he was very, very pleased! What's more, they had said they might use him again for similar 'security work' – that was how they described it to him – in the future."

Dominik took another sip of his drink, before continuing, Emil kept silent, listening, indulging Dominik's story-telling.

"I don't know how many drinks Reiner had already had, but after a couple more he started opening up. He knew he was pretty obvious to the police because of his size, but he thinks that's why these guys, the yanks, hired him in the first place, along with his mates. They wanted the police to chase them, to distract the police away from what they were doing. Not that they said as much. This was Reiner putting two and two together."

"Sounds like any larger calculation might have been a bit challenging for him …"

"Now, now, don't be unkind, he was very helpful to us. Anyway, Reiner realized pretty quickly that he'd have no hope avoiding identification if the police got anywhere near him, so he legged it from the confrontation pretty quickly, not down Selnaustrasse where the rest of them went, but along the pathway next to the Schanzengraben, then stepped into the first dark doorway he could find and hid there until all the action had passed. And what do you think he could see from where he hid in the darkness?"

"I hope you're about to tell me, Dom. I'll throttle you if you keep me in suspense any longer!"

"Why, he saw his American friends, of course, and they were dragging something that looked suspiciously like a body down the ramp to the water. He said they took it along to where they had a dinghy with an outboard motor, then they dumped it in the bottom of the dinghy, covered it with a blanket or sheet or something, and motored off quietly in the direction of the lake."

"And you're saying that body was me?"

"I'm not saying anything. Just repeating what Reiner told me."

"Well, if it's correct, it takes us a little further forward, in that we know something about our assailants. They had American accents. Still, it doesn't prove that I was kidnapped, unless we could persuade Reiner to make some sort of sworn statement, which by the sounds of things is unlikely."

"Emil, my friend, you've forgotten that we're following the money. I haven't told you the best part of Reiner's story yet!"

"OK, ok, I'll shut up."

"Reiner was quite chuffed when he told me this, it had really tweaked his sense of humour. He said that he was called out of the blue by one of the Americans. It was the guy who had recruited him and his friends in the first place. He had been very apologetic about the mix up in Zürich and Reiner being taken in for questioning, then deported. Reiner said he told the guy he was unhappy about not being paid and the guy said all that would be sorted out. He just needed to give him his bank account details and it would be there the next day. So when Reiner checked his account, well, there it was – double the amount he'd been promised."

"Generous indeed."

"My guess is that Reiner was given the share of the two Swiss guys, but I didn't say that to him, since I was supposedly there on their behalf – he might have become less friendly, which I really didn't want to happen. Besides, the thing he was most amused about, when he saw the money in his account, was where the deposit had come from. He found this very amusing: it had come from the very place that he'd been hired to cause trouble for … it came from BKZ!"

30

Dominik finished off the last of his drink and retrieved two more bottles from the little refrigerator in the corner of the open, airy room that doubled as sitting room and kitchen.

"By the way, a sworn statement from Reiner is out of the question. This morning, before you arrived, I received a text from a friend in Berlin. The police pulled Reiner's body out of the Landwehrkanal on the weekend. He'd been garrotted – throat cut from ear to ear. Almost completely decapitated, they said."

The guest house was surrounded by wide awnings that covered a verandah onto which large shuttered doors opened, and beyond which was a well-tended garden of bushy shrubs, substantial trees providing a canopy around the fringes. The late afternoon was hot and dry, but noticeably more bearable where they were, even with the doors opened wide. They each drank from their bottles, before Emil spoke:

"Why didn't you tell me any of this in Luxembourg?"

"It wasn't much, but I was going to tell you what I had found out by then – that was my other purpose in setting up the meeting. But you were so negative, non-committal about joining me – and then that car showed up, so I just thought I would keep going by myself a bit longer, until I had something more tangible."

"OK. BKZ is not a normal bank. From what you've found out, we know that these American sounding guys must be connected with it somehow, if it's paying out their contractual arrangements. Unless, of course, they're extorting the money from it, or from Beckwith, or someone else who works there. But let's put that possibility to one side for a minute and assume they're connected. How does that bring us here, to Hyderabad?"

"My former colleagues at BMU were very interested to hear that a Swiss bank company had been financing German hooligans who have been smashing up climate change events. Admittedly, in this case, it was to cause trouble in Switzerland, not Germany. But Reiner and his friends were already well and truly in the sights of the German police for their activities in Germany. So my friends asked their Swiss counterparts to make some inquiries, which elicited the type of unhelpful, evasive responses that we know, from our own experience, are to be expected from BKZ. However, the bank inadvertently gave away one crucial piece of information. As a reason for not answering, BKZ indicated that, to fully answer the regulator's inquiries, would necessitate costly and time-consuming data retrieval from the bank's data storage facilities in Hyderabad, India."

Emil sat up in his chair, forehead crinkled by a frown.

"Oh no, Dominik, I think I can see where this is leading and I don't think I like the sound of it."

"Well, I've come this far, so at least let me finish. It was serendipity that my friends are located here, as well as the data facility used by BKZ. I initiated enquiries through them, and we now have a contact at the facility used by BKZ."

"Dominik, I can't believe I'm hearing this from you," said Emil, suddenly indignant. "We're talking about data theft here, aren't we?"

"Not by us. But we will get the product."

"What's the difference? I'm amazed that you seem so blasé about proposing that we carry out such a criminal act. In a foreign country. That you've lured me here, halfway across the world, and put me in this position. I just can't believe you'd propose such a dangerous, stupid thing, as this."

"Emil. Now listen. I've just provided evidence of the fact that these guys actually planned your kidnapping in Zürich. God knows how many of them at the function were laughing at you behind their hands, swigging at their drinks, knowing that you were about to be drugged and hauled off by these thugs. Who knows what these thugs did to you while they had you? And all the while, the people who were paying for it, were the same ones putting on the function that you'd been invited to. Now this is our chance to find out what's really going on with this so-called bank. And let's not forget the reason we're doing it – this is the link to PNG. Remember our old friend, our former colleague, our dead colleague? Isn't that reason enough to find out, even if it means bending the rules a bit?"

"Jesus, Dominik! Fuck! Listen to yourself! Your career has been spent making sure people obey the rules. Now you're advocating we do some serious law breaking ourselves."

He stood up and paced around the perimeter of the room.

"I've been covering for you at the office, misleading Betty G about my contact with you, my knowledge of your whereabouts. I've responded to your request – no – plea, by coming out here when I could have been with Johanna. And when I get here, I discover that you've suborned me to join you here in a criminal conspiracy. In India. Havinder Singh would love this!"

He turned on himself and paced back the other direction.

"Fuck! My position at GCMO is tenuous enough without this, isn't it?" he said, voice terse, throwing up his arms and staring at Dominik, but the question was half-rhetorical.

Dominik sat motionless, staring out into the garden where the last of the afternoon's sunlight was rapidly dwindling. He said nothing. Emil walked out to the verandah and stared out into the garden. Then he was pacing again, muttering under his breath to himself, as he covered the garden's perimeter.

It was dark inside the guest house by the time he came in. The garden, too, was dark, but giving forth a symphony of buzzing and croaking and cheeping and clicking. Dominik was still sitting in the same position, motionless, staring out into the dusk.

"I had to come in before I was eaten alive," said Emil, the emotion gone from his voice.

"I can give you something to keep them away, if you need it. Or do you want me to take you back to the airport instead?"

Emil sat down and picked up his bottle, examining it in a faint glint of light coming from somewhere outside. It was empty, but he put it to his lips anyway, receiving the last couple of drops it offered.

"No, Dom, I don't want to go to the airport," he said with a note of resignation, putting the bottle down. "I'm here now and you're right, this is the link. If there really is something rotten in the state of PNG, it's far better that we find it, before someone else does. Even if we're not responsible, if it relates to the trading arrangements we'll be implicated, whether we like it or not. That would be the end of the MIU."

"It would be the death-knell for the entire organisation, in some circles."

"Well, let's see what we come up with. Hopefully, something good enough to persuade Betty that we need to rethink the endorsement."

"Don't fool yourself, Emil, she might be just as likely to sweep it under the carpet, if she thought she'd get away with it!"

"OK. Whatever. I've agreed we should try it, at least. So what happens next?"

"The contact has been made by an associate of our host, so the data centre worker who has agreed to provide the data doesn't know you or I exist. They had a preliminary meeting and have discussed, but not agreed, a price, which our host has said he will provide in rupees, when required."

"That's pretty extraordinary! You must know our host pretty well."

"Well, let's just call it an advance that he's making us."

"So does that mean he's got a stake in the information, or that we'll be in hock to him?"

"He's interested in us successfully getting to the bottom of what's going on, so relax, it's not some sort of mafia thing where he'll come calling on us to repay the favour, or something like that."

"OK, so they had this meeting…"

"Yeah, it was agreed that there would be another meeting and the guy would bring a sample. If the sample looks OK, then we agree the price, he would provide more and be paid for it."

"How do we know this isn't some sort of set up?"

"We don't. But our intermediary is pretty sure the guy is genuine – in the sense, that is, that he's just doing it for the money. Anyway, we're one step removed from the whole set up, so it shouldn't be a problem for us."

Someone was approaching the guest house from across the lawn and stepped up onto the verandah, still hidden by the darkness.

"We might be considered to be a developing country, but we can afford electric lights!"

Dominik jumped up and found the light switch.

"Amitabh! Hi! We were talking and hadn't noticed that it was dark. Allow me to introduce my colleague who arrived only this afternoon, this is Emil Pfeffer. Emil, this is Amitabh Venkat. Amitabh is the General's personal assistant."

"And I assume the General is our host?" asked Emil.

"Yes, correct, Mr Emil," Amitabh replied with a wiggle of his head. "Mr Dominik, I have come over to advise that, unfortunately, it seems someone else has taken an interest in your presence here."

He produced a digital camera and, turning it on, handed it to Dominik.

"This motor vehicle has been parked just down from our entrance gates since not long after you arrived back from the airport."

The first photo was of a white four wheel drive, with successive shots revealing close-up images of its occupants' hard, square-jawed, tanned faces and closely cropped hair.

"They look like military, just like in Luxembourg" said Dominik, passing the camera to Emil. "Recognize them?"

Emil nodded. "No, and I wouldn't fancy meeting them on my own, which might happen if you were to take me back and leave me at the airport."

Amitabh advised them that a meeting had been arranged with the contact from the data storage facility for the following afternoon. It would be at the Golconda Fort, just before sunset, and the contact would bring a sample of the information. They would need to be there to check the material and, if it was acceptable, the first transaction could take place.

"I thought we were going to be kept one step removed from

this?" said Emil, unsettled by the thought of direct involvement in the transaction.

"No need for you to be worried, Mr Emil. You and Mr Dominik will merely be tourists visiting the famous Golconda Fort, if there is a problem," Amitabh reassured him, "but I'm sure that there will not be a problem and everything will be as smooth as silk."

Emil was worried. But having agreed to stay, and with two goons sitting outside, he probably didn't really have any option now, other than to go ahead and see what came of it.

31

Golconda Fort lay south of the Jubilee Hills, on the western side of the city, just past the Qutub Shahi tombs of the dynasty that ruled and resided within its walls for part of its more than thousand year history. It rose above what had once been open countryside, though now the city was gradually creeping towards it with the relentless inevitability of an ice age glacier. For the moment, however, and in spite of its age and the assaults suffered over time, the fort sat imperiously on the hill from which it took its name, aloof from the human hub-bub beyond its massive outer fortifications which, in former times, had kept attackers on elephants at bay.

They weren't meeting until just before sunset, but they left several hours earlier to give themselves time to see the fort and get their bearings. They also wanted to make sure that they weren't being followed or if they were, to be able to clearly identify who it was that was following them.

"You should take a guide and do a tour of the famous Golconda, Mr Emil. Don't worry about this fellow you need to meet, he will be able to find you," Amitabh advised.

This made Emil even edgier than he already was, as it meant that, somehow, the contact had the means of identifying them.

"Look, Emil, don't worry. You're being overly sensitive," Dominik told him. "We'll stand out anyway, like – what's that expression you use – like a dog's balls? Is that it? Yes, we'll stand out like a dog's balls anyway, so why do you worry about it?"

Muhal, their driver, dropped them at the main gate to run the gauntlet of the waiting hawkers, trinket vendors and the gaggle of map selling tour guides, from which they managed to select one and agree a price. The man was quite pleased with the deal he'd made, making Emil think that they hadn't driven a hard enough bargain, but when he worked out that they were paying him the equivalent of less than two euros, he thought they should probably have agreed to pay him more. He resolved to tip the man another two if he was any good.

Above them, the hill stood swathed in its fortifications, the crenellated walls running back and forth like folds of material, overlapping between the buildings and massive upright plugs of grey-brown rock that were dotted round it. The guide was in no rush, taking his time to explain every facet of the fort's ingenious engineering features. Emil was only half listening to the man, who was saying something about the acoustics allowing a clap at the main portal gate to be heard a kilometre away at the highest point of the fort, which Emil found difficult to believe. He stopped trying to follow what the man was saying, instead concentrating on scrutinising the tourist groups following them, as they edged their way along, first through the outer grassed courtyards and former gardens, past the derelict buildings that had been residences, halls, stables, climbing gradually up through the fortifications, to the inner palace and temple areas, formerly inhabited by the rulers of Golconda, now all just the empty shells of what had once been there. Dominik was right, Emil thought as they worked their way forward, they did stand out from the other visitors. Or was he just being overly self-conscious? The others all seemed decked out with the paraphernalia of tourists, cameras and backpacks and water bottles, none of which they had.

Even for late afternoon, it was sweltering in the sun. This should have been the coolest and driest month of the year in Hyderabad. But the temperature was more like May, and the August humidity seemed to be lingering on, without sign of abating. Despite the measured pace, their sweat-soaked shirts stuck to their backs and Emil could feel the damp legs of his jeans beginning to chaff the inside of his thighs by the time they reached the mosque near the highest point of the fort. If he were to stay here much longer, he would need to get some shorts. In the shade of the hall at the very top, an occasional breeze graced them, but in the tourist crowd it was a battle to find a space clear enough to benefit from it. The guide described what they couldn't see in every direction through the dusty heat haze, before heading down the eastern side of the fortifications, away from the setting sun, by a long, wide set of stairs that zigzagged down to more derelict buildings, in a series of walled courtyards.

At the bottom of the stairs, they passed through a high wall into the first courtyard, along the left side of which ran a stone colonnade with a low vaulted ceiling. The other tourists seemed to have all turned and gone back the way they had come up, so now Emil found he was actually listening to the guide and observing what was being described to him, instead of focusing on the other tourists for people following them. As a result, he was startled when a figure stepped out of the shadows of the colonnade, very close to them, and spoke to their guide. He was a young man, casually but neatly dressed, with a leather satchel slung over his shoulder. More like a professional out of an office, than another tour guide.

The two men finished their brisk conversation and their tour guide asked Emil for his fee. Emil duly paid, then tipped him the same amount again, eliciting a torrent of effusive gratitude, until the newcomer cut him off. When the guide had been hurried away, without introduction the newcomer simply picked up the tour, continuing to describe the surrounding ruins as they sauntered along, as if he had been their guide from the beginning. As they walked, he reached into his satchel and produced two wads of papers, one of which he passed to each of them. They continued edging their way towards the high wall of the next courtyard, their steps slower and slower as they examined their samples: selections of BKZ financial transaction data and related email correspondence.

"This is dynamite!" Emil said, closely examining a page of financial data. They'd stopped walking and were standing leafing through the pages, pointing entries and items out to each other from the pages they held.

High on the upper part of the stairs they'd come down, the two man team that had been tracking them around the fort was observing their progress through the ruins below. They hadn't seen the change, but they noticed that the guide now was not the one that had been with Emil and Dominik earlier. One of the two waited higher on the stairs, watching for the approach of any tourists who might be unfortunate to follow them down this side of the fortifications, but all the tourists were heading back the way that afforded a view of the sunset. His partner, lower down, was leaning over the wall of the stair, obscured from above by the stonework, making the final tightening twists of the silencer on the barrel of the rifle he'd been carrying in sections in his backpack. He settled into the shape of the battlement perfectly, after all, this was probably the precise purpose for which it had been designed. Shielded from any unwelcome view by the imposing blocks of stone around him, he could easily have been mistaken for a tourist taking photographs. He surveyed the targets below through the telescopic sights, slowly moving the cross-hairs from the back of the tour guide's head, to Dominik's temple, to the bridge of Emil's nose, then finally in a measured, deliberate line down to the centre of Emil's chest.

"Dom, you were right to follow the money," said Emil waving the papers in his hand at Dominik, then to the newcomer, "how much more of this can you provide?"

"A great deal more, if you can pay. But before I can let you have anything, first we need to agree the terms," he said, reaching over to take the pages from Emil's hand.

As he leant forward, his shoulder exploded out of his shirt. Blood and sinew and fragments of bone sprayed their faces. The man uttered a half scream that faded into a groan as he slumped to the ground. Emil threw his hands up to his face, to wipe his eyes, but Dominik grabbed his arm and pulled him down to the ground. A puff of dust rose off the wall directly behind them, then another, chunks of stone and dirt showering down. Holding Emil's arm, Dominik scuttled in a crouch behind the nearest stone column, dragging Emil with him.

"Fucking hell!" gasped Emil, wiping his face on the sleeves of his shirt. "'No problem', he said! 'Nothing to worry about, Mr Emil'. Nothing except getting bloody-well shot!"

The newcomer was still on the ground where he had slumped in a half-sitting, half-squatting position, supporting himself with his good left arm and making a low moaning sound. Emil looked quickly around the column then back at Dominik.

"We can't leave him there like that."

Dominik ventured a quick look. "The shots seem to be coming from somewhere higher up. They're probably coming down to get closer."

"We sure can't stay here."

"We need to get those papers, too."

The papers Emil had been holding were now on the ground under the man.

"Well, we better make it fast, before the bastard shooting at us gets any closer."

"OK," said Dominik, "I'll get in front of him, you loop his left arm over my shoulder and I'll carry him on my back. You get the papers and go ahead to see how we get out."

He had his mobile out, dialling as he spoke.

"Muhal, we've got a problem. Someone is shooting at us. Can you meet us where you dropped us. We'll be there in two minutes. We need to leave fast."

He looked around the column again, then to Emil: "OK, let's go."

If he'd thought about it, they could have been jumping out straight into the line of fire for all they knew. But Emil didn't think. He didn't know why, perhaps Dominik was just faster-thinking in a crisis, but he seemed to have instantly taken control. Emil just dutifully followed his instructions.

They scuttled bent half forward, Dominik with the weight of the man on his back, into the next courtyard. Then from colonnade to colonnade, across another courtyard, and down more steps.

Emil stopped and waited under an archway for Dominik to catch up. He didn't really know whether their route would lead to the main gate, it just seemed like the right direction.

Dominik had to get his breath back.

"Just a quick rest," he gasped, slumping to a squat under the colonnade where Emil was waiting for him.

"Keep watching for them."

The man's shoulder was bleeding profusely, the back of Dominik's shirt soaked red. Emil tore the other arm off the man's shirt and made a pad, then tore the arms from his own shirt, using them to tie the pad over the gaping wound. He could feel his sweaty jeans chaffing the insides of his thighs raw, but that was the least of his worries. He looked around for the shooter, but he could have been anywhere in the maze of ruins surrounding them. Then they were scuttling again, the bumping, as Dominik ran, making the wound bleed more. Out of that courtyard, through another, then into the final grassed area inside the main gate by which they'd entered.

They slowed to a walking pace, having picked up a crowd of following onlookers, some offering assistance, others just looking, but at least they made it less likely the gunman would be able to shoot them. Outside the gate the car was waiting, Muhal standing at the driver's door. When he saw them, he started towards them, but Dominik shouted for him to get back in the car and drive. They lifted the man off Dominik's back, not worrying about the wound, there was so much blood everywhere it was a matter of time, putting him across the back seat. Emil got in the other side cradling his head and pressing the pad to the ragged mangle of bloody flesh that had been his shoulder. Dominik jumped in the front.

"Go! Go!"

Muhal put his foot down and the car lunged into the morass of traffic on Bada Bazar Road, weaving around and past trucks, buses, motorcycles and other cars that seemed to sway towards, then away from them, before disappearing behind their vehicle.

"We must get him to a hospital, fast!" Dominik glanced over his shoulder at Emil and the man in the back seat. "He's losing lots of blood."

Muhal produced his mobile phone, holding it up in one hand and dialling with his thumb, steering their wildly swaying course in and out of the traffic with his other. Dominik had both hands on the dashboard, anticipating the worst, Emil wondering if any of them would survive this ride, keeping the pad pressed down on the wound, but it was so wet it was probably having little effect. He could feel the warm dampness on his lap through his jeans, the lower part of his shirt had turned vermilion.

Muhal jabbered urgently into his phone, listened, then finished just as quickly.

"We go to Nizamia General Hospital. We leave him there and he will be looked after. The General has a friend in the emergency there."

They were heading east, away from the safety of Jubilee Hills.

"Where is it?" asked Dominik.

"Shahalibanda Road, near Charminar, Mr Dominik."

"That's a long way from Jubilee Hills."

"I know Mr Dominik, but that is where we need to take this man."

Bada Bazar Road turned into Fort Road and they passed a large military hospital, of no help. Maybe their pursuers might think they'd gone in there. Fort Road became Golconda Road, became Karvan Road. Past another hospital, the Government Maternity Hospital this time.

"We'd better get this guy there soon or he's dead anyway," said Emil, breaking the silence.

The man's body was going into shock, his convulsions making it harder for Emil to keep pressure on the wound.

"We'd better get there soon or we might all be," said Dominik, looking into the wing mirror, urgency in his voice. "There's a large, white four wheel drive I've been watching – it's been slowly gaining on us for the last couple of kilometres. It's still a fair way back. It looks pretty much like the one Amitabh showed us."

"We are almost there, we can go the rest of the journey through old city," said Muhal, swinging their vehicle sharply right across the on-coming traffic off Hussaini Alam Road and into the back streets of the Old City, throwing Emil's head and left shoulder into the door with the suddenness of the movement.

It quickly became apparent that this wasn't a good move, the streets getting smaller and smaller the further they delved into them, market stalls intruding into the little remaining road space, people walking through the near stationary cars, small tabletop trucks and donkey-drays until eventually the traffic came to a complete standstill. Someone was trying to turn into the stenosed thoroughfare they were in, but with vehicles completely gridlocked in front and behind, drivers honking, tooting, swearing, arms waving out windows, cigarette smoke rising from open windows, exhaust fumes from tailpipes, there was nowhere to go.

Dominik looked over the back seat, out the rear window.

"We've got to get out of here now or we're dead!"

Behind, in the distance, he could see two military types were out of the four wheel drive and working their way up the mess of stationary vehicles, people and animals towards them, looking in each vehicle as they went.

"Go up to Shahalibanda Road, go past Charminar and the Nizamia to the Laad Bazaar, Mr Dominik," said Muhal. "I will call you when I have dropped him at the hospital, then I will come and collect you there."

Dominik looked at Emil.

"Keep your head down when you get out, we'll go down that alley," he said, pointing.

They got out of the car and keeping bent double ran for the alley, hoping their departure was unnoticed from behind. When Emil stood up in the alley, he looked like he'd been sitting in a vat of claret.

"Jesus, I'm not going to be hard to find, am I?"

"C'mon, don't worry about it, let's get out of here."

32

Back down the street they'd just left, behind Muhal's car, the two man team knew that their quarry was caught somewhere up ahead in the wash of vehicles, animals and people. They'd almost lost it in the traffic, but just caught sight of it when it turned out of Hussaini Alam Road into the Old City. Now that ploy had worked to their advantage and they were moving in for the kill. Methodically and cautiously one on either side, they were working their way up the line of vehicles. They didn't expect the targets to be armed, but no point in taking risks. Each had a hand in the outside pocket of his flak jacket, finger on the trigger guard of his pistol. A quick glance passed between them when they reached the rear of Muhal's car. One looked in the back window while the other covered the back of Muhal's head with his pocketed gun. Apart from Muhal and the man in the back seat, covered in blood, the vehicle was empty.

"They've gone."

He opened the back door and checked the guy unconscious on the back seat, went through his pockets, found his wallet, and took it. At the same time, with one massive hand, the other man was dragging Muhal out of the car by the scruff of the neck, like he was a kitten.

"Where are they? Where did they go?"

Muhal quaked beneath the mound of unbridled threat towering over him.

"I don't know, sir, I don't know. They just ran off, sir."

The same massive hand forced the back of Muhal's neck down towards the ground, like it was disciplining a dog. Removing the other hand from his pocket he put the small, silenced pistol to the back of Muhal's head and squeezed his index finger twice. He let go and Muhal slumped forward onto the ground, half under his vehicle, almost as if he was trying to see where some problem noise was coming from under there. The man then lent into the car over the driver's seat, putting the end of the barrel against the head of the man lying there, again squeezing the trigger twice.

As he pulled back out of the car, his partner spoke: "Over here."

There were fresh blood spots on the ground heading up a side alley. They set off following the trail, but it quickly petered out. It was clear where they were heading. Without needing to speak, the two ran up towards Shahalibanda Road as fast as they could, but by the time they got there, it was too late. A swarm of humanity, the crowd swelling and dipping like a choppy ocean swell, was pouring out of the Makkar Masjid mosque adjacent to the Charminar. Their quarry had been swallowed by it – and escaped – for now.

33

Laad Bazaar. They'd set out running, but once they hit the crowd on Shahalibanda Road, could only make their way by easing around people, squeezing through the more congested groups; hunching over to make the most of the cover, trying not to look around in case the pursuers picked out their faces in the crowd, but unable to resist doing so all the same. It was forty minutes since they'd left Muhal, but there hadn't been a call. They were swimming in their sweat-drenched garments. More problematically, both were pretty well soaked in the man's blood. It was darker now, but not dark enough to hide the glistening wet rouge of their clothes – even more obvious once they reached the lights of the bazaar street, where the crowd was marginally thinner.

"You stay here. I'll try to find something we can put over these clothes," said Dominik.

They'd found a side alley that was dark in shadow. He left Emil there, trying to be as inconspicuous as possible: if anyone had taken the trouble to look, Emil was about as inconspicuous as Santa Claus would have been standing there. Further into the bazaar street, Dominik found a fabric and sari shop, where he bought a couple of kaftan-like garments. Back where he'd left Emil lurking in the shadows, there was no sign of him. In the background, sirens were screaming out of the Charminar police station, as first response vehicles started heading down Shahalibanda Road. Something was up. But where had Emil gone? He pulled out his mobile, then remembered Emil didn't have one with him. He began heading back in the direction they'd come, but then thought, no, why would Emil go back there – closer to where their pursuer's might be – so he headed back in the other direction again, towards the shop he'd just come from. As he passed the darkened alley, he heard something.

"Psst. Dom, pssst."

He found Emil about twenty metres up the alley in darkness.

"What are you doing up here?" he asked, when he reached him.

"Those two goons came past," he whispered. "It was lucky I'd wandered back up here a bit, they missed me. I didn't know where you were, so I just stayed back out of sight. Thank God they didn't see you."

Dominik was looking anxiously at the end of the alley.

"We can't afford to wait for Muhal, we'll have to find another way back to Jubilee Hills."

He began to thumb the keypad of his phone, then froze. Neither moved, neither breathed. Their pursuers were at the end of the alley, one peering up into the darkness. The man stood there, looking, for seconds that passed so slowly, Emil began to feel like he'd reverted to that stage of his childhood when time seemed to take forever to pass. Eventually, the man moved on, out of sight. Emil and Dominik stayed rooted where they were for more long seconds before, looking around, Dominik signalled to move further into the darkness. Suddenly, torchlight stabbed out from the end of the alley. Dominik pushed Emil into a gap between the buildings, sliding in after him. They found themselves in a warren of narrow passages between decrepit walls, feculent ooze squishing beneath their feet. They kept going, as fast as the squelching would let them, bumping off the walls as they squeezed along the narrow passages, around each new corner as it presented itself, until they could see street lights ahead of them. They stopped and waited, listening, but no squelching sounds chased them.

"We'll have to take the risk, we can't just wait in here all night in the hope they won't come by again. These will help, too," he said producing the kaftans from a plastic bag. "Here, I got the ochre-coloured one for you."

"Thanks, that'll really fool them!" said Emil with a sardonic smile, pulling it over his head.

They peered out into the street. They were back at the bazaar street, further along from the alley where they'd entered. The lights here were brighter from the preponderance of gaudy jewellery and bangle shops and there seemed to be more people. They moved quickly out into the middle of the crowd, heading even further up into the bazaar, trying not to stand out, but Emil feeling exceedingly self-conscious all the same.

Dominik, slightly taller than Emil, walking in front and stooping so that his head wouldn't stick out above the surrounding crowd, abruptly stopped and turned, bending even lower.

"They're in front of us!"

Emil scanned the sea of heads and faces in front of him. Over Dominik's shoulder, about fifty metres away and standing out above the adjacent throng, he could see the backs of two crew-cut heads extending out of flak jackets, constantly turning left and right. Then, to his horror, they both turned and started back towards them.

"Oh, fuck, they're coming back," he said, reflexively ducking his head below the level of those in front of them.

"Quick, in here."

He grabbed Dominik's arm and guided him into the nearest adjacent shop.

It was a bangle store, long and narrow, with hundreds of long pegs loaded with red, yellow, orange, green and other iridescently coloured bangles protruding from either wall, floor to ceiling, highlighted by strong down lights. There was absolutely nowhere to conceal themselves along its full, dazzlingly bright length.

At the back of the store the shopkeeper sat on a stool behind the counter, speaking on his mobile phone. They raced down the store to him, Dominik pointing to the door behind him.

"Where does that go?"

Emil was watching the entrance to the store.

"Shit, the white four wheel drive just went past – slowly – they might have seen us!"

Not waiting for the shopkeeper, Dominik moved behind the counter and opened the door. Outside was the stinking open sewer they had just left, but their pursuers would probably have its exits well and truly covered this time. He tried again with the shopkeeper who, with the commotion these two crazy Europeans were making, had given up on his phone conversation.

"Is there another way out of here?"

Urgency, desperation, in Dominik's voice – perhaps responding to the sound of it, or maybe just anything for a quiet life, he pointed upwards. Above their heads, dangling from the ceiling, was a dirty brown cord, knotted at the end. Dominik pulled it and a trap door in the ceiling opened, then an old wooden ladder slid down. By the time its legs hit the floor, Dominik was vaulting up it, two rungs at a time, Emil following him. Dominik hauled Emil up the last couple of rungs into the space, then pulled up the ladder. He reached down, grabbing the knot in the middle of the trap door, hauled it shut, pulling the cord up through the trap door as well. In the half-light filtering in from the street, they could see they were in what looked like the shopkeeper's office-cum-living quarters. There was a desk and chair, filing cabinet and divan bed with clothes folded neatly on shelves at either end of it. In the corner was a sink. From the contents of the surrounding shelves, it was both bathroom and kitchen. Immediately below, they heard boots moving quickly from the front to the back of the shop. They froze, rooted to the spot, like the monoliths they'd seen at Golconda, not daring to draw breath. The door to the alleyway was open, as Dominik had left it. The boots went straight through, without a word. Emil was just about to speak when Dominik urgently held up his hand, nodding furiously. Emil stood mouth open, below the boots were back. Light was filtering up between the floorboards. Below, through the gaps, he could make out two cropped heads directly beneath him. Then a hard voice.

"They can't get out. I'll get the others to start working in from each end. You stay here in case they come back this way."

Then one set of boots was running out of the front of the shop.

Emil pointed to the divan. Behind it was a window, open onto the next couple of adjacent rooftops, which continued until there was another building with the luxury of an upstairs room. Without moving his feet, in case his shifting weight caused the floor to creak and expose them, Dominik lent over onto the divan. No sound.

Gently he lifted a foot and placed it on the end of the bed, cautiously testing it for taking his weight. No sound.

He shifted his full weight onto the foot on the bed and lifted his other foot off the floor. No sound.

He took a quick look out the window, assessing their options. Outside there was plenty of ambient street noise, surely enough to mask their escape across the rooftops. Inside here, with one of the pursuers immediately beneath, the slightest creak could give them away.

Emil was a little further from the divan than Dominik had been. It was going to be a real stretch for him to follow the same technique, with his slightly shorter legs. He had to risk taking a step first.

On the floor he could just make out the line of nail heads across the floorboards, indicating where there was a joist. He cautiously lifted a foot and placed it down further along the joist towards the divan. No sound.

But now his legs were practically pointing in a straight line. He felt himself starting to topple backwards, arms waving like a windmill picking up speed as he silently, frantically, tried to maintain his balance. Just as his foot moved to restore his equilibrium, Dominik's hand shot out catching a waving arm and taking Emil's weight. He stopped suspended there, foot still hanging in the air, sweat exploding out of every pore, beads of it dropping onto the floorboards either side of the cracks through which he could see the cropped head, immediately below. A single drop. It would only take one, single drop to thread one of those gaps and they would be done.

Below, a hand went up to the head, quickly brushing back and forth over the bristles. Was that a drop? The man looked around, still rubbing his hand over his bristly scalp. If he looked up, he would see the trapdoor with the knot, for the cord, in the middle of it. If he looked a bit harder, he might even make out Emil's face staring down at him through the gaps in the floorboards.

Emil couldn't stay where he was, he had to move.

With Dominik still holding his weight, he carefully placed his foot back down and moved his other foot onto the end of the divan, then shifted his weight onto it. In a second, Dominik was out the window and onto the next roof, Emil following, the cooler evening air inducing a shiver, as he was suddenly aware of the wetness soaking through every garment on him.

They worked their way along the rooftops until they reached the end of the block, the street noise covering their movements across the sheets of iron roofing.

"I don't think we should risk going down onto the street again until we have transport out of here," Dominik whispered hoarsely, as he dialled his mobile.

A large tree emerged from the roof of the last building on the block, the building having been constructed around it. They could use it to get down, once it was safe and their transport arrived. In the meantime, its thick foliage afforded them a hiding place.

So they waited.

34

Adrenalin drained, exhaustion was overwhelming them by the time they got back to the guest house. When their car had arrived, Dominik's phone rang once, the signal it was safe for them to descend. They'd been forced to stay hidden in the tree for hours. The return journey was largely a silent one, Emil trying to take in what had happened, Dominik keeping his thoughts to himself. Both alert to any passing vehicle and its passengers. This time they weren't taken in the main gate, but through a maze of tiny back streets and alleyways which somehow eventually found its way into the compound.

There was another vehicle parked outside the main gate now, they were informed by Amitabh on their arrival. A different pair of Europeans inside, observing. The General wanted to discuss the situation with them, Amitabh also advised. They washed, cleaning the blood off their bodies and excrement off their legs and feet, changed their clothes and followed him through the garden, black as pitch, but alive with its nocturnal symphony, into the main building. It was in darkness and silent. Upstairs they found the patriarch of the family, the General, sitting quietly behind a large old teak desk, working under a single desk light.

The office from where he presided over the family-owned conglomerate was modest. Emil immediately warmed to the man, not because he was their generous host, but there was something about his manner. Dignified, courteous, simply but smartly dressed even at that hour, as if he'd just come from a business meeting. On the desk, in-tray and out-tray both piled with papers, documents and reports, behind him a row of metal filing cabinets that might be found in any government or company office anywhere in the world. Unembellished, other than on one wall, a small shrine garlanded with fresh flowers, containing a dog-eared, slightly faded photo of, what Emil assumed, were his parents. He was introduced, and only referred to, as the General.

"I have to give you some very bad news, I am afraid," he began. "Both Muhal and the man you were meeting have been killed. 'Executed' is how the police are describing it. Each was shot in the head."

Emil felt another brief involuntary shiver, like someone had walked over his grave. These were people he'd been in physical contact with only hours before. He felt sick at the thought that these two human beings had had their lives snuffed out so violently and callously. 'Executed' – it sounded so matter of fact. He shook his head.

"You can't have any doubts now about what we're dealing with," said Dominik.

"Does, did, Muhal have any family?"

"Why, yes," said the General, in the same even tone in which Emil realized later he said everything, "he, and they, are part of our family."

"Of course, I'm sorry."

"I am sorry, too, that our source of information on these criminals has been eliminated. Did you get anything from him?"

The now torn, scrunched up, blood stained pages the man had given them to look at when they were at the fort, were produced. They began running through, with the General, what they had thought – at that time – might be incendiary information for BKZ and the PNG projects. There were payments in and out of various accounts, and for different entities, which they would need time to analyse in detail. Many of the names seemed to be disguised – in a sort of code – the problem being, they quickly realized, they didn't have a way of deciphering that code.

Dominik slumped back in his chair.

"We've got to get more. I don't think we'll be able to get much out of this on its own."

"Maybe this will help," said Emil, producing a laptop hard-drive.

Dominik and the General looked puzzled.

"I lifted it out of his satchel, when I was nursing him in the back seat," Emil went on, sheepishly.

"Well that's a fine cup of tea! That's the last time you admonish me about stealing data. Really, taking a hard-drive out of a wounded man's satchel, honestly Emil I'm surprised at you!"

Emil knew Dominik was teasing, but coloured all the same.

"You shouldn't worry about it, Mr Emil," said the General. "These people need to be exposed and stopped. This man was going to sell something to you anyway."

"Let's get it connected to a computer and see what's on it."

Amitabh was called in to assist. It didn't take long for him to access the drive. This was what the man had come to sell. Highly compacted, it had the BKZ financials from its establishment several years before, together with supplementary information – invaluable archived emails and correspondence. The source had obviously collated the information from a number of different database storage locations within the facility. It was going to take days, if not weeks, to sift through it all but, even from the few minutes they spent scanning through it, questions were emerging.

"What on earth are they doing there?" asked Emil. They were looking at a file of paid invoices apparently related to the REDD projects.

"We must go there and find out," replied Dominik, without lifting his eyes from the screen.

Emil didn't respond.

"The first thing we must do is to make some practical arrangements," said the General. He called Amitabh back into his office.

"Here, take this hard-drive and make back-up copies of the contents. Firstly, find two spare laptops and copy it onto the hard-drive of each. Then I want you to make several back-up copies on DVDs."

There were only a few remaining hours of darkness, so the General adjourned their meeting.

"We will need to speak again, but I have a busy day of meetings ahead of me and we all need to sleep."

Back in the darkened guest house, Emil gratefully shed his clothes and climbed under the sheet, oblivious to the buzzing and cheeping and croaking that carried on outside. His head had barely touched the pillow when he was asleep, but then, almost as immediately, it seemed he was being shaken awake again. Dominik was standing over him:

"Quickly, you must wake up. The police will come soon, Amitabh said we must go. It's not wise for us to stay here."

It was after four. He'd been asleep barely two hours. They quickly packed their belongings by the thin light filtering in from outside the cottage, rather than attract the attention of any watchers outside. Leaving the same way they had arrived the preceding evening, their new driver took them to an apartment in a low rise block, adjacent to the Hussain Sagar lake in the middle of the city, facing out towards a huge statue of Buddha on an island in the lake. Again, they didn't bother to use the lights, once the driver had left, Emil quickly fell asleep again.

He opened his eyes. It was much brighter now, even with the shutters closed, and there was a lot of noise coming from outside. He looked at his watch, it was mid-morning. In the kitchen of the apartment he found Dominik making coffee, chatting with Amitabh.

"Do you ever sleep, Amitabh?"

"Oh, certainly, for sure, Mr Emil," he replied with a smile and wiggle of his head. "A little here and a little there."

"Amitabh brought laptops, one for each of us with the hard-drive copied," said Dominik, pouring out three cups of his potent smelling brew. "The General has the hard-drive itself and has other copies as back-up."

Emil sat down opposite Amitabh. In his drowsy state, the previous day's events were streaming back into his consciousness, along with the realization that he had no choice but to continue. There was no opting out now and going back to work in Bad Eschbach, as if nothing had happened. He'd been involved in the theft of data; he was associated with the deaths of two Indians, one of them, their driver. He freely took the decision to join Dominik, now he would have to live with the consequences of that decision. Provided, of course, they could avoid the people who were trying to kill them.

"As expected, the police visited Jubilee Hills early this morning, when they had run a check on the vehicle registration. They will be calling again, for sure," said Amitabh. "The General thinks it is too dangerous for you to stay in Hyderabad any longer."

"They've made arrangements for us to get out of India," said Dominik. "We'll go to Chennai tonight. The company has reserved two tickets to Singapore on tomorrow's flight."

Emil was too quiet.

"It's the right thing to do. We need to find out what's going on there. We need to find out for Davies."

Before Amitabh left, Emil used his phone to text Johanna, to say everything was alright; if she needed to contact them, she could get a message to them via this number. They spent the next few hours sifting through the wealth of BKZ financial information that was now at their disposal. After running backwards and forwards over the volumes of material, they decided they needed to be more scientific in their approach. Clearly, the company called Bishopsgate Complete Carbon Solutions LLC, was one thread they needed to follow. A major part of the accounts was devoted to its financial arrangements. Dominik recalled it was the entity managing the two project sites. He took on the task of searching for any Bishopsgate leads in the data.

Emil was more interested in the large numbers of smaller payments, some one-off, others periodic, that BKZ had been making. From the emails stored on the drive, he began following trails for payments which appeared to be going to individuals, which he hoped could lead further. His first task, however, was to find a way to decipher the code which concealed the recipients' identities.

Mid-afternoon the General called in to say goodbye. Their new driver had tickets for them and would take them to Secunderabad, he advised.

"Even if the railway platforms at Hyderabad are being watched

– we will check that, but I think it's unlikely – I do not expect they would be checking stations down the line in every direction. The Hyderabad-Chennai Express overnight will leave Secunderabad at 17:15 and arrive at Chennai Central at 05:55."

From there, he advised they should go directly to Chennai airport.

"Once you arrive at the airport, go to the Air India ticket counter. The seats have been reserved in the name of my company. You will need identification and the tickets will be issued only then in your names. After that, I cannot help you any further, you're on your own." He shook their hands. "I wish you well."

When they had boarded the train and were on their way, Emil couldn't contain his curiosity any longer.

"So what's the story with the General? Is he DG?"

"Let's just say he shares our common concerns and commitment. He supports those activities he sees as being important and worthwhile out of his own personal resources."

Emil had to smile at the irony of it. Someone from a developing country providing financial support to first world environmental activists. He wondered, though, whether you could still really call India a developing country. A glance out the train window answered his question, as the express rattled past endless shanties fringing the railway in urban areas and rural settlements alike. Yes, there was a certain irony in it all.

Little opportunity arose for sleep on the overnight express. Between the comings and goings of their fellow passengers, the jolting, rattling and, at times, shunting progress of their express train, they needed to keep alert for any European looking faces amongst their travel companions. From Chennai Central they made their way by local train to Tirisulum station at the airport, avoiding taxi ranks or places that might be watched for them and, following instructions, obtained their tickets to Singapore.

By the time they boarded the plane, Emil felt like he was the walking dead, but then regretted the analogy as soon as he'd thought it, his mind conjuring images of Muhal and the bloodied, ragged shouldered data seller. On the flight he slept, not the restful, tiredness-induced sleep he wanted, but filled with dreams of being pursued, relentlessly, ending with the ruthless, faceless pursuers catching him. He woke, with a start, on the descent into Singapore, feeling like he'd been ten rounds with a prize fighter in a sauna.

Now they were without contacts, or friends, to help them out. Hotel rooms were at their own expense, so they found a hotel away from the city centre, along the Changi Road. Modestly-priced, clean and quiet, and there was a hawker market nearby where they could eat cheaply. Once they'd checked in, Emil texted Betty G using Dominik's phone to say he'd be taking longer than the week they agreed, but there was no immediate reply.

For the next two days they hardly left their rooms, working their way through the BKZ information. If they did go out for food or a break, they took the laptops with them, carrying them in nondescript plastic shopping bags. The other guests at the hotel were mostly backpackers, or Asians, who paid them little attention. By the end of the second day, they reckoned they had probably deciphered enough for the time being.

"These payments to Bishopsgate are extraordinary. They can't be justified. The government really needs to be able to explain what's going on there," said Dominik.

"You mean Hudson. He's the one who needs to explain it. Along with all the payments being made to individuals. I'm going to enjoy this."

"There's definitely something more than one or two forest conservation projects going on. But we really need to go there and see it for ourselves: we need first hand evidence."

"Unfortunately, I think you're right. We can't rely only on this stuff. Incriminating as it is for them, it's just as incriminating for us to have it ..."

"We just need something corroborative. Better still, something that shows those boys were at the site. If we could get that, it might be enough to convince Betty G of the need to open things up again. Then we could use what we know, from this data, to ask the right questions."

"OK, so the first step is to get to the project sites and obtain evidence. But then what do we do? Whoever's there may not like it. We really ought to have some sort of back-up, in case there's trouble."

The question was how: how to get there, how to get some back-up? Coming in through Jacksons Airport in Port Moresby would expose them immediately and put Hudson and the project operators on notice. The alternative was to enter less conspicuously – but illegally – over the border from Irian Jaya. But with the Indonesian military constantly on patrol for Free Papua Movement rebels, that would be daunting.

"I can contact some people who might put us in touch with the OPM," suggested Dominik. "They might be able to get us through, but it would be highly risky, and there's no guarantee how long it might take to arrange."

They were tossing around these ideas when a text message arrived from Amitabh:

Stories beginning to appear in Indian press. Two Europeans seen leaving vehicle in which two Indians found murdered – shot execution style. Descriptions are good fits for you, Mr Emil and Mr Dominik. There are eyewitnesses who saw two bloodstained Europeans in the Laad Bazaar that night. It may not be long before the authorities trace you to Chennai and then Singapore.

Just as they were pondering this development, Dominik's phone buzzed again. He opened the text, then held out the phone to Emil:

"It's Betty, responding to you."

Emil read the long missive, then exploded.

"Jesus Christ Almighty!"

Dominik took the phone back and read it. She began that, while under the circumstances she could just about accept Emil's leave extension, the police were wanting to know where he was and when he'd be back. They wanted to question him further about the explosion that killed Frau Hoerler and the other tenant. A suggestion had arisen that he was in a tenancy dispute with Frau Hoerler and that he could have set off the explosion. She couldn't say where this was coming from, but his absence did not help quell the gossiping. According to the police, the second explosion was apparently due to petrol cans and cleaning material Frau Hoerler had stockpiled under her stairs around the heating oil tank. And rumours that Dominik was involved with the perpetrators of the PNG ceremony fiasco persisted. These rumours were doing serious damage to the organization both internally and externally. Unless both he and Dominik returned by the end of the week, she would have to ask the IOS about terminating their contracts. She regretted that she would be left with no other option.

"I should ring or text her and tell her what we've found. That would shut them up," said Emil when Dominik finished reading.

"That's the last thing you should do! We can't be certain that she won't pass it on inadvertently, or worse still, that she isn't the one who's actually spreading these stories!"

In the end, Emil agreed that they should leave things where they were in Bad Eschbach. That would have to wait until they had sorted out what was happening in PNG.

They went to the hawker market for a meal, then stretched their legs walking along the foreshore beyond the East Coast Parkway. With the monsoon imminent, this was the only place to find some relief from the humidity. Dominik began counting the vessels moored at anchor out in the Singapore Strait, but gave up once he reached fifty. They walked on in silence until Emil spoke over the hum of traffic from the Parkway.

"I've got an idea how we can get there without raising attention. There's a guy, Rory McDonald, an old contact. He used to be with Steamships Trading Company, running the coastal trading vessels. I know he's in Hong Kong now, running a much bigger shipping operation. He might have something we can get a passage on to the New Guinea coast – Vanimo or Wewak maybe. Then we could pick up a domestic flight over to Daru or somewhere nearer the sites."

"Good thinking! It's worth a try."

"The idea came from you counting all those rust heaps anchored out there."

They returned to the hotel and Emil settled in to track down his old friend. He had a response from Rory's mobile phone almost immediately. An exchange of several more emails, a telephone call, and Rory had come up trumps: one of his trading vessels would be leaving Singapore the day after next for Zamboanga in the southern Philippines, then Vanimo, Wewak, Lae and eventually around to Port Moresby. They could take paying passenger berths, so long as they didn't mind helping out with the night watch for pirates on the stretch around the Zamboanga Peninsula.

The only hitch in the plan was that it would be another week before they made land in PNG. Then they would have to work out how they were going to get across to the Papuan side of the highlands, where the projects were located. They were wrestling with these logistics when Dominik's phone buzzed again. It was another message from Amitabh, this time forwarding a message from Johanna:

'Leaving for POM day after tomorrow to finalise closure/packing/ storage of library. Staying at EU official residence for next week if you need to get in touch. J xxx'

Emil looked at Dominik when he'd read it.

"OK, that's settled that. Let's check out flights to Moresby. I'm not going to sit on a ship somewhere at sea while she's there."

35

It was past the due time for the monsoon in south-east Asia, but better late than never. Very soon the rain clouds sweeping their way down from the sub-continent, over the Indonesian archipelago would reach the island of New Guinea. But at the moment, it was just the precursory wind that was coursing in that direction, providing a welcome tailwind for their flight. The Air Niugini Airbus crossed the coastline and swung into a dipping arc over the Coral Sea, mimicking in converse the path of Emil's last arrival at Jacksons International Airport.

Emil and Dominik produced their diplomatic passports at the Immigration desk, but instead of being waved through as they were accustomed, the immigration officer gave both documents careful scrutiny, before asking them to wait. He disappeared into the office behind the arrivals booths and returned minutes later with his superior.

"Mr Pfeffer, Mr Baumann, our apologies for the delay, please follow me," said the senior officer, handing back their passports and leading them down a corridor to what looked like an interview room, where he left them. Emil took the opportunity to send a text message to Johanna, so that she would have Dominik's number for contacting them directly. He didn't know whether she had arrived yet, although by his guess work it should be that same day.

An hour later they were still in the room, waiting.

"This is getting beyond a joke," said Emil. "I think I'd better go and stir things up, otherwise we'll be here all night."

"They've probably forgotten they put us here," was Dominik's predictably sanguine response.

Emil found the officer who had left them there, back in the office behind the immigration booths. He noted it had a two-way mirror window, so arriving passengers could be discreetly scrutinised.

"Is there some reason why we're being kept here?"

"Oh, ah, Mr Pfeffer," said the officer looking up from the newspaper he was reading. "Someone is coming from Waigani to collect you."

"Who said we want to go to Waigani?"

"Er, I think they want you to go up there."

"Who are 'they'?"

"Ah, someone in the government. I don't know, sir."

"Well, even if we'd taken a bus we could have been there by now. How much longer do we have to wait here?"

"I'll check. Er, could you go back to the room and wait. I'll come down when I find out where they are."

Emil returned to the room, then Dominik went out to find a toilet. At least they weren't under arrest or about to be deported, not yet anyway. For the moment, it just seemed like someone in the government wanted to see them. Gregory Hudson, no doubt. Well, Emil was prepared for him if it was.

The immigration officer appeared again with the advice that the car had arrived and, shortly after, they were on their way to Waigani. As he had expected, their driver pulled up next to the buai strained pavement leading to the OCC building. A brand new sign outside the main entrance indicated that the building had been officially dedicated as the 'Sir Gideon Kukuraimi Building' and opened as such by the Prime Minister, even though it had been there, open, used and abused for a number of years already. Just like Heinrich-Heine-Weg, thought Emil. I wonder if Sir Gideon would be pleased with this prematurely aged and unmaintained pile as his memorial.

Their driver led them up to the OCC offices on the seventh floor, Emil experiencing a sense of déjà vu as he again read the yellowing building directory in the lift, noting the Department of Justice Executive was still there. This time there was no nervous and quietly spoken Thomas Siroi to greet them, just an empty waiting area, on the edge of the empty office. They had been there less than a minute when the door swung open and Gregory Hudson whirled in, sleek and business like.

"Is this an official visit gentlemen?" he asked. "If so, why has there been no prior notification, no arrangements made for your itinerary?"

"Thanks Gregory, it's nice to be welcomed," retorted Emil.

"How can we welcome you when we don't know you're coming?"

"But obviously you did know we were coming, otherwise why would you have arranged for us to be held at the airport on arrival? Which begs my next question, why were we held at the airport – and for so long – when our papers are all in order."

"It may have escaped your notice, but Papua New Guinea is an independent sovereign state, which means the government can obtain information on who is trying to get into its territory, can decide whether it wants to let them in, and if so, on what terms to let them in."

"I don't need you to lecture me on international law, thanks all the same."

"What is the purpose of your visit?"

"We are making a spot check on the Debepare projects, as part of our on-going MIU monitoring, pursuant to the GCMO endorsement. We request that you provide us with transport and access to the project sites immediately, and any other support necessary to carry out this purpose."

For the first time in their brief acquaintance, Hudson hesitated, as if he'd almost tripped himself up.

"This is outside your remit."

"The GCMO will decide what's inside and outside its remit."

Hudson again stopped himself, before he responded.

"This is highly irregular. I will need to check. However, in the spirit of cooperation I'll see if we can accommodate you."

With that, he left them alone on the empty seventh floor.

The lift doors opened a short time later, but instead of Hudson returning to tell them that he checked with the GCMO and knew that Emil had made it all up, Gerry Johnstone bowled out, grabbing them each by an arm and leading them to Thomas Siroi's empty office, closing the door behind them.

"What the fuck are you two doing here?"

"No, Gerry, my turn to ask the questions. You tell me what the fuck is going on here? The Debepare project set up is completely crooked. Even the auditors seem to be in on it."

"That's all been centralized under Hudson, you know that. I don't have any involvement or control. What do you mean they're 'crooked', anyway?"

Emil opened the plastic bag holding his laptop and pulled out the crushed, blood smeared papers that he had been given at Golconda.

"I'll tell you what I mean," he said spreading and flattening the pages out on the desk.

He turned a couple of pages then poked his finger at some lines in the accounts.

"What do you know about these?"

Gerry bent over and looked closely at the small print.

"What do you mean?"

"Gerry, c'mon. How long have we known each other? There's an account here into which your friends in Zürich, BKZ, have been making some regular and, I'd say, pretty generous payments. An account with a Swiss bank that has something of a reputation for providing services that you'd normally get from a laundromat. The name on that account started to ring bells for me the second I saw it: Count Raggi, the name of one of the types of Bird of Paradise found here in PNG. In fact, the most significant, since it's the national emblem. And the pseudonym that you frequently used to go by back in the bad old days – am I right?"

Gerry remained silent just looking from Emil to Dominik and back to Emil. Dominik staring at him in silence.

"So, Count, you've been caught out. It's time for you to come clean with us."

Gerry slumped back into a chair with his head in his hands. "Fuck. I knew it was going to come unstuck sometime or other.

It was just too fucking good to be true."

"What was 'too fucking good to be true'?"

"When all this REDD business and carbon trading stuff kicked off here, the PM was hot-to-trot on it, they wheeled in Gregory and said he would be dealing with everything. To buy off my complicity, I suppose, and that of a few other people who should know better, they said we'd be looked after. All we had to do was stay out of it, not ask too many questions – in fact, not ask any at all – and let Gregory get on with it, including any aspects that should properly come under our administration. In my case, the management of those two inquests was a case in point. In return for this, a nice little nest egg would be growing in Zürich for me."

"So, Count Raggi rides again."

"Yeah, that's the name I gave them for the account. But I just take the money to not get involved. I really have no idea what's going on."

"Gerry, you're up to your ears in it, whether you know what's going on or not. You'll get crucified just on the strength of this – they can hang you out to dry, dump you in it, blame it all on you any time they like, you idiot."

"It was Diana, mate, she just spends money like there's no tomorrow! I only agreed so that I could keep her satisfied. Don't get me wrong, she's great. I wouldn't begrudge it to her. God knows, staying here with me, she deserves it! But it's been almost impossible for me to keep up with her spending, on just my government salary. Bloody overdraft was getting completely out of hand. The money's been a Godsend. You know I never got into those property deals. Not like the others."

"Yeah, Gerry, you just settled for the ladies."

All three were silent for a few moments.

"You better watch out, Gerry, they'll kill you if you look like you're going to cause them any trouble."

"You still haven't told me what you're doing here?"

"We're going up to Debepare, to do a spot check – a surprise audit, if you like."

"Are you sure that's a good idea?"

"It's our job. But judging by what we've found out already, it might be a good idea for us to have back-up. You can help us: if we're not back here – or if you haven't heard from us in, say, three days – send up a squad of police."

"Dawani is back: I'll brief him in the morning."

In the quiet of the empty building, they heard the lift whirr urgently into motion.

"That'll be Hudson coming back, I'd better not be seen here with you," he said.

With that, Gerry was out of the office, had dived into the stair-well and was gone, before the lift doors opened. Dominik looked at Emil:

"I don't believe he could have been that naïve."

36

"Gentlemen," said Hudson, almost congenially, as he emerged from the lift. "I have made the necessary arrangements to accommodate your request, highly unusual though it is. You will need to be at the airport domestic departures terminal by no later than seven in the morning. I will have the project manager meet and look after you at the site."

"Thanks, Gregory," said Emil. "Now, if we can leave, can you get your driver to take us back down into town?"

Hudson pulled out his mobile phone and dialled, quickly issuing instructions for the driver who was waiting outside, ushered them into the lift and bid them a perfunctory goodnight.

"That was all a little bit too easy, don't you think?" said Dominik, in German, in case part of the driver's task was to report back to Hudson on their conversation.

"Perhaps," replied Emil. "But does it matter – our objective is to get up there, isn't it?"

"So long as we do reach there and aren't pushed out the door of the aircraft, en route."

"You heard Gerry: he's going to brief Dawani in the morning. He might have been stupid to take the money, but he's professional. And an old friend."

"By the way, where is this guy taking us now, we don't have a hotel booking?"

Emil spoke to the driver in English.

"You can drop us at the Crowne Plaza, thanks."

"No expense spared!" said Dominik.

"Not when it's on your own account," said Emil, again in German. "Let's hope they have two rooms available."

Rooms were available and when they had checked in and freshened up, they met again in Emil's room. He had been trying to reach Johanna, without success. He opened a couple of beers from the mini-bar and they sat down to plot their next move.

"Don't you think it was odd that Hudson wasn't interested in where we were staying, or how long we intended to be – either here or up at the site?" Dominik had been chewing things over. His investigator's way of thinking made him suspicious.

"He might just have been pre-occupied with something else. Did you see the headlines in today's newspaper, when we were at the reception desk? The opposition is bringing forward a parliamentary motion of no confidence in the government. Maybe that's distracting him."

"Maybe."

Dominik's mobile phone rang. Johanna's number, he passed it to Emil.

"Hallo, I've just got into Port Moresby, I see you've been trying to call."

"Yes, we need to talk."

"Aren't you worried about my phone being tapped any more? Where are you, anyway?"

"If you're back at the residence, less than a kilometre away!"

"What! Where are you? Are you here in Port Moresby?"

The sound of excitement in her voice had him instantly aroused. Emil wrestled his thoughts back under control.

"In the Crowne Plaza. Dominik is here, too. Can you meet us, sometime tonight?"

"Sure, what about dinner? We can relive our last famous evening together there!" she laughed.

Hearing her, Emil wished Dominik was somewhere else, anywhere but here right now. Once she had freshened up, she had her driver drop her at the hotel. They met up in Emil's room, a restrained embrace. He gave an abridged version of what had happened in Hyderabad, not elaborating on the provenance of the information that was now in their possession, but explaining its significance. She could probably work out where it came from, anyway.

When he finished, she was at first angry, then concerned, then both at once.

"Why have you put yourselves at such risk coming here? These people who were after you, they must surely know you're here now."

"We must get up to the site and confirm our suspicions, even if it means taking a risk. How else can we do it?"

"You can wait for the police, or your own organization, to support you, to protect you, can't you?" she implored, looking at them earnestly.

"If they suspect they'll be exposed, they'll hide things, cover up. Our only chance is to surprise them. By just the two of us going, they'll think they have us covered and may not worry about hiding things. We have a better chance of catching them out," said Dominik.

"And we've arranged for the police to come if they don't hear from us in three days."

"What good will that do if they *kill* you?"

Then, all of a sudden, she began sobbing and turned away from them.

Dominik said he'd see them in the restaurant and left. This was definitely not how Emil had been imagining things earlier, being alone again with her, in his room. He held her tightly to him, until she said he was squashing her and she couldn't breathe, which made them laugh.

"If you two want to take these risks, you don't need to suffocate me first!" she said, shaking with sobs again.

"You know if there was another way to do this, that's what we'd do. Don't worry, we'll be careful – at least we'll be able to watch each other's back. I'm more worried about you, here in Port Moresby."

"Oh, I'll be alright. I have my security detail. As usual."

"I really didn't want you involved in all of this, but you're here now, so I guess that can't be avoided. You can do something to help us. Take this laptop, if anything happens to me, or if you haven't heard from me before you're scheduled to leave," he said scribbling on a scrap of paper as he spoke, "contact this person in Frankfurt and give it to him. A journalist, he'll know what to do with it."

They stayed as they were, holding each other, unaware of time until Johanna said she was tired from her journey and wouldn't stay for dinner, so he walked her to the car and waiting security detail.

"Here take this number, as well. It's Gerry Johnstone's," said Emil scribbling again. "He's the head of the Justice department. Remember he's that old friend I told you about. He's organising to send the police if we need them. If there's an emergency, you can call him."

As he waved her car off, in the back of his mind he was experiencing niggling second thoughts, wondering whether Gerry really could be trusted. But then, just as quickly, he put them out of his head. Yes, of course, Gerry could be relied upon: it was just whether he could be trusted with Johanna! At least now there was Diana to mitigate that risk.

By the time he got to the restaurant, Dominik was on his third, or was that his fourth beer, sitting up at the bar.

"This South Pacific lager is not bad," he said as they settled down at a table.

"I hope you're going to be alright for this flight tomorrow – don't forget we've got an early start."

"Yes sir!"

37

They presented themselves on time the next morning and were greeted by a matter-of-fact, no bullshitting, broad shouldered, clean cut American, their pilot, who, without removing his Ray-Bans, introduced himself as Bruce. Their transport to the project site, however, did not match its pilot's sharp lines. Waiting outside a hanger at the end of the tarmac was a very old Cessna 185 single prop 6-seater.

"In this li'l ole baby it'll take us about four hours, depending on the headwind. So if you boys need to take a leak, now's the time to do it," Bruce informed them, pointing to the outside wall of the hanger.

Dominik took up the offer. Minutes later, they were taxiing out onto the main runway.

Once airborne, they followed the coastline west from Port Moresby up over Kerema, on the Gulf of Papua, before tacking west-north-west in a direct line for the project area. It was all flying by sight in aircraft like this. They were lucky it was a clear morning. They had to reach their destination before the cloud came rolling in, because once it did, Bruce explained, they would have no hope of finding their destination and he didn't fancy flying around blind, with all the mountains in the vicinity – they'd have to land somewhere else below the cloud.

They were almost halfway there when it dawned on Emil that they must be going to land at the actual project site, unless at the last minute Bruce was going to divert to somewhere like Kiunga, or even Nomad. But Emil didn't know whether smaller places like Nomad had landing strips. If the project site had its own landing strip, that was going to be the first piece of evidence they'd collect: there hadn't been any mention of it in any project related documents, or auditor's reports, and it certainly wasn't part of the approved project arrangements.

The Cessna was noisy and draughty and rattled a lot, but they were getting there. Sitting in the co-pilot's seat, Emil looked over his shoulder to where Dominik was sitting behind Bruce. He had his head against the window, eyes closed and looked slightly green. Oh, well, that was his introduction to the local brew, Emil thought. Those little bottles with the long necks packed more of a punch than he'd realized. About three hours into the flight, great stacks of grey cloud began to loom ahead of them over the horizon and a steady headwind began to increase in strength, buffeting the creaky little aircraft.

"We'll make it ahead of that cloud – just, but it's gonna be a bit bumpy going in," Bruce crackled in Emil's ear through the headset.

Emil turned around and passed on the message to Dominik who'd woken with the increasing turbulence. He nodded an acknowledgement and closed his eyes again.

An hour of shaking and jolting later they were circling down towards what looked like just more forest, but then as they lent into another wide descending arc, Emil was amazed to see what looked like landing lights on a strip of cleared land, standing out in the gathering gloom. He was even more astounded to see another aircraft, bigger than the one they were in, taxiing, then taking off beneath them, as they swung lower towards their final approach.

"What was that?" he asked.

"That would have been the PAC750. They'll be getting the last of the workers out."

"Why are they doing that?"

"Once the rains come, they can't do anything much, gets too muddy."

The question burning in Emil's mind was, exactly what did these workers do that might have required them to go out in the mud anyway? He thought the idea was just to conserve the trees. He didn't bother Bruce again, he was talking on the radio to someone on the ground, anyway, preparing for his final approach.

When they were on the ground bumping their way up to the end of the strip, he thought he'd see what else Bruce might reveal.

"Can't be too many bush strips with lights like this – how long have they been in?"

"As far as I know, this is the only bush strip with lights. Been in as long as I've been flying here."

"How long's that?"

But Bruce just smiled. OK, looks like that's the end of the tether with Bruce, he thought.

The Cessna pulled up at the end of the strip, on the edge of the cleared trees, near a small prefabricated hut. As they stopped, the landing strip lights went out and the heavens opened right on cue.

"Head for the hut," shouted Bruce over the din thundering on the roof of the cabin like thousands of hammer blows.

Emil opened the door and stepped out under the high wing. It provided protection from only the most directly overhead of the downpour. He looked around as Dominik passed him his bag then followed him out the door. They nodded to each other then bolted for the hut, rain stinging like tiny darts, it was coming down so hard. It was fewer than thirty metres, but they were wringing wet, clothes pasted to their bodies, in the short time it took them to reach the verandah. A figure stood in the doorway, almost filling it, silhouetted by the light inside.

"I hope you brought you' raincoats," he said, in a thick European sounding accent, capped by a humourless chuckle.

Bruce joined them on the verandah and Emil noticed that he, like the hulk in the doorway, was wearing an oilskin, Bruce's running with water.

"This is a nice reception you've organized for your guests, Wiebe."

"You take what you get here," Wiebe growled back.

"Can we get inside out of this rain?" asked Emil.

Wiebe scowled at him, then moved back into the room.

"Don't drip fuckin' water all over the floor. This is my office."

"OK, OK. We just need to get out of the weather for a minute," said Emil as they squeezed inside the doorway, consciously not moving too far into the room.

In the light, they could see his face was as ugly as his tone of voice. His head, thought Emil, was like a piece of chewed gristle with a couple of coffee beans for eyes, set too close together in the middle of it. Under the oilskin his body filled out in jungle green camouflage fatigues, like some sort of overly fed guerrilla fighter, rounded muscular hands hanging at the ends of solid, stumpy arms.

"I assume you're the site manager?" said Emil, trying to retrieve a sense of authority and composure.

"No, I'm the fuckin' queen of England…"

"Gregory Hudson should have told you about the purpose of our visit. We shouldn't trouble you for more than a day or two. We're here to conduct an audit of the project, to make sure things are on track."

"That's nice," said Wiebe, "but you didn't choose you' timing too fuckin' well. You' not goin' to see much more than the inside of the huts this time of year, unless you want to walk 'round in the rain. Can't take any vehicles out, they just get bogged."

This wasn't going well. Emil looked to Dominik for help.

"Perhaps we can just get dry and change our clothes, then we can talk about what can be achieved," said Dominik. "Is there some accommodation we can use?"

"Sure, place is empty now, 'cept for me ant my boys."

"And you wouldn't have any spare oilskins we could borrow while we're here, would you?" asked Emil hopefully.

Wiebe looked at Bruce and shook his head in disgust. With a wave of his thick hand he shooed them out of his office, turned off the lights, slammed the door shut and strode off the verandah out into the now easing, but no less drenching, downpour. Bruce indicated they should follow, Wiebe leading them along a track through the bush which eventually reached a large clearing, at the far end of which was a cluster of more prefabricated huts.

"You can stay here," said Wiebe when they were adjacent to the nearest of the huts, and pointing at the hut two along, "That's the mess."

Then he left them.

38

"If it's still operating, let's see if it's still here ... somewhere."

Dominik was logging onto his laptop. They had just returned to their hut after spending an awkward couple of hours with Wiebe and Bruce the pilot in the mess. The food – pre-cooked and reheated rice with tinned tuna, a staple of the locals – was edible, just barely. The conversation, on the other hand, didn't even reach that level. Any of Emil's or Dominik's questions about the projects and the arrangements either elicited a monosyllabic grunted response, or were ignored entirely. In the end Wiebe told Emil to shut the fuck up and let him eat in peace, the only words passing between them after that being Wiebe's direction for them to clean up after themselves, delivered with the advice:

"We don't keep fuckin' servants here!"

It was apparent that whoever was funding this operation wasn't cutting corners when it came to the infrastructure. The set up at the airstrip was evidence enough of that. The hut they were in was relatively comfortable. They found oilskins hanging behind the door and wellington boots, which they promptly appropriated. So far as they could make out in the watery gloom, there seemed to be about six or so other similar huts, although a couple of the others were considerably larger, all being of the type commonly found on construction or mining sites. With the rain continuing to fall, the clouds sitting heavily and offering no sign of respite before nightfall, there had been nothing else to do but return to their hut, given Wiebe's distinct lack of cooperation, bordering on outright aggression. Bruce the pilot could have Wiebe all to himself.

There was no longer any signal from the boys' GPS. Dominik delved into his bag and pulled out what looked like a slightly larger than normal yellow and black smart phone and placed it next to his laptop. It was the handheld GPS device the guys at TURD had sent him. The two boys had been using a less sophisticated version than this one. TURD had said he'd be putting it to good use if he could find its 'little brother'. The slush of footsteps approaching the hut outside reached them over the drumming of the rain on the corrugated iron roof. Dominik dropped the GPS device back into his bag a split second before the door was swung open by Wiebe.

"Don't you knock?" Emil challenged him.

Wiebe glared at Emil.

"This is my place, I'm the boss ant I do what I fuckin' like! Got it?"

Then he seemed to ease slightly.

"If the rain clears in the morning, I'll show you around the camp like Mr Hudson said. Until then, you stay here. If my boys catch you outside at night, that's you' funeral."

Emil felt an instant urge to challenge Wiebe if that was how the two boys from TURD copped it, but he could feel Dominik's eyes on him. Instead he asked:

"What if we're hungry – is the mess out-of-bounds?"

"You just fuckin' finished eating ant already you' thinking about more. This isn't a fuckin' holiday camp."

He looked Emil up and down, as if sizing him up for a fight.

"Get what you want from there before dark. You' got about two hours. After that, like I said – you' funeral."

The door slammed shut behind him and they heard him slush off in the direction of the airstrip and his office. Dominik retrieved the GPS device from his bag. They had checked online the previous evening for the coordinates from which TURD had last received a signal. Dominik checked the coordinates TURD had emailed, then turned on the GPS.

"This is a professional instrument. The specifications say it should give us our position to between two and five metres. So if the last signal from the boys' device came from here, we should be able to get pretty close to where it was – and presumably, where they were, as well."

He fiddled about with the program controls, tapping the touch screen and periodically referring back to the laptop where he'd downloaded the operating manual. Emil stayed clear so as not to get in his way, concentrating on looking out in case Wiebe decided to come back, periodically checking outside the door for any signs of his 'boys'. So far, he hadn't sighted them. It would be good to get an idea of what they would be dealing with, if they decided they needed to make some nocturnal investigations.

Dominik interrupted Emil's thoughts.

"This is brilliant. It has an in-built camera and, if I use the right settings when I take still photos, it automatically associates the photos with the global positioning. Amazing. It's a phone and it's got Wi-Fi and Bluetooth."

"So if we can piggyback on their satellite connection, can we email photos?"

"I don't see why not. But first, I need to work out how to use this thing …"

An hour later, Dominik was satisfied he could operate the device. In the meantime, Emil had paid a visit to the mess, where he interrupted Bruce the pilot and Wiebe, deep in conversation, and retrieved some food supplies and bottled water. At least in his absence they wouldn't be sneaking up on Dominik. As he reached the hut, his peripheral vision caught a movement in the bush at the edge of the clearing. It was almost dark, so he couldn't make out any more than a dark shape and what could have been the glint of a blade. Hmm, so they're actually there, not just Wiebe's bullshit, he mused. Maybe they'd bide their time on the nocturnal snooping side of things.

"We've got eight hours battery with this thing on full GPS, before we need to recharge it. I haven't been able to find any power sockets in here, so I don't fancy our chances of recharging it if we need to. Anyway, let's see how we go now."

Dominik pressed the touch screen a couple of times and the device began reading out the coordinates of their location at full volume.

"Turn it down! Turn it down before they hear it!" Emil blurted, as Dominik frantically hit the touch screen a few more times before managing to mute the device.

"Well, we can't be too far away," he said looking from the GPS to his laptop and back. "It looks like we're more or less same latitude, maybe a little bit further west, I think, of where the signal came from."

Emil looked over Dominik's shoulder at the screens.

"I reckon that would put it back over near the airstrip somewhere. They might have been loading them onto an aircraft or something. Or it could've been Wiebe's hut. We'll need to walk around with this thing tomorrow until we get nearer those coordinates, but for now I guess we'd better save the battery."

"Well, I think I'll try to get some sleep," said Dominik turning off the GPS device. "I'm still feeling the effect of those beers from last night."

While Dominik dozed, Emil went back through the BKZ data on Dominik's laptop, continuing the examination he'd begun, sifting through countless folders and files, stored emails, accounts, notes to accounts, transaction records ...

They were both woken by the sound of the aircraft engine. The light was still on in the hut, but there were signs of light outside.

"I must have nodded off," said Emil getting up and opening the door.

Outside the sky was clear and fresh and the morning bush cacophony was in full swing, competing with the aircraft engine. It seemed to be receding. Emil turned to Dominik, who was rubbing his eyes with the butts of his palms.

"Shit, that's Bruce! He's leaving!"

He leapt out of the hut and began running down towards the airstrip, Dominik loping behind. They reached Wiebe's office hut just in time to see the Cessna lifting off at the far end of the strip. Wiebe came out to the door of the hut.

"Where's he going?" Emil demanded.

"Back to Moresby, where else?"

"What about us? He was meant to stay and transport us back when we're finished here."

"That's not my problem. If you didn't sleep in so long, you could have taken it up with him. But it's too late now."

Emil looked at his watch. It was only six fifteen and barely light.

"Get him on the radio," he ordered. "Tell him to come back."

Wiebe looked at Emil contemptuously then, smiling to himself, slowly and precisely locked the door of his office and began heading back up the track to the clearing and the other huts.

"Fuck, that's great," Emil said looking at Dominik, but he wasn't listening. He'd pulled the GPS device out and, making sure Wiebe was far enough away not to notice, took the coordinates and a photo of the hut. They then headed back up in Wiebe's wake. At their hut, Dominik checked the reading he'd just made against the coordinates TURD had emailed. They were virtually identical.

"We know where to begin our search, at least," he said showing the two screens to Emil. "Provided we can get access."

"Well, from what we've seen so far, we're going to have to be a bit more subtle than just bowling up to him and demanding it."

"Let's get him to give us the tour he promised last night. Looks like we'll be here at least another day."

They found Wiebe in the mess hut. There was cereal and toast, and even filter coffee, for breakfast. Dominik had a go at engaging him in conversation, since they'd decided between themselves that Wiebe had taken a severe disliking to Emil, so it was unlikely he would get anywhere with him. Dominik was only marginally more successful, although he did at least manage get Wiebe's agreement that after Dominik and Emil had cleaned up after themselves - because there were no fuckin' servants and this wasn't a fuckin' holiday camp - he'd show them around, provided it didn't start fuckin' raining again.

As luck would have it, as they finished cleaning up their breakfast things the rain began pelting down and, like a curtain drawn on the day's activities, continued to do so. They spent most of the day in their hut, taking turns to use the laptop, trawling through the BKZ information, discussing items of correspondence or accounting entries they'd come across that looked useful, making notes of salient documents. At least there were plenty of food supplies in the mess, even if they were in some instances not terribly palatable and could only be secured by encountering the even less palatable Wiebe.

The following day dawned bright and sunny, as had the previous, but not to be caught out again, they were out of their hut and into the mess as soon as there was sufficient daylight to avoid an unscheduled meeting with Wiebe's 'boys'. The previous day they'd seen his boys wandering around the fringes of the clearing, trying to keep as dry as possible under makeshift shelters of branches and leaves. They were short and squat, but looked sufficiently intimidating nonetheless, machetes dangling at their sides, long bows and clutches of even longer arrows slung across their backs. Wiebe grunted an unwilling response to Dominik's greeting and as soon as he finished he got up to leave.

"Can you show us around this morning, given the rain seems to have gone for now?" asked Dominik as Wiebe went to step out the door.

"I'll be back by nine."

39

The tour began with the other huts in the clearing. A couple of the others were for accommodation, one for ablutions which they'd already found, one was Wiebe's, and the other larger huts were what he called storage and works buildings. All told, there was accommodation for twenty, although they'd only had that full number there for one short period. It seemed personnel would come and go on a regular basis. They moved on to the machinery compound which was located at the opposite end of the clearing from the airstrip, but linked to it by a road that ran through the bush skirting the northern side of the clearing. The scale of the operation took them by surprise: apart from a grader, a tracked digger and several high wheel base four-wheel drives, there were vehicles that looked suspiciously like logging machinery, all new and well-maintained. Wiebe made no attempt to disguise their purpose.

"That's a cable skidder ant that's a tracked harvester," said Wiebe pointing to each vehicle.

"So you're felling and harvesting timber?" interjected Emil.

"When we need to."

The compound was surrounded by a cyclone wire fence and along one side was a sheltered area for working, chainsaws and other pieces of equipment sitting on a long work bench. This area also doubled as quarters for Wiebe's 'boys' and a couple of them were trying to rest, weapons as sleeping companions, on mats laid out on the higher dry ground beneath the work bench. From the gate of the compound a road stretched off eastwards to the town-ship of Nomad, about six hours away. With a few more days of rain, Wiebe explained, it would get very difficult to travel along the road in the four-wheel drives. Another week or two of rain and even the tracked vehicles would be at risk of getting bogged.

Wiebe led them back around the road linking the compound to the airstrip. It was well constructed with a loam surface and showed no adverse effects from the rain. He took them to his office where he spread out a map of the region, the project areas etched out in red hatching. Emil left it to Dominik to ask the questions.

"So when they're here, what do all the workers do? After all, these projects are just about conserving the forest, aren't they?"

"It's in the auditor's reports. Read them," said Wiebe, gesturing to the folders on a bookshelf.

"We have, but we'd just like to hear from you, as the site man-ager."

Wiebe folded the map, looked at his watch.

"Like I said, it's in the auditor's reports."

In the distance, the sound of an aircraft could be heard.

"That's the end of the tour."

Behind his desk there was a doorway to a smaller inner room from which came the crackle of a radio. Wiebe went in, held the headset up to one ear then spoke quickly and inaudibly into the microphone. He listened again, then spoke again, this time clearly enough for Emil to make out what he said.

"I'll guide you in. There's some soft patches as you get closer to the hut. You need to avoid them."

Dropping the headset back on the table he strode out of the office as if Emil and Dominik didn't exist, continuing down towards the end of the airstrip. Emil stood at the door watching his receding figure.

"Stay there and keep watch," directed Dominik, already begin-ning to rummage through the desk. It gave up nothing of use, the drawers containing scraps of paper and other bits of stationery. There were cupboards either side of the room, both stacked with papers and office miscellanea, but nothing that might indicate the two murdered boys had been there.

Emil watched as a smart little Beechcraft King Air C90 bounced a couple of times down the strip before managing to remain on the ground, taxiing towards where Wiebe stood signalling to its pilot.

"Eureka!" he heard from behind his back.

Dominik had pulled a large cardboard box from the bottom of another cupboard in the inner room and was standing over it adjusting his GPS device to camera mode. Emil went in and looked into the box. A laptop, two mobile phones, a digital camera and yellow and black GPS device, similar to the model in Dominik's hand.

"Quick, hold it up so I can photograph the serial number," pressed Dominik.

"Which one?"

"Any, quick, just hurry up!"

Emil turned the laptop over and held it so Dominik could line up a photo. He grabbed the GPS device from the box and held it in front of the one in Dominik's hand, then photo taken, replaced it with the digital camera from the box.

"What the fuck are you cunts doing?" screamed Wiebe from the outer doorway, then marching towards them: "Get the fuckin' hell outa there, you fuckin' cunts."

Reaching the inner doorway he elbowed Emil out of the way and stood facing off Dominik, the cardboard box of items on the floor between them.

"What the FUCK are you doing in here?" Wiebe repeated.

"We're carrying out the audit we came here to do," said Dominik, evenly, composed. "Whose equipment is this?"

"I'll tell you whose fuckin' equipment it is," said Wiebe as his fist came swinging up in a hooking haymaker arc at Dominik's head.

But he wasn't fast enough as Dominik easily swayed out of its reach, although Emil couldn't avoid its follow through in the confined space between Wiebe and table housing the radio set, Wiebe's huge fist catching him on the shoulder blade, where he'd been hit in Stuttgart, making him wince as he crashed against the radio table.

A familiar voice called from the outer office.

"Alright, that's enough. Come out here. Wiebe, bring them out here."

Gregory Hudson, looking his usual sartorially smooth self, stood at the outer doorway, frowning. Wiebe grabbed Dominik by the shirt and thrust him into Emil's back as he went through the doorway, making them both stumble out in front of Hudson.

Emil, holding his aching shoulder, decided attack was the best form of defence.

"Hudson! It's just as well you're here. There are some serious questions that need answering ..."

"You mean like 'What's your little charade with Baumann here all about?'?"

"No. Like what's the property of the two boys who were murdered doing in this hut?"

"What property? Wiebe, do you know what he's talking about?"

"No idea, Mr Hudson."

Emil pointed at the box on the floor of the inner room. "Look for yourself."

"That stuff's mine!" said Wiebe. "Everything here is mine."

"Can we take that as an admission of guilt?' asked Dominik.

Wiebe glowered fiercely at him, but looked perplexed as to whether he should answer or not.

"So there's your answer, it's Wiebe's. Now, what about answering my question?" Hudson went on.

"Sure, but it's your charade that's over, Hudson. We know that gear in there belongs to those boys, irrespective of what he says," said Emil. "And we can prove it if we need to. So why don't you come clean with us – what's really going on here? You don't need teams of workers out in the bush for REDD projects, you don't need airstrips with landing lights and you certainly don't need cable skidders and harvesters."

"I see Wiebe has been showing you around." He looked at Wiebe. "Have you shown them the work hut and storage hut?"

"No, not inside."

"That's alright, Wiebe. Perhaps it's time we showed them?"

Wiebe smiled, as if this was some sort of inside joke between him and Hudson, but Hudson just went on again:

"Get your 'security detail' here just to make sure Messrs Pfeffer and Baumann don't do anything stupid, and we'll show them around a bit more."

Wiebe disappeared out the door and bellowed some pidgin English. When he returned with his 'boys' in tow, Hudson spread his arms like some magnanimous host, addressing Emil and Dominik.

"After you, gentlemen. We wouldn't want your "special audit" to overlook anything, would we?"

They walked back up the track to the clearing and the storage hut, Wiebe's boys tracking Emil and Dominik like a Melanesian Praetorian guard. Wiebe unlocked the door and immediately their noses were assailed by the overpowering stench of accumulated animal urine and excrement. Inside all sorts of small animals in cages were stacked on shelves, rodents, smallish marsupials, tree kangaroos, cuscus, quolls. Further down the room there were birds in larger cages, birds of paradise, various parrots and, at the end of the room, in the largest cages, even a couple of Harpy eagles. They all looked a bit worse for wear.

"Wiebe, you'd better get some ventilation through here or they'll all be dead soon," instructed Hudson.

"What the hell are you doing here Hudson? You're meant to be protecting the forest for these birds and animals, not trawling it for them."

"A very simplistic approach to REDD, I'm afraid," replied Hudson, looking around the hut and moving in to examine the inmates of a couple of the cages more closely.

"Well, you'd better tell us what your sophisticated one is, because as far as I'm concerned what you're doing here is completely outside REDD."

Hudson ignored him and stepped back out of the hut, Wiebe prodding them into following him, to the works hut. Hudson again instructed Wiebe to get some air into the place. It was set up as a field laboratory. Well set up, Emil noted. Work benches with sinks and gas outlets for Bunsen burners ran down the middle, on one side the walls were lined with glass-fronted cabinets in which labelled bottles of chemicals were arrayed, on the other, the glass cabinets contained an assortment of snakes and spiders. There must have been dozens of them. Emil's eyes fixed with trepidation on one particular group of glass cases in which were housed a number of hairy eight legged monsters, each of their abdomens alone the size of one of Wiebe's muscled hands.

"Ah, I see you're taken by the mygalomorphae," said Hudson.

"Excuse me, the what?" Dominik hadn't noticed them yet.

"The bird-eating spiders," Emil informed him, pointing at the cases.

"Jesus Christ!"

"I'm advised they have a painful bite. Wiebe, take note, we've a couple of arachnophobes here. That'll be useful later on, so long as you don't damage the goods. That lot have already been snapped up by a very keen buyer in the States."

"'Buyer in the States'? What the hell are you talking about Hudson?" said Emil, spurred on as much by fear driven adrenalin as by the anger and indignation he wanted his words to convey. "Whatever you're doing here isn't REDD. No credit will ever be traded on the basis that it's generated here – I'll personally make sure of that. And what's more, I'm going to put an end to your illegal export of this fauna."

"Who said anything about illegality? You two are the only ones acting illegally, so far as I can see. Coming here on a false pretext, fraudulently claiming to be acting for the GCMO. I know you have no authority. On the other hand, export licenses are issued for all the items being exported from here. Signed by the authorized signatory under the Act, Sam Kaumi."

"That stool pigeon!"

"In fact," Hudson continued, "over time, this little area is going to become something of an export hub for PNG. It will be a whole lot more beneficial for the development of this country than locking up the forests and their resources for centuries, condemning their inhabitants to remain in their current pre-historic state."

Emil opened his mouth to speak, but before he could Hudson went on, warming to his topic.

"You see, not only is PNG embracing these new age ideas like REDD and carbon trading, but with the help of its friends, it's going to take them to new levels the originators could never have conceived, even in their wildest dreams. What you see here now is just a pilot phase, but if all goes as planned, it will be ramped up into quite a production site in the coming years. The scientists working here have already made outstanding discoveries that, eventually, are going to be worth a lot of money. Easily enough to warrant the risk of investing in these activities."

"Which are what? The usual rape and pillage of the environment – selling off endangered species to collectors in the US? No doubt any money will be going straight into the pockets of the 'friends', not the locals."

"Everything is so profane for you, Pfeffer, isn't it? What you're privileged to be seeing is the pilot for the shift to the real new agenda, a model which *will* work. Not like the hopeless unworkable models that are propagated by organizations like yours. You bureaucrats love acronyms – UNFCCC, CDM, REDD – well, here's a new one for you: our working name for this project is CEASE: 'Comprehensive Evaluation and Structured Exploitation'. Building on our success here, we'll be rolling it out in Equatorial Guinea and the Central African Republic next, then Dominica, Dominican Republic, Belize – all through Central America, in fact, every tropical rainforest country, if possible."

"Is this your idea of a joke, Hudson?"

"There's nothing joking about it, Pfeffer. We're very serious, deadly serious in fact."

"You take *yourself* very seriously, Hudson. That's about the extent of it."

"There are serious people backing this venture – people more serious than you can imagine. People who aren't going to sit around doing nothing, while all this climate change claptrap eats into their businesses like a cancer."

"The people who attacked your ceremony know the PNG government has to be stopped, but they have no idea how off the rails things here really are," said Dominik. "The whole idea of REDD is that the forest products are renewable, they provide sustainable development – for the indigenous people."

"Is that so? Well, Herr Baumann, you see the difference is that we're doing this in a *comprehensive* and *structured* way, looking at *all* the resources this area has to offer, not just one of them, and then planning their exploitation over time to maximize the value that can be extracted from this place.

"Take for instance the pathetic little cottage industry extracting 'essential oils' from Waria Waria trees, further down from here, on the savannah grasslands. It's been going on there for years. Generates income that wouldn't even cover costs, if the villagers' labour was properly valued. To you, that's sustainable development. Reality is it's a complete waste of time. Who wants these rubbish essential oils, anyway? They'd do better ripping the whole lot out and putting in palm oil plantations."

"Is that what you've got planned for here? That won't earn you too many conservation credits."

"That won't be a problem. We need the time to lay the groundwork, so to speak. And all the time we're doing that we have these REDD credits which will help defray the costs. Eventually the trees will all be logged, anyway, before the mining phase begins. Yes, there are mineral resources here, too. In fact, the most important carbon trading PNG will do won't be in some poxy credits, it'll be in the real thing. Hard, black and tangible."

"Too bad about the environment, the people who live in it and actually own the trees, the animals, and everything else you're stealing from here – their minerals, their intellectual property, for instance, their carbon credits. Listening to you, Hudson, makes me sick."

"Pfeffer, you're a fool, a naïve and unthinking fool. These people will take a very, very long time to get around to developing these resources, if they ever do. The resources are here, for developing now, and that's exactly what we're going to do with them."

"It's theft, Hudson. Environmental rape and theft."

"The locals will get their cut from this development. The difference is they'll have the money now, not in some far distant generation in the future."

"No, what you mean, Hudson, is that you and your masters will have the money now."

"The people here will get their share when the investor who's providing the up-front capital gets a return on that risk investment. That's business, Pfeffer."

"We know who your real paymaster is and we have all the accounting information we need to prove it," said Emil.

"I work for the Government of Papua New Guinea."

"Is that so? Well, it looks like you've been receiving corrupt payments then, just like poor old Sir Gideon. Just like a number of your colleagues still are, all coming ultimately from the same source, good old BKZ. They've been paying off a lot of people, as well as providing the funding for this nice little operation. Now where do you suppose they might be getting their money from? I'd hate to think it might be traceable back to somewhere like, say, the United States, because the US has this nasty habit of applying some of its laws extra-territorially – like, for instance, the Foreign Corrupt Practices Act. Sounds a bit unfriendly, doesn't it, Greg? Wouldn't take too much for the US authorities to catch up with a Canadian like yourself. Look at Conrad Black. All his money couldn't save him. Then you might not only lose all the loot they've been stashing away for you, but you and your cronies could be looking at lengthy stretches in chokey in the US. Not nice, Greg."

Hudson's eyes bored into Emil's.

"And exactly who do you think is going to contact the US authorities? Not you. You two aren't leaving here, I'm afraid. Messrs Pfeffer and Baumann are about to have an unfortunate accident, brought on entirely by their own irresponsible behaviour, while undertaking an unauthorized, illegal incursion into a security area. Acting, what's more, in complete contravention of the directions of their own organisation. The press will have a field day with this – especially as persons matching your descriptions are already wanted by the Indian authorities in connection with the murder of two Indian nationals in Hyderabad, and the theft of confidential data that one of them was carrying. Then, of course, there's that other small matter of the explosion that killed your landlady and fellow tenant. I hear the Hessen police are keen to speak to you – were very concerned when they discovered you'd skipped the country. You've left a veritable trail of death and destruction behind you."

"DG was right to try to stop you," said Dominik.

"Yes, we musn't forget you and your criminal associates, Baumann. The police are just as interested in finding you and them. However, they won't. Not alive, at least. Not after you tell us their names and where we can find them."

"It's too late, Hudson, others already have the information for passing on to the authorities."

"Oh, you mean your little girlfriend, Dr Dorn. Sadly she won't be able to help you either. I'll be asking the Department of Justice to issue a warrant for her arrest, when I get back to Port Moresby tonight. So she'll soon be in custody. Handling stolen goods, accessory after the fact. The Indian authorities will be very grateful to the PNG Government for its assistance."

"She's not involved."

"You should have thought about her earlier. You know, if you'd just stuck to your day job, instead of nosing around, heeded just one of the warnings you were given, you and her could have lived happily ever after. But it's too late for that now."

Emil began to move, his instinctive reaction to lunge at Hudson, but it never happened. The thought had barely even had time to register in his own mind, when the blow dropped him to the floor, stunned, Wiebe standing over him with a kosh in his hand, his other hand held up in warning to Dominik:

"Yeah, c'mon, let's see you try, fucker!"

40

Drumming on the roof roused him. His friend, the rain, had returned. If only he could get out into it. Then he could wash all the animal piss and crap he'd been left lying in off his face and from down the front of his shirt.

At first he thought he'd been asleep. His subconscious trying to shield him from reality. But then, as his mind had fought its way back to awareness, he began to appreciate his predicament. He remembered Hudson telling them they would never leave Debepare, that they would die there. He remembered that when Hudson left, Wiebe had decided it was time for 'no more Mr Nice Guy'. Emil had become his punching bag, tethered to a tree. But that was all he could remember. He must have passed out. He had no idea what else had happened, but his head and body ached all over: and this bloody stinking muck all over his face, he really had to get it off before it drove him crazy.

His eyes scanned the floor around him. Dominik. Where was Dominik? How long had he been here? He rolled on his side and looked up. He was in the storage hut. The animals and birds in their cages were still active: it looked like there was still some light outside. His hands were tied tightly behind his back, making it difficult for him to manoeuvre into a position where he could stand up. He wriggled on his side over to the wall of the hut, to his frustration encountering more puddles as he went, his shirt on that side was wet through, smeared with a pooey paste. These poor creatures, the place was disgusting. And Hudson was only interested in getting them shipped out while they were still alive. Then they'd be someone else's problem.

Emil inched himself up against the wall. He sat there gasping in the fetid air – his hands were so tightly constrained it was making it difficult to suck enough into his lungs – but when he did, his sides hurt so much he coughed it out. Painfully, slowly, he worked his legs up underneath himself and pushed up until he was in as straight a standing position as his bruised torso would allow. He started edging his way around the wall feeling the surface and any beams of the wooden framework with his hands and his side.

"Ow, shit!" He found what he was looking for.

The protruding tip of the nail was just a little higher than the height of his hands behind his back. Bending forward he raised his hands until he found the tip then began working the twine tying them up and down on it. The position was awkward, his bruised arms and torso crying out for him to stop, but fear was driving him: fear for Dominik; fear for himself. And he just had to get that muck off his face, the stink was driving him out of his mind.

He worked the twine back and forth across the nail tip with increasingly slower, laboured sawing, pushing himself in spite of the pain. He felt it tear and begin to slacken. He pulled his hands loose and immediately ripped off his shirt and wiped his face on the only unsoiled patch of it. Then he had to rest. Trying to suck the air into his lungs, without being convulsed by coughing.

How long was it since they left Moresby? Must be more than three days. Where the hell was Dawani and his squad of police? Must be on their way, by now. Just wished they'd bloody-well hurry up and get here. Unless Hudson had found out and stopped them. Or something had happened to Gerry, before he could organise it.

He thought about taking a peek out the door. But if one of Wiebe's boys was standing guard, that would give him away. The hopper windows were on winders just below ceiling level. They offered no escape route, but at least he could see what was happening outside. Hopefully, without being seen himself. Awkwardly, he climbed over and around the cages and peered out of each window, trying to place the boys. He could see three of them, lurking around in the vicinity of the huts.

He couldn't see Dominik or Wiebe, but there were lights on in the works hut. He could hear Wiebe's cursing. Suddenly, a full-bodied, guttural scream set his spine tingling. Dominik! What strength they had seemed to drain away out of his legs. He felt his entire body weaken. Fear bored into his gut. For a second, he didn't think he could control it. Thought he was going to shit himself. Get a grip, come on, Emil. He had to get a grip on things, he told himself, if they were going to get out of there alive: whether or not Dawani showed.

The animals and birds were getting agitated. His movement over their cages was making them jump and flutter about. Escape was on their minds, too, no doubt. He clambered back down and surveyed them. Yes, we all want to escape. But we need a weapon, don't we? What was clear – he couldn't sit around and wait for Dawani. He had to get to Dominik, before Wiebe did any more damage to him – or finished them both off. Resolve, come on, Emil: a weapon. He needed a weapon.

None of the cages had locks, just bolts. He tried one and found that the bolt could easily be pulled right out, leaving the cage door free to open and the bolt as a potential weapon. Think. He walked up and down in front of all the cages again. They were all the same, but what good would be a few metal bolts if Wiebe had a gun, or against the bows and arrows and machetes his boys were carrying? Still, there was something beginning to nag at the back of his mind, what was it? Thoughts of Johanna kept jumping into his head; no, it wasn't her: it was something she had said. Think. He looked around again at the windows and the cages – then it came to him – he was standing almost directly in front of it – a cage with several bright orangey-red coloured birds with black heads. Were these the ones she'd told him about? Shit! Should've listened more carefully to what she was saying, instead of just ogling at her.

He combed his memory, desperately trying to piece together what she had said. She'd shown him photos. Oh, for fuck's sake, they'd all just looked the same to him – but what was it she'd said? Something about another species that resembled them, or were there just two different sorts? He stood there looking at the birds. No, these were the ones, they had to be, he was sure of it. There were gloves on a peg in front of the cage – it had to be right. He'd just have to take that chance.

41

In the works hut, Wiebe was warming to his task. This was the part of his job he enjoyed more than any other. He wouldn't tell that to Hudson. Or any of the pilots who called in, of course. And he definitely wouldn't let on to the technicians working here. They mightn't understand, might think he was a bit weird, that there was something wrong with him. He could have been a surgeon, he would tell himself. But then, if he was, they probably wouldn't have understood him either. No, it was better this way. He could do what he liked and there was no-one to challenge him. In fact, Hudson's parting words were to do whatever was needed to find out the names of Baumann's accomplices. So that's exactly what he was doing.

After he'd given him a few slaps to make him more compliant – not so many that he'd pass out like that other little fucker – just enough to let him know that he meant business, he'd tied him face forward over one of the work benches. His pants were pulled down around his ankles and Wiebe had been making use of a pair of wooden salt and pepper shakers. He'd picked them up from the Arts and Crafts shop in Port Moresby, on one of his visits. It was beyond him to understand why tourists would want to buy salt and pepper shakers, carved out of teak, in the shape of a large circumcised penis. But he certainly had a use for them. They were perfect for a job like this, the prominent carved foreskin creating a nice hard lip that tore at Dominik's sphincter each time Wiebe shoved it in and ripped it out.

"Just tell me the names ant I'll stop, you fuckin' cunt!"

Wiebe shoved one of the shakers in again as far as he could, twisted it violently and yanked it out. The lack of any reaction now, other than a low groan, then air sucked in through Dominik's clenched teeth, incensed him even more.

"I'll put both in together if you don't start fuckin' talkin'!"

Wiebe stood back, looking around the benches and shelves for inspiration. The writing pad lying on the bench next to him was still devoid of names. This fucker just wasn't going to talk. Wiebe's eyes fixed on the gas outlet pipe in the middle of the bench. Or was he? He walked around to the front of the bench and pulled Dominik's head up by the hair and glared into the puffy, partially closed, blackened eyes.

"No, I've got a much better fuckin' idea for you," he said, smashing Dominik's face back down onto the bench top.

He went over to a cabinet and pulled out a long length of rubber hose to the end of which was fitted a Bunsen burner. Attaching it to the gas outlet pipe on the bench top, he turned on the gas bottle below the bench then lit the burner. He waved the blue flame just above Dominik's head, singeing the top of it. There was a sudden, pungent smell of burning human hair.

"Had any hot curries lately? Make you' arse burn? No? Well now you gonna find out what a burnt arse really feels like if you don't gimme those fuckin' names."

Wiebe walked back around behind Dominik with the burner, waving it menacingly just above his buttocks, close enough for Dominik to feel the intense heat.

Before he could do more, there was the sound of a commotion outside the hut. He could hear his boys running around, calling out excitedly. He put the burner back on the bench and extinguished the flame, then stomped over to the door and flung it open.

"What the fuck…" the words were left hanging as he watched animals and birds exiting the door of the storage hut, his boys running around ineffectually after them in the rain.

"Fuck! FUCK!! What the fuck's going on?" he screamed at them.

His boys stopped, rigid with fear, pointing at the door, then disappearing into the bush to hide. Wiebe stalked over to the storage hut, with each step the anger welling up through him like lava up the stem of a volcano; blood making his face puce with malevolence. That little fucker in here is going to pay dearly for this. He raged in through the open door, only when his eyes adjusted to the dimness inside noticing the stacks of now empty cages that flanked either side, too late seeing the arms swing from above him. Emil's gloved hand, holding a clutch of Hooded Pitohui feathers, stabbed their points into Wiebe's eyes, his nose, his mouth, quickly, savagely hard, again and again and again, scratching them across whatever soft tissue there was, in his other gloved hand, the partly plucked Pitohui, rammed into Wiebe's face, forcing its little body, skin and remaining feathers across the tiny scratches and gashes. Wiebe, caught unawares, flailed at the stabbing hand, giving Emil precious seconds to work the little body over his face. Recovering, Wiebe lashed out furiously sending the stacks of cages over, bringing Emil crashing down on top of him. Emil had a hold of Wiebe just as much as Wiebe did of him, working the Pitohui's skin and feathers over Wiebe's face as hard as he could, the bird screeching in terror, claws scratching, pecking wildly at anything but connecting mostly with Wiebe's ugly face. They fell together amongst the crashing cages, the shrieking bird still in Wiebe's face clawing at it, Emil still stabbing at it, until Wiebe hit out at Emil with both arms, sending him sliding across the excrement covered floor. Wiebe scrambled to his feet, looking around for Emil, then starting at him slipped in the accumulated exudation, dropping back to one knee, recovering and coming again. The slip gave Emil just enough time to get one of the cages, still holding a squawking, panicked Harpy eagle, between them. Both men pushing the cage, with the screaming, flapping bird, at the other, Emil straining every sinew of muscle to resist the force against him, Wiebe's greater strength manoeuvring Emil into a corner trapping him behind the cage. Through the bars and the flapping bird wings Emil could see Wiebe's inflamed, bleeding face, he could feel Wiebe's drawn out halitotic breathe in his face, sense the crazed frenzy behind the narrow red slits of eyes, the frenzy to rip Emil apart, limb from limb, with those thickly muscled hands.

Then the pressure against him eased.

There was a palpitating, quivering sensation in the middle of Wiebe's chest, his arms relaxing in reflex. In that split second loss of focus, a miniscule dose of neurotoxic steroidal alkaloid, imparted by the terrified bird, was manifesting itself in his cardiac muscles, was working its way into his peripheral nervous system. Wiebe momentarily became aware of the intense stinging over his raked, bleeding face. Both hands went up, but he couldn't make his fingers work, with a shock realizing he couldn't feel them, couldn't control his arms, or the jumping beat in his chest.

To Emil, it looked like Wiebe's body was pushed down by a giant invisible hand. He slumped over on his side, contorted, gurgling for breath. After a couple of seconds' hesitation, unsure whether this was some sort of ruse by Wiebe to draw him out, Emil mustered what strength he had left and, keeping the cage between himself and Wiebe, worked his way to the door. Wiebe didn't show any sign of getting up to stop him. Seeing the Pitohui on the floor where he'd dropped it, he grabbed it in his still gloved hands and gave it another hard, quick working over the flailing Wiebe's face, before jumping out of his reach. The unfortunate, stupefied, dying bird would be doing the world a great service if it took Wiebe with it.

Forcing his legs to run, he made it over to the works hut and slammed the door closed behind him.

"Jesus!"

Dominik was stretched across the work bench, dark blood running down the inside of his legs from his bruised, red, naked arse. His bloodied head moved at the sound of Emil's voice. He's alive, Emil thought. He started pulling out drawers, opening cabinets, until he found a knife. Cutting Dominik free, he eased him down off the bench, feeling each wince of pain from him as he did. He lay him on his side on the floor as carefully as he could.

There was a first aid box on the wall at the end of the hut. He started towards it, but the door flung open and Wiebe lurched in through it, a pistol in his hand, face florid with weals, criss-crossed by innumerable small bleeding lacerations. He was trying to say something, but his mouth wasn't moving, the words incomprehensible. He lurched first into one bench, then another, trying to lift the gun, pointing it in all directions, incapable of aiming or pulling the trigger, arm waving about wildly, uncontrollably.

Wiebe's determined fight against the tiny, but terminal, quantity of batrachotoxin coursing through his nervous system ended there. His left shoulder hunched up, bloodied eyes staring wildly, open wider than at any other time in Emil's short acquaintance of him, he stumbled backwards into the glass cases of mygalomorphae. The back of his head crashed through the first of them, the rest of his bulk smashed the fronts of the others. He slumped down sitting on the floor, propped up by the frames of the broken cases, for the moment still conscious, impotently rigid, the release of acetylcholine triggered by the toxin destroying synaptic vesicles, the nerve and muscle membranes of his body flooding with sodium ions, rendering them impotent.

After a moment's hesitation, the hairy giants began cautiously dropping onto his head, using his motionless body to make good their escape. They were heading directly towards where Dominik lay on the floor. Emil jumped in front of Dominik's prone body, stomping his feet at the nimble hulks, driving them towards the open door. One lingered over Wiebe's torso, puzzling perhaps over the Pitohui scent which would have now permeated his face. The thing was hovering about right next to where Wiebe's pistol had dropped from his hand, which Emil wanted to recover. He found a broom and poked at it, until it disappeared around behind Wiebe's slackening torso. Let it stay there and I hope it bites the bastard, Emil thought, retrieving the gun. But suddenly it appeared out the other side, making him jump away and as he did, Wiebe's inert body collapsed on its side, sending the thing scuttling away under a cabinet.

Emil shut the door of the hut and, keeping one eye on the base of the spider's cabinet, collected the first aid box and tended as best he could to Dominik's injuries. It looked like there could be internal injuries, making him reluctant to do much. He stuck a wodge of cotton wool wrapped in gauze between Dominik's purpling buttocks and pulled up his jeans, only then, noticing Dominik's hair and the smell.

"God, that smell, Dom. What's the bastard been doing to you?" he asked rhetorically. "Can you stand?"

Dominik gingerly pulled himself up on the work bench, his face betraying pain, not uttering a sound. Emil went back over and searched Wiebe's pockets, extracting a set of keys.

Dominik was trying to say something:

"Police ... come?"

"No. Self-help time. I'll see if I can find the keys to those vehicles. You stay here and I'll come back for you."

Dominik nodded his agreement and hobbled to the door behind him. Emil opened it and peered out. The light was fading fast, the rain still falling, shadows and shapes moving in the foliage, any of Wiebe's boys indistinguishable against the background. He stood there and listened, eyes adjusting to the light. Nothing. He was just about to move when he heard the low whistle, instinctively dropping down to a squat. A long arrow thudded into the hut wall at chest level. He scanned the dim surroundings, spotting the bowman fitting another arrow to the bow.

Even though he'd never even held a gun before, it was in his hand and he didn't think. Flipping the safety catch off, he raised it and fired. What he intended as a warning shot hit the bowman in the chest, lifting his small body and dumping it a couple of metres backwards, where it lay unmoving.

"Oh, bugger! Sorry, mate."

Only then, Emil noticed the other bowmen ranged around him in the semi-darkness. He raised the gun again, higher this time and fired over their heads. The bows and arrows dropped, Wiebe's remaining boys disappearing into the bush.

Emil pulled the door shut behind him.

"Keep it shut until I get back."

Running to Wiebe's hut made his sides and back shriek with pain: his body insisting on reminding him of the pummelling Wiebe had given it. He unlocked the door and began rifling through Wiebe's effects for where he might keep the keys to the vehicles. The place stank. It had the pungent chemical smell of something vaguely recognizable. He couldn't immediately think of what it was. There were cupboards against the wall on either side of the room. He ripped open the doors of the first.

"Fucking hell ..."

Large specimen bottles lined the shelves. One had what looked like a penis and scrotum floating in some sort of liquid. The one next to it the same. Another had what looked like what might be part of a brain – formalin – that's what he could smell. On the shelf below, there were several more preserved male genitals. Unlike the two above, these were darker skinned. Other jars had a severed hand, a foot and what could have been human organs. More bits of brain. A liver.

He turned away, he couldn't look at it. He opened the other cupboard, slowly, in expectation of the same, but finding instead, amongst Wiebe's mephitic underwear and socks, all the vehicle keys and a box of bullets. There was a bag on the floor into which he threw the keys and bullets and, being careful that Wiebe's boys hadn't returned, headed up to the vehicle compound.

When he got back to the works hut, he found Dominik trying to keep the bird-eating spider at bay with the broom. They left it there with Wiebe's cadaver, Emil helping Dominik up into the cabin of the high wheel base four wheel drive, where he'd already put their gear and some food and water retrieved from the mess.

"Box of the boys' gear ... Wiebe's office," said Dominik.

Emil drove down the track to the airstrip, it being clear from even this short journey that driving anywhere was going to be an extremely painful experience for Dominik.

"We can try radioing, but what if Hudson, or some his cronies, pick up on it?"

"What about police," Dominik squeezed out through gritted teeth.

"I'll try to get Gerry."

But Gerry wasn't answering on any of the numbers Emil had for him and the calls just rang out. He tried the EU residence but the result was the same. There wasn't even a connection from the radio phone to Johanna's mobile. The rain, which had been light but consistent, was increasing in intensity.

"If we don't get moving we mightn't get through on this road.

There's a radio here in the cab, so we can see who we can reach once we get going."

Darkness had closed in, but the vehicle had powerful spot lights on its front bull-bar and across the top of the cabin. Emil had them all on, so it was lit up like a Christmas tree. Wiebe's boys would have no trouble finding them, if they decided to follow, but that was too bad if they did: the last thing they needed to do was to hit some unseen hazard or get bogged. Emil took pillows from their hut and got Dominik to lie across the rear seat on them. At least this might reduce some of the jarring and bumping from the road, if you could call it that. Just after midnight the rain stopped, the sky clearing to a brilliantly starry night, making the drive marginally easier; but it was almost dawn, before they could see the outskirts of the tiny township of Nomad.

As it turned out, Nomad had an airstrip. They parked up there and waited until the town began to rouse itself. Someone showed up eventually and told them there would be a 'milk-run', delivering mail and fresh food items which should arrive about 8:00 a.m., since there was a clear sky. They'd be able to get a lift on it back down to Daru.

Once in Daru, they checked into the airport motel and while Dominik rested, Emil again unsuccessfully tried to phone Johanna and Gerry, then spent a sleepless night fighting off mosquitoes and legions of other insect invaders, which had no difficulty circumventing the poor excuse for wire mesh on the windows of his room.

Late the following afternoon they were on a commercial flight to Port Moresby, what awaited them when they arrived, or how he would deal with it, Emil wasn't sure. All he could focus on was getting medical attention for Dominik. And making sure Johanna was safe.

42

By the time they landed, Dominik was having trouble moving, so Emil hunted down a wheelchair for him. The terminal building was surprisingly congested, the air buzzing with lively conversations in pidgin, motu and tok ples, all drowning out the flaccid flight and public safety announcements. Ex-pats and nationals alike standing around, waiting, anticipating, expectant. Even with Dominik in the wheelchair, he was having trouble getting the crowd to let them through.

"Can you help me get through," Emil asked a policeman. "I need to get this man to the hospital."

The policeman seemed to be just another one of the milling throng trying to see whatever was happening, rather than marshalling the crowd, which was probably what he was meant to be doing.

"Ah, sir, sorry you'll have to wait a minute until they take this man through."

Cameras started flashing and the crowd crushed back towards them, with the policeman's help moving around Dominik in his chair, rather than falling into his lap. A phalanx of uniformed police was coming in the main entrance doors of the terminal building. In the centre of it, Gregory Hudson. Hudson not looking his usual sartorially smooth self. A strand of black hair had fallen down across his perspiring forehead, but he was maintaining an air of arrogant dignity in spite of the buffeting he was getting as the contingent pushed its way through the crowd.

For a second, Hudson's black stare met Emil's gaze, without recognition it seemed to him at first, then the same crooked mouth, half-cocked smile from their first meeting crossed his face and he was gone.

"What's happening?" Emil asked the policeman.

"That man is being deported."

"Deported?"

"Yes, the new government is deporting that man. They say …"

Emil wasn't listening – new government? The no confidence vote – of course! He felt himself slump, as if he'd taken a drug that relaxed every muscle in his body, releasing the tension like a stopper removed so it could flow out.

The crowd thinned enough for him to wheel Dominik outside. Dominik seemed to be in a world of his own, framed by pain. The night air was still warm. It swarmed with the usual array of moths and beetles, but it was fresher than the sweaty congestion inside. Emil squatted down beside the chair.

"Did you see who it was? That's Hudson being deported! The opposition must have won the no confidence motion and rolled the government."

"That's great," replied Dominik through clenched teeth, his eyes tightly closed.

"That probably explains why we haven't been able to get anyone on the phone. OK, let's get you to the hospital."

Standing up he saw Robert, the Justice Department lawyer Gerry had assigned to him during his previous visit. Robert waved and made his way over.

"I heard that you had come back – unannounced! Hey, you look terrible. Have you been in a fight or something?"

"We've been up at Debepare. They were going to kill us. This is my colleague Dominik: he's badly injured. Can you help me get him to the hospital?"

"Sure, sure," said Robert quickly pulling out and dialling his mobile phone. "Hoko is here with the car."

Despite his reservations about leaving Dominik in Port Moresby General Hospital, Emil had to see Johanna. A clean bed had been found for Dominik and his injuries examined, assessed, dressed so far as they could be, and painkillers, penicillin and a saline drip administered. Emil left him to sleep. Robert and Hoko volunteered to take Emil to the EU residence to see Johanna. He still couldn't get her to answer her mobile, which was beginning to irritate him. En route, Robert filled him in on how the political developments unfolded.

"Back when the Opposition first started agitating for the no-confidence vote, the PM wasn't worried – he had the whole bloc of Highland MPs in his pocket. He'd arranged for them to get 'special' enhancements over and above the usual Electoral Development Fund payments they were getting."

"You mean slush funds on to top of the slush fund?"

"Yeah, you could put it that way. Anyway, the Opposition latched onto a story about Sir Gideon's death not having been accidental. They started asking some very pointed questions in Parliament, about the government's knowledge and involvement. Then the press got going on it. After that, it became a question of how long before tribal loyalties swayed the Highlands MPs. By the time of the vote, they'd decided to cross the floor as a bloc, out of respect for Sir Gideon."

"And I wonder how the Opposition got onto that story…" said Emil, giving Robert a quizzical look.

"Beats me, mate!" Robert smiled back from the front seat.

Emil wondered whether this might have been the outcome, anyway, without the benefit of their trip to Debepare and near deaths at the hands of Wiebe. Probably. So what had they achieved? They'd found evidence related to the two boys, they'd exposed Hudson's real agenda. But they still had no idea who was funding it all, who really controlled what happened.

"After this, I'd like to go and see Gerry, if you don't mind being my chauffeur tonight, Hoko. And if that's OK with you, Robert?"

"We don't mind driving you, but you won't get Gerry," answered Robert, looking over his shoulder. "As soon as it started looking like the Opposition might be going to win, Gerry announced he was taking early retirement. By the next day he'd flown out."

"What? But what about Diana, what about his life here?"

"Who's Diana?" asked Robert, turning around.

"His partner – he told me he had a partner called Diana, who had expensive tastes and cost him a lot of money."

"No, that's not Gerry. You know what a bullshit artist he is. He must have been pulling your leg. Gerry still lived in the same old bachelor pad accommodation the department had provided for him since his marriage ended years ago. That's how he could up and leave so quickly – he didn't have anything to take with him except a couple of suitcases."

Emil's mind was racing.

"Where'd he go?"

"He left on a flight to Singapore, but I don't know if we have a forwarding address for him yet."

They had arrived at the EU residence. Hoko buzzed and the security guard opened the gates. With an increased sense of concern, Emil jumped out of the car and raced up to the door, finger on the bell until someone opened the door.

"Dr Dorn, is she in?"

"And you are?" responded the grey-haired gent who had opened the door.

"My name is Pfeffer, Emil Pfeffer, I'm her boy… partner."

Then realizing the man was looking at him curiously.

"You'll have to excuse my appearance, I've been up in the western highlands since, ah …"

He tried to remember when they gone, but he'd lost all track of time.

"About a week or so… at Debepare. I've just returned."

"Well, I'm afraid you've missed Dr Dorn, Mr Pfeffer. She had to leave her work here and return to Brussels several days ago."

"What do you mean, 'had to return'?"

"She was called back. But look, if you are her partner, you should be able to contact her there, shouldn't you?"

There didn't seem to be anything more to be said. Emil thanked the man and walked back down to where Hoko and Robert were waiting.

"Is everything OK?" asked Robert.

"I hope so."

Like the families of the local patients in the ward, Emil slept next to Dominik's bed, although he confined his slumbers to an armchair rather than setting up a mini bedroom under the bed, as others had. Some even looked like they'd established mini squatter settlements, around and under their loved ones. By the morning, Dominik appeared much better, although still in pain. Steve Grahame called in to visit them.

"You sure you don't want a bed, too? You look worse than he does!" he said, looking askance at Emil.

"No, Steve, I value my well-being too much to have a sojourn in here," responded Emil, trying to make it sound like a joke but meaning every word of it.

"Thanks, thanks a lot!"

"No offence, but I can't get the image of those shipping containers out of my mind. Just don't want to end up in one. Have you got them fixed yet?"

"No offence taken," said the affable Grahame. "Yep, they're up and running, full to capacity as usual," Grahame sounding like a cheery shopkeeper enthusing about his well-stocked storeroom.

He made a brief examination of Dominik's injuries.

"You'll need surgery on those tears when you get home. I'd recommend you getting back to Germany and having a specialist look at it as soon as possible. Unless, if you want to go down to Sydney, I can recommend a good surgeon there."

"I have to face up to the journey at some stage, so I think I'll get it over and done with sooner rather than later," said Dominik.

"Well, other than that, all I can do is advise you to stay out of the S&M clubs for a while. You blokes look like you're too old for that sort of stuff anyway …"

It suited Emil to be heading back to Europe. He needed to see Johanna and was getting increasingly frustrated at not being able to reach her by phone. He couldn't understand what would be so important that she would up and leave, without even trying to get a message to him. But, then again, maybe she did. Maybe she had left a message with Gerry and the bastard had just forgotten, or not bothered with it, when the political drama got too hot for him. Emil was simmering over what he was going to say to Gerry, when he caught up with him, when Robert and Hoko hurried into the ward.

"We've just heard that Herbie's on the move – probably going south, back to Queensland. Apparently he's put the Motor Lodge on the market. We thought you'd want to know."

"Bloody hell! That means Hudson's gone, Gerry's gone and now Herbie's following them. He knows more than he's letting on. We've got to keep him here – at least until he can be questioned properly under oath."

He wasn't going to let another one slip away. Three-quarters of an hour later, turning in through the sawn log gateway, they were greeted by an apparition: the kumo vehicle with its tinted windows stood facing them, doors and tailgate open as items of luggage were stacked inside by the barman-cum-waiter-cum-porter.

"Shit, that bastard Herbie's got some answering to do!" shouted Emil as he jumped out of the car and charged into the main building, Robert and Hoko following close on his heels.

Herbie was coming out from around the bar, having just emptied the contents of the till into his pockets.

"Stop right there!" Emil shouted at him, catching him by surprise. "You're not going anywhere until you've answered some questions."

"Like fuck I'm not!" he roared back, recovering from Emil's surprise appearance, then barrelling across the room straight at Emil as fast as his legs could move him.

Even if he'd been expecting it, Emil wouldn't have had time to react and get out of the way. All he could do was draw a leg up, knee lifted high, defensively, in self-protection. As Herbie reached him, instinctively he lashed out kicking at Herbie with all the force he could muster. It was a poorly directed kick, delivered with eyes closed, landing only a glancing blow. With the momentum of Herbie's one hundred and sixty kilo plus bulk, even at the moderate pace at which he was moving, there was only ever going to be one outcome. Emil landed hard against the wall, but at least out of Herbie's path. Herbie let out a cross between a scream and a howl, reverberating around the room, sending Robert and Hoko staggering back even further out the door through which they were already retreating.

Clutching at, but unable to reach his knee, from which Emil's misdirected kick had just dislocated the kneecap, Herbie toppled forward face-first onto the ground and lay there howling.

"Hey, it's Jackie Chan!" enthused Robert, racing back in to help Emil up.

Emil shook himself free of Robert and leapt onto Herbie, dropping down onto one knee, on Herbie's gross, triple-chinned neck, somewhere under which was his throat.

"You murderous bastard! You killed the Minister and Davies," he snarled, putting his full weight on the knee on Herbie's neck. "You ran them off that road in that truck, you fucking mongrel dog!"

"Not me ... no ... wasn't me!" Herbie gasped under the force being applied through Emil's knee. "I rang Hudson. That's all. Hudson sent someone. That's their truck ... left here ... when they skipped the country."

"Just like you were about to do ..."

Before Emil could do more damage to Herbie, Robert hauled him off.

"We've got a witness who saw that truck run the Minister and Davies off the road. The same vehicle tried to run us off the road. That's a lot of charges you're facing, Herbie. That's a long stretch in Bomana. So you better start talking!"

"OK, OK. I'll tellya what I know. Just get me to a fuckin' doctor, willya? Yev fucked me knee!"

An hour's worth of Herbie's moaning later, Emil watched an ambulance escorted by police cars, sirens and blue lights flashing, leave the Motor Lodge. The Justice department could deal with that bastard now.

Emil and Dominik managed to get seats on a flight to Singapore the following day, unfortunately with a ten hour layover until their onward flight to Frankfurt. Having checked into the Changi airport transit hotel, Emil decided it was time to face the music and call Betty G. Predictably, he found her in the office even though it was barely six in the morning in Frankfurt.

"So, the prodigal returns. What happened to you? Where are you? We thought you'd gone to Brussels, but the police eventually found out you'd taken a flight to India."

"It's a long story. Have you heard the PNG government has changed."

"Yeah, I'm aware of that."

Emil wondered whether that innocently meant she was keeping up with the news media, or as he had long suspected was more likely the case, her US government contacts had briefed her on what was going to happen before it happened.

"Did you know Gregory Hudson has been deported by the new government?"

"No, issattafact? I didn't know that. Where are you Emil, you're not in PNG are you?"

"As I said Betty, it's a long story. We'll be back in the office in a couple of days time."

"We? Who's the 'we', Emil? Is Dominik there with you?"

"Yeah. On second thoughts, he might take a bit longer to get back to the office."

Emil thought it better to leave things there. He could explain it all properly when they got back, so he finished the call. She'd probably have found out most of the story from her sources by the time they got back, anyway.

43

Arriving in Frankfurt to snow and sub-zero temperatures a day later, he suddenly remembered that he was carrying with him all his worldly possessions and no longer had a home to return to. It was all slightly unreal after the events of the previous fortnight, but if he didn't want pneumonia, the first things he would need were more warm clothes. All he had was what Johanna had bought him after the explosion. So he headed for the department stores on the Zeil.

Sabrina jumped up from her desk and hugged him when he walked in. His office was as he left it, musty from being closed up. He tried calling Johanna's apartment and mobile without success. He rang her office in Brussels and was holding the line when Betty G came in and closed the door behind her.

"OK thanks, I'll call back," he said, ending the call when they said they couldn't find Johanna.

"Welcome back. I thought you were having a holiday, but you look like someone put you through the mangle," said Betty when he hung up.

"Thanks Betty, I've felt better. But that was before Hudson's people tried to kill me."

She sat down in the chair opposite him and crossed her legs.

"This sounds like it'll be interesting! You can start your long story now."

An hour later, he'd told her everything, having tip-toed around the question of how they came across the source of information on the BKZ accounts and having left out the fact, which he still couldn't get his own head around, that he'd killed two people in the course of the preceding week.

Before they'd left Port Moresby, he'd briefed Robert and the new head of the Justice Department about what they'd found at Debepare. The new government had already decided to re-open the inquiries into the deaths of the two boys and Sir Gideon and Davies. Robert had been promoted to oversee the investigation. Based on Emil's feedback, and their own inspection of the project site, the Debepare projects and the previous government's carbon trading arrangements were suspended. A full investigation by the government auditor would be initiated, in conjunction with the GCMO. At least MIU would still have a role, Emil thought, when Robert rang him later with the news.

He finished his narration and sat looking at Betty G for a reaction, but she was deep in thought.

"Well, I didn't notify IOS in the end, so you've still got your job," she said, finally, without breaking her stare into the middle distance. "But I don't know whether we're going to be able to cover any of your costs. You were both on your own time. If you haven't got anywhere to stay, we can continue the hotel arrangement here for you a while longer until you find an apartment."

"Thanks, Betty, I appreciate your support. Or at least, perseverance. I'll take you up on the hotel, too, for the moment. So what's been going on here while I've been away?"

She looked at him. "Oh, here, nothing quite so action-packed, I'm afraid. Orlando suddenly quit this week, you probably wouldn't have heard that yet. So I'm looking for a new assistant."

So I was right about him, Emil thought. He *was* the mole Dominik had warned about.

"He was following Otis, who quit the day before. So we're looking for a new director for the Government Liaison Unit."

Shit, maybe it was both of them!

"He's no loss, Betty. I never trusted him anyway. The way he used to suck up to that Hudson character was pathetic."

"Well whatever your prejudices Emil, we need to replace him.

The Employment Office is working on it, but it takes an age to get anything back from New York. Don't you go doing anything silly now. Let's hope we get that Dominik Baumann back here as soon as possible. We need him."

She stood up to leave.

"Oh, and by the way, you may be interested to know that the cyber attacks on us have miraculously stopped. Amazing. It was just like somebody had turned off a tap."

Emil sat looking out his window when she'd gone. It was like business as usual for her and the other people here. The hacking had stopped, OK move on to next problem. PNG was done and dusted, OK move on to next problem. He had just killed two people, OK move on to next problem. He and Dominik had almost been killed themselves, OK move on to next problem. Dominik, oh shit, better find out how he's doing.

When he finally got through to his mobile, he found Dominik had been admitted to hospital and was being treated with large amounts of antibiotics to counter the infections which had developed in his injuries. He would be in hospital for some time to come, he was told by the nurse who answered the phone. When the infections were under control, he would need surgery.

He rang Johanna's work number again and eventually was put through to the head of her unit. "No, no, Johanna has not returned here yet, " he advised. "As far as we know, she's still finalizing matters in Port Moresby."

Emil suddenly felt empty, like a hole had just been bored through his middle. It was an effort to speak.

"But, but at the EU residence they said she had been called back – the man's words were 'had to return to Brussels'. I know, I was there, he told me face-to-face."

"Well, Herr Pfeffer, all I can tell you is what I know. We are not expecting her back until next week at the earliest. But look, I will check and call you back."

Emil rang Johanna's family in Berlin, but they said they hadn't heard from her – they thought she was in Brussels. He spent the night in his office, sleepless, making calls and turning over in his mind what that bastard Hudson had said, something about a warrant for her arrest and handing her over to the Indian authorities. Fuck! Why hadn't he thought of this before. He should have realized Hudson wouldn't walk out without doing as much damage as he possibly could.

And that fucking Gerry Johnstone, he really was up to his eyeballs in it. Emil was going to have some serious words, when he caught up with him.

But Emil's conscience wouldn't let him escape from his own role in the predicament, his own responsibility.

Why, he reproached himself, why had he given her that laptop? What could he have been thinking? It just made her even more of a target.

He rang the EU delegation in Port Moresby several times. Eventually he established that she had received a call from a colleague in Brussels, informing her of the need to return. They didn't know who it was that called, but they were able to pin it down to a particular day. She had flown out the following morning. He rang Robert and asked him to see what he could find out from his contacts at the airport. A few hours later, Robert called back.

"I was able to get hold of the passenger manifest for the flight to Singapore the day you said. It shows she boarded that flight. But get this, mate, that was the same flight Gerry took."

"Jesus!"

"That's not all. My wantoks were able to tell me the ticket was purchased in the US. It was POM-Singapore-Frankfurt-Brussels, but she never took the second or third legs. They know, because the second leg was delayed while they took her luggage off. As far as they know, it's still being stored in Changi airport waiting to be collected."

By morning he was exhausted and dozed fitfully for a while with his head on his desk. When he woke, he knew what he had to do. He took out the laptop that the General had given Dominik and, as soon as they arrived, dragooned the two best analysts on his team.

"I've got a special project for you two. Absolutely your top priority until I tell you otherwise. Highly confidential – no-one, not even … no, especially not Betty, is to know about this, OK?"

They nodded.

"Right. There's a huge amount of information on here from BKZ," he said, holding up the laptop. "Accounts, emails, correspondence, scans of invoices, you name it. Don't ask me how we came by it. What I want you to do is make a forensic analysis of all the separate accounts, entries, payments into and out of BKZ. Split the work between you. Firstly," he said addressing one of them, "I want to be able to identify, separately if possible, all the individual payees."

Then to the second of them:

"And I want to find out as much as we can about where BKZ's funding was coming from. OK?"

They nodded.

"I want you to identify the money trails, both to and from BKZ, track them back and forward as far as you can. BKZ was only a pass through: what I want is the identity of the source, or sources, and a list of the recipients.

"Dominik and I have already been through a lot of this. You'll find some notes we've made in files on the hard drive. But I need a really thorough analysis to extract as much as we can. There's about three years' worth of accounts data. But whatever you do, not a word to anyone about what you're working on."

When they had left, he tried Dominik's mobile but it was switched off, so he headed off to the hospital. He found Dominik alert, but still in pain.

"God, that bastard Wiebe did a job on you, didn't he?"

"Have they caught him yet?"

Emil hadn't appreciated just how far off the air Dominik had been. Being careful not to be overheard, he filled in the blanks.

"Christ! You mean bits of us would have ended up in that cupboard as well?"

"It's a strong likelihood."

Dominik just stared at him.

"I need to thank you," said Emil. "I just didn't read the signs. Some of these things should've been obvious, but I guess I just wasn't looking at things the right way."

He told Dominik about the outcome of his night of calls.

"I'm worried these bastards have done something to her or

taken her somewhere. We've got to track them down. Can you get your BMU friends to contact the Swiss authorities again? We need to get the accounts that BKZ was making these payments into blocked, before they get away with the money."

"So, now Emil, you agree: 'follow the money'."

"Have you ever doubted it?"

44

Emil returned to his office and began compiling a report for the Executive. He was driven, pushing himself to keep on going, unable to stop for food or sleep until his body threatened to shut down if he didn't minister to its needs. He was just finishing his report the following day when Dominik called.

"I have some bad news. The Swiss financial regulator visited the BKZ offices this morning, but there was hardly anyone there. Just a couple of junior staff shredding papers and generally getting ready for the furniture removalists."

"What! Where are they moving to?"

"Nowhere. They've ceased trading. The Swiss said that court documents have been lodged for winding up the company."

"Fuck, no. They're covering their tracks. Dom, we've got to find out who they are. Can your mates get anything more from the Swiss, like who the shareholders were, who's petitioning the winding up, anything ..."

"I'll try. But you should also know I had a text last night from Amitabh. There was a fire at the data storage facility where our source worked. A lot of workers were trapped inside because of the security. They're saying as many as fifty might have died in there. The Indian police say it was lit deliberately."

"Bloody hell."

"And I asked my contacts to follow up on that 'Count Raggi' account, as you asked. It's been cleared out. It was done by a series of electronic transfers of smaller amounts, over the past week, so as not to attract too much attention from the Swiss central bank."

"Fuck no!"

"But, but – before you go crazy – the overall amount was significant enough to attract its attention. So all the registration details of the party making the transfers, recipient bank, and a lot of other information had to be reported. It's going to be sent to me by my mate in BMU. Should be with you by this afternoon."

When Betty G dropped by his office later, she found Emil tidying his desk. She closed the door behind her and lent against it.

"I've spoken with the Office of Internal Oversight Services people. They've suspended their investigation into Davies' death and the fallout from your trip to PNG – the official one, that is – pending your report on the latest developments, and further inquiries they want to undertake with the new PNG government. This doesn't address the Governing Council members who are still baying for your blood, I know, but for the moment, the message is that you're in the clear," she smiled. "You and the MIU should just get on with work as usual."

Emil swung his chair back from the desk. Whatever he did now, he thought, after what had happened, for him it could never be business as usual again.

"Thanks, Betty. Here's my report," he said, handing across the desk the pile of papers that had been sitting on top of his keyboard. "I've just sent you the electronic version. I had an email overnight from my contact in the Justice department in Port Moresby. He said they've already had some breakthroughs in their re-opened inquiries. The owner of the hotel where Davies and the Minister met has given sworn evidence backing up his admissions that he called Gregory Hudson and told him they were there. And the witness I told you about, the one the police had warned off, well, he's been found and he's agreed to give evidence about what he saw.

"So when you put that together with what we found at Debepare, it more or less ties Hudson into all four deaths. Wiebe was taking his instructions from Hudson. And it's reasonable to assume Hudson arranged the accident for the Minister and

Davies. I know the new inquests haven't taken place yet, so I've left all this as conjecture, in the report. But it all seems to be fitting together, doesn't it? The unanswered question is, of course, who was Hudson taking his instructions from?"

"Yes, it would be interesting to answer that question. But that's not the MIU's or the GCMO's job. We need to stick to our internationally agreed functions. That's what the GC members want to see."

"That's what *you* need to stick to, Betty. Not me. The last two pages that you're holding in that pile, one is an application for extended leave, the other is my resignation. It's your choice which one you accept. Dominik should be back on deck within the next few weeks, he's more than capable of taking over."

"Emil, don't. What're you going to do?"

"Johanna is missing. She received a call to return to Brussels, but it must have been a trick: no one there knows anything about it. She seems to have left the flight in Singapore and just disappeared. I've got to find her ... to do that, I'll need to find Hudson."

45

He was halfway down the path, from the front door of the building to the kerb, when his mobile rang. It was Johanna's mobile.

"Where are you? Are you alright? What happened?"

The voice at the other end was slow and precise in responding. But it wasn't Johanna.

"Listen to me, Mr Pfeffer, listen very carefully and don't interrupt. If you value Dr Dorn's life, if you want to see her again, you will do as I say. You will collect the data that you stole – the hard drives, CDs, DVDs – any and every copy that has been made from every location to which it's been copied. You will have it all in your personal possession within seven days. Once it has been recovered from you, you will forget about BKZ and anything or any person related to BKZ or the PNG projects. Dr Dorn will be kept as insurance that you comply. Seven days from now."

The line went dead.

Emil stood where he was, as if he'd become stuck to the spot. He stayed there for quite some time.

They'd won. The kumo people. For now, anyway. He couldn't afford to risk anything happening to her. Anything more than what had already happened. Might be happening. What had Dominik said? Something about Gerry not being so naïve. No, that was a joke! And the joke was on Emil. He was the naïve one and Gerry had played him out like a fool. But he would find Gerry Johnstone. He would find Gerry, eventually. He would find Hudson and his paymasters, too. And, somehow, he would stop them.

Behind him, at the window of her office, Betty G stood watching him. She had watched him walk out the door of the building to embark on his vigilante crusade. Then she had watched him as he stopped to take a call on his phone.

Now she watched him standing on the path leading to the kerb, not moving. She watched him standing there for long minutes. He seemed to be transfixed, staring down at something on the ground in front of him.

Across the road, she could see the dismantling of the anti-market protester encampment was continuing, oblivious to her and to him, uninterested.

Then after what seemed like an age, she saw him turn around and, still staring down at the ground in front of his feet, slowly and deliberately retrace his steps back into the building.

END

Appendix

The UN Global Carbon Market Organisation

The GCMO is the product of a United Nations sponsored treaty between the participating countries under which the Constitution and the funding arrangements for the organisation have been agreed.

The governance structure of the organisation consists of the Governing Council and an Executive Board, which is headed by the Director-General.

The Governing Council itself consists of the Director-General plus nine Ministers from participating members states, who themselves are appointed on a rotating basis from the General Council, in which the Ministers of all participating member states sit.

The Executive Board is made up of the unit directors and their deputies headed by the Director-General. The Director-General answers to the Governing Council, which represents the General Council of all Treaty signatory members.

Mission/charter:

The GCMO charter is to:

- Improve the functioning of the carbon market by ensuring sound, effective and consistent level of regulation and supervision on a global basis;

- Ensure the integrity, transparency, efficiency and orderly functioning of the carbon market globally;
- Strengthen international supervisory coordination across the carbon market;
- Prevent regulatory arbitrage and promote equal conditions of competition;
- Ensure that the taking of carbon investment and other risks is appropriately regulated and supervised across and between member states.

Roles and functions:

The role and functions of the GCMO are to:

1. Set market policy across carbon markets for the primary objective of maintaining stable carbon prices in furtherance of the environmental policy objective (of limiting the risk of dangerous anthropogenic climate change) (Policy Unit)
2. Gather and publish data across all markets and undertake carbon market analysis (Economic Analysis Unit)
3. Evaluate new proposed market arrangements (MIU) and monitor on-going market operations (MIU) with a view to limiting attacks on market integrity (in conjunction with national regulatory bodies through Liaison Unit)
4. Liaise with national regulators (Liaison Unit)

Glossary of Selected Terms

BKZ - Bankgesellschaft Kohlenstoffermäßigungen Zürich

BMU - German Federal Ministry for the Environment, Nature
Conservation and Nuclear Safety

BRIC - Brazil, Russia, India, China – rapidly developing nations

CDM - Clean Development Mechanism (of the Kyoto Protocol)

GC - Governing Council (of the GCMO)

GCMO - Global Carbon Markets Organisation

IGO - Inter-governmental organisation

IMF - International Monetary Fund

IOS - UN Office for Internal Oversight Services

LNG - Liquefied natural gas

NGO - Non-governmental organisation

OCC - PNG government Office of Climate and Carbon

PNG - Papua New Guinea (aka Papua Niugini)

REDD - Reducing Emissions from Deforestation and Forest Degradation

UNFCCC - UN Framework Convention on Climate Change

Author's Note

This is a work of fiction. All the characters are fictional and any resemblance to any person, living or dead, is unintended and purely coincidental. The GCMO does not exist, nor does, and never did, the BKZ, *C-world*, Lynx Cable or TrueUpREDD: they are purely creations of the author. Similarly, places such as the Owen Stanley Motor Lodge, Bad Eschbach, the Frankfurt-burghof and the Debepare conservation projects exist only in the pages of this novel.